Praise for *Midnight at the Blackbird Café*

"Perfect for fans of *Like Water for Chocolate* and *Fried Green Tomatoes at the Whistle Stop Cafe.*"   —*Bustle*

"Full of family secrets, undeniable charm, and that particular touch of magic so often found in the South . . . Webber creates a town as dynamic and real as her characters. I savored every word."   —Kristy Woodson Harvey,
national bestselling author of *Feels Like Falling*

"A tantalizing, delicious delight."
—Kristin Harmel, international bestselling author of
The Book of Lost Names

"This novel is as warm as the cup of coffee you'll surely want to settle down with as you pick up this book and read straight through to the ending."   —*Bookstr*

"Webber infuses her charming Southern small-town tale with lighthearted magic and gentle humor. . . . Readers of Sarah Addison Allen and Joshilyn Jackson will enjoy spending time at the Blackbird Café."   —*Booklist*

T0008462

Forge Books by Heather Webber

In the
MIDDLE
of
HICKORY
LANE

Heather Webber

TOR PUBLISHING GROUP
New York

IN THE MIDDLE OF HICKORY LANE

A Forge Book
Published by Tom Doherty Associates/Tor Publishing Group
120 Broadway
New York, NY 10271

www.tor-forge.com

Forge® is a registered trademark of Macmillan Publishing Group, LLC.

The Library of Congress has cataloged the hardcover edition as follows:

Names: Webber, Heather S., author.
Title: In the middle of Hickory Lane / Heather Webber.
Description: First edition. | New York : Forge, 2022. |
"A Tom Doherty Associates book."
Identifiers: LCCN 2022008311 (print) | LCCN 2022008312 (ebook) |
ISBN 9781250774651 (hardcover) | ISBN 9781250774668 (ebook)
Subjects: LCGFT: Novels.
Classification: LCC PS3623.E393 I52 2022 (print) |
LCC PS3623.E393 (ebook) | DDC 813/.6—dc23/eng/20220224
LC record available at https://lccn.loc.gov/2022008311
LC ebook record available at https://lccn.loc.gov/2022008312

ISBN 978-1-250-77467-5 (trade paperback)

Our books may be purchased in bulk for promotional, educational, or business use. Please contact your local bookseller or the Macmillan Corporate and Premium Sales Department at 1-800-221-7945, extension 5442, or by email at MacmillanSpecialMarkets@macmillan.com.

First Forge Paperback Edition: 2023

Printed in the United States of America

0 9 8 7 6 5 4 3 2 1

For everyone who believes in second chances

If I had a flower for every time I thought of you . . .
I could walk through my garden forever.

—Alfred Tennyson

IN THE MIDDLE
OF HICKORY LANE

Chapter

1

January 13, 1962: Levi and I found ourselves a ten-acre piece of land near US 98 in Sweetgrass to build our first home. I knew the moment I stepped foot on it that it's real special. I'm right proud these days at how far Levi and I have come so quickly. Newlyweds. New town. New house. New job for Levi. I'm living my dreams.

Emme

In the middle of Hickory Lane grew a neighborhood garden, a circular patch of vibrant land that fit snugly into the footprint of the wide dead-end street, a cul-de-sac. The landscaped island rose from the surrounding asphalt road, lush and verdant, beckoning for a closer look, a long stay. It was impossible for me not to notice, however, that among its gravel pathways, trees, shrubs, planter beds, trellises, and flower meadow, a secret had once been planted as well. One that was slowly being exposed with each thrust of a shovel into rich soil as a newly discovered grave was unearthed.

As I made my way on foot past police tape that roped off the top of the lane, I adjusted the strap of the backpack slung over my shoulder and kept tight hold of the large wheeled suitcase that trailed loudly behind me as it protested a missing wheel with loud scraping and a constant tug on my arm, as if begging me to turn around, that nothing good could come of being here.

It had taken every ounce of my courage and determination to make this trip south to Sweetgrass, Alabama, so I hoped the suitcase was wrong, that it was simply used to nothing good coming from *anywhere* I went.

While that had always been true, this move was my chance to start over and make something good of my life. I longed to plant roots, even if they were shallow ones, and I was willing to overlook a lot to make that happen, including an apparent grave site.

Pulsing blue and red in the warm mid-April afternoon were the emergency lights of six police cars, two fire trucks, and an ambulance, and surprisingly there was plenty of space for the vehicles to park. As I glanced around, it seemed to me that Hickory *Lane* was a misnomer. This street felt more like a quaint residential boulevard, one that had been stretched long and wide to accommodate the garden island.

I kept my chin up as I walked, trying to hide my dismay that tiny bayside Sweetgrass had such a considerable police force. If I'd known ahead of time, I might've had second thoughts about moving in with my grandmother, Glory Wynn. Police had a habit of looking at me apprehensively, as if knowing with a sixth sense of sorts that I was bad news.

Shading my eyes against the bright sunshine with my hand, I searched for house numbers along the tree-lined street, looking for number seventeen. This was an old-fashioned kind of neighborhood, built up with the best materials, and it had aged with pride, grace, and beauty. Mature trees shaded large yards, roses bloomed in colorful hope, and lawns were neatly kept with clean edge lines. This was the type of street where people *cared*. These were the types of homes where doors were left unlocked. It was the kind of place where no one anticipated anything bad ever happening to them and theirs.

Fools, all of them.

As I half rolled, half dragged the reluctant suitcase, I collected bits of information from the crowd gathered, flutters of words caught on the wind, dispatched by sincerity and sympathy and fellowship.

A human bone if I ever saw one.

Early this morning. Sinkhole. Near the gazing pool.

Took almost sixty damn years, but still.

May she now rest in peace.

I took a moment to wonder about the woman who'd been missing for so long and how she'd come to rest in the garden. I felt a twinge of sympathy, empathy, for a person I'd never known—and a surge of camaraderie for this neighborhood, which on first glance had looked picture-perfect. But now? Now I knew I'd fit in here just fine.

Hickory Lane had a dark past.

Just like me.

"Needing some help, miss?" a deep voice asked.

Up a brick walkway, a man stood on the top step of a wraparound porch, his shoulder resting against a wooden column, his arms folded, his curious gaze narrowed on me. The house, 5 Hickory Lane, was a large cottage, painted pale gray green with creamy trim, the colors perfect for a community like Sweetgrass, a speck on a map alongside Mobile Bay, just north of Fairhope. The cottage's only visible flaw was in the emerald-green grass, where a half dozen or so shallowly dug holes marred an otherwise lovely lawn.

I took quick stock of my new neighbor. *Inquisitive*, I instantly surmised, noting to keep my distance from him. In my world, inquisitive meant dangerous. He was especially more so, because he didn't look like a threat on the surface. I guessed him to be early to midthirties, and he stood a bit taller than average, with shoulder-length sandy-brown hair, a high forehead, slightly off-center nose, deep tan, and five-o'clock shadow that was just a hint lighter than his hair color. His lanky body was dressed in jeans and a tight white T-shirt. His feet were bare.

With the easy-breezy way he leaned against the porch column, everything about him screamed that he was comfortable in his own skin, confident. *Approachable.* Maybe for others, he was. But I knew better. I pegged him as some kind of law enforcement straight off—criminals, even somewhat reformed ones, had a sixth sense, too.

On the porch next to his feet, a white shepherd watched me

with bright brown eyes, and I suspected I'd found the source of the strange holes in the lawn. A faded, ratty green tennis ball was in its long mouth, and a furry tail thumped loudly against the porch's floorboards. The dog's friendly gaze was the first bit of welcoming warmth I'd felt since arriving, and it melted away some of the ice-cold dread that had followed me southbound.

I lifted my chin and forced myself to meet the man's questioning gaze. "I'm looking for Glory Wynn's house."

Something that looked like suspicion flared in his eyes but he shuttered it quickly, instantly revealing that he was used to—and good at—hiding his thoughts. Slowly, he uncurled his arm and pointed toward the heart of the cul-de-sac. "The middle house."

I could practically hear his thoughts as he sized me up, much as I'd done to him.

What he saw was trouble, plain and simple.

He wasn't entirely wrong.

I squinted against the sunlight at the house that felt like it was still a half mile away. "The white one?"

"Yes, ma'am."

"Thanks kindly." I smiled as innocently as I could. My mother always said a smile was one of the best weapons of distraction. She had deployed it religiously.

Giving the dog a wistful glance, I pushed on, threading through the people who'd collected on the sidewalk to gawk and gather gossip, hoarding it with the thoroughness of birds lovingly collecting twigs for nesting. These people were my new neighbors, and I was grateful that they were too occupied with being busybodies to pay me much mind. It had been a long, hot trip from Louisville, Kentucky—eighteen hours on a bus to Mobile, then a forty-minute taxi ride across the bay—and I was in no mood to field questions about myself, my raising, or my parents, all topics that deserved to be questioned.

Eleven houses—a mix of cottages, bungalows, and transitional farmhouses—lined the lane, and Glory's place was located smack-dab at the bottom of the street. With its hip roof, three dormer windows, and wraparound porch, it sat like an old Southern lady, dolled up and ready for visitors to come calling. An American flag flapped in the wind and hanging ferns swayed in the breeze. There was a pair of white rocking chairs near the front door and another set near the side door, and suddenly I longed to sit and rock for a while.

To the right of the house, set back some and shaded by a tall hickory tree, stood a detached two-story garage, a smaller likeness of the main house. The apartment above the garage would be my home for the next little while, and even from a distance I could tell it was going to be a sight better place to live than any other residence I'd ever called home. A far sight.

The house to the left of Glory's had a small group of older women standing on the front lawn, gathered beneath the protective leafy arms of an oak tree. I hoped the women wouldn't pay me any mind, but as soon as I started up Glory's driveway, I realized it wasn't to be.

"Oh my days!" one of the women in the group exclaimed. "Emme? Emme Wynn, is that you? Of course it's you. I dang near forgot you were arriving today. This police business has thrown me all out of sorts. It's me—Glory!"

The woman, who looked to be in her late seventies, peeled away from the others and seemed to glow, as if sunlight and goodness shined straight out of her. As she hurried forward, her gait a bit uneven, the hem of her lime-green day dress hugged short, thick legs. Her white hair was cut into a choppy asymmetrical bob, which hinted at a playful personality, and bright-blue eyeglasses sat atop her head and glinted in the light like a jeweled tiara.

Loving was the first word that came to mind as she drew closer, and it filled my heart with hope.

I wasn't sure when my ability to identify a person's personality at first glance had started, but it wasn't until I was older that I became aware the talent was something special. Special because it was never wrong.

As Glory closed the distance between us, big, round apple

cheeks popped up and wrinkles multiplied as she smiled. When she finally stood in front of me, her gaze searched my face, and in her eyes, I saw her seeking familiarity in my features, looking for *family*. Looking for her son, who had passed away years ago after being hit by a car when walking along a busy Las Vegas roadway.

One of her pale eyebrows dipped in disappointment as she said, "Spitting image of your mother," before she opened her arms for a hug. "Get on in here, honey."

Swallowing back the sadness at her disappointment, I stiffly stepped forward, leaning down a bit because she was a good three inches shorter. Squeezing me close to her plump body, she enfolded me in warmth, and I awkwardly accepted the embrace, letting go of my luggage and forcing myself to return the hug. I didn't know how to return affection, but I wanted to learn, and it seemed like Glory was going to be a good teacher.

Exaggerating the motion, she rocked me back and forth and said, "It's been too damn long."

The sting of tears in my eyes and a rush of emotion reminded me that this was why I'd agreed to come here. This connection. I could see myself getting used to her hugs, her affection, the unconditional love I'd craved my whole life long.

Only after Glory pulled away, but still held on to my shoulders, did I realize I hadn't uncurled my fists to return her hug properly. I clasped my hands together, linking my fingers, and hoped she hadn't noticed.

Blue eyes flecked with green and tinged with sadness skimmed and scanned as she gave me a good look over. "So skinny! We'll fix that. How was the trip?"

"Just fine," I answered, then belatedly added, "thank you."

I needed to be more open, friendlier. It was going to be a challenge, since I wasn't an overly friendly type unless I was faking it for one reason or another. Otherwise, all my life I'd tried really hard to make myself invisible. Here in Sweetgrass, I was going to have to become part of this community in order to finally plant those elusive roots.

Sunlight sparkled prettily on delicate earrings imprinted with a design that reminded me of flower petals, the aged gold most likely antique, as the corner of Glory's lip lifted with amusement. With a gentle squeeze, she dropped her hands from my shoulders. "I can imagine how fine it was. I sure do wish you'd taken me up on my offer to pay for a plane ticket."

The kindness in her gaze encouraged me, and I smiled as I said, "And miss the humanity lesson? I couldn't have possibly denied myself."

Her eyes narrowed a fraction as if judging whether I was joking, then she laughed. "I'll show you your room so you can drop off your luggage; then I'll introduce you to some of your new neighbors." She waved a hand toward the women gathered under the oak tree, who were openly watching us.

I offered them a small, hopefully *friendly* smile.

"We'll be right back!" Glory called to them, then turned me away from the group.

Drawing back my knotted shoulders, I lifted the suitcase instead of dragging it through the velvety grass, and I swore it breathed a sigh of relief.

As Glory led me across the lawn, she said, "I was so pleased you took me up on my offer, Emme."

Her offer. A job at her side at an outdoor market called the Sweetplace and a place to live. Here. Right next door to her.

Roots.

I'd jumped at the invitation and was holding it tight.

"I have to admit I was surprised to get your call." I still wasn't sure how she'd found me, and I felt that darn rush of emotion again as I said, "But it came at a good time. It's been a rough"—I wanted to say "lifetime" but didn't want to come across as too dramatic, even though it was true—"stretch. I was between jobs." I didn't want to mention that I'd been recently fired. Fired because I spoke up when passed over for the promotion I'd been promised, one I'd been counting on for the financial breathing room to finally get a place of my own.

Because of that promise, I had let my guard down, laying it

at the feet of hope and possibilities, and I'd paid the price. My mother would have had zero sympathy for my plight. "Trust no one, Emme," she had always said. "Everyone lies. *Everyone*."

Of all people, she would know. She wore her lies like diamonds, so brilliantly dazzling they blinded people to the truth.

Glory's driveway was constructed of sandblasted bricks laid out in a herringbone design. Several determined dandelions had wedged themselves up through cracks into the fresh air, adding a splash of green and yellow to the muted red expanse, and I was careful not to crush any of them as we made our way along.

She tut-tutted in sympathy. "Hard to find the right fit sometimes, but I believe you'll love it here. The gazing pool in the garden, especially. It has a way of sharing with you something you didn't even know you needed."

I threw a wary glance over my shoulder at the garden, at the throng of police, and looked away quickly. Despite my curiosity about what was going on across the street, I didn't even want to mention the police to Glory in case my voice gave away something I wanted to keep hidden.

"Do you garden?" she asked as we strode along a walkway on the right side of the garage where friendly fern fronds brushed wide flagstones.

I realized suddenly that she seemed to be avoiding mention of the police presence as well. Perhaps she thought it might scare me off. Little did she know that it would take much more than that to let go of the chance at roots that she'd given me. "Not really."

She tutted again. "We'll fix that. I'll teach you all I know. Glory's Garden Lessons, coming right up."

I liked the sound of that as we climbed a dark metal staircase flecked with spots of rust. In front of the apartment door, which was shaded by a peeling wooden awning dotted in silvery moss, Glory breathed raggedly and let out a series of barking coughs.

"Are you all right?" I asked, not sure whether I should pat her back or call for help.

Holding in a cough, she reached for the door handle. "Oh, I'm just fine, honey."

Because her face was turned, I hadn't been able to see her eyes, but I sensed she was lying. "I can imagine how fine," I said, echoing her earlier words to me.

Looking over her shoulder at me, she smiled before pushing the door open. Unsurprisingly, the door had been unlocked. "Sadly, this spring chicken isn't so springy anymore, but as long as I've still got some pluck, I'll make do. As you know, pluck can see you through many challenges."

"You think I have pluck?" I'd surprised myself by asking the question. So personal. So *hopeful*.

Her eyes sparkled. "You're here, aren't you?"

Swallowing hard, I nodded.

Glory walked inside and threw her hands outward as if making a grand reveal. "It's small but hopefully suits your needs."

Small? Hardly. This place was practically palatial compared to my last one—a rented room in a run-down duplex in a seedy area of Louisville.

Air-conditioning hummed, cooling the cozy living space that held a sofa, two chairs, and a coffee table. The whole room was drenched in light that accented a vaulted ceiling covered in whitewashed wooden planks and the scarred oak floor. An outdated kitchenette was tucked into an eave. A bedroom was set in the back corner along with a bathroom and walk-in closet.

I slid the backpack from my shoulder and rested it on top of the suitcase. "It's beautiful."

"You're the picture of kindness, Emme. It needs a lot of TLC that I meant to have done before you arrived—some updating, some paint—but I haven't had the time, between work and . . . life." Her cheeks plumped as she grinned, and I instantly knew I'd never tire of seeing her smile.

"I have time. Just tell me what you want me to do. I'm happy to help. Truly. I'm fairly handy."

Assessing me with the lift of one pale eyebrow, she said, "I'll take your offer under consideration. Do you need any help un-packing? When are the rest of your things arriving?"

I nodded toward the two bags at my feet. "This is all I have."

Before I left Louisville, I'd sold what big items I owned: a table, chair, small desk, and a bookcase—all items I'd salvaged from other people's trash and fixed up. What few household items I'd accumulated while living on my own I'd donated to the homeless shelter where I'd once lived.

Shadows crossed Glory's eyes, darkening those green flecks, before she said, "It sure will be easy to unpack, won't it? Take your time putting up your luggage. I'm going to make a few calls. Come on down once you're ready, and I'll introduce you to some of my dearest friends." She took a deep breath and gave me a warm smile. "I'm sure glad you're finally here."

I couldn't stop myself from saying, "Thank you for being so nice to me. You don't even know me. Not really."

"Nonsense," she said. "My heart knows you just fine."

With that, she gave me another quick, awkward hug and was out the door and plodding down the steps, her footfalls echoing on the metal treads.

Once I watched her disappear into the main house through the side door, I locked the apartment's front door, then carried my bags into the bedroom. I lugged the suitcase into the walk-in closet, laid it down on the floor, and pushed it into a corner under a silver rod full of empty wooden hangers. I twisted numbers on the luggage lock's dial until the hinge popped open, and I then pulled the lock free. I unzipped the frayed canvas, pulling strings from the zipper teeth, and opened its top, leaning it against the wall.

I stared at all my worldly possessions, packed neatly, almost obsessively. Travel light, my mother had always cautioned when I was younger, and I hadn't yet broken the habit.

I closed and locked the bag again, then hurried back into the bedroom, not wanting to keep Glory waiting too long. A tall chest of drawers stood between two oversized windows that gave broad views of the beautiful backyard. I opened the bottom drawer of the chest and placed the backpack in it, taking a moment to unlock and unzip it to take inventory of its contents—my most important and prized possessions.

Inside was a tattered hardcover copy of *The Lion, the Witch and the Wardrobe* stolen from a library in Georgia, a Winnie the Pooh night-light, a crossword puzzle book, an old switchblade, a thin envelope that mocked my life's savings, and a zippered folder that held my general education diploma, my social security card, and my birth certificate.

I opened the folder and let my gaze linger for a moment on my birth certificate. *Emme Halstead Wynn*. I ran my finger over the raised seal, across my parents' names—Rowan Dean Wynn, Kristalle Fay Halstead—and along the two strips of Scotch tape that held the torn paper together. Finally, I put everything away, zipped the backpack, and gently closed the drawer.

Trying to ignore the guilt needling me from the inside out, I walked into the living room and looked out toward the cul-de-sac. With my bird's-eye view, I could see that the intricate garden was clearly a labor of love, with its gravel pathways that twisted and branched throughout the island, which was divided into four sections with a ring of green space set smack-dab in its center.

My vision blurred with unshed tears, and I took a deep breath, let it out slowly.

Since I'd been on my own, I'd worked so hard to change my life. To unlearn all the lessons my mother had taught me. To become a better person. A deserving person. I'd struggled. I'd gotten therapy. I'd dared to dream.

And with just one phone call, I had been willing to sacrifice it all.

Simply because Glory had offered me everything I'd ever wanted in life.

Spitting image of your mother, Glory had said earlier.

And though it pained me to consider it, maybe she wasn't wrong.

Chapter
2

 *Glory's Garden Lesson #1*

Your first lesson, Emme, is going to focus on, of all things, moss. Yes—moss. It grows mostly around the stones of the gazing pool, on the north side of the stone garden shed, and at the base of the old live oak tree just yonder, where it cushions the ground as if inviting someone to sit down and stay awhile. Some people consider moss a nuisance, but I find it to be utterly beautiful in its simplicity. Moss symbolizes a charitable nature and a mother's love, and every time I see it, it makes me remember my mama. She's the one who taught me—and Bee—all about the language of flowers. And now I'm going to teach it to you. You know, like moss, all mamas should provide a soft place to fall, but some, like your mama, must have missed that memo.

Cora Bee

Portfolio tucked under one arm, my tote bag draped over the other, I walked quickly but carefully along the uneven brick sidewalk, fighting the urge to add a little skip to my step as I headed toward my car, one of many parked diagonally along Third Street.

My meeting had gone well this morning at Turner & Gebbes, T&G, the only commercial architectural firm here in Sweetgrass. Better than I could've hoped, considering I was a relatively new designer—and also relatively new to this area.

I'd been completely surprised by the request for a meeting. And even more astonished this morning when T&G presented me with an interesting opportunity after looking over my portfolio. They'd extended an invitation to an exclusive competition they were holding for three select designers to create a color concept and brand, including a name, for an upscale outdoor shopping and dining attraction that was going to be built in the community.

As a color consultant primarily for residential design, I had never attempted any projects on the scale they proposed. So yes, I'd been surprised. Shocked, even. And giddy, like my whole body was filled with glossy iridescent bubbles that nearly made me float straight up out of my seat. That buoyant happiness lasted right up until they revealed the project was to be built on a site near the Sweetgrass River where the old Yardley Brick Company had once stood.

One by one the bubbles popped.

Sure, the old brickyard had been razed long before I moved here, but a ghost of its past was never far from my thoughts.

T&G must have sensed my sudden reticence because they promptly disclosed that, as representatives of the Yardley Brick Company, they were aware of my family ties to the former brickyard and hoped I would be able to put the past behind me to focus on the future of my up-and-coming business.

Sure, winning this competition would really put my company, Southern Colorways, on the map, which was something I'd been working like a dog to do since I moved to town from Gainesville, Florida, nearly three years ago, eager to start a new life—and heal from my old one. But putting the past behind me was impossible solely because of my grandfather, Levi, who had once been a partner at the brickyard some sixty years ago.

Levi Gipson. Embezzler. Abuser. Murderer. Fugitive.

Just thinking about him and what he'd done to my family made me queasy. So, no, forgetting the past was out of the question.

But could I work under his dark cloud on the Yardley project for the sake of my fledgling company? The company that held my whole heart and soul and was the only reason I even rolled out of bed some days?

Framed that way, it was hard to say no, so I accepted the invitation.

Once I'd made the decision, I allowed myself to feel hopeful. Excited, even. While I wanted to win, even the second and third place prizes weren't too shabby: a decent cash award and plenty of press. But still, I'd like to be in the top spot. However, I had to wait a bit before I could start designing—until the firm sent over the architectural renderings of the shopping center. I couldn't choose colors for the project without seeing what I was working with, and I certainly couldn't create a brand concept without knowing the colors. Fortunately, I had plenty to keep me busy until the files appeared in my in-box.

I smiled at people as I hurried past them, bidding a cheerful good morning but not stopping to chitchat with the few faces I recognized. I rarely stopped. I liked to keep moving.

Sweetgrass was practically buzzing with activity this morning, and I'd been glad to find a parking spot relatively close to the T&G office building, since the Sweetgrass Marketplace, known by most as the Sweetplace, was located only a block away, housed on the weedy lot behind the courthouse. The marketplace, a maze of tents and booths and an eclectic collection of vendors, was busiest on Saturdays, and its own parking lot filled quickly. Side streets were often crammed with the overflow.

The courthouse loomed large in the late-morning light, rising up and hulking over the small town with its orange-brown brick facade and imposing clock tower. And I'd be damned if that brick wasn't begging to be lightened up. Absolutely *pleading*. A mortar or lime wash would do wonders to soften its first impression. In my mind, I could already see it transformed, and it stood proud and hospitable instead of harsh and dreadful.

However, despite the fact that Sweetgrass was where my mama had been born and raised, I knew if I ever dared to suggest painting the courthouse, I'd be run straight out of town with a sickly sweet *bless her heart*. People around here took their brick seriously—because the Yardley Brick Company had put this town on the map.

As I reached my car, a cheer rose from a nearby youth soccer game being played behind the middle school down the road a piece, and I glanced over my shoulder toward the noise. People swarmed the school's parking lot, coming and going, accompanied by the echoing bounce of soccer balls and the clicking of cleats.

My gaze caught on one face in particular, a boy, nine or ten years old, trailing behind a small group of older kids. *Wiley?* My heartbeat jumped into my throat, and I opened my mouth to call out his name only to realize I'd lost sight of him in the crowd as it shuffled toward the fields.

I took a deep, calming breath. It was just as well he'd disappeared. The child I'd seen couldn't have possibly been Wiley, because he'd been gone from my world for three years now, having stayed in Gainesville with his father and new stepmother. Since Florida law didn't allow *former* stepparents any kind of legal visitation, I'd been completely cut out of his life. It was a wound that still bled.

What did he even look like now? Had his light-brown hair darkened? Had he grown it out? Did he still like peanut butter and potato chip sandwiches? Was he still scared of spiders? Did he miss me? Did he know how much I loved him? How much I still loved him?

Feeling foolish and suddenly deflated, I willed away the questions, the pain, and forced myself to refocus. To stay busy to keep the thoughts at bay. I had two in-home client consultations booked for this afternoon, one here in Sweetgrass and a second one in Fairhope. I also needed to pop into Fibery, the local yarn shop, to replenish my stash, and then do a bit of grocery shopping. I'd also promised my great-aunt Glory I'd have supper with her and my estranged cousin, Emme Wynn, who was supposed to arrive sometime today. If all that didn't keep my mind focused where it belonged—here in the present—then there were always my crochet projects, too innumerable to count.

Busy hands, quiet mind.

As I fished around in my tote bag for my keys, which were

hiding somewhere in the dark leathery depths, I couldn't help wondering about my cousin Emme. Where had she been all this time? What kind of person was she? The last I'd seen her, she'd been a newborn. I'd been six years old and immediately smitten with the new baby. But soon enough, her mother had taken her away—breaking all our hearts—and neither had ever returned. Until now.

Aunt Glory asked so little of me that I couldn't say no when she requested I be extra friendly to Emme, to help her feel welcome. Of course I'd be *friendly*—I was an expert at it—but that's where I needed to draw the line, for my own peace of mind.

As my fingers finally closed around my keys, my phone lit up, illuminating the inside of the bag. It had been silenced during my meeting, and as I pulled it into the sunlight, panic rose when I saw numerous missed calls and text messages. Most were from my mother, and instantly I thought of my navy admiral father, who'd had major rotator cuff surgery earlier this week and had spent two nights in the hospital.

I set my art portfolio on the roof of the car and quickly dialed my mother. My pulse raced wildly as I paced the narrow, rectangular stretch of pavement between my car and the one next to it, waiting for her to answer.

"Cora Bee, she's been found," my mama said by way of a hello, her voice strong but scratchy as it carried across nearly two thousand miles from San Diego.

Anyone nearby surely heard her as well. Lillian Gipson Hazelton wasn't what anyone would describe as a soft talker. As I squinted against the bright sunshine, my shoulders loosened their tight knots, releasing the worries I'd quickly gathered about my father, letting them drift away like cottonwood fluff caught on the wind.

Confused by her greeting, I asked, "Who's been found?"

Her voice caught, wavered. "Your *grandmother*, of course. Who else?"

A rush of air whooshed out of me, and I leaned against the car, then jumped away from it as the metal scorched my bare arms. My grandmother, Barbara Elizabeth, who went by the nickname Bee, had been missing since 1965. "What? Where? When?"

"A couple hours ago. In her garden on Hickory Lane, by the big rhododendrons near the gazing pool. A sinkhole, of all things, opened up, revealing just enough to arouse suspicions. The police were called. They've been digging for more than an hour now." Mama's voice was thick with emotion as she added, "All this time and she had been there with us all along."

"Oh, Mama."

It was all I could seem to say. My chest hurt and my eyes filled with tears.

She sniffled and my heart broke all over again. She rarely lost her indomitable composure, and I hated the thought of her crying. More so, I hated the reason behind the tears.

My mother had been only a year old when Bee and my grandfather Levi had gone missing on a dark, drunken night that left everyone believing his temper had finally gotten the best of him.

Now, after what felt like an eternity, Bee had been found.

"Where have you been?" she asked, and I imagined her clutching a tissue, dabbing her eyes. "Half the town has been trying to reach you."

Another cheer rose up at the soccer game. I threw the fields an angry glance, annoyed with the liveliness in light of this upsetting news. "I had a meeting. My phone was off."

"Oh my Lord, you're not driving right now, are you?"

I sighed. "Mama, no. I'm not driving."

She sniffled again. "Thank heavens."

Immediately, my back ached from memory alone, and I fought the urge to run a fingertip along the ridged scar on my scalp, hidden beneath my hair. "What now?" I asked. "With Bee I mean?"

I'd always called my grandmother Bee, something I picked up from everyone else—except my mama—calling her by the nickname. Aunt Glory, especially. After Bee disappeared, Aunt Glory had taken over raising my mama and had assumed a grandmotherly role with me as well. She'd always been a constant in my life. My rock. My soft place to fall when my own mama wasn't around. I could only imagine how she was dealing with this news. Bee had been her older sister, after all. I needed to cancel all my afternoon appointments and head straight over to see her.

Mama blew out a long breath. "The police are still digging in the garden and then forensic testing has to be done. It could be months before we have a proper service. And the irony of it all? We'll likely place her ashes back near where she was found. The gazing pool was her favorite place in the whole world."

Starting to feel queasy, I began pacing again. The hem of my sleeveless linen dress swirled around my legs, its laurel pink color blurring through the tears in my eyes. "I'm so sorry," I said, mourning a woman I'd never known yet loved deeply.

"Me too, darlin'."

"Have you tried to reach Cain?"

My older brother had followed in my father's military footsteps and was currently incommunicado on a submarine somewhere in the middle of the Pacific Ocean.

"I've sent word, but who knows when he will receive my message? And even when he does receive it, it'll be months before he can make it back to the mainland. If there's a silver lining in having to wait on the police investigation, that would be it. He won't miss his grandmother's funeral."

I unlocked, then opened the back door of my car and placed my portfolio and tote bag inside, both feeling much heavier than they had only minutes ago. "Have you spoken with Aunt Glory? How's she handling this news?"

"I spoke with her only briefly. I've mostly been communicating with Nannette this morning. She's been calling or texting with updates every half hour or so."

Nannette, a neighbor of Aunt Glory's, was a dear family friend and one of my mama's closest confidantes. They'd grown up together on Hickory Lane.

Mama said, "According to Nannette, Aunt Glory is being

a mite stubborn. She's refusing to accept that the grave found this morning belongs to my mother. She won't even entertain the thought of it and is refusing to discuss the matter until the forensics report comes back." Her voice cracked once again. "You know how she always hoped my mother would be found alive one day, living it up on a white-sand beach, drinking daiquiris or some such."

In Aunt Glory's eyes, abandonment was a sight better than believing her sister had been the victim of domestic violence. Denial was a double-edged sword when it came to mental well-being.

"A part of me wanted to believe that my mother simply ran away, too. That life in Sweetgrass had become too hard for her," Mama said, her voice thin and distant. "But I never quite accepted that theory, because when I lived on Hickory Lane, I always felt a motherly presence around me. Now I know I wasn't just imagining that."

My chest continued to ache, for my mama, for all she had lost, and for Bee and all she'd lost as well. "I'll see what I can do to make Aunt Glory see reason. Avoiding the topic for months isn't going to do any of us any good."

"I'll speak to her as well, but since it's a conversation best had face-to-face, I'm coming home. I'll likely stay in Sweetgrass until we can lay Mama to rest so I can be kept up-to-date on the investigation. Since Glory's apartment is currently taken," she said with a dark undertone, "I was hoping to stay with you."

Panic nudged aside my grief, rising up in me, hot and uncomfortable. *Months.* Mama had said it could take months before a funeral service could take place.

"It'll be good to be back home for a while," she added, "and it will also give me the chance to meet Emme, the little gold digger, and run her straight back out of town before she tries to scam Aunt Glory out of her life savings."

"Mama," I began, but didn't know where to take the sentence. A lecture on how she shouldn't judge Emme for her mama's sins? At least, not until she met her to see if they were cut from the same cloth. And I certainly couldn't protest Mama living with me for *months*, though, dear God, I wanted to.

Ultimately, I said, "You know it wasn't Emme's idea to move here."

"And? Just because it wasn't her idea doesn't mean she won't take advantage. Has Aunt Glory told Emme of her grand plan?"

"I don't think so," I said. "She wants to see how Emme fits in first."

"Aunt Glory is asking for trouble."

I fought back tears as I thought of my great-aunt, at all she'd endured health-wise these last few years. It wasn't trouble she was asking for now. It was closure.

But my mama didn't know how bad the circumstances were. Aunt Glory had gone out of her way to create the illusion that all was well in her world when it most certainly was not. Only I knew the truth of the situation, a secret safely entrusted to me, just as my secrets had been entrusted to her.

Mama said, "I'll email you the information when I've booked an airline reservation. There won't be an issue with picking me up at the airport, will there?"

"What about Daddy?" I asked quickly, trying to make *her* see reason. "He's just had surgery." The last I heard, he still needed day-to-day help. He couldn't yet dress himself properly, and he certainly couldn't drive.

"He's healing well. Well enough that he's making me a little crazy. He's a lousy patient. I'm on the hunt for a good home-healthcare company to look after him. He can join me when he's well enough to travel, since he has six weeks off to recuperate. It'll be so good to see you, Cora Bee," she said, the words drifting wistfully through the phone on a sigh. "It's been too long. Quick weekend trips go by much too fast for this mama's heart. I've missed my baby girl."

I had missed her, too, and desperately longed for one of her hugs. But the weekend visits had been purposely designed by me to be quick. In, out, hugs, kisses, no need to linger to see things that would only cause concern and raise questions.

Her being here for *months* was going to make my secrets impossible to hide.

"Mama, I know this news about Bee has been a shock, but Daddy . . ." I couldn't believe she was planning to leave him, lousy patient or not. It was so unlike her nurturing, somewhat overbearing personality that it made me start questioning everything I knew about her.

"He's given me his blessing, Cora Bee." There was a hint of a pout in her voice. "In fact, he's currently looking up flights as we speak."

Suddenly, I smiled. Now I understood. Daddy might be a lousy patient, *or* Mama might just be the most annoying nurse ever. A story always had two sides.

"Mabel! Mabel, *stop*!" someone shouted, the high voice punctuating the air with a mix of anxiety and irritation.

Turning toward the shout, I saw Mabel, who appeared to be a chocolate Labradoodle, running all willy-nilly up the middle of the street, looking like she was having the time of her life. Her tongue lolled, her ears flapped, and freedom blew through her dark curly fur. A purple leash trailed behind her, as did a young girl dressed in a shiny, bright grass-green soccer uniform.

"What's that shouting?"

"There's a loose dog running up Third Street. I've got to go help, Mama."

We quickly said our goodbyes, our I-love-yous, and, *heaven help me*, our see-you-soons. I tossed the phone into the backseat and hurried toward the street, happy to see no cars coming. "Mabel! Here, girl!" I said loudly, patting my thighs and hoping Mabel didn't have an aversion to strangers.

Mabel took one look, altered her course slightly, and ran full speed ahead toward me for a proper hello, joy shining in her brown eyes. It was still shining as she barreled into me, knocking me to the ground with her enthusiasm. She covered my face with wet kisses.

"Mabel, get off!" the girl shouted once she'd reached us,

quickly grabbing up the leash. She then said to me, "I'm so sorry! Are you okay?"

"I'm—" I hurt, actually. I tentatively sat up, setting my dress to rights before half of Sweetgrass saw what color underwear I was wearing, then wiped the dog kisses off my face and took stock of potential injuries. I'd scraped my palms, and they stung, but there was a shooting pain in my foot making me wince. "I'm sure I'll be just fine."

I'd survived worse. Much worse.

Mabel took my words as an invitation to resume kissing and slurped my cheek and chin. I couldn't help but smile through my distress. I patted her head and said, "That's quite enough, Mabel."

The girl took hold of Mabel's collar and tugged the dog backward into a sitting position. Mabel happily started sniffing cleats and shin guards, suddenly enchanted with scents that had come from the soccer field.

Glancing at my foot, which was quickly puffing up, the girl blanched before shouting over her shoulder, "Dad! Over here— hurry!"

Her short light-brown hair was scraped back in a stubby, sweat-dampened ponytail, but defiant wisps had escaped their confines and framed an elfin face. Her color was high, darkening pale cheeks and complementing deep-blue eyes.

I gently pulled off my sling-back high heel as the swelling blossomed, and I willed my foot to calm down, because I didn't have time to deal with an injury. "No, really, I'm okay." I attempted to stand, but as soon as I put weight on my foot, the pain was too much to bear, and I wobbled.

The girl grabbed my elbow and helped me shimmy backward toward my car to lean against the trunk. She looked over her shoulder. "*Dad!*" she said in the same anxious, irritated tone she had used on the dog.

A man jogged toward us, dressed in athletic shorts, T-shirt, and ball cap, and I immediately recognized him as one of my neighbors, as he was highly recognizable. Tall, at least six foot three, and lean with a thick mop of brown hair that was now curled around the brim of the cap. He'd moved onto Hickory Lane only recently, just a couple of weeks ago, and until now I'd only seen him in passing, though I'd dropped off a basket of welcome-to-the-neighborhood muffins last week.

Only days after he'd moved in, neighborhood gossip had quickly revealed his single-dad status, and at that bit of news, I'd tuned out the rest of his particulars. That status was also one of the reasons why I'd barely brushed my knuckles against his front door when I dropped off the muffins and had left quickly before anyone even had a chance to answer.

As he approached, his worried gaze evaluated the scene, sweeping quickly across me to focus on his daughter, then the dog. "You caught her. Good job, Alice," he said, then turned his attention downward. "*Mabel*," he chastised without much heat, "you can't be runnin' off like that."

Apparently having zero regrets for her adventure, Mabel happily thumped her tail against the ground.

He rubbed her ears, and immediately I pegged this giant of a man as a big softie.

Up close, I noticed that even though he was lean, he was muscled. Not bodybuilder buff, but in an athletic kind of way—muscles that came from running. Or swimming even, considering the breadth of his shoulders.

"*Dad*," Alice said. "I didn't catch her. This nice lady did, and Mabel knocked her over, and her hands are bleeding, and her foot is hurt, and we should call an ambulance and . . ."

"Whoa, Al, breathe," he said, setting his big hand on her small shoulder as his milky-blue gaze finally landed squarely on me.

As our eyes met, something shifted painfully in my chest, like it was rigging up a perimeter of caution tape around my heart.

"Ma'am." He smiled like I was an old friend and tipped his hat just before dropping into a crouch to gently lift my foot onto his rough palm. "We're mighty grateful for your help and quite sorry for Mabel's overzealous greeting. She's a puppy and still learning."

Heat bloomed in my cheeks as his hand roamed over my foot, prodding yet tender. "You don't have to . . . I mean . . . I'll be fine," I said, injecting some of my mother's firm tone into the last word before pulling my foot away from his hand. Using my big toe for balance, I set my foot gently on the ground.

The roughness of his palm had me wondering what he did for a living. Those kinds of hands came from hard work. Construction? Ranching? Cabinet making? Suddenly, I was curious. More than curious, which prompted a harsh reminder to mind my own damn business.

Standing, he said, "If I were a betting man, I'd say it's broken."

"No, no. It's just a little *tweaked*," I insisted. "I'm sure I can walk it off."

The sun caught on the blue in his eyes, making them appear oddly opalescent. "I've seen tweaked. That's not tweaked. Best you visit a doctor and get it checked out. Where's the closest urgent care? We'll take you over and of course cover all costs."

"Good idea," Alice piped in, nodding.

At the earnest concern glistening in her eyes, I almost gave in. Almost. I drew my shoulders back. "You're right kind, both of you, and I appreciate the offer, but I'm fine. I'll drive straight home, ice it, elevate it, rest it. It'll be good as new in no time. No problem."

His eyes narrowed a smidge and the opal turned to steel. He wasn't as big a softie as I first thought.

"Is that so?" he said with a smug smile as he set his hands on his hips.

I instantly despised that smugness.

"It's so." I gave what I hoped was a friendly smile and wave and added, "I'll be seeing you around." I turned from them, took a deep breath, and forced myself to put one foot in front of the other as I limped away. Tears of pain quickly gathered in my eyes as I tossed my shoe into the backseat and pulled my car keys from my dress pocket.

"Tweaked," I whispered to myself, willing it to be true. If my foot were broken, that would likely mean a cast and crutches and . . . no easy way to get around town.

"Perhaps you should call someone for a ride," the man said before I even pulled open the driver's door. "Considering it's your right foot that's injured."

I glanced down at the offending limb, cursing it a blue streak in my head, as if it were its fault I was in this predicament. In addition to the swelling, it was now turning a lovely shade of purple. The thought of using it to press a gas pedal turned my stomach. There was no way I could drive. Not very far, at least.

I curved my fingers around my keys, squeezing them tightly. With everything that was going on over on Hickory Lane, I'd likely have to call a taxi or rideshare.

"For what it's worth," he said, "I still think a trip to the doctor is in your best interests."

"Same," Alice piped in, and I swore I heard her mutter *stubborn* under her breath.

Alice had sass. I liked that about her.

"Even if it's *tweaked*," the man said, "your foot likely needs medical attention. The sooner you see a doctor, the better. Get that swelling under control."

"I once had to wear a big ol' boot for six weeks because I sprained my ankle playing soccer," Alice added. "And my foot didn't look near as bad as yours does."

"Alice," the man said under his breath.

She shrugged. "It's true."

A boot. A boot could be workable. I could probably even drive with a boot.

"My offer to take you to a doctor still stands," he said. "We'd need to take your car, though, since Al and I walked over to the soccer game this morning. I'm James, by the way," he said, pressing his hands to his broad chest. "My friends call me James." He paused a beat. "I'm just kidding. They call me Jamie."

Alice groaned.

"And," he added, "this is my daughter, Alice, who loves my humor. You of course have already met Mabel."

Mabel licked my hand. I patted her head and tested my weight again, nearly groaning aloud when pain radiated up my leg. As I studied the bruising, I supposed it was in my best interest to get the injury looked at. Reluctantly, I held out my keys to him. "Sweetgrass Hospital is a few miles away. I'm Cora Bee."

Alice's eyes widened. "Cora Bee of the chocolate chip muffins? *That* Cora Bee?"

I nodded. "I live a few houses down from you."

"Those muffins." She sagged dramatically. "So good."

"That's real nice of you to say." I ducked into the backseat to move my portfolio, phone, and purse. "It's one of my great-aunt's recipes. You've met Glory Wynn, right?" I gestured for her and Mabel to climb on in, and there was much excitement on Mabel's part to be going for a ride.

"Oh yes!" Alice said. "She brought by a pan of brownies when we first moved in. I like her."

I smiled. "I like her, too."

"Cora Bee," Jamie said as he helped guide me to the passenger side of the car, "it's nice to meet you in person." Shadows played in his eyes and his voice softened as he added, "I heard your name a lot this morning at the soccer game. I'm real sorry about your grandmother."

I swallowed over a sudden lump of emotion in my throat. "I appreciate your kindness. It's turning out to be quite the day."

"As bad days go, you can't get much worse."

I thought back to three years ago on a rainy day in Gainesville, a slick road, and overwhelming pain and hopelessness.

As Jamie pulled open the passenger door, I mustered up a wan, hopefully agreeable smile. But as I slid into the seat, I couldn't help thinking that today wasn't even close to my worst day.

Not by a long shot.

Chapter
3

December 18, 1962: We named the private lane that leads to our house Hickory Lane for all the hickories on the land. The house is finally finished and we moved in over the weekend. I'm hopelessly in love with this land. Was surprised to find that a small, beautiful natural spring broke through the earth a good bit behind the house. Will build my gardens around it. I also want to get bees. This land is practically crying for bees and it just seems fittin' that someone named Bee should have an apiary. Levi seems to be liking his new job at the Yardley brickyard. It's hard to tell sometimes. He's a bit moodier than I realized when we were dating. Here's to hoping that he does like it. Because I like it here on Hickory Lane. I like it a lot.

Emme

As I once again followed Glory across her yard, early afternoon sunlight caught on the dandelion blooms in the driveway, making them look like precious flowers rather than weeds. Glory reached for my hand, tugging me forward, and I wondered if the action had been prompted by a surge of affection . . . or the need to grab hold so I didn't run off. Either way, she clearly sensed my nervousness to meet my new neighbors, and I was grateful to have her to hold on to.

"They aren't likely to bite, honey," she said, then chuckled. "Most of them anyway. Nannette is a calling card."

"A calling card?" I echoed as I walked beside her.

She cast a puzzled glance my way. "What? Oh! Darn slip of the tongue. A *wild* card. She's a wild card. You'll see."

The three women I'd seen standing with Glory earlier still remained beneath the oak tree, watching what was happening across the street with great interest. Soon, though, one nudged another, and their attention swiveled to Glory and me as we approached.

"Don't worry any. We'll make this short and sweet," Glory said with a smile under her breath.

Friendly, I reminded myself. I could do this. I could be the person I had always wanted to be.

"Emme, honey," Glory said as we sidled up to the women, "meet Nannette and May. This here is their lawn we're standin' on. And this is Dorothy, who lives up the street a few houses. These wonderful women are some of my dearest friends."

Dorothy, I noticed, held a small hot-pink-handled shovel in her hand, and for one horrifying moment, I thought she'd been the one to discover the grave this morning. Then I remembered the talk of a sinkhole and realized she had probably been pulled away from her gardening by the tumult of the morning and had forgotten she was still carrying it around.

"Everyone, this is Emme Wynn, my long-lost granddaughter. Rowan's daughter," Glory proclaimed as she released my hand and threw an arm around my taut shoulders.

Long-lost.

I hadn't been *lost* so much as cut off. Not by Glory, but by my mother, who had dragged me all over the country as a child, leaving Sweetgrass behind when I was only a month old. She had no roots keeping her here—she'd been an orphan and had grown up in the foster care system—and had decided that my roots were best left untethered by a complicated family situation.

With the flick of a glance, I assessed the women standing before me as easily as I breathed. *Prim; generous; mischievous.*

With a twinkle in her eyes, Dorothy stepped forward, took my hand, and shook it vigorously. She was dressed in a bright-blue cotton housecoat, and had short, fluffy, curly white hair so thin it revealed a pearly pink scalp. "So you're the bastard! It's nice to finally meet you after all this time."

I slid a look to Glory, who shook her head and tightened her arm around me. With a heavy dose of censure in her voice, she said, "*Dorothy.*"

Dorothy blinked innocently. "What?"

"Our apologies." May swooped in to pull Dorothy back into line. "Dorothy had a bit of an accident a while back. Sometimes she loses her filter."

Looking from face to face, Dorothy asked, "What did I say now?"

No one answered her.

"I'm sorry to hear about the accident," I murmured, not sure what else to say. There was no refuting that I was an illegitimate child. My mother didn't believe in marriage. And I rather liked Dorothy's frankness, truth be told, but my first impression of her made me wonder how much of her candidness was due to the accident and how much of it was a product of her mischievous personality. Finally, I added, "I like the color of your shovel."

She waved it around menacingly. "If you see the varmint around, let me know."

I stole another look at Glory, who said, "Dorothy has squirrel issues."

Nannette murmured, "Don't get her started on the topic. It's nice to finally meet you, Emme." She gave me a tight smile as she linked arms with May.

By the lie in her eyes, Nannette was most certainly *not* happy to meet me, but I had expected my new neighbors to be cynical at best. At least they weren't openly hostile—something I had worried about during the bus ride down here.

As with my ability for first impressions, I also didn't know at what age I'd started recognizing lies—or whether the skill was innate or learned from eighteen years spent at my mother's side. I suspected the latter. One of the few gifts my mother had ever given me. All I needed to see was someone's eyes while they were talking to know if they were lying. It was an ability that had come in handy more times than I could count.

Nannette didn't even seem to be trying to hide the fact that she had fibbed, her eyes now full of suspicion. She looked to be in her midfifties and had deep olive-toned skin, short brown hair with sunny highlights, and vivid, serious brown eyes. She was dressed in crisp dark jeans and a pristine white blouse that was tucked in at a slim, belted waist.

There was nothing about her, not a single thing, that said *wild card* to me. In fact, she seemed the opposite of wild, which made me wonder if Glory had been mistaken in the assessment.

"I hope the police presence doesn't scare you, Emme," May said, her sea-blue gaze not nearly as distrustful as her partner's.

With her generous nature, she was apparently willing to give a stranger the benefit of a doubt. She had long curly brown hair streaked with silver strands and wore a peasant blouse and an ankle-length boho skirt. On her feet were lived-in Birks that looked to be as old as she was.

"It's not the norm around here," she added. "We're usually a peaceful neighborhood."

With a shake of her head, Glory faced me and said, "A little thunder doesn't bother someone who's lived in a storm. Isn't that so, Emme?"

I could only nod, taken aback by Glory's words, her knowledge that I'd lived through my share of storms. Exactly how much did she know about my past? There was no way she knew everything . . . *No way.*

Eyes widened all around, and Nannette's hand went to a strand of pearls resting at her throat. May coughed and looked upward, as if seeking guidance from the old tree.

We stood in awkward silence until Nannette said, "Lillian texted me, Glory. She said she tried to call you a few minutes ago but it went straight to voicemail."

Glory stiffened slightly. I probably wouldn't have even noticed, except she still had her arm around me. I recognized the name Lillian from reading Rowan's online obituary, which I'd all but memorized. She was his cousin, Glory's niece.

Nannette went on. "I told her there was nothing to update as of yet, and she suggested you might want to go speak with one of the detectives to see—"

Glory held up a hand, effectively silencing her. "All in due time, Nannette."

"Glory," she said, still sliding her index finger along her pearls, "you can't possibly—"

Glory cut her off by saying loudly, "There's plenty of time to get to know everyone, Emme. Let's get you inside, get some food in you. *Skinny.*" She pasted on a bright smile and aimed it at the three women. "We'll see you lovely ladies later."

With that, she turned me around, marched me toward the house. "They seem nice," I said, hating the sudden heavy silence. "No one even came close to biting. I barely saw any teeth at all."

It took her a moment, but she let out a gentle laugh as we climbed the porch steps. Behind a screen door, the front door stood open. "You won't find more caring, loving friends."

"They did seem rather concerned. Not only about me being here, I mean. But about you, too."

The house seemed to exhale a cool sigh as we stepped inside. A heady, pleasant scent of vanilla filled the air as I glanced quickly around. In the living room there was a large photo on the mantel of a younger Glory holding the hands of a small boy and girl. They all wore big smiles. Was that Rowan? It had to be—he had Glory's kind blue eyes. There was another photo, more recent, where he was crouched low, his arm around a golden retriever. He was laughing in the shot as the dog licked his face, and I smiled, feeling the joy in the moment. Rowan had been a big bear of a man, but that softness in his eyes made me think he was more teddy bear than grizzly.

"It's this police business they're concerned with," Glory said as she continued on into the kitchen.

Even as I hurried to catch up with her, I noticed the inside of Glory's house seemed to reflect the woman herself. Full of light and color, it pulsed with life, practically buzzing with it. It should've been dizzying but instead was calming. Soothing. Comforting. Loving.

The kitchen was especially cozy. It occupied a back corner of the house and was primarily decorated with windows. I'd never seen so many windows in a kitchen. I counted twelve of them, not including the glass-paneled side door. Light saturated the room, soaking the wood floor in golden tones and highlighting whimsical wallpaper patterned with flowers, leaves, butterflies, bees, birds, and rabbits.

I tried to take it all in as I said, "It seems serious."

"*Mm,*" was all she said to that as she poured me a mason jar full of sweet tea and ushered me toward an L-shaped bench behind a small turquoise-colored table tucked into a corner. "You sit yourself down while I fix us some lunch."

"I can help you—"

"No, no, you sit on down, honey. There will be plenty of time for you to help later. Let me spoil my granddaughter a minute."

Reluctantly, I sat. I'd much rather be standing. Doing. I wasn't used to people waiting on me. It was an unfamiliar feeling, and it made me itchy. Antsy. Suspicious. I wasn't used to people being kind without wanting anything in return.

I noticed the end of the bench closest to the side door was weighted down with three stacked wooden boxes full of baked goods. In the top one were cupcakes and cookies and fudge and caramels, all delicately wrapped in clear packaging, tied with twine, and labeled with a gold sticker that had an image of a vintage-looking bee in midflight and said GLORY & BEE in dark-purple lettering.

My gaze shifted to the backyard, which was just as beautiful as the garden across the street though not nearly so large. There were plenty of flowers and shrubs tucked around the yard and it also had a long raised vegetable bed that sat in a sunny puddle of light, full of leafy foliage and a few tomato cages.

Before I knew it, Glory had bacon frying in a large cast-iron pan, and its scent edged out the note of vanilla in the air. She set out a loaf of bread and collected lettuce from the fridge.

I couldn't take the growing silence—it reminded me too much of all the time I'd spent alone—so I said, "I heard some people in the neighborhood talking as I walked down the street earlier. About why the police are here."

Her hand stilled as she pulled a tomato from a wire basket on the counter, and I saw her chest heave as she drew in a deep breath. For a moment, I didn't think she was going to say anything, but finally, she spoke. "People around here are thinking the grave found in the garden today belongs to my sister, Bee, your great-aunt, who disappeared in the nineteen sixties."

I couldn't imagine the pain that had come with not knowing where she had been for sixty years—and also the pain that came with finding out. "I'm real sorry for your loss."

She stood in profile, so I couldn't see her whole face, but I caught sight of the way her chin jutted, as if she was steeling herself against an onslaught of emotions. "That poor soul out there is not her."

"I-I mean . . ." I didn't know what to say, so I stared into my tea glass.

"I'd know if it was her, plain and simple," she said, each word clipped. "It's not her."

Was she right? Or was she simply attempting to shield her emotions from the truth? To keep the pain of grief at bay? By her resolute tone, I knew not to push the matter. Everyone had their own ways of dealing with pain. If hers was denial, so be it. Time would tell whether she was right or wrong.

"I hope you don't have plans for supper," Glory said, decisively changing the subject. She put four slices of bread into a toaster and pushed the lever down. "I've asked your cousin Cora Bee to eat with us tonight. I'm eager for you two to meet, and it's my dearest hope that you'll become fast friends."

Friends. I'd never had a true friend. My mother and I moved too often and then there were the secrets I had to keep. When I was older and on my own, I found that old habits died hard. I had trouble opening up to anyone, allowing them into my life.

"Cora Bee lives right next door." Glory's chin nodded toward the charming cottage that stood on the other side of the garage. "Her older brother, Cain, is career navy like his daddy and is currently on a submarine somewhere in the deep blue sea. You won't be meeting him for a while yet, though I have plenty of pictures I'm happy to share with you."

The thought of being enclosed on a submarine in the dark ocean made me break out in a cold sweat. I wiped my hands on my jeans.

"They're Bee's grandchildren," Glory added as she took a bag of potato chips from the pantry. "Their mama, Lillian, and her husband, Simon, live out in California."

"My mother never talked about them."

"I'm sure she had her reasons," she said diplomatically, though the pinch of her lips undercut the neutrality of the statement. "Cora Bee should be here anytime now—she had an early meeting, and I'm sure her phone's been off. Gossip travels fast in a small town, though, and it's only a matter of time before she hears the rumors and hurries on home."

The rumors. I studied Glory's face, looking for any hint that she believed, somewhere deep down, that the rumors were actually true. Sure enough, I found uncertainty written in between the lines of her face, belying her steady assurances that it wasn't her sister out in the garden. She talked a good game, but there were doubts she couldn't quite hide. Doubts she obviously preferred keeping to herself.

As my thumb slid up and down over the raised letters on the front of the mason jar, I suddenly felt like I should leave. This was such a deeply private family matter, and I didn't want my presence to add any stress to the emotional load Glory already carried. "Maybe it's best to postpone the dinner you'd planned. In fact, I can make myself—"

"No, no." She shook her head, cutting off my offer to make myself scarce until things settled down awhile, allowing her and Cora Bee to sort through this tragedy without an outsider hovering over their shoulders. "Being with the two of you will be just the thing I need to take my mind off what's happening outside. Distraction is good for the soul."

Distraction and denial. I couldn't say I blamed her, but I worried if she'd ever be receptive to the truth.

With a weak smile, she took the bread slices from the toaster and set them on a plate. "Search parties combed this land after Bee disappeared, every bit of ten acres, but *especially* the garden. Bee had been putting in drainage and irrigation using a neighbor's tractor, so the land was all tore up, but nothing was found. So you see, I'm not simply brushing off what everyone else is so easily ready to accept, despite the circumstances of her disappearance."

My curiosity got the better of me. "Circumstances?"

She set out a wooden cutting board and placed the tomato on it, then used a butter knife to try to slice it. "Dorothy, who you met earlier, was Bee's best friend."

I glanced at the full knife block that sat next to the stove top alongside a pair of ceramic chicken salt and pepper shakers and wondered why she hadn't chosen a sharper knife.

"Bee had called Dorothy the night she went missing, begged her to come over. Told her Levi—he was Bee's husband—had been drinking and that she was scared to be alone. Levi had developed quite the temper after they married."

I absently reached up to my cheek, felt a thin scar barely visible to anyone else, thanks to skilled emergency room doctors.

Setting the butter knife aside, Glory added, "He had already broken her arm, though she told most people she had fallen in the garden. Those who knew her best suspected it was only a matter of time before he went too far, but she loved him and always believed he'd change." She glanced at me, her eyes wet with tears. "Through the haze of love, sometimes it's hard to see reason."

In my short time in shelters, I had met several women who'd eventually gone back to abusive spouses, thinking they had no other options, thinking love could fix it all. The little girl in me, the one who believed closets led to mystical lands where good ultimately conquered evil, wanted to believe love *would* fix it all.

The grown-up me, however, hoped those women were safe.

"By the time Dorothy arrived at the house, Lillian, who was barely one at the time, was sound asleep in the car parked in front of the house and the house was on fire." Glory turned off the flame on the stove and moved the pan to a trivet on the countertop. Working quickly, easily, Glory slathered the thick pieces of toasted bread with Duke's mayonnaise, then piled the sandwiches high with lettuce and bacon. She skipped the tomato. "There was no sign of Levi or Bee, and for a while it was believed that they both perished in the fire, but investigators combed through the ashes and couldn't find any sign of either of them."

Which made sense now, I supposed, considering what had been found in the garden.

"Dorothy made sure people kept looking for Bee. Dorothy's late husband Gil was the police chief back then, and he had the clout to get things done. But for as close as Dorothy was to Bee, Gil was to Levi. There was talk back then that Gil had actually found Levi and let him run with a warning to never return. Levi had the money to disappear, too, since he'd embezzled cash from his workplace that he'd squirreled away somewhere. Not long after all this happened, there was supposedly a sighting of him at a strip club in Florida. Dorothy had herself a full-on hissy fit when she heard and threatened to leave Gil. He denied any involvement with Levi's disappearing act, of course. What else could he do?"

"If Levi—" I'd started to ask if Levi was on the run, then where did she think Bee had gone? But at the distraught look in her eyes, I decided the question didn't need to be asked after all.

Glory set two plates onto a tray, then added the sandwiches and chips. She carefully tucked cloth napkins next to the plates. "Eventually, Dorothy let it go. We all had to let it go for our peace of mind."

Carrying the tray to the table, she put it down and then eased onto a cushioned chair across from me, a deep frown on her face as her gaze drifted away. I suspected she was looking at a long-ago memory and finding it to be unpleasant.

"I'm sorry," I said again. Even if it wasn't Bee in the garden, her sister had still gone missing. With her emotions so close to the surface, it was easy to see in Glory's eyes the anguish that loss had caused.

Her head came up and she puffed out a deep breath. "That's enough distressing talk. We'll give ourselves indigestion. Let's talk about something happier. About you being here."

Distraction. If chatting about me would chase even a bit of that sadness from her eyes, I was more than willing to play along.

She passed a plate to me, then took the other for herself. She set her napkin in her lap, and I copied the movement, though I rarely used such manners when I ate alone.

"I feel like we have so much catching up to do," she said, "but I don't want to pepper you with deep questions straight off, so maybe we'll just start with the basics. What's your favorite color?"

I couldn't help smiling. When she'd said basics, she meant *basics.* "Purple. Yours?"

"Gold. Favorite food?"

"Peanut butter. You?"

"Oh Lord, honey. I can't choose. I love it all. Favorite movie?"

I tilted my head left, then right. "*Pretty Woman.* You?"

"*Miracle on 34th Street.* I believe! Book?"

"*The Lion, the Witch and the Wardrobe.*" I took a bite of the sandwich and nearly groaned with how good it tasted, even without tomato slices. Yet, I couldn't help but wonder why she'd abandoned the tomato on the counter. "Thank you for this."

"My pleasure, hon. Do you cook much?"

I shook my head. "Not really. Noodles and the like, mostly. I'm not a big foodie. I pretty much live on peanut butter."

"What is this I'm hearing? Not a *foodie*? No grandchild of mine would say such a thing." She laughed, a hearty sound that

made me smile despite my sudden loss of appetite. "I'm guessin'
you just haven't had enough exposure to good food. We'll fix
that while you're here."

I shifted uncomfortably on the bench. My appetite had been
replaced with a cold, hard knot in my stomach. I forced myself
to take another bite, a small bite, of the sandwich, then said,
"You said the search party scoured ten acres. Did this street not
exist back then?"

"It didn't. When Bee disappeared and Levi took off, I became
guardian of this property and of Lillian. At first, Lillian came to
live with me in Georgia, and the land sat untended but watched
over by Dorothy and Gil. But not long after Rowan was born,
my marriage fell apart. So the three of us moved back here to
a trailer on the land. Financially strapped, I had to make some
hard decisions. One of them was dividing this property into
tracts. I knew Bee wouldn't want anything but quality on her
land, so I made sure to find the best builder around to create this
neighborhood. And I knew I could never pave over her garden.
She loved that garden. So we worked it into the plans. I created
a trust for Lillian—this was her inheritance, after all, and eventually I bought this house and the garden from the trust."

"That's a lot for you to take care of on your own."

"I do hire out help for mowing and the like, but it's become
a community garden through the years. Some neighbors are
happy to get their hands dirty by claiming a raised planter box
while others simply enjoy the beauty it brings to the neighborhood."

The skin on Glory's hands was sun-drenched and spotted.
I had no doubt she was someone who didn't mind getting her
hands dirty.

At the sound of a car turning into the driveway, Glory stood
and walked over to the kitchen door. "Street must be reopened."

Some of the tension eased from my shoulders. An open street
meant the police were one step closer to moving along.

Sunlight flashed off the windshield as the car rolled to a stop
in front of the garage. "Oh! It's Cora Bee."

Glory pushed open the screen door and trundled out onto the side porch and down two steps to the driveway. I stood and followed, too curious to sit still. Outside, I rested my shoulder against a shaded porch column as a man emerged from the driver's seat of a small blue car and a young girl and a dog popped out from the backseat.

"Jamie, Alice, what a surprise!" Glory said to the pair. "I wasn't expectin' you to be with Cora Bee."

"I don't think Cora Bee was expecting it, either," Alice said with the flash of an impish smile.

"Hello, Miss Glory," the man—Jamie—said, giving her a smile as the dog strained its leash in an effort to reach Glory.

I immediately pegged Jamie as *honorable* and Alice as *bright*. So bright she practically twinkled.

The passenger door of the car swung open, and out came the top of one crutch, then another. A head came up next, just as the man said, "Whoa now, wait for me, Cora Bee."

"I can do it," she said, her irritated voice carrying easily as she rose fully out of the car.

Jamie, apparently wise as well as honorable, backtracked.

With her shoulders pulled back, stiff and determined, Cora Bee set the crutches under her arms and took one tentative step, then another. Slowly, she made her way around the car. She had auburn hair that was pulled back in a loose, low bun, a pointed jaw, and a heart-shaped face. She stood taller than Glory by more than a few inches, so I guessed her to be about my height, five foot six.

At the full sight of her, I smiled, recognizing a somewhat kindred spirit. *Softhearted.*

With my upbringing, I shouldn't have a soft heart, a tender anything. Yet, I thought my empathy for others was what helped me survive my mother's way of life. Caring when she didn't made me realize how different we were—and that I didn't want to be anything like her.

Yet, a soft heart in a hard world was challenging, and I learned quickly to hide my true self. It was that or risk getting picked apart by people who preyed on soft emotions. People like my mother.

As a child, I hadn't realized she was taking advantage of my talent for first impressions, using it to choose her marks. I'd believed it was just a game we played when we went somewhere new, a bonding routine. When I was older and I realized what was happening, I didn't want to play anymore. It *hurt* to play. It took two months of purposely bad guesses before she believed I'd lost the ability to read people. She'd pouted for weeks. But truly, she hadn't needed me. She knew how to choose her victims just fine. Always had.

"What in the world happened to your foot, Cora Bee?" Glory exclaimed.

"Mabel," Jamie and Alice said at the same time, looking pointedly at the dog.

The dog leaped and barked happily, seemingly oblivious to their disapproval.

"Down, Mabel," Alice said sternly, exasperated. "*Down.*"

Mabel did not sit down. She kept straining her lead on the leash until Glory stepped toward her to pat her head.

"It was a rescue mission gone awry," Cora Bee said.

Alice jumped in to explain. "Mabel got loose, and when Cora Bee tried to help catch her, Mabel was all excited and ran right over to her. Then right over her. Knocked her down flat."

"I can absolutely see that happening," Glory said, rubbing the dog's ears. "You're such a happy boy, aren't you, Mabel? Oh, to have that kind of pep in my step again."

I almost smiled at the slip of the tongue, of her calling Mabel a boy, until I saw the twin looks Jamie and Alice slid toward Cora Bee. The glances, which were a mix of pity and empathy, along with the way Cora Bee's shoulders deflated, told me clearly that something wasn't quite right with Glory. I'd suspected it earlier with the coughing fit, and then with the cutting of the tomato, but it hurt to see it confirmed in their faces.

"That she is." Cora Bee kept her tone light. "She's the happiest dog I've ever had the pleasure of meeting, though I do wish our first meeting had been a touch more . . . gentle."

She held her hand out to Mabel, and the dog happily licked it, her tail wagging so fast I thought I felt a breeze.

Regret bloomed in Jamie's pale eyes. "Mabel's newly enrolled in an obedience class. Seems as though the first few classes haven't quite sunk in yet."

"Mostly, she just sniffs the other dogs," Alice said with a shrug.

I studied Glory, top to toes, looking for anything that would reveal what was wrong with her, but nothing was glaringly apparent. My knack for first impressions hadn't prepared me for this. All I'd sensed from her was her loving spirit.

Glory laughed. "Mabel's a lover, aren't you, darling?" Mabel's tail wagged as though she knew she was being praised, and she slobbered Glory's hands with kisses. "She loves big. Best to accept her as is instead of trying to change her. You don't want to go breaking her spirit."

She loves big. My breath caught at the words, so heartfelt that I knew immediately someone had once tried to break Glory's spirit. Maybe one day she'd share the details of her failed marriage with me. Even though it was none of my business, I wanted to learn everything I could about this woman.

"Her spirit is too big to let that happen," Cora Bee said, her voice strained as though close to tears.

Glory stepped over to her, patted her cheek lovingly. "How long will you be on crutches, hon?"

"I'm not sure yet." She didn't look too pleased about not knowing. "It's . . . it's broken."

Glory gasped. "No! I didn't see a cast, so I thought it was just sprained. Or tweaked."

Cora Bee pressed her lips together tightly, as if holding back a whole lot of what she really wanted to say.

"The splint is temporary until Cora Bee can see a specialist after the swelling goes down," Jamie explained.

Fatigue creased Cora Bee's face but she pulled her shoulders back, lifted her chin, and said, "I'll make do."

"Of course you will," Glory said. "Well, come on; let's get you inside to sit down and prop that foot up. You too, Jamie, Alice, and Mabel. I've just made lunch and there's plenty."

Jamie held up his hands. "Thank you for the offer, Miss Glory, but we best get home."

Alice looked like she wanted to argue but thought better of it when her father gave his head a shake.

"Call if you need anything," Jamie said to Cora Bee.

She nodded and said, "I will."

A lie. I lifted my eyebrow at how easily it had come out, without a trace of insincerity. Impressive.

As the trio walked down the driveway, Glory threw her arms around Cora Bee, crutches and all. There was no hesitation, no awkwardness, and the unexpected stab of envy I felt had me looking away, turning to study the police in the garden, still digging, still searching.

"My mama called," Cora Bee said. "About Bee."

Glory pulled back. "I'm real sorry for the shock that call must've given you."

"Shock is putting it mildly. It's all so . . ." She shook her head. "It's a mix of emotions is what it is. Sadness but I'm also glad Bee's been found after all this time so we can lay her to rest right and proper. Mama also mentioned—"

Glory held up a hand, the same way she had with Nannette earlier. "I know what you're going to say, and I love you dearly, but I don't want to hear it."

At that moment, Glory's earlier words drifted back to me. *Through the haze of love, sometimes it's hard to see reason.* Her denial of what was happening was born from love, pure and simple.

"Aunt Glory," Cora Bee said on a sigh.

"Let it be, honey. Now, come on inside." She turned and immediately saw me standing there. "Land's sake!" she exclaimed as she tossed her hands in the air in exasperation. "I've forgotten my manners. Emme, I'm so sorry, hon. Come meet Cora Bee."

I stepped forward into the sunlight, and Cora Bee stared openly for a moment before she said, "Wish you were visitin' during a happier time, but welcome."

"I'm sorry about your grandmother."

Glory sighed loudly.

Cora Bee nodded. "Thank you."

Her eyes were a light-brown color that held flecks of green and a great amount of sadness. I wanted to write it off as expected, because of what had happened to Bee, but this sadness went deeper. It haunted her.

We all turned at the sound of approaching footsteps. An older man strolled forward dressed in jeans and a short-sleeve dress shirt, a badge and gun clipped to his belt. A seasoned police detective was my guess. I tried not to fidget when his glance landed on me for a second longer than the others.

"Glory, you got a moment?" he asked.

Her jaw clenched for a fraction of a second, then resolutely loosened. "Sure do, Bob. You girls go on inside, sit down, eat. I'll be only a minute."

I held open the door for Cora Bee and she crutched inside, banging into the doorway, and I heard her curse under her breath. It was such a mild curse that I suspected she didn't curse often.

After I pulled a chair out for her, she swiveled to sit, and her pink dress flared out before falling prettily against the chair legs. As she maneuvered, she dropped a crutch in the process. The bang echoed. As I picked it up and leaned it against the wall, she closed her eyes. When she opened them again, they were awash with moisture.

The day's shocking turn of events coupled with the frustration of her injury were obviously taking a toll.

I dragged another chair over so she could prop up her foot and pushed Glory's plate aside, out of the way. "Crutches take some gettin' used to, I imagine. I've never used them myself."

She settled her foot onto the seat cushion. Her toenails had been painted a light pink, and not a single one had chipped, despite the morning's ordeal with Mabel. "Me neither. And I don't particularly want to be on them now."

I sat down on the bench, then stood up again. "Are you hungry?"

"Not really, thanks."

"Sweet tea? I can grab you a glass."

"Honestly, I'm a little queasy. Partly from the foot pain, partly from everything that's happened today. It's been . . . a lot."

"Understandable," I said. I sat back down, unsure what to do, what to say, and suddenly feeling more out of place than usual. I'd never really felt comfortable anywhere.

"Do you know much of what's going on?" she finally asked. "In the garden?"

I fiddled with the edge of a cloth napkin. "I overheard some of the neighborhood gossip when I first arrived, then Glory gave me the CliffsNotes version of events of what happened in the sixties. As for what's going on today, she said she doesn't want to talk about it."

"I heard." Her forehead creased with dismay. "A sinkhole—who'd have thought? The last time a sinkhole opened up here . . . Well, the last time that happened was the year Bee disappeared. I read about it in her journal—one of the few things we have left of hers." She took a deep breath and slowly shook her head as though unable to believe the coincidence.

Even though Cora Bee wasn't much older than I was, I could tell that we'd had vastly different upbringings. She sat perfectly straight in the chair, not a hint of a slouch in her shoulders. Her skin was lovely, unmarred by violence; her auburn hair was streaked with gold, which could've come from the sun, but I suspected it was at the expert hands of a skilled stylist. The loose bun at the nape of her neck was casual but elegant. Her makeup, even after the day she'd had, still looked flawless. Not a mascara smudge to be seen. She spoke evenly, clearly, and slowly with perfect enunciation and articulation, so different from my clipped, rushed way of talking.

My natural posture was atrocious, as I liked to curl up to disappear into myself most of the time. The only time I truly ever stood straight, shoulders back, chin up, was when I was walking alone. To give the illusion of confidence, to make myself seem *bigger*. A don't-mess-with-me attitude that I'd been forced to adopt a long time ago. Sometimes it worked . . . and sometimes it didn't.

My hair was naturally blond and had never been professionally cut. I favored loose pigtail braids and messy buns that were messier than most. I didn't wear makeup. Too much time in the sun had given my freckles a life of their own. The sound of my voice wasn't anywhere near cultured, but it was good enough for someone who lacked a proper education. My mama hadn't been a big believer in schooling, but she had been a big believer in libraries. Mostly as a place to while away time. To use the Internet. To meet people, even. *Marks*. The poor unsuspecting souls.

For me, the library had been my Narnia, a magical place that took me away to another land, where I learned more than I had ever hoped. Librarians instinctively took me under their wings, protecting me as much as they could from the evils inherent in my mother's way of life. Books had become my refuge, my only friends, my family, my escape from my everyday reality.

Cora Bee finally said, "You'll be working at the marketplace with Glory?"

I nodded. For four days a week, I'd be helping with her stall at the Sweetgrass Marketplace, which she called the Sweetplace for short. "I'll likely need to find another part-time job as well if I ever want to get a place of my own."

Her gaze held steady on me. "How long do you plan on staying around these parts?"

I had the feeling she was asking more than the obvious and I struggled with how to answer. Finally, I said, "As long as y'all will have me."

I was afraid a little of my heart had leaked out with that answer, so I quickly shifted my gaze to the wallpaper, where it skimmed across the bright flowers and mischievous rabbits and landed on one of the bees in the print. I swear I saw its wings flutter. I reached out to touch it only to realize the bee was warm under my fingertip.

"Do you like the wallpaper?" Cora Bee asked. "Some people think it's too busy, too colorful, too much."

I turned to face Cora Bee. "It's not any of that. It's *perfect*."

Though her eyes were tired, haunted, she smiled. "I think you'll fit in around here just fine, Emme."

And I smiled, too, because I knew she wasn't lying.

Chapter
4

🌿 *Glory's Garden Lesson #2*

Take a look at these beauties, Emme. Doesn't it seem like the thin green stems won't be strong enough to hold its heavy flower cluster? But it is stronger than it looks. See all the tiny white flowers? There has to be at least a hundred individual flowers in every cluster, each with four petals, and some are even tinted with pale-pink dots, like they're trying to set themselves apart from the others. They're so pretty it's hard to believe they're even real. They're hydrangeas and are believed to represent heartfelt feelings, persistence, and thankfulness for being accepted. Let's snip a few and take them over to Nannette and May. It's their favorite flower.

Cora Bee

"Looks pretty as a picture." Glory stepped back from the queen-size bed and surveyed the guest room. "Don't you think?"

I took stock of the room, which was freshly dusted and swept. The linens had been changed, the pillows fluffed. "It looks wonderful. Thanks, Aunt Glory. This would've taken me hours on my own."

Maybe longer. I was struggling on the crutches, catching them on the edge of rugs, door frames, and table legs. I prayed my foot wouldn't require surgery (a possibility) or a cast (a probability) and that I could get away with an air boot for the six to eight weeks of healing the ER doctor had predicted.

Six to eight weeks.

Good heavens.

And to think that at dinner earlier I'd tried to decline Glory's offer to help get the guest room in order for my mother's arrival. Foolish of me, considering my predicament. But being Aunt Glory, she'd waved off my words with a flick of her hand and a staccato "nonsense."

Emme had offered to help, too, but I turned down her offer with a broad excuse of how there wasn't enough to do for three people. At her look of dejection, I'd felt a swift, sharp stab of guilt but hadn't changed my mind. I needed to figure out where to set my boundaries where she was concerned.

The space closest to my heart had been closed off long ago, locking in those who were already housed inside and keeping out everyone else. It hadn't been an easy choice, but it was the only way I had been able to move on with my life after my divorce, after my accident.

Still, Emme was family. Keeping her at a safe emotional distance was going to be a challenge, especially when she lived right next door.

Aunt Glory scooted in close to me. "What's family for but to step in when you need a little help?"

She was forever stepping in. Stepping up. Shouldering the burdens of others without a thought to herself, her emotions. I envied that about her. How she made it look so easy to give of herself. I knew it wasn't. I knew the risks.

"Speaking of, what did you think of Emme?"

Knowing my great-aunt, she'd been fit to burst with wanting to ask my opinion but held off until our work was done. My thoughts went to Emme, to her cautious eyes, her bitten fingernails, the scar on her cheek, and her galaxy of freckles.

Her hard life, her painful life, floated around her in tiny black spots of ash, telling a story only I could see. But it was a story she'd *lived*. Her life had been steeped in pain and sadness. There were many colors floating around her, more than I usually saw with others. It was the juniper green that I was most curious about. That specific color represented a secret. Not just any old secret—a guilty one. She was hiding something she was ashamed of. Which, considering the black floating around her, could mean just about anything.

I've been able to see colors around people and objects my whole life long. Through my eyes, colors drifted around people, like softly falling snow, offering glimpses of personalities. Floaters, I called them. It had taken me years to figure out the language of the colors, their meaning. Take Alice, for example. Orange floated around her, telling me of her playful, energetic personality.

But after my car accident, other colors, secondary colors, had become sharper, clearer, *louder.* They were emotional colors and were nearly impossible to ignore. After Mabel had knocked me down, around Alice there had been sparks of dark plum. Remorse.

"Were you able to see her personality?" Glory asked, her thin eyebrows raised high.

Only close family knew how I could see color—it was too hard, too strange, to explain to others. However, my abilities weren't the least bit odd to Glory, who knew where to plant a flower seed simply by looking at it, or to my mother, who had never been lost a day in her life because she instinctively knew which direction to go. We came from a long line of people who had enhanced intuitions connected to nature.

I shook my head. "Her innate personality is shrouded by darkness, and I can't see beyond that."

Her breath caught. "What color darkness?"

Though most of the time I appreciated being able to see people's personalities—I often knew who to avoid at all costs—sometimes it gave me more information than my soft heart could tolerate without breaking.

"Blackness mostly." I let that sink in before I finally said, "I'm glad she's here. I think she needs you."

"She needs *us,*" she corrected. "I won't be around forever."

Carefully balancing on my crutches, I leaned into Aunt Glory, into her strength. I had no idea how I was going to live without her.

She put an arm around me. "It'll be okay, hon. *You'll* be okay," she said as if reading my mind.

"Promise?" Because right now I couldn't see how.

She nodded and smiled. "Well, once you get used to Lillian being here."

I groaned.

"You know," Glory said, "you can always tell her what happened. It would take the weight off your shoulders."

I shook my head. "No. No one needs to know. I just haven't figured out how to keep her from seeing it for herself."

How long could I hide myself, the person I'd become after that dark day three years ago, from her? A week? Maybe I could do it. It would take effort, but I could do it. Months, though?

Aunt Glory tutted. "Just take it day by day." She gave my cheek a peck and said, "Best I be getting back. It's been a long day, and I'm ready to put my feet up."

A long day was putting it mildly. It had been an emotional roller coaster.

At dinner, Glory had once again declared to Emme and me that until the forensic testing was completed, she would not tolerate talk of it having been Bee found in the garden. Plain as day, she stated that she refused to put her life on hold while we waited for an identification.

Essentially, she was refusing to grieve.

She'd been refusing for nearly sixty years now.

As far as coping mechanisms went, it had worked for her so far, but by denying what was so glaringly obvious to the rest of us, she was setting herself up for a hard fall. A hard, painful fall. One from which I wasn't sure she could recover.

Not long after she left for home, my cell phone rang, and I crutched as quickly as I could into the living room where it sat charging on an end table. I sighed as I spotted my mother's name on the screen and answered.

"Aunt Glory's not picking up her phone," Mama said by way of a hello.

"Hold on, Mama." I put the phone down, then dropped onto the sofa, letting out a whoosh of breath as I landed heavily. My foot was throbbing. The ibuprofen I'd taken at the hospital had worn off, and I hadn't taken any of the prescription medication Jamie had insisted I fill before we left the hospital premises.

Jamie. Mr. If-I-Were-a-Betting-Man. It was a good thing I wasn't a gambler or I might've lost my shirt. The sudden image of me losing that shirt in front of Jamie made me blush, my cheeks suddenly fiery hot. I didn't have the wherewithal to dissect why my brain had decided to go *there*, so I pushed the images away, banishing them forever.

I set aside the blasted crutches, then picked up the phone again. "I'm back."

"Where'd you go? What was all that commotion? Where are you?"

"I'm at home." I lifted my foot onto the large square tufted ottoman that served as a coffee table. As much as I didn't want to tell her about my injury, there would be no hiding it once she arrived, so I decided to get the worst over with. "It's kind of a long story, Mama, but I broke my foot today."

I winced, already knowing what her reaction would be.

"What?" she cried. "How? Why didn't you call me? Did you have another car accident? Oh Lord."

"Mama, no." I tightened my jaw, then forced myself to relax it. "I fell. That's all."

"Are you okay? Are you in much pain? Are you in a cast?"

I looked around my living room, my gaze landing on the picture of my parents that sat proudly on one of the built-in bookshelves that flanked the fireplace. The photo had been taken ten years ago at my wedding rehearsal dinner. They were facing each other, smiling as if sharing a private joke, and at the time I took the picture, I wished more than anything I'd have a marriage like theirs.

I let my thoughts drift to my ex-husband, Lucas, for a moment, before shaking them loose. No need to go there right now, either. Or ever again. I should really put the photo of my parents into an album, out of sight, but I kept it out as a reminder that once in a while, if the stars aligned, true love was possible. And it was beautiful, even if it didn't happen for everyone.

Mama went on. "Are you able to drive? I can call a car service to pick me up at the airport on Monday. I have an early flight out, connecting through Houston. I'll be landing late. I'll send you the itinerary."

"Mama," I said, "it's truly not necessary for you to come out right now. I know you don't really want to leave Daddy in the condition he's in. Plus, Bob Graham—you remember him, right? The police detective? He told Aunt Glory tonight they're done in the garden but because the state crime lab is backlogged, it could be up to *six* months before we hear anything, before we can plan a funeral service. Six months! Surely you don't want to put your life on hold for *six* months."

"Six months does seem excessive," she finally agreed, "but a month or two seems perfectly reasonable."

I stifled a groan. "But Daddy . . ."

"He'll be joining me there once he can fly, Cora Bee. The navy doesn't care where he finishes his medical leave. Now, shall I call a car service for Monday?"

Slumping with defeat, I said, "I'll be at the airport one way or another, Mama; don't worry about that."

"Now that we have that settled, tell me how supper went with the little con artist."

"Mama." Every last bit of weariness I possessed came out in that one word. "Her name is Emme and dinner was fine. She seems . . . scared. I don't think she's had a happy life."

Emme's fear had floated around her in shades of red. I'd been impressed that she'd masked it so well outwardly. Usually there was a tell-tale sign. Fidgeting. Twitching. Twiddling of thumbs. But Emme tended to sit stoically still, as if afraid of calling attention to herself.

"Have you considered that she's playing the poor pitiful victim trying to get on your good side? You didn't know Kristalle the same way I did, Cora Bee. Apples don't fall far, young lady."

It was hard to believe that my mother and Kristalle had once been friends. Or, rather, my mother had considered Kristalle a friend. No, not a friend. Family. Mama had considered her *family*. But it turned out my mother had simply been yet another pawn in Kristalle's game of life.

I knew the feeling of being betrayed by someone I loved, someone I considered to be family, so I knew why my mama was currently acting the way she was. But taking her pain out on Emme wasn't the least bit fair.

"I saw the darkness around her with my own eyes, Mama. And besides, she's also Uncle Rowan's child." Even though Rowan was technically Mama's cousin, I'd always considered him an uncle since he and Mama had been raised together like siblings.

I waited for my mother to repeat the rumors that had circulated through our family—and this community—that Emme *wasn't* Uncle Rowan's child. Rumors that Kristalle had lied to him because she'd been looking for a sugar daddy and had run off when he asked for a DNA test. After meeting Emme, I wasn't so sure those rumors were true.

I quickly added, "Emme has his freckles." I recalled how those freckles swept her cheeks and across her nose, glowing gold on her fair skin, glinting in the light like they held a thousand secrets.

"Is that so?" she said, a hint of softness in her voice.

"They're mesmerizing. And so far, I can't find fault with Emme. She's been the picture of kindness and friendliness."

Mama sighed. "You need to be careful, Cora Bee. You're too tenderhearted, always believing the best in people."

I wanted to argue that compassion wasn't a bad trait, but I'd learned the hard way that wasn't true. I decided not to tell my mother about how Emme had touched one of the bees on Aunt Glory's wallpaper and had felt how unique it was—the wonder on her face had been genuine. Mama would only try to explain the moment away, and I didn't want to hear it.

This neighborhood was special, buzzing with charm, but not everyone could feel it. From flowers that sometimes bloomed out of season to the barely perceptible tremors underfoot to the gazing pool. Especially the gazing pool. Although almost everyone had heard tales of what the gazing pool had to offer, not everyone who sat on its stone ledge experienced its enchantment. It seemed to reveal itself only to those who truly felt a connection to nature.

"Did Emme say where she's been all these years?" Mama asked. "Has she agreed to a DNA test?"

"No, and I didn't ask, on either count. Supper wasn't the place for an interrogation. Especially not today."

"Hmm," she said, as though she believed otherwise. "How's Aunt Glory doing? She rushed through every one of my calls today. Were you able to help her see reason? Nannette said she tried and failed."

I quickly explained that Aunt Glory was unlikely to budge on the matter of Bee. At least, not until the investigation was complete. Then I added, "Physically, she's doing okay. A few slips of the tongue today. Her unsteady gait was a little more pronounced, but it always is when she's tired, and it's been an exhausting day."

"When's her next checkup?"

I swallowed hard, hating to lie. "I'm not sure."

"I'll be glad to spend some time with her. I've missed her almost as much as I've missed you."

"We've missed you, too, Mama."

"Perhaps a six-month-long visit isn't unreasonable after all."

I laughed because I hoped she was joking. "I should get going, Mama. I have some work to get done tonight before I turn in, some designs I want to finish up. And I have a big project on the horizon I should start prepping for." A shiver of excitement broke through the exhaustion of my day, reminding me how much I loved my job. Of how my job had saved me. My job . . . and Aunt Glory.

Since there'd been enough tumult today, enough thoughts of Levi, I'd wait to tell my mother about the specifics of the Yardley contest until she was here in person. Talking about the Yardleys always meant thinking about Levi. They were forever linked.

"Work? But it's the weekend, Cora Bee."

I fought a yawn. "Is it?"

"Don't sass. Why are you working at all? You should be taking time off to recuperate properly. Healing can't be rushed. You of all people know that. Besides, with you on medical leave, it'll give us more time to spend together. I'm more than happy to make calls on your behalf if you need me to. Your clients will understand if you take some time off."

I broke out in a cold sweat at the mere thought of Mama calling *anyone*. "That's not necessary. Thank you, though. It's just my foot that's hurt, so I doubt it'll affect my design capabilities at all."

"Cora Bee, you're not going to be stubborn about this, are you?"

I heard the front porch door squeak open, then snap closed, and then the doorbell rang, saving me from answering my mother's loaded question. "I really have to go. Someone's at the door. Bye!"

I hung up quickly and let my head drop back on the sofa cushion just as the person at the front door knocked softly on the door frame. I threw a glance at my crutches and simply couldn't summon the energy to stand up. "Come in!" I shouted, knowing my voice would carry easily, since the pine door stood ajar.

A head tentatively looked inside. "Cora Bee?"

"Alice! Come in, come in." I waved her inside. "Is Mabel with you? Should I brace myself for kisses?"

"No, she's home with Dad." Smiling, she stepped into the living room carrying the basket I'd dropped off at her house last week, a bouquet of flowers, and lingering plum-colored sparks—she was still feeling guilty about Mabel knocking me over.

"I brought back your basket," she said. "It's full of cookies. I made them myself. My mom always tells me that you shouldn't return someone's basket or bowl or casserole dish empty. Do you like chocolate chip cookies?"

"Love them, and that's good advice from your mother. My mother taught me the same."

She thrust the flowers forward. "And these are from Mabel."

"Mabel has good taste. They're beautiful," I said, taking the sleeve of flowers from her. Nestled inside layers of tissue paper was a small bouquet of pink hydrangeas, pink roses, and gardenias that smelled amazing. I pulled the note from its clip and opened it.

It read *I'm sorry. Woof woof.*

I smiled. "Mabel might need obedience training, but it seems her etiquette is just fine. Please tell her thank you from me."

"Oh, I will. Should I put the flowers in a vase for you?"

"No, no, but if you could put them on the kitchen counter for me I'd appreciate it." I held the bouquet out to her.

"I can definitely do that." She took the flowers and hurried into the kitchen.

A second later she was back and because those plum-colored wisps still colored the air around her, I added, "Why don't you come sit down and let me try one of those cookies."

She tentatively sat down. "I don't mean to be rude, but you look a little pale. Are you feeling okay? I can call my dad—"

"No, no, I'm fine. It's been a long day is all." Talking to my mama had given me a headache, and I was starting to panic about what she'd said—about making phone calls to my clients. I wouldn't put it past her. I really wouldn't. "Cookies are just the thing to perk me up."

The purple faded a bit.

Alice's hands were clasped on her lap, and she was picking nervously at a hangnail. "I heard about your grandmother. I'm real sorry."

"Me too, Alice." I held up the half-eaten cookie. "This is delicious. Did you brown the butter?"

Her head bobbed, pleased that I'd noticed. "My mom taught me."

"You'll have to teach me sometime. I always burn the butter."

She grinned. "I'd like that." Then she hopped up. "My mom

also says a guest should never overstay her welcome. I'd really like to help you out while you're on crutches. I'm happy to do any of the chores that you can't. Like take out the trash—things like that."

Earnestness fluttered around her as lovely as hummingbird wings, and I told myself to turn her down gently. Instead, I found myself saying, "My flower beds will likely need some attention since I won't be able to pull the hose around."

Maybe my mama was right—I was too softhearted. I was inviting heartache by allowing Alice to come over here every day, but I told myself I wouldn't get attached. I'd let her help. That was all.

"I'll be here tomorrow right after school." She pulled a slip of paper from her pocket. "Here's my phone number. Text me if you need anything, okay? More cookies, kisses from Mabel, an extra set of hands. Anything."

I took the paper and curled my hand around it, feeling its warmth, its caring.

"You're real sweet, Alice. Thank you." I shimmied to the edge of the couch and stood up. She handed me my crutches, and I made my way to the door with her. "Maybe when you come tomorrow, you can bring Mabel with you?" I found I rather liked the cheerful, fluffy dog.

Her wide smile could've blinded the sun. "I will. I promise."

With a wave, she was off. As soon as she turned up her driveway, I headed for the kitchen to put the flowers in a vase, and my thoughts once again turned to my mama's upcoming visit.

I grabbed a vase, set it on the counter. As I reached for the faucet handle, my hand stilled as my gaze fell on the prescription bottle that had been sitting on the windowsill. Outside, shadows bloomed in the growing twilight, but the windows in the apartment above Glory's garage glowed with an inviting golden hue. Suddenly, I heard Aunt Glory's voice in my head saying, *What's family for but to step in when you need a little help?*

Suddenly filled with the craziest of ideas, I quickly crutched out the back door. I carefully made my way across the stone patio, through the open side gate, and along the flagstones that ran beside Aunt Glory's garage. When I reached the stairs going up to the apartment, I realized I'd reached my limit. There was no way I could make it up those steps.

I worried my lip for a moment before my gaze fell on the pea gravel that bordered the walkway. I picked up a stone and tossed it at the living room window. Then another and another. "Emme!" I called out.

Finally, Emme lifted the sash and peeked out with a bewildered, somewhat panicked look on her face. "Cora Bee?"

"Hi, Emme. Sorry to bother you, but can you come down for a sec? I have a proposition for you."

Chapter
5

March 1963: I'm buzzin' with excitement. I bought some bees from a neighbor who keeps hives. I have two hive boxes and was more than happy to start bee-talkin', which is a whole lot like sweet-talkin', which is appropriate since it's supposed to help the bees produce honey. Levi keeps mocking me for how much I care about the bees. He just doesn't understand, but that's okay. I love the bees enough for both of us and hope they'll be happy here.

Emme

The last place I expected to wake up this morning was in Cora Bee's guest room, but here I was. I rolled and sat up, teased by the scents of coffee and cinnamon. A thin yet cozy quilt fell to my waist, and for a moment I wanted to lie back down, pull that quilt over my head, and simply enjoy the warm safety of the cotton cocoon. The bed was the most comfortable I'd ever slept in. The linens so soft. The down mattress heavenly.

But Cora Bee was already awake, so I slipped out of bed, my bare feet landing on a plush area rug. I quickly made the bed, which took only a moment because I had hardly stirred during the night, too fearful of my unfamiliar environment, the odd noises, the comfort I didn't deserve.

An old-fashioned clock sat on the nightstand and amber light filtered through the curtains. It was almost six in the morning, and I had hoped to be up and about before Cora Bee woke up, but judging by the clomping noises coming from the kitchen and those tempting scents, I guessed she'd been awake for a while.

In the attached bathroom, I brushed and flossed my teeth, washed my face, and pulled my hair into a loose topknot.

Back in the bedroom, I unplugged my night-light and carried it to the closet, where the click of the closet door echoed in the quiet morning as I pulled it open. I crouched down to open my suitcase and set the night-light inside and grabbed an old cardigan I'd had forever. Slipping it on over my nightshirt, I hugged it close, feeling a sense of relief and familiarity rush over me.

With a deep breath, I pulled open the bedroom door and stepped out into the hallway. The TV was on in the living room, its sound turned down low.

In the kitchen I found Cora Bee at the sink, her crutches resting loosely under her arms. A cup of coffee steamed from the countertop, and a dozen perky muffins sat on a cooling rack.

In Cora Bee's hand was a prescription bottle, and she was staring at it like it was an old friend.

My voice was scratchy with sleep as I said, "Good morning."

She jumped, nearly falling backward until she grabbed hold of the kitchen sink. "Sweet baby Jesus!"

I rushed forward to steady her. Her skin was soft, warm, pulsing with feverish guilt under my fingertips. "Sorry. I didn't mean to startle you."

She quickly set the bottle onto the windowsill, then pressed her hand to heart. "No need to apologize. Just for a moment there I forgot I wasn't here alone. Coffee?"

"Yes, please, but I can get it." I opened an upper cabinet and took down a mug, feeling her watchful gaze on me. I fought the notion that I was doing something wrong. Opening cabinets I had no right opening. I had to wonder how long this would last, the sense that I was an outsider, an interloper. That I shouldn't be here. Not in Cora Bee's house. Not in Sweetgrass. It felt as though I was someone living a life that didn't quite belong to me. Maybe because it didn't.

But only last night Cora Bee had shown me around the house in an effort to familiarize me with the layout. She'd pointed out where the mugs were kept, the plates, the fancy dinner napkins I couldn't imagine dirtying.

My eyes had welled up when she'd given me a set of house keys, but I hid the tears away before she saw. She'd shown me how to work the TV remote, to set the DVR, how to run the washer and the dryer. She'd been thorough, and I'd paid attention to even the smallest details. How she kept her stack of magazines neat, largest on the bottom to smallest on top, their right corners all at a perfect ninety-degree angle. I'd stood in awe in her cozy office, with its swatches of colors, drafting table, computer, bookshelves, desk, and the cubbies full of luminous yarns.

She'd told me very little about her company, a color-consulting and design firm, and full of curiosity, I had so many questions about it. But there would be time enough to ask. Plenty of time, since I'd be staying with her for the foreseeable future.

A proposition, she'd said last night when I opened the window to her rock throwing. In reality, her offer had felt like so much more.

As I poured the coffee, I inhaled the steam, breathing it in, letting it wake my senses and clear away those feelings of unworthiness from my mind.

With a nod of her chin, she gestured to a small blue ceramic pitcher on the countertop, its glaze crackled from age. "There's cream there if you'd like it."

"Thanks, but I take it black."

She made a sour face, twisting her lips and wrinkling her small nose. "I could never. I need the sweetness of sugar, and the richness of the cream cuts that lingering bitterness, you know?"

I did know, but creamer was a luxury I could seldom afford. The only time I ever used it was the rare times I treated myself to a coffee from a fast-food place or gas station, when the cream was free.

Looking up, I let my gaze linger on a painted wooden sign that hung above the sink window. It was a garden scene, the flowers painted in ethereal colors, part abstract, part impressionist in style. A delicate bee flew above the blooms and among the words DAY BY DAY, which had been brushstroked in pale gold, barely visible.

"Glory commissioned that sign for me from May. You met May, right? She has a gift store out on Main Street and dabbles in all kinds of arts and crafts."

"It's beautiful. She's really talented for a *dabbler*."

Cora Bee's eyebrows lifted with amusement. "May's greatest gift might be her humility." She nodded to a cooling rack on the countertop. "Apple cinnamon muffin? They're fresh from the oven."

"They smell incredible." I picked one up, peeled back the liner, and took a bite before wondering if I should've put the muffin on a plate. Used a fork. A napkin.

With the warm bite in my mouth, I stared at the muffin as if it held an invisible etiquette lesson. I swallowed, feeling the muffin catch in my throat. Suddenly, I questioned why I'd come here, why I ever thought I could set roots in Sweetgrass. I wasn't like these people. I would *never* be like them.

Glancing up, I found Cora Bee watching me, and I suddenly felt like running. Like running and never stopping. But then she smiled, a slight quirk of her lips, and she reached over and grabbed a muffin, too. Using her crutches for balance, she peeled back the liner, and took a big bite.

She tipped her head side to side, as if weighing a decision. "Needs a little crunch, I think. Maybe some pecans next time?"

Moisture stung my eyes as I made a point of looking at the muffin as if studying it closely, while I forced myself to remember why I *had* come to this little bayside town. It was because I *wanted* to be like these people. I wanted roots. I wanted connections. I wanted family. I wanted to grow. I wanted to *belong* somewhere. "I think it's real tasty the way it is."

"You're the picture of kindness, Emme." She tossed the rest of the muffin in her mouth and dropped the liner into the metal waste can that sat next to the oven, sending its lid swaying. "But pecans next time, most definitely."

I eyed her. She was fully dressed already, wearing black flowy linen pants and a pristine white T-shirt that had the barest hint of an embroidered detail on the cap sleeves. Her hair was pulled off her face, combed back into another loose but fancy knot at the nape of her neck. She had makeup on, even lipstick.

Lipstick at six in the morning.

"How long have you been awake?" I asked.

"I'm an early riser," she said, not really answering my question.

And also a night owl. I'd heard her crutching around her office well after midnight last night, hours after she'd convinced me to move in with her, hours after I'd turned in, my heart finally calmed down after thinking the sound of the stones on the window had been someone trying to break into the apartment.

Her proposition had entailed me moving in with her, helping her around the house while she recuperated, and acting as an assistant of sorts, driving her to appointments and such. When I wasn't working with Glory, of course. In return, Cora Bee was providing room and board and a nice weekly wage as well.

But it hadn't been the money or my innate desire to help her through her injury that had me lugging my suitcase over here. It had been the thought of companionship, the hope of friendship.

Glory had been thrilled by the plan when she found us standing in the driveway talking over details and promised Cora Bee she would come straight home from the Sweetplace and not dillydally like usual. Apparently the Sweetplace was a social hot spot.

I did *social* about as well as I did affection, so working at the marketplace was bound to be a challenge. But I'd give it my all, determined to learn.

Breathing in more coffee steam, I said, "Are you sure your mother isn't going to mind staying in the garage apartment and not here with you?"

Cora Bee glanced at me over the rim of her coffee mug. "She won't mind."

It was a whopper of a lie.

"My parents usually stay in the apartment when they're in town," she added. "My mother will quickly see it's better this way for all of us. She's . . ." She searched for the right word. "Headstrong. Thoughtful and caring but headstrong. With this injury of mine slowing me down, she won't think twice about stepping into my shoes. Taking over how I clean my house, how I file work folders, how I meet with clients. It's just how she is."

"And you're sure you want me to drive you to the airport tomorrow to pick her up and not go with Glory?"

It seemed to me Glory would be the better option, but it was becoming clear that once Cora Bee had an idea, she stuck with it. She seemed the planning type. Organized. A doer.

Yet, there was a dreamer in her, too. I saw it in half-completed yarn creations and inspiration boards full of color and whimsy. Refined whimsy, but whimsy nonetheless.

"It's best my mama gets to know you straight off. I mean, as an adult, that is. You were just a baby the last time we saw you."

This was news to me. "You knew me as a baby?"

Cora Bee nodded. "I was only six at the time, but I remember holding you and being afraid to drop you." She flashed a smile. "I didn't, by the way."

"I didn't realize you lived here back then. I thought Glory said your dad was in the navy."

"My mama, Cain, and I spent that summer here with Aunt Glory while my father was deployed overseas."

My stomach started hurting. "So you knew my mother?"

She tipped her head side to side. "I have vague memories of her. Big hair, big personality. My mother, however, knew her pretty well. She took Kristalle under her wing, befriending her. She bought Kristalle maternity clothes and baby items and talked nursing and nurseries. She had been a young mom, too, and knew how hard it could be. Besides all that, she was thrilled to have another baby in the family. My mama loved you the second you were born, and she was blindsided when your mother took you away. Brokenhearted. Then angry. I don't think all those feelings have completely gone away."

I swallowed hard. "I'm sorry."

"It's not your fault, Emme."

That might be true, but I felt like it was just the same. "I know part of my job is to drive you around, but maybe it's best if you ask Glory for a ride to the airport."

Her gaze softened. "You'll be fine, Emme. Besides, Aunt Glory doesn't drive anymore."

This was also news. "She doesn't? How does she get to the marketplace?"

"The kindness of others," she said with a smile. "She'll be seventy-eight on her next birthday, and she's just not comfortable behind the wheel any longer. But I'm sure now that you're here, she'll have you drive her SUV."

By the look in her eyes, what she said about Glory being uncomfortable driving wasn't an out-and-out lie, but it wasn't the full truth, either. I tried to gather up some courage to ask about Glory's cough, the misspeaking, but it felt too personal a question, one I didn't have the right yet to ask. Instead, I looked down at the splint on her foot, which peeked out from the wide hem of her pant leg. "How's your foot today, pain-wise?"

"About the same. Throbbing. And now my armpits and hands hurt, too." She let out a breathy half-hearted laugh. "Who knew crutches were painful in their own right?"

I glanced to the prescription bottle. "Are you keeping up with your medication?"

"Yep," she said brightly.

Another lie.

Suddenly it became obvious that I wasn't the only one around here used to hiding. Maybe Cora Bee and I were more alike than I first thought.

"Anything I can do to help you out right now?" I asked.

"If you could carry this mug into my office, I'd appreciate it. I'd like to get some work done this morning."

I put my mug down on the counter and took hers from her hand. "Is it a color project or a design project?"

"Actually," she said as she crutched down the hallway, "it's a dream project. I shouldn't even be working on it today, since I don't have all the materials I need, but I just can't help myself."

I was hoping she'd say more, but she didn't elaborate.

In her office, I set the mug on a coaster on her large desk while she sat down in an upholstered swivel chair, patterned with boldly colored flowers. I took her crutches and leaned them against the edge of the desk—out of her way but close enough for her to grab when she needed them. Then I carried a small ottoman away from a cushy-looking armchair and placed it by her feet, set a throw pillow on top of it, and motioned for her to prop her leg up.

As her foot hit the pillow, she let out a weary sigh. "What an ordeal this is. Thanks for your help, Emme."

"I'm happy to help."

"And I'm grateful to have you here."

I felt a well of warmth bubble up at the truth in her eyes.

"I'll be working for a while, so you don't need to hang around if you want to go out, explore, or simply want to watch TV. Make yourself at home."

Home. I waited for a warm, fuzzy feeling to accompany the word, but thoughts of unworthiness clawed their way back in, leaving me feeling cold. I drew my sweater tighter around me.

"Truly," she added. "This is your home for the next few months or so, give or take."

The plan was that I wouldn't move back to the garage apartment until she no longer needed crutches or until her mother left town, whichever came last. The timetable was up in the air because we didn't know how long Lillian planned to stay.

"Holler if you need me," I said, unsure what to do with myself. The only item on my schedule was supper at Glory's house. Sunday suppers, according to Cora Bee, weren't to be missed.

She threw a small smile over her shoulder. "I will."

I took a step, stopped, turned back to her. "Do you know if the local library is open on Sundays?"

"It's not," she said. "Sorry. But there are a lot of books on the living room shelves if you're interested."

"Thanks."

I wandered into the living room, feeling once again out of sorts and out of place, despite the fact that Cora Bee was thankful to have me here. I scanned the bookshelves, which didn't hold solely books. There were vases, candlesticks, a steampunk art piece that I studied for a good five minutes, amazed at its intricacies. There were also picture frames and photo albums. Unable to help myself, I opened one up.

It was a family photo album that had a black-and-white photo of a young Glory on the first page. She was holding a blanket-wrapped infant while a tiny girl clung to her leg, and she hadn't changed all that much in, what? Nearly sixty years? Her plump cheeks popped as she smiled at the camera, her eyes held a touch of sadness, and she seemed bathed in glorious light.

The little girl had to be Lillian. She had light ringlets that framed serious eyes, as if at such a young age she already understood the tragedy that had befallen her life. The baby in Glory's arms had to be Rowan, but it was hard to see anything other than the tip of a tiny nose. I wished I could read the personalities of young children more easily, but because the early years were all about formation, true personalities didn't start showing up until nine or ten years of age.

As I flipped the pages, there were fewer pictures of Glory and more of Cora Bee and a person who had to be Cain. Pictures that documented milestones. Christmases, birthdays, dances, graduations. There was one singular picture of a wedding on a beach. Cora Bee had been dressed in a barebacked lace gown as she smiled at the man who held her hands in his. I studied his face.

Egotistical.

Knowing so, I could easily imagine why they weren't married anymore.

My gaze fell on a small boy who couldn't be much older than a year, who sat at the man's feet, holding a velvet pillow. He had a sweet face with big eyes filled with adoration as he gazed at Cora Bee.

Near the end of the album, I'd been captivated by one photo in particular. It was of Rowan sitting at Glory's turquoise kitchen table. In front of him sat a pile of nuts, bolts, springs, gears. He'd been looking at the camera in the picture, his eyes full of happiness. Dozens of freckles glinted playfully in the sunlight. As much as I wanted my freckles to resemble his, mine were smaller, lighter, more numerous.

With an inward sigh, I finished glancing through the rest of the pictures. As I went to place the album back onto the shelf, a photo slipped out, falling onto the floor. I bent and picked it up, losing my breath at the image in my hand. It was a Polaroid-type picture of a broken Cora Bee in a hospital bed, hooked up to all kinds of tubes and monitors. Her eyes were swollen shut. Part of her head was shaved and at least a dozen staples were visible on her scalp. A large brace was wrapped around her torso that oddly reminded me of a medieval breastplate. In the white space at the bottom of the photo, *Day by day you find your way* was written in a slanting script, along with a date from three years ago.

I wanted to run back into Cora Bee's office and hug her, and I wasn't a hugger by nature.

Shame filled me as I thought about how I'd admired her flawless skin that had never seen violence. It was a painful reminder that I shouldn't judge books by their pristine covers. That even though I had a knack for first impressions, I didn't know every detail of that person's life.

I tucked the photo back into a random page of the album, unsure where it had fallen from—I thought I'd scanned every picture. I gently set the photo album back on the shelf and quickly skimmed book titles. I pulled out a worn copy of *Pride and Prejudice*, grabbed my coffee from the kitchen counter, and headed onto the screened front porch, to the swing I'd seen out there last night.

Bold purple flowers with yellow centers climbed trellises in front of the porch. Birds sang as the sun climbed, throwing its light along the garden across the street where noisy sprinklers watered the grass. Bright yellow police tape flapped in the morning breeze, a reminder of yesterday's shocking discovery.

I pulled my sweater tightly around me, thinking about Bee on the night she disappeared, calling for help and not getting it in time.

My heart hurt for her, for those who loved her.

My gaze drifted to Glory's house, to the ferns hanging proudly.

I didn't know how Glory had found me, because I hadn't called her for help.

All I knew was that she'd shown up at just the right time, when I had been at my lowest, wondering if anything in my life would ever work out for the good. I'd been ready to give up on my hopes and dreams. Ready to give up altogether.

Now I was here on Hickory Lane, and I wasn't going to let my feelings of unworthiness get in the way of finally feeling like I'd found a loving home.

Chapter
6

Glory's Garden Lesson #3

Over here on the east side of the stone shed you'll find a bed filled to its borders with one of the more unusual flowers in the garden. Parrot lilies. *Alstroemeria psittacina.* As you can see, hummingbirds love to sample from the red trumpet-shaped blooms. Crouch on down here and take a close look at the inner bell of the flower. Some people say it resembles a parrot—hence, the name—but it looks like butterfly wings to me. It's believed *Alstroemeria* represents friendships that have deep roots—strong relationships chock-full of support and devotion. That's why I call this little bed Dorothy's garden.

Emme

By late morning I found myself at loose ends. I'd already done what few dishes had been in the sink, swept, and dusted while Cora Bee had closed herself up in her office. I finally decided I'd take a walk around the neighborhood. Tomorrow was trash day, and there were already several bins lined up along the curb in preparation. Up near the top of the street, close to the main road, I could see some sort of furniture piece leaning against a trash can. A dresser. Or bookcase. It was too far away to see from here, but I wanted a closer look. A nonchalant look. An I'm-just-window-shopping look.

I told Cora Bee I was going out to stretch my legs and started up the street, my gaze fixed on my true destination. I was hoping the furniture piece was a big clunky dresser. Or maybe a buffet or credenza. Something that I wouldn't want to pick up and carry back to Cora Bee's. Something I could walk away from easily.

But it wasn't to be. My steps slowed as I walked past, my gaze affixed to the three-shelf bookcase. With its orangish hue, it appeared to be solid oak, and I didn't see any big flaws. Just expected wear from years of use. It would be perfect for my bedroom in the garage apartment.

Yet, I forced myself to keep walking. I was new to the neighborhood and really wanted to make a good first impression on my neighbors. Somehow, I didn't think picking through their trash would be applauded.

It hurt to walk away. Physically hurt. Anger sprouted, too, at what some people considered trash. There wasn't anything wrong with that bookcase that a little love wouldn't fix. Why toss it in the trash rather than donate it?

By the time I looped around the street, my anger had faded some, but my desire to rescue the bookcase had only grown. While I tried to talk myself out of marching up the street and claiming the piece for myself, opinions be damned, I spotted Glory in the island, walking amid the small field of wildflowers, a basket in hand. She looked up as though sensing she was being watched and lifted a hand to wave me over.

I threw a longing look at the bookcase and crossed the street, my flip-flops slapping against hot asphalt. As I stepped onto the island, I felt a faint buzzing beneath my feet, a gentle rumble. The vibration wasn't unpleasant or alarming but oddly soothing. It took the edge off my irritation with the bookcase situation and provided a sense of calm I'd rarely felt before.

As I followed the meandering path toward the flower meadow, I came upon the yellow police tape that cordoned off an area near a shallow pool of water. Beyond the police tape, there was no sign of a sinkhole, only destruction. The earth had been turned up and over and shoveled into piles. A big shrub had been upended from its bed and set aside, its roots weeping clumps of dirt. In that same bed, daisies and black-eyed Susans had either been dug up or trampled.

As I gazed at the mess, sympathy ballooned in my chest.

The buzzing beneath my feet intensified as I neared the small pool of water. This had to be the gazing pool I'd heard about. Sheltered by tall, skinny evergreens and shrubs that held heavy clusters of small, delicate white flowers, it was shaded by the canopy of an old live oak tree that had moss growing at the base of its trunk.

Curiosity drew me in. Faint ripples pulsed along the water's surface as the small pool burbled gently, peacefully, as if relieved to be unburdened of its long-held secret about Bee. I studied the burbling, wondering what caused it, because it didn't appear that anyone had placed a running hose beneath its surface. There was no equipment at all. Just clear water.

A knee-high mossy stone wall enclosed the pool, and ferns grew along its foundation, nestled snugly, their fronds rustling in the warm breeze. Suddenly I felt the urge to sit and stare into the water, and I absently smiled, thinking the *gazing pool* had been appropriately named.

"There you are, hon! I had a feeling you'd been sidetracked by the gazing pool. It has a way of drawing attention, of drawing you in."

With her back to the police tape and upturned earth, Glory sat down on the stone ledge and patted the spot beside her. She let out a sigh and placed her harvest basket on the ground. "It's nice to sit for a moment and just listen to nature. Are you listening?"

Smiling, I sat where she'd motioned, turning my body so I could watch the water. A bee flew by, leaving its crackling buzz in its wake. An airplane flew high overhead, a lawn mower droned on from down the street, a dog barked. "What am I listening to?"

"Life, Emme. Life." She closed her eyes and tilted her head backward toward the sky, and for a moment I thought the eyeglasses perched on top of her head were going to fall into the water.

The bee buzzed past again, flying in spirals toward the water. I followed it with my gaze, hoping it didn't plunge into the pool, as I didn't think bees could swim. It turned out I needn't have worried, as its fuzzy yellow body simply skimmed the water's surface. As I stared at the bee, it seemed to me its yellow bands began to glow brightly. When I blinked, the bee was gone and the water had clouded over, darkening. The bubbling stopped. The water flattened.

I squinted as an image of a man appeared on the water, coming slowly into focus. An angry man, wearing dark trousers and a white T-shirt, stomping toward a small apiary consisting of two white beehive boxes sitting side by side, resting on planks held off the ground by stacked cinder blocks. I also saw the gazing pool, though it looked different. There were no evergreen trees around it, no shrubs, and the live oak tree was smaller. The land was oddly bare compared to what it was now. When steam puffed out of the man's mouth, I realized it was cold, most likely wintertime, and I watched in horror as the man shoved the bee boxes off their supports, one quickly after the other. As the boxes hit the ground and split open, I felt a deep throbbing pain in my chest. Heartache.

"Amazing, isn't it?"

My head snapped up, and I noticed I had my hands pressed to my chest. "What is?"

"Life, honey."

I looked down at the water. It was clear and once again burbling peacefully. "I—"

I didn't know how to describe what I'd just seen without sounding like I'd been hallucinating.

Maybe I had been.

Glory looked at me, her eyes damp. "This was Bee's favorite spot in the whole world."

Still reeling from what I'd seen, it took me a moment to reply. "I can understand why. It feels . . . special."

"The last time I sat here with you, you were just a baby with pink cheeks and big green eyes, and so skinny even back then. It was the last I saw of you until yesterday. Of course, it's unlikely you remember the visit. Which is for the best, I reckon."

"Why's that?"

"Let's just say Kristalle and I didn't part on the best of terms."

My mother rarely parted with anyone on good terms. Not even me.

"Had she asked for money?" It wasn't a great leap of imagination to suppose so.

Glory looked off in the distance and wrinkled her nose. "Not from me. She wanted something I couldn't give her and used you as leverage. She wanted me to talk Rowan into marrying her or else she'd take you away forever."

I was grateful she wasn't trying to protect me from knowing the cold, hard truth. Sometimes there was no repainting an ugly past. It was what it was, and there was no hiding its big, bold swatches of disgust and shame and embarrassment. No one knew that better than I did. What surprised me most was that my mother had wanted to get married. I could only guess that there had been an ulterior motive, most likely a financial one, since she wasn't the marrying kind. I'd lost count of the men who'd fallen for my mother, only to be left behind, heartbroken and broke.

"Had they dated long?"

Glory's eyebrows shot up. "Oh, honey, they hadn't dated at all. Kristalle chased after him for a good while, but he always turned her down gently. He was a good ten years older than she was, and she wasn't his type."

When I was younger, I'd looked up Rowan Wynn on a library computer, hoping for a glimpse of my father. It hadn't taken long to learn that he was a professional gambler who was worth a small fortune—so it was no wonder my mother had been interested.

"Yet," I said, hoping my voice didn't crack, "I'm here."

"Apparently you happened during one drunken night." She drew in a deep breath. "All Rowan remembered about it was waking up the next morning with Kristalle beside him. Next thing we knew, she was pregnant. While she was pregnant, and with the agreement that there would be a DNA test once you were born, he paid all her bills, medical and otherwise, and rented a nice place for her to live. They did not continue a relationship."

"And once I was born?" I asked, my heart in my throat.

"Rowan fell in love with you. We all did. No one even talked about the DNA test anymore. We all just wanted you in our lives. It was then that Kristalle started pushing for marriage and issued her ultimatum."

It never ceased to amaze me what my mother would do in the pursuit of money. Marriage. She'd been willing to marry Rowan, a man who clearly didn't love her, to have open access to his wallet.

"No one thought she'd really take you away. Not until she left—and never came back. It was a horrible situation with you caught in the middle of it all."

How different would my life have been if Rowan had married my mother? I couldn't even begin to imagine—and I had a good imagination. "Sounds like you were caught in the middle, too."

"Not like you were, just an innocent little baby, having no say-so."

The police tape flapped in the wind, catching my attention, which then quickly shifted to the shrub that had been dug up, its weeping roots now exposed.

Glory followed my gaze. "That rhododendron and the two identical ones next to it are some of the few plants here that are original to Bee's garden."

"Will you be able to save it?"

"I hope so, hon."

I hoped so, too. I didn't push my luck by asking anything more about the police investigation. Not after she'd made it quite clear that she didn't want to discuss the matter.

A dog playing fetch on the green space barked happily and Glory turned her head toward the sound. "Come along with me to the cutting garden," she said, passing her basket over to me before lifting herself off the wall with a slight groan. "I still have a few more flowers I want to snip before I need to head inside and freshen up for supper."

I glanced into the basket at a pair of beautiful pale apricot-colored flowers. "Are those roses?"

"They look like roses but they're ranunculus. Stunning, aren't they?" She picked them up, holding them close to her face as she wiggled her pale eyebrows. "They symbolize attractiveness and charm. Can you see why they're one of my favorites?"

The humor in her eyes made me smile. "Absolutely. I've never heard of them before, but they're gorgeous. If you haven't been able to tell already, I don't know *anything* about flowers or gardening."

She flicked a disbelieving look my way. "You've ever grown *anything*?"

"You mean other than my disdain for people who dog-ear library books? No."

She laughed lightly. "We certainly have that in common."

As we walked away from the gazing pool, I glanced back over my shoulder, wishing I could stay a while longer. "Where does the gazing pool water come from?"

"It's from a small underground natural spring. This particular pool formed not long after Bee first moved here. She was delighted."

"An underground spring? Is that why the ground vibrates? It feels like there's buzzing under my feet."

Her gaze swept over my face, and surprise glinted in her eyes. "Not everyone feels the buzzing. Bee said it felt like bees were living underground, but the vibration is most likely from the spring."

Bees. The image of the man pushing over the bee boxes filled my head again, and I shook it away, wishing I could banish the heartache that had come along with it.

Glory said, "All the women in our family have a special connection to nature. Mine is with flowers. Cora Bee's is with color. Have you ever noticed a particular connection?" She lifted her pale eyebrows in question.

I swallowed a hard lump and shook my head. "Only if being able to feel the buzzing counts."

"I'm surely counting it," she said with a wink.

As we walked, my gaze swept across the island, which was divided into four free-flowing sections, big slices of pie that blended gracefully from one area to the next. At the top of the island, shade trees canopied a pergola that housed a picnic table and benches along with Adirondack chairs and a fire pit and barbecue grill. Another section held the small wildflower meadow and the cutting garden. Another held the vegetable garden, which was dotted with raised planter beds and support trellises. The last held the gazing pool and a stone shed that sat tucked into a copse of evergreen trees. In the middle of the island, thick grass grew on a small expanse of lawn, perfect for picnics or kite flying.

I stuck my hands into my pockets. "Speaking of Cora Bee . . ."

"Yes?" Glory said.

"Well, I mean, I have no right to ask this, but I saw a picture of her earlier. It fell out of an album. It was of her in a hospital bed, and honestly, she looked at death's door. It broke my heart. Do you know what happened?"

Glory tutted. "A bad car accident in Gainesville, where she lived before moving here."

"That's terrible."

She put her arm around me. "They were dark times, but sometimes it is in the harshest conditions that the most beautiful flowers bloom."

We'd just reached the metal arch that led into the cutting garden when a large dog, a white German shepherd, galloped playfully toward us, a faded green tennis ball in his mouth. I realized he was the dog I'd seen when I first arrived on Hickory Lane and was happy to see the welcoming look in his eyes hadn't dimmed.

"Emme, this is Orville." Glory patted the dog's head and flopped his ears back and forth. "He's a good boy. A very good boy."

"Hi, Orville." At the sound of his name, his backside wiggled this way and that, and it was impossible not to smile.

As Glory reached for the ball in his mouth, Orville pulled it out of reach. She laughed. "If you want me to throw it, you need to let it go. Drop it!"

Orville danced left, then right, obviously enjoying this game of keep-away. I enjoyed hearing Glory laugh, so lighthearted, as if for a moment forgetting the sorrow that had been dug up yesterday.

"He's always had a soft spot for you, Glory," a deep voice said.

I tensed as the man who'd given me directions to Glory's house yesterday strode toward us. The man who had a cop's eyes and an inquisitive nature.

"You best watch out, Chase, because one of these days, I might just keep him as my own."

This sounded like a familiar conversation between the two.

"Chase, this is my granddaughter, Emme. Emme, Chase is Dorothy's grandson and is staying with her a spell."

Although it was said simply, I could tell by Glory's tone that there was more to the story of why he was living with his grandmother. It took everything in me to meet his unwavering gaze. "We've met. Kind of. Thanks again for the directions."

"No problem," he said.

Up close, Chase looked strangely familiar, as if I'd seen him before yesterday. It wasn't only his eyes, those slightly hooded, long-lashed blue eyes, but there was also a faint scar above his right eyebrow. Somehow I knew there would be a dimple when he smiled—only one—in his right cheek.

I searched my memory, especially the times I'd crossed paths with law enforcement, but came up empty. "Have we met before?" I finally asked. "Before yesterday, I mean?"

"No."

Orville circled Chase's legs before finally dropping the ball and nudging it toward Glory. She dutifully threw it and with one graceful leap, he took off.

"Chase gets that a lot," Glory said. "You might've seen his face on his books. He's famous."

Color rose high into his cheeks. "I'm *not* famous," he said to me.

"Don't be so humble." Glory elbowed him. "Chase writes true-crime books. He's even been on TV to talk about them. We're real proud of him around these parts. The town council is even planning on naming a road after him."

My eyebrows went up as my brain quickly connected the dots. He was Chase Kistler, a former police officer. When he was injured in the line of duty and had to leave the force, he turned to writing. He was the author of two true-crime books that had made national headlines for the cold cases they'd helped solve. "Impressive," I murmured.

"It's an alleyway," he said.

I couldn't help smiling at his deadpan tone.

His right eyebrow—the one with the scar—lifted ever so slightly. "A dead-end alley."

I didn't want to like him, but he was making it difficult with his self-deprecating humor. I needed to remember that he'd been a cop once, and now he investigated things people wanted to keep hidden.

The last thing I needed was him digging too deeply into my past.

"You're from Kentucky?" he asked.

I stood stock-still, not so much as twitching. I. Would. Not. Fidget. "Most recently, yes. How many books have you written?" Even though I already knew, I was in full deflect mode.

"Two so far. I'm currently working on a third."

"Is that why you're staying here? Are you researching what happened to Bee for a book? Your grandfather was the chief of police back then, right?"

I clamped my lips closed, realizing I was talking too much, trying to keep him from asking about me or my old life. There was no bigger tip-off that I was hiding something than rambling.

It was a rookie mistake, but his humor had thrown me off my game.

Orville's tail thumped as he dropped the ball at my feet. I was more than happy to throw it for him, to divert attention away from me. After he went running, I glanced at Glory and noticed her face had paled.

"Chase came back home to look after Dorothy. Since her accident, she can't live alone . . ." Her voice trailed off and she gazed up at him. "Right? You're not writing about Bee's disappearance, are you? Chase? It's too personal."

"No, ma'am."

Interesting. It wasn't a blatant lie, but it wasn't the whole truth, either.

He cut a look my way, one part exasperated, another part wounded—as if I'd just ratted him out, betraying his trust.

Which was ridiculous for a number of reasons.

Yet, I suddenly felt guilty and looked away before I did something truly foolish like apologize.

He whistled for Orville. "Orville and I need to be getting back home to Dotty."

Dotty. I nearly smiled, thinking how grandchildren in the South rarely called grandmothers *Grandma*.

"We'll be seeing you for supper, right?" Glory asked.

Mentally, I groaned. What had I done to deserve this kind of punishment?

But I already knew that answer.

"Wouldn't miss it." He tossed another glance at me, gave a nod, and strode off. Orville trotted ahead, his tail still wagging happily.

Glory stared after him before flashing me a bright smile. "How would you like a bouquet to take back to Cora Bee's? To brighten up your room?"

"I'd like that," I said softly. "I'd like it very much."

Walking under the vine-covered arbor that led into the cutting garden felt a little like stepping into a magical land. On each side of a long stone walkway were five raised beds, lifted about two feet off the ground, each having just enough space between them to move around easily. Every bed but one was full of flowers. Some were in full bloom, others had buds, some were still growing, having only leafy green stalks.

"What's your favorite flower?" Glory asked me.

"It's an answer bound to change now that I'm here, but I've always loved daisies. They make me smile."

"A wonderful selection! They often represent new beginnings, and I can't think of anything better for you to plant in your own bed." She'd stopped at the empty bed and smiled at me. "This one is ready when you are."

"Really?"

"Of course. There's no better learning than by doing."

My own flower bed. It filled me with excitement, but also a bit of anxiety, wanting to get it just right.

As we walked around, planning my bed and pausing every so often for Glory to snip a bloom, in the distance I saw Chase and Orville go into their house. "Glory, would it be the worst thing for Chase to write about Bee? From what little I've heard, there are some powerful lessons in her story."

The basket swung on her arm as she faced me. "The *worst* thing? No, of course not. But truly, it's no one's business but our own. Bee wouldn't want her mistakes shared with the world."

"What kind of mistakes?"

Glory sighed. "Mistakes like marrying Levi. Or staying with him after he turned violent. Or possibly running away and leaving a small daughter behind."

Possibly. The word hung between us, full of painful acknowledgment, before Glory turned away.

As she walked along the rows of flowers, among the reds and yellows and pinks, I couldn't help but wonder why she'd lied to me. Because if the look in her eyes was any indication, it would, in fact, be the worst thing in the world for Chase to write about Bee's disappearance.

But why?

Chapter
7

May 10, 1963: My gardens are coming right along. There's so much to do that sometimes I feel like it'll never be done. But I read somewhere once that planting a garden is like believing in tomorrow. I like the notion of believing in tomorrows. Of being optimistic. I admit my spirits have been a bit low lately. Levi's moodiness is worrisome. Being out in the garden helps. I built a stone sittin' ledge around the natural spring, which I'm calling the gazing pool because it's mesmerizing. The bees love it, too. I often see them flying near it, and sometimes, and I know this sounds strange, they seem to take on a golden shimmer when they're near the water. I planted some ferns at the pool, too, because some believe ferns represent magic, and it sure feels magical out there to me.

Cora Bee

"I don't know, Aunt Glory. Do you think ten pounds of potatoes is enough?" I asked with a teasing lilt as I sat on a counter stool that had been pulled up to the sink. I wielded a shiny stainless-steel peeler, sliding it across the skin of a potato, grateful to have a chore to do to keep my hands busy and my mind off my troubles.

Aunt Glory swatted me with a dish towel as she set a canister of flour onto the island. "Be sweet. Don't go being a bad influence on Emme with that kind of sassiness. She's still young. Impressionable. What will people think?"

Emme glanced at me with a quirked eyebrow as she sliced a cucumber. A smile played on her lips.

My heart swelled with love for Aunt Glory, at how easily she embraced people, making them feel at ease. Welcome. At home. Emme smiled so rarely, but here in this kitchen I'd seen several already, some so big they revealed a slightly crooked front tooth that I found absolutely charming. It gave her face such character, and it made me want to see her smile all the time.

I said, "They'll think it's a family trait. I've known you to be sassy a time or two, Glory Wynn."

She barked out a laugh. "Hush your mouth."

I glanced at Emme, hoping to see her enjoying the conversation as much as Aunt Glory and I were, but her smile had fallen away as she concentrated on keeping the cucumber slices even.

I had noticed Emme took great care in everything she did. From the way she washed dishes to the way she folded the throw blanket on the sofa. Even her handwriting was neat and precise. It had taken a lot of encouragement from me to get her to add what she wanted to the grocery list on the side of the fridge, and I'd never seen *dental floss*, *apples*, and *peanut butter* spelled out so beautifully. Which was saying something, as I'd done my fair share of work with architects who prided themselves on their printing.

I'd teased her a little about the dental floss, about how she'd made it a priority, and she said she blamed it on the movie *Pretty Woman*. When she'd watched it years ago, she'd been fixated with Julia Roberts's character caring so much about flossing, even though she was dirt-poor, struggling to make ends meet. Ever since, Emme had made it a point to floss. And I had to admit, her teeth, even the crooked one, were beautiful for someone who had never seen a dentist. She'd inherited Uncle Rowan's smile, that was for sure.

And it was nice to see her care about her teeth, because otherwise, she was a bit of a hot mess. With the loose pigtails she wore, it was easy to see that the ends of her hair were choppy and uneven, and not in a modern kind of way. I suspected she'd cut her hair herself. Her clothes were drab and didn't fit her slim frame, all slightly too big, too loose, and too worn. She wore little to no makeup. Her fingernails were short, afflicted with hangnails, and bare. Her feet had Y-shaped suntan lines from cheap flip-flops. I smiled, though, at how her second toes were slightly longer than the big toes, just like mine.

While I knew she didn't have much extra money, I had to wonder why she didn't put a little more effort into her appearance. With her fair skin, big green eyes, and those stunning freckles, it wouldn't take much to banish her current street urchin look. Because even as she was, all raw and unpolished, it was easy to see she was a natural beauty, almost bohemian in nature—a modern-day flower child.

I smiled at the thought of her wearing a crown of daisies, because if anyone could pull it off, she could, and she glanced my way, a question in her eyes.

"Who all is coming for supper, anyway?" I asked over my shoulder to Aunt Glory, to turn Emme's attention away from me. I'd hate for her to think I was judging her. I wasn't. I was simply observing. "This is a lot of food for just the three of us."

I'd spent every Sunday since I had moved to Sweetgrass eating supper at Aunt Glory's table. It was rarely only the two of us, as we were often joined by friends and neighbors. Her door was always open, her generosity endless.

Aunt Glory tossed the dish towel over her shoulder. "As far as I know, it'll be the three of us, Dorothy and Chase, May and Nannette, and Jamie and Alice."

Of course she'd invited Jamie and Alice. It was typical Glory to envelop anyone who wandered into her world. Honestly, I should've expected it the moment Jamie drove my car onto her driveway.

Glory crossed to the double ovens and opened the bottom door to check on the roasting chicken inside. "*Hmm.*"

I swiveled on the stool to face her. "Something wrong?"

"The chicken is taking its sweet time. I'm afraid supper's going to be a mite bit late."

Emme walked over to take a look, then frowned deeply. "The chicken's still raw. Is the oven on? I don't feel any heat."

Glory's jaw dropped as she looked at the control panel. Then she burst out laughing. "No, it's not. That would certainly explain it! No harm, no foul. Or in this case, fowl. F-o-w-l. Get it?" She jabbed a playful elbow into Emme's arm, then took the roasting pan out of the oven, and set it on the island.

It was impossible not to laugh along with her, but underneath the cheerfulness lurked a great blue melancholy, wide and deep and dangerous. I blinked and looked away before I fell headfirst into its depths. I'd done so once, years ago, and I almost didn't survive.

Aunt Glory merrily preheated the oven, then wandered into the dining room to set the table, humming a happy tune under her breath. Emme returned to her spot beside me and picked up the knife she'd been using to slice the cucumbers. I felt her look my way, but I kept my gaze on the potato in my hand, though it was hard to see through the tears in my eyes.

Aunt Glory hadn't wanted to tell Emme of her health issues—at least not at first—but she hadn't planned on them being too hard to keep hidden. It was clear to me that Emme sensed something was wrong.

I doubted she had any idea of the cancerous tumors that grew inside Aunt Glory's head. Inoperable masses that would one day take her life. There had already been years of treatments. Radiation and chemo and pills and hospital stays and utter exhaustion. Earlier this year she had finally had enough, as the treatments were making her sicker than the disease itself—and barely prolonging the inevitable.

Any bouts of forgetfulness or clumsiness were explained away as side effects of her long fight. Though every time she stumbled, physically or mentally, people worried. And I was finding it harder and harder to keep Aunt Glory's secret. The secret that she didn't have much time left. Six months more, give or take.

It had already been six months since Glory had walked away from the medical world. Six months since she had decided *she'd* be in charge of how she wanted to live the rest of her life. Her first order of business had been telling everyone she was in remission. Then the hard work began. Getting her affairs in order. Her bucket list completed. Finding Emme.

My cell phone rang from its spot on the kitchen table, and Emme automatically grabbed it for me, not even glancing curiously at the screen as she handed it over. I thanked her and tried to hide my anxiety at seeing MAMA pop up on the caller ID.

Feeling like the worst daughter in the whole world, I tried to inject some cheer into my voice as I answered. "Hi, Mama."

"It's been a day, Cora Bee," she said on a long, drawn-out sigh. "A weekend, really. I need a stiff drink. A margarita the size of my head. Yes, that's just the thing."

Honestly, a monstrous margarita sounded wonderful to me, too. Too wonderful. I shifted, suddenly uncomfortable on the stool. "What's happened today?"

Emme slid me a worried glance.

"It's your father," Mama said.

"Is he okay? I thought he was healing well." Well enough for her to leave him to the care of someone else.

"He woke up with a slight fever, and his wound is looking a touch red. I'm sure it's nothing, but I'm just not comfortable leaving him until we know for sure. I have a call in to his surgeon. Long story short, I'm postponing my visit for a bit. A week. Maybe two."

My emotions warred. I worried for my father, but relief swirled like lustrous snowflakes around me.

Mama said, "When I know more, I'll let you know. Give my love to Aunt Glory."

We said our goodbyes and I hung up.

Glory stepped into the kitchen holding a stack of placemats. "Is everything all right, Cora Bee?"

I quickly explained the situation. "If it is an infection, it was caught early."

After a moment of listening and tut-tutting, Glory said, "I can see at least one silver lining in this situation. Lillian putting her trip on hold gives me an opportunity to get those updates done on the apartment. At least some of them. I mean, assuming Emme isn't moving straight back in."

"Do you want to move back, Emme?" I asked her. "I can let you out of our deal if you want."

She faced me. "I'd like to stay with you if that's okay."

The look in her eyes nearly did me in. The hope, the fear. Suddenly I knew she'd never lived anywhere that she felt truly *wanted*.

I held her gaze. "I'd love it if you'd stay with me."

Glory clapped her hands and said, "Then it's settled." She was smiling ear to ear as she headed back to the dining room.

Emme called out after her, saying, "My offer still stands about helping with the apartment. I'm real handy with a paint brush."

"All right, you've worn me down," she yelled back. "Later on, we'll talk about what all needs to get done."

As Emme went back to slicing cucumbers, I swallowed hard over a lump in my throat and pretended not to see the sheen of moisture in her eyes or the relief that swirled around her in delicate white wisps.

Slowly but surely, all was going according to Aunt Glory's plans. Emme's arrival had been a huge burden lifted from Glory's shoulders, as she was the foundation for most of what Glory wanted for the future.

But only time would tell if all would fall into place with Emme the way Aunt Glory hoped.

Or if it would simply fall apart.

Emme

I was in hell.

It was beautiful, this hell, but still hell nonetheless.

The dining table had been decorated with jars full of flowers of varying colors, heights, scents. Caladium, salvia, violas, snapdragons, or "snaps" as Glory called them. I'd learned their names—and forgotten half a dozen others as Glory and I had strolled through the garden earlier.

Votive candles set into pale-pink glass holders flickered along the table runner. The glass- and silverware sparkled in the early evening sunlight, while dust motes floated lazily through the air. The roast chicken and whipped potatoes, pull-apart rolls, green bean salad, and cucumbers and onions soaked in Italian dressing had been consumed. Or picked at, as the case had been for Cora Bee and me. Apparently, neither of us had much of an appetite.

The dinner conversation had been pleasant, surprisingly so. There had been plenty of talk of Lillian's upcoming return and of the Sweetplace. I'd learned that Nannette was as tightly wound as my first impression had intimated. She was an attorney for a local nonprofit, and I had no doubt she was good at her job. May owned a small gift shop in town, and Alice was a delight, full of life and charm. Chase had shared some amusing anecdotes about his book tours, and Jamie seemed on a quest to make Cora Bee laugh—with little to show for his efforts. Dorothy and Glory, who sat at the head and foot of the long farmhouse table, had been quiet, soaking up the conversation but rarely contributing much other than a word or two.

Because Glory had laid down the law about discussing the matter, any mention of what had transpired in the garden yesterday had been avoided, and no one asked much of me at all, other than generalities. It was almost as if it had been agreed upon beforehand to give me breathing room, which I appreciated more than words could ever say.

However, once the dinner dishes had been cleared, and Glory, with the help of Dorothy, went to fetch dessert, the inquisition began.

"How long do you plan to stay in Sweetgrass, Emme?" Nannette asked, her voice tight, as if the words were being pried from her lips.

I fought to keep my facial expression neutral, to hide the anxiety that coursed through my body, but my toes curled on the beds of my flip-flops. "As long as Sweetgrass will have me," I answered, repeating a version of what I'd told Cora Bee only the day before.

Nannette let out a small, amused huff. "One certainly can't beat free room and board. Glory has always had a soft spot for the unfortunate, and it seems Cora Bee is carrying on the tradition."

The unfortunate. I wanted to slide under the table and hide. If not for my resolution to be more outgoing, friendly, I might have gotten up and left. Starting a new life was harder than it looked. "I'm grateful Glory reached out to me," I said instead. "It was time for a change."

"A change from what?" Nannette leaned in. "What were you doing before?"

I could sense everyone's eyes on me and could feel the mix of suspicion, curiosity, and pity that hung in the air along with the scent of rosemary and thyme. I longed to say something truly snarky, like grave robbing, because by her tone I could tell that's what she expected. But I reminded myself of how hard I had worked to change myself, the years of effort. The years of low-cost counseling I'd received through a community program in Louisville. I didn't want to revert back to what I had once been— well, no more than necessary. It was easy to be defensive. It took effort to understand that Nannette was only looking out for her friends. It didn't mean it hurt any less, but understanding brought shreds of patience. "My last job was at a department store's call center."

The job had been utterly dreadful, but it had paid the bills. Barely. The promotion I'd been promised would've changed everything. I would've been able to start a savings account, one earmarked for a down payment on a home to finally call my own.

"What kind of schooling did you have?" May asked. "Did you go to college?"

In the seat next to me, Cora Bee sighed softly and threw a longing glance at the wine bottle standing in the middle of the table. She'd declined a glass of wine with dinner, murmuring something about her medication, and I suspected she now regretted the decision, harmful interactions be damned.

From my spot, I could barely see Glory and Dorothy standing at the kitchen island, their heads bent together. What in the world was taking them so long?

When I looked back at the table, I noticed Chase studying me, and my hands began to dampen. I set them in my lap and twisted the cloth napkin around my fingers. "No. My mother didn't much believe in academics."

Nannette continued to lean forward. "What does that mean? Did you drop out of high school?"

If she leaned any farther, she'd practically be sitting on my raffia placemat. "No, ma'am." I continued to twist the napkin until my fingers hurt. "I didn't drop out, because I didn't go. I've never set foot in a school as a student."

There was no point in hiding the fact—it wasn't as harmful to me as some other aspects of my life that I was choosing to keep to myself.

"Wow." Alice looked impressed. Her eyes were wide as she stared at me with wonder, and I almost smiled. While most kids would enjoy a no-school lifestyle, I had longed to go for a few reasons—namely, my desire to stop living on the road, my thirst to learn, and it would've been nice to make friends.

Jamie nudged his daughter with his arm. "Don't get any big ideas, Al."

"My mom would kill me dead if I didn't go to school," she said, her voice perfectly cheerful. "She's a teacher."

May frowned, the lines around her mouth pulling downward in dismay. Shock shone brightly in her blue eyes. "No school at all, Emme? That *has* to be illegal."

I lifted one of my shoulders in a slight shrug. "My mother also never cared much for matters of the law."

An understatement to be sure. Somehow Kristalle Halstead always managed to wiggle out of consequences. At the first sniff of trouble, she'd be on to the next town, the next mark, the next *sucker* before anyone noticed she was gone.

"I ended up getting my GED," I said, which on its surface sounded like no big deal. But it had been a very big deal. "That then allowed me to find a decent job."

"Customer service is such an under-appreciated industry," Cora Bee said quickly.

I glanced over at her and found earnestness in her eyes. She was trying so hard to soften Nannette's sharp edges.

"That's the truth if I ever heard it." Jamie gave Cora Bee a warm smile. "With our family business, we've learned that a good rep is worth their weight in gold."

I couldn't help noticing the way Cora Bee pretended not to see the way he looked at her. She nodded agreeably, but it seemed all surface and no substance.

Glory had mentioned that Cora Bee had been divorced for a few years now, and I wondered if she had yet to start dating again. Her body language said no. Practically screamed it.

"Where's your mother now, Emme?" Nannette asked.

"I'm not sure," I said. "I haven't seen her in a while."

A while equaled seven, almost eight, years. The last time I had seen her was on my eighteenth birthday.

"What kind of work does your mom do?" Alice asked, and Nannette beamed at her as if she were a prized student.

"It varies," I answered and threw another look at the kitchen as I braced myself for the next prying question.

I'd been jailed once, and this experience was infinitely worse—at least emotionally.

Chase, who sat next to Cora Bee, pushed his chair back and set his napkin on his seat as he stood up. "Emme, don't you think we ought to see if our grandmothers need help?"

Nannette opened her mouth, but whatever she planned to say was silenced by May's hand on her arm. May's warm gaze met mine. "That's a splendid idea. I'm more than ready for one of Glory's hummingbird cupcakes."

Chase stood at the foot of the table waiting for me, and I was surprised to see the flicker of compassion in his eyes before he hid it away. He had heart. And while I still knew to keep my distance, right here and now he was an easy choice over Nannette's interrogation.

Practically jumping out of my seat, I headed for the kitchen.

Chase fell in step behind me, and I could feel him, his presence, his heat, like it was an energy field that pulsed around him.

As I rounded the kitchen corner, I heard Glory, who'd been in the middle of whispering something to Dorothy, exclaim, "What timing! We were just talking about how this platter was too heavy for us to carry. Chase, would you, hon?"

The lie glowed in her eyes like shiny blue glitter, and it made me wonder what they'd really been discussing.

Dorothy licked a bit of frosting off her finger and squinted at me. "Who are you?"

"The bastard," I answered, not even caring.

A huge smile creased her face and she winked at me. "Ah, yes. I remember now. You're all right. I like you. You can stay."

That statement wasn't a lie, and I warmed from the inside out. "Thanks, Dorothy."

Chase picked up the platter full of beautiful cupcakes. "Emme's been under attack in the dining room, so if you lovely ladies don't mind rejoining us and putting Nannette in her place, we'd all surely appreciate it."

"Perhaps not Nannette," Dorothy said, shuffling off.

Chase laughed and dutifully followed his grandmother.

"I'm so sorry I stepped away for so long, Emme," Glory said, remorse in her gaze. "Was it terrible?"

"It wasn't great. I . . . I don't like talking about my past. It's painful. Plus"—I swallowed over a big lump in my throat—"I've done things I'm not real proud of."

She cupped my cheek with her soft palm. "We all have pasts, Emme. Some more colorful than others. We do what we have to do to get by. To survive. To live. No one's going to shame you for that. Not around me, at least. You're smart to leave the past behind you. Otherwise, if you keep looking over your shoulder at it, you might miss what's right ahead of you." She kissed my forehead, let go of my face.

"Thanks, Glory," I said, my stomach tangled up in a knot of guilt and love. "What were you and Dorothy up to in here with all that whispering?"

Glory's eyes lit. "We were just cooking up a little plan."

"What kind of plan?" I asked.

"Oh, you'll see soon enough."

For some reason, I didn't like the sound of that.

She smiled and then headed for the dining room.

I threw a longing look at the side door and fought every instinct screaming that I should walk straight out, and keep going, back to my old life.

Until I remembered that there was nothing left for me there.

Suddenly it felt like there might not be a place for me anywhere.

"Emme?" Glory called. "There's a cupcake here with your name on it. Come and get it, honey."

I wasn't sure yet that I'd made the right choice in coming here to Sweetgrass, but at least here there were cupcakes and Glory's flowers and Cora Bee's kind smiles.

And hope for the future, where there hadn't been any at all before.

Chapter
8

Glory's Garden Lesson #4

Take a whiff of this, hon. It looks like summer with its green velvety leaves and these magnificent stacked white flowers that look like an ice-cream cone. But doesn't it smell like Christmas? Stock's scent is reminiscent of clove. It represents beauty everlasting and a joyous, happy life. It also symbolizes a lasting, loving bond. *Hmm.* If I'd had some stock in my wedding bouquet, maybe my marriage wouldn't have been an utter disaster. Promise me you'll carry it when you get married. Don't argue with me—I'm an old woman. Just promise. That's a good girl.

Cora Bee

I woke up in the pitch black with a familiar sense of impending doom crushing my chest. I gasped for air and pulled myself into a sitting position. My mouth was dry; my head pounded. I glanced at the clock on the bedside table. Two fifteen in the morning. I let out a breath and leaned back against the pillows, wishing I could close my eyes and go back to sleep. But it wasn't that easy. It had never been that easy, but especially so since my accident. Sleep had become like silky smoke, a whisper in the night, a soft fleeting caress.

While I loved the darkness, I'd do just about anything for a good night's sleep. A doctor once told me that sleep helped heal, and I was desperately in need of healing. Physically, with my foot, and mentally for pretty much everything else.

Leaning back against the pillows, I pressed my hands to my

heart, willing it to slow its rapid beating. The crushing doom wasn't real—just a memory that was occasionally dredged up to torment me.

Or at least it felt that way.

Glory once advised me to switch up my way of thinking— that rather than viewing my car accident as a painful memory, to *choose* to think of it as a reminder of my survival. Of my strength.

I'd never admitted to her that my survival had never felt like strength. Not my own, anyway. Maybe hers, as I credited my survival to her. She'd raced to Gainesville when she'd heard what happened, had taken one look at me, broken and defeated in the hospital bed, and had somehow known exactly what I had done.

There had been no judgment. Only love. Care. Support.

By the time my parents had arrived from where they'd been stationed in Singapore, Glory had concocted a plan. I'd move to Sweetgrass and live with her while I fully recuperated from my broken back. Then I'd leave the past behind me and start rebuilding my life, my hopes, my dreams. I'd open my own business. I'd heal.

But as much as I tried, I'd yet to fully recover. I was stronger, yes, mentally and physically, but there were still struggles. And my hopes and dreams still lay broken and scattered, like shards of rainbow glass.

Noise came from the hallway and I sat up again, listening intently. Footsteps. What in the world was Emme doing out and about at two in the morning? Immediately, my mother's voice sprang into my head. When she'd called earlier to share that my father had been prescribed an antibiotic for a mild infection, I finally told her about Emme staying with me before she heard it from Nannette. Mama hadn't been pleased with the news, and I spent ten minutes attempting to calm her down, trying to convince her that Emme wasn't going to rob me blind and disappear into the night.

Now I was suddenly having doubts about Emme's intentions. Maybe I *was* too trusting. Too naïve. Too softhearted.

I swung my legs over the side of the bed and cursed the splint on my foot. I slipped my other foot into a house slipper, then grabbed my robe from the foot of the bed and pulled it on before picking up a single crutch from where the pair rested on the footboard. I could move faster with only one.

The squeak of the front door being pulled open cut through the silence of the night. As I crutched as quickly and quietly as I could down the softly lit hallway, I took mental inventory of my valuables. Heirloom china. Silver. My paternal grandmother's diamond necklace. My wedding ring set, including a two-carat engagement ring. My TV. My laptop. It was the thought of the computer loss that made me move even faster. My work life was on that computer. And work was my life.

The front door stood open, and I stepped onto the porch. The outside lights had been switched off. As I took a moment to let my eyes adjust to the darkness, a sense of calm came over me. The night was a balm to my soul, even now.

Much to my relief, Emme wasn't hopping into a getaway car idling at the curb. She was standing stock-still on the walkway, dimly lit by dull light thrown from the lamppost in front of Glory's house. Her hair was hidden under a dark ball cap, and she was dressed in black leggings and a black T-shirt. She certainly looked the part of a burglar, except for her feet. I doubted any respectable burglar would wear pink flip-flops while breaking and entering.

It was only when I noticed the crimson wisps of fear drifting around her in the soft light that I started to worry. "Emme? Are you all right? What're you doing out there?"

She folded her arms over her chest, hugging them to her body. "It's silly."

By her reaction, I didn't think whatever had drawn her out here was silly at all. I pushed open the wooden porch door and took one cautious step down the wide-planked stairs, then another. "What is?"

"There's a bookcase," she said, jerking her head up the street. "In the trash. I saw it on my walk earlier. It's a perfectly nice bookcase. Oak. Three shelves. Sure, it has its scars and scuffs and outdated carvings, but I can fill in the carvings, paint it . . . make it shine."

As my brain took a moment to connect the pieces of what she'd said, I walked stiffly toward her, trying to keep from putting too much pressure on my hurt foot. "You want the bookcase?"

"It's not like I'd be stealing it," she added quickly. "Anything that's left out at the curb for trash is free for the taking. It's just sitting there waiting for someone to see that it's not trash at all. A little love and it'll be good as new."

Because she sounded so defensive, I said, "Of course you wouldn't be stealing it. I just don't understand why you didn't take it when you saw it earlier."

"And have the neighbors see me picking through their trash the day after I arrived? I can only imagine the reaction."

"I can see your point," I conceded. Something like that was sure to get tongues wagging. "But why're you standing here now if you want it? Why not just go get it?"

She swallowed hard and kept on hugging herself. "It's so dark out here. I thought with the streetlamps it wouldn't be so bad, but there's no moon, and . . ." She shuddered.

"You're afraid of the dark?"

"A little."

A lot if her body language and those red floaters were any indication. It hurt my heart, her fear, because I found so much peace in the darkness.

"Let's just go back inside," she said. "I really don't need the bookcase. It's not a big deal. There's not anywhere to put it anyway. I won't be moving back to the apartment for a while, and I'm sure you don't want that kind of clutter around your house. Besides, I don't even know if it's still there."

I watched her ramble on, her gaze darting down the street to where I assumed she'd seen the bookcase earlier, and made an easy decision. "We'll go together to see if it's still there." I took a few tentative steps up the walkway.

"You're in your robe, Cora Bee. And you only have one crutch."

"And you're stalling, Emme. You'll be filled with regret if you don't even check. Come on."

She hesitated for a second, then took a deep breath and stepped forward. "All right, fine. Let's just get this over with."

"That's the kind of enthusiasm I love."

She cracked a smile.

I kept talking, to distract her from her fear. "I think darkness can be peaceful. Sometimes you can see more clearly in the dark than you can in the light. The absence of color makes you focus more intently."

"I thought you loved color. Glory mentioned something about it, that you had a natural way with it or something."

"When you see color the way I do, sometimes it's nice to get a break from it. It crowds my senses. Nighttime, darkness, evens it out. It's all about the balance for me."

"How is it that you see color, exactly?"

I was thinking about how to answer when Mabel started barking as we passed Jamie and Alice's place. I tossed a look at their house, hoping Mabel didn't wake anyone up. Namely, Jamie or Alice.

"Oh! It is still there," Emme said, the words coming out bright and sparkly, floating into the night air like golden butterflies.

Rushing forward, she inhaled deeply as she ran her hand over the top of the bookcase, as if lovingly reassuring it that it wasn't going to the landfill. She quickly set her arms inside the piece and lifted, letting out a little grunt when the bookcase barely moved. "It's heavier than I thought."

"Solid oak, probably. No veneer for that baby."

Mabel kept barking, and I wanted to shush her even though I knew she couldn't hear me. She was going to wake the whole neighborhood.

"I think so, too." Emme crouched down, her back to the

piece. "Can you tip it toward me? I'll get it up on my back and carry it home that way."

"Are you out of your ever-loving mind? I think that bookcase weighs more than you do. You'll be a pancake. *That* will really get the neighbors talking. I have a hand truck in my garage. We'll go back and get it."

Slowly she stood. "All right, but we're getting your other crutch while we're there. You really shouldn't be walking around without it."

"Yes, *ma'am*."

She grinned, and my resolve to only be friendly—and not her friend—shook like there'd been an earthquake.

We turned to head back to the house, and a long shadow emerged from the darkness. Emme immediately latched onto my arm, gripping it tightly, and fear coursed from her fingers into my skin, burning it.

"It's okay," I said under my breath, recognizing the man right away. "It's just Jamie."

"Sorry if I startled you," he said, tossing a glance at Emme's death grip as he stepped onto the sidewalk. "Mabel's barking woke me up. I was surprised to see you out here. Is everything okay?"

He had bed head, his hair sticking out every which way, and wore only a pair of loose knit shorts. I tried to keep my gaze off his chest, but it kept slipping back down until I turned toward the trash cans. "So sorry we woke you. We were just rescuing this bookcase for a little upcycling project Emme's wanting to try."

Emme nodded. "Upcycling."

"At two thirty in the morning?"

I shrugged. "We were up. It seemed the thing to do. But we need to go back for a hand truck. It's a little too heavy for Emme to carry alone, and I'm currently useless."

"Probably solid oak," he said, giving the piece a good once-over.

Emme finally released my arm and glanced at me with a

slight smile on her lips, no doubt recognizing that I'd said the exact same thing. There was a twinkle in her eye that suggested she had matchmaker aspirations.

Nope. No way. I had to put a stop to that right off the bat.

"Thanks for checking on us, Jamie, but you can go on back to bed. We've got this under control."

He walked over to the bookcase, bent, and lifted it easily. "I'll just take it for you right now. Save you the trip back." He started off down the sidewalk.

"Show-off," Emme whispered in my ear as we followed him.

"What exactly is upcycling?" Jamie asked over his shoulder.

"You know how people flip houses? Upcycling is basically furniture flipping, but with a fancier name. Trash to treasure, that kind of thing."

"What're you planning to do to it, Emme?"

"Paint it," she said. "Maybe fill in some of those carvings to give it a modern look. Probably add some wallpaper on the back panel."

Goose bumps rose on my arms at the dreamy sound in her voice. It was as though she could already see the finished product in her mind and was already in love with it. "What color are you thinking?"

"I'm not sure. I didn't let myself dream that far," she said. Then she blurted, "Teal. Something's telling me that it should be teal."

My heart fluttered a bit. Teal was the perfect color.

"Will you keep it? Or sell it at the Sweetplace?" Jamie asked. He seemed awfully chatty for the middle of the night.

"Keep it," Emme said. "Do they even sell furniture at the Sweetplace?"

I smiled. "They sell a little of everything there."

He said, "I'd love a chance to see it if you decide to sell. I've been looking for a bookcase for Alice's room—something fun and quirky. Unique. But I can't find anything that's just right."

Teal was a perfect color for Alice, too. It was almost as though it had been meant for her all along. Then I recalled the love I'd heard in Emme's voice for the bookcase and doubted she'd part with the piece once it was done.

Jamie walked the bookcase up the driveway and waited for me to punch in the code on the outside garage door opener. The door slid open, the light coming on automatically.

My car was parked on the left side of the garage, but the right side was completely bare. Remembering Emme's dreamy tone, I turned to her. "What do you think about using this side of the garage to work on the bookcase and any other pieces you find? We can set up a workshop area for you."

Her eyes widened, then she blinked away the happiness that had flared up, dousing it quickly. "That's real nice of you, Cora Bee, but I don't want to mess up your whole garage."

"You're not messing it up. You're creating. I'm all for supporting the arts."

Jamie set the bookcase down and put his hands on his hips. "Me too. I have some tools you can borrow if you need them. Saws and sanders and just about anything, really."

It was awfully nice of him. Emme must've thought so, too, because there was a fine sheen of tears in her eyes. "Thanks."

Jamie gave us a nod. "I need to get back. I closed Mabel off in my bedroom to keep her from barking, and I'm guessing my pillows are shredded by now. You never met a dog so enamored with pillow stuffing."

With that, he was off, and we watched him go, his long strides making quick work of the sidewalk that linked our houses.

Finally, Emme turned to me. The moisture was still in her eyes. "Really, Cora Bee. I don't need all this space. The backyard is fine. That way I won't worry about getting paint on the garage floor."

"Instead you'll have gnats and grass in your paint, a sunburn, and sore muscles from hauling the bookcase back and forth from the garage to the backyard. In here is perfect." She looked ready to keep on protesting so I added, "I insist."

Glancing around, she said, "I'd only need a small corner."

I couldn't help laughing. "We'll figure all that out later on.

Right now we should get to bed for a few hours' sleep. We both have a long day ahead."

She ran her hand over the top of the bookcase, a small smile playing on her lips; then her lip trembled and she wiped her eyes with the heels of her hands.

"Are you okay, Emme?"

She nodded, and for a moment I didn't think she was going to say anything, but she finally whispered, "I'm not used to people being so nice. Thank you."

Suddenly I realized how alike Emme and that bookcase were. She needed someone to see beyond her rough exterior, to see her value.

All she needed was a little love to fully shine.

Chapter
9

*June 22, 1963: What an amazing way to kick off sum-
mer! We're finally having a baby. Levi wants a boy but
I'm hoping for a girl. I'm due in February. I hope the baby
will love flowers and bees as much as I do. Speaking of bees,
I got to talking to Mr. Yardley at the company picnic and told
him about some interesting kilns I'd seen in a magazine article.
They looked like beehives! He seemed fascinated enough, but
Levi told me later Mr. Yardley was just being nice and that
the next time we saw him I shouldn't bother him with my bee
nonsense. Still. I think Mr. Yardley truly was interested.*

Emme

"You're already earnin' your keep, honey," Glory said over her
shoulder as I pushed a hand truck over hard-packed, cracked dirt
dotted with limp clumps of weeds and grass. "I've gone to battle
with that dolly more times than I care to admit and lose nearly
every time. I named her Suzanne after Suzanne Sugarbaker because you know she would rather die than do manual labor.
Seemed appropriate, considering the sass that thing gives me."

The morning sun sat low in the sky and lazy sunbeams
skimmed the tops of booths and tents that were set up on a
fenced lot behind the courthouse. Lingering dew dampened the
tops of my feet, tickling my toes. As we passed under a wooden
sign branded with SWEETGRASS MARKETPLACE in swooping
font, I asked, "Suzanne who?"

Glory looked over her shoulder again. Today she wore a

lightweight blue dress that matched her eyes, coupled with a chunky necklace and sturdy leather sandals. In her ears were the same antique flower-patterned earrings she'd worn every day since I met her. A straw hat with a curled brim and white grosgrain ribbon band shaded her broad face. "Sugarbaker. She's a character from the show *Designing Women*. Have you never seen it?"

"No, ma'am."

"That's a tragedy. We'll fix that." With a stumble, she stopped in front of a booth and grabbed the counter for balance before smoothly righting herself. She pointed an accusatory finger at the hand truck. "Just know if you ever hear me cussing Suzanne out, that's who I'm talkin' about."

I worried about Glory's balance issues, but because she'd treated the stumble as though it hadn't happened, I thought it best if I did as well. Eventually, I was going to have to start asking some hard questions, but for right now I was happy to live with Glory in the land of denial and carry on with the day.

Five wooden crates were stacked on the hand truck and seven thoughtfully placed bungee cords held them in place. At first I thought the amount of bungees was overkill, but then I tried to steer the cart, and it became clear that the amount of cords had been determined by painful experience. The hand truck seemed to have a mind of its own and was more than willing to throw its weight around. I'd been pushing the blasted thing for only five minutes and I'd nearly tipped it over four times, banged up my shins and ankles, and had run over my toes twice.

There was a sixth crate still in Glory's SUV that I needed to go back for, and I was grateful it was one I could carry. It was packed with mason jars full of petite flower arrangements. When I first saw them this morning, I'd wanted to take the whole box back to Cora Bee's and dot her house with the small pops of beauty. I'd never considered myself much of a flower person, but there was something about Glory's flowers—and the way she arranged them—that sent happiness buzzing through me.

Glory held out her arms toward the booth like she was aiming to give it a hug. "This one is ours."

Ours.

It wasn't ours. It was hers. Yet her desire to include me warmed my heart and packed my head with thoughts of roots and love and family. "It's charming."

"I think so, too."

The wooden booth looked like it was part lean-to, part lemonade stand. There were no side walls, but it had a plank floor and a caged fan that hung from a timber ceiling. Floating dark wooden shelves lined a shiplap back wall that had been whitewashed at some point. There was a cutout in the center of the wall that housed a large purple-and-gold GLORY & BEE sign. The wooden countertop was worn and scarred, its rounded edge rubbed smooth from time and usage.

Several other booths identical to this stall dotted the wide lanes of the marketplace, and mixed in between were a couple dozen matching white canopy tents.

"It's a prime location, that's for sure." Anyone coming into the marketplace would have to pass by this stall—and I questioned how anyone could resist Glory's treats. I'd already eaten three pieces of red velvet fudge and it wasn't yet eight a.m.

"Helps to know the people who started the Sweetplace way back when. *Waaaaaay* back when." When I didn't say anything, she let out a loud laugh. "It's me and Dorothy. We're the ones who started it."

I smiled at how she laughed at her own joke. Her humor was contagious. "I had no idea. How long ago?"

She released a bungee cord and the wooden crates sighed in relief. "A good fifty years ago. We were both young moms looking to spread our wings a bit. We started small. Roadside-stand kind of small, which is an idea I stole straight from Bee. Slowly our business grew. And grew and grew. We'd taken a chance. And it paid off."

I placed one of the crates on the countertop. The box was full of accessories. Tablecloths, runners, doilies, stands, trays, and several empty mason jars. "A success story, then."

With a touch of pride in her eyes, she glanced around the lot. "For the most part. There've been some ups and downs. Mostly ups. We've been lucky that the town has supported us for so long, lettin' us lease this land on the cheap. But that's going to be changing soon."

I set another box onto the countertop. "Change how?"

"The town's decided that Sweetgrass needs a municipal building and community center on this lot more than it needs us. The Sweetplace is fixin' to move across town next month. Buck's Drive-In has offered us a short-term contract to set up there. We'll have to pack up and clear out every day, so it's not ideal, but I'm mighty grateful we won't have to shut down until we find land of our own."

I lifted another crate. This one was filled with clear plastic bags stuffed with treats. Each bag was labeled with a beautiful GLORY & BEE sticker and tied at the top with gold ribbon. There were cookies, caramels, fudge, divinity, peanut brittle, truffles. I wanted to sample them all. "It doesn't seem right to kick you out after fifty years."

"The community center will have public meeting rooms, fun class offerings, a gym, an indoor pool, a big outdoor pool with slides, a toddler pool, and a splash pad. Even *I* voted for its approval."

At her honesty, I smiled.

"Sometimes change is a good thing, Emme." She winked at me before sorting through a box.

Change. I'd had so many changes during my lifetime that I was more than ready for stability. For predictability. For routine.

I'd been hoping the last change in my life for a while—a long while—would be moving into Glory's garage apartment. But then I moved in with Cora Bee. And now in a month, my workplace would be changing locations. It suddenly felt over-whelming, like I was caught in a riptide, being carried along and trying not to drown. How was I going to be able to set roots if

I was constantly moving? It was as if the universe were working against me. Telling me that until I told the absolute truth, I'd keep getting dragged along.

It was an unsettling thought.

"Good morning!" a woman said as she easily pulled a collapsible wagon behind her.

With its all-terrain wheels, the wagon rolled smoothly, barely even jostling the small pallets of bagged bread nestled inside its high walls.

I bet she hadn't once run over her toes.

"Mariella! Meet my granddaughter. Emme, this is Mariella Saunders, one of the best bakers in the South. She specializes in bread. All kinds of glorious bread."

Mariella's dark cheeks lifted high at the compliment. "It's a labor of love. Nice to meet you, Emme. Welcome to Sweetgrass."

Mariella seemed to be assessing me the same way I was her. *Amiable* was the word that came immediately to mind. With her big eyes, wide smile, and full cheeks, she had a friendly face— inviting. She was the type of person who probably had people lining up at her stall not only for bread but to chat about the weather or ask where they could find okra in the marketplace.

She'd be an easy mark.

Hers was the kind of personality con artists loved to take advantage of. Suddenly, I wanted to warn her to be careful of being too open, too friendly. Yet, there wasn't a trace of suspicion in her gaze as she looked at me. Only curiosity. Somehow I felt seen for the first time in a long while and that made me want to thank her like she'd given me a gift.

The push and pull between my old life and my new one was proving to be confusing . . . and slightly painful.

"Thank you," I finally said, meaning it. "It's good to be here."

Her eyes squinted when she smiled. "I'm sure I'll be seeing you around."

Glory said, "I'll be by later for a loaf of rosemary bread, so be sure to set one aside."

"Sure thing," she said with a wave and strode off, her wagon following obediently at the slightest tug from her hand.

I watched her go, eyeing the roll of those wheels. "I think I have wagon envy."

Glory laughed. "Suzanne will grow on you."

I had my doubts.

For the next ten minutes, Glory and I worked quickly and efficiently to set up her display, as if we'd done it together a thousand times before. I marveled at the result. The shelves were filled with baskets of goodies, and mason jars had been loaded with beautiful honey lollipops, their amber color almost translucent. There were tiered trays full of boxed cake slices and stunning cupcakes topped with playful fondant bees, clear packaging showing all the delight inside. An old tobacco basket on the countertop was brimming with sugar cookie sandwiches filled with various types of frosting.

A shallow wicker basket held the only merchandise for sale at the stall that Glory hadn't made or grown. It was full of crocheted pieces done in bright, playful colors. Coasters, doilies, hot pads, washcloths, a floppy bunny. I picked up the rabbit, studied it closely. It was primarily crafted from pale purple yarn, but there was some silver mixed in as well. It had long lop ears, wide-set friendly eyes, and a delicate white yarn nose. Attached with twine was a brown craft paper tag that read CORA BEE'S CROCHET. The bunny was priced at twenty dollars, and if I didn't need to buy paint and supplies for the bookcase, I'd have bought it then and there.

"Cora Bee has a way with yarn, doesn't she?" Glory asked as she stepped up next to me.

I set the bunny back into the basket. "Most definitely. The bunny is my favorite of what's here."

I'd been hesitant to leave Cora Bee this morning, but she insisted she'd be fine for a few hours on her own. She had moved her morning meetings to the afternoon and planned to work on existing projects while I was gone.

Glory said, "I don't know how she does it. She tried to teach me how to crochet a few times, and all I ended up with was a ball of knotted yarn. Won't be long before she tries to teach you."

I smiled. "Another of her bad influences?"

"You have to keep a close eye on her."

For a moment our gazes met, held. It almost felt like a hug, and for some reason it made me feel like crying. I wasn't sure whether from happiness or sadness.

I jerked a thumb over my shoulder. "I should go get the flowers before they start wilting. Should I close the windows and lock the SUV when I'm done?"

She waved a hand as she set up her cash drawer and pulled out a computer tablet that had a credit card reader attached. "No need, honey."

Glory had left the windows down in the SUV and the doors unlocked, and it had taken all my willpower to walk away from it so . . . unprotected. Glory was tempting fate, leaving the vehicle wide open. Just on my quick survey of the interior on the drive over, I'd seen a couple of dollars in the console, loose change scattered about, a crystal sun catcher dangling from the rearview mirror. There was a toolbox she kept in the backseat for emergency repairs at her booth, a couple of lawn chairs, sunglasses, a GPS device, and worst of all, her garage door opener. With that, thieves could access whatever Glory kept in her garage, and I was suddenly thankful that her garage wasn't connected to her house.

Not that it mattered all that much, because she kept those doors unlocked, too.

I wanted to shake sense into her, into all these unsuspecting people, but I had the feeling they'd only smile and tell me that Sweetgrass was a safe place. Maybe it was safer than most, but no place was immune from the dangers in the world. The tragic discovery in the garden over the weekend proved that.

As I headed for the small parking lot adjacent to the courthouse, I couldn't help noticing the courthouse's clock tower. It loomed above me, radiating disapproval, as though it knew I didn't belong here, in this town. It might be right, but I was staying as long as I could, so I ignored it, even as I wondered who in their right mind thought that dark brick was a good idea.

I passed by other vendors heading for their stalls and offered small smiles, hoping they came off as friendly and not as painful as they felt. I opened the back of the SUV and was reaching for the crate of flowers when I felt the air shift around me. I whirled around, my hands fisted, and came face-to-face with Chase Kistler.

He held his hands up. "Hey now. Friend not foe."

I wasn't sure about that but released my fists. "Sorry. Old habits. But you should really clear your throat or something when you approach someone from behind."

Of all people, a former police officer should know that, and I sensed he *did* know, that he'd been testing me somehow. I didn't know whether I'd passed or failed.

He gave an easy smile and glanced at my hands, which had fisted again. I reached for the crate of flowers so my hands would have something to do.

"My apologies," he said. "I thought you heard my footsteps. Dotty always teases me about how I clomp around the house."

I didn't want to admit I had been lost in thought, so I simply nodded my acceptance of his apology. "I didn't take you as a clomper."

Dorothy, I noticed, stood not too far away, chatting with a woman I didn't recognize. Neither were paying us any mind.

"Compared to her birdlike steps," he said, "I'm practically a one-man marching band. Also, when she fell and hit her head a few years ago, it not only affected her mind but her hearing as well. Amplified it. Here, let me take that." He reached for the crate.

"It's okay. I've got it."

He grabbed hold anyway. "I insist. It's the gentlemanly thing to do."

"Are you a gentleman?" I asked.

"I'm working on it."

I released the crate. Not because of his smile but because I didn't like standing so close to him. It was the easiest way to separate myself. I closed the hatch and couldn't help myself from locking the doors. Still, I eyed the open windows. They weren't all the way down but someone with a skinny arm could certainly reach inside.

"Something wrong?"

"Nope."

"It's killing you keeping those windows open, isn't it? More old habits?" he asked.

I didn't like how easily he saw right through me. I tried for a light shrug. "Glory said to leave them open."

"Where'd you learn these habits of yours anyway? You don't seem the type to throw a punch."

I glanced at Dorothy and silently begged her to wrap up her conversation. "Nowhere in particular."

"I think I've passed through there a time or two."

I tucked Glory's keys in the pocket of my shorts. "I knew you looked familiar."

He smiled. It wasn't one of his usual easy, lazy smiles but one that reached his eyes and lit them up. One that made the dimple show.

I took a step away and again glanced over at Dorothy, who was still chatting up a storm, her arms swinging this way and that as she related a story that didn't seem to be ending anytime soon.

"I should get these flowers to Glory." I held out my hands for the crate, more than ready to flee. "Looks like shoppers are arriving."

"Just lead the way," he said.

"Don't you need to wait for Dorothy?"

Something flitted in his eyes before he turned and said, "Dotty, I'll be right back."

She waved a hand at him, shooing him along.

He laughed. "She hates when I hover."

"How does she feel about you living with her, then?" I asked before I could stop myself.

For a second I didn't think he was going to answer, but finally he said, "Mixed emotions. But I'm a sight better than having to move to assisted living, so she tolerates me."

I was starting to feel emotionally invested in this conversation, wanting to ask him a dozen more questions, each more personal than the last, so I picked up my pace and pressed my lips together.

"Are you ready for today?" he asked. "There's bound to be a crowd just wanting to catch a glimpse of you. It's not every day Glory's granddaughter makes an appearance."

"As ready as I'll ever be."

To avoid someone coming the other way, he moved in close to me and didn't step back afterward. Uncomfortable with the closeness, I veered to the left. Thankfully he took the hint and didn't glue himself to my side again.

As we approached Glory's stall, she grinned as she looked between Chase and me. "Delegation! I love it. You've got some good leadership skills there, Emme honey."

I said, "It wasn't so much delegation as appropriation."

Chase's eyes widened in surprise and then narrowed as he reassessed me. "Hold up now. I was being a *gentleman*."

Glory laughed and took the flowers from Chase. "Whatever it was, I'm glad you two are gettin' on so well since you'll be spending a fair amount of time together."

I froze. "What's this now?"

"You didn't tell her?" Glory asked Chase.

"Didn't have the chance. I was too busy appropriating."

I clenched my fists and heard him chuckle. "Tell me what?" I asked.

"Chase is going to help you with the garage apartment redo. Wanted to tell you himself, but I guess the cat's out of the bag now. Isn't that nice of him to help?"

My gaze slid to his. He watched me carefully.

"So nice," I said through clenched teeth. This had to be the little plan she and Dorothy had cooked up in the kitchen last night.

"You two should be able to get started in a week or so. I've been online shoppin', and I'm just waiting until everything comes in before you get started. There's nothing so frustrating as gettin' started on a project only to have to stop because you don't have what you need."

It was mean of me, but I hoped the items were back-ordered for a while. A long while.

Chase scratched the stubble on his chin and smiled. "I should get back to Dotty. I'm looking forward to getting to know you better, Emme."

"*Aww,*" Glory crooned.

I said tightly, "Can't wait."

He laughed as he walked away, and as I busied myself behind the counter, I wondered why I couldn't stop thinking about his dimple.

↘↙

By noon I decided that if an arts-and-crafts show and a farmer's market had a baby, it'd be the Sweetplace. You could find just about anything here from handcrafted furniture to garlic bulbs pulled fresh from the dirt. I longed to wander the pathways, visit every booth, but stayed put alongside Glory.

She had an easy way about her I tried to emulate, because I certainly didn't have the people skills to be as charming as she was. Throughout the morning, I'd pasted on a fake smile while suffering through endless introductions to other Sweetgrass residents. I'd never remember all the names, but I'd be able to recall my first impressions. *Amusing. Empathetic. Arrogant. Intelligent. Wise. Funny. Cautious. Faithful. Genuine. Dramatic.*

Interestingly, every single one of the booth's visitors had inquired after Glory's health in one way or another, whether it was a direct question or a more indirect, "You're looking well, Glory!"

It quickly became clear she had a set of prepared responses that ranged from *doing just fine*, *right as rain*, and *better than ever* to *every day is a good day to be alive*. After which, she'd redirect the conversation, asking about their health or spouse or child or work.

It felt like everyone knew a secret that I wasn't privy to. I was going to have to ask about Glory's health sooner rather than later, but asking Glory to her face was something I couldn't bring myself to do, especially since she seemed happy living in her land of denial. I'd ask Cora Bee. This afternoon.

With thoughts of Cora Bee, I glanced toward the crochet basket and felt a deep pang of sadness to see that the darling little bunny had been sold.

Chapter
10

 *Glory's Garden Lesson #5*

Take a gander at these lovely ladies in this bed. Zinnias. You've never seen such saturated colors. Oranges, pinks, reds! Look at those petals, hon, how they stack up, like they're lying down atop of one another. And oh, such delicate yellow pollen florets in the center of each. They're a wonder. Give them a little more time, and this bed will be absolutely bursting with color. You'll actually see them around the whole garden island, peeking out here and there to share their beauty with others. They represent endurance, remembrance of a dear friend, and everlasting affection. It'll probably come as no surprise to you that I planted them for Bee.

Cora Bee

"You always come up with such fresh, clever concepts, Cora Bee, so I'm not sure what you're worrying about. It's not as though you're planning to name the new shopping center the Brickyard, which has been so overdone."

It was just past five in the morning on Mama's side of the country, but her voice came through the speakerphone of my cell loud and clear, burrowing under my skin uncomfortably. Frowning, I glanced at my sketch pad, at the bold words I'd penciled in at the top of the page. *The Brickyard at Sweetgrass.* I grabbed an eraser to obliterate the idea altogether. "Of course not." I tried to laugh but it stuck in my throat.

Mama was right about using the word *brickyard*, and I was

glad I'd told her of the contest and my concerns about coming up with a name for the complex when she'd called with an update on my father, who was still a bit feverish.

Reaching for my laptop, I typed in "brickyard + shopping." More than a dozen hits popped up for shopping centers, apartment complexes, or plazas named The Brickyard, including one in Birmingham.

Suddenly I felt like a hack. Honestly, it was silly of me to even be brainstorming. This wasn't how I usually worked. I needed to see the building's renderings before I could see its colors. Yet, I couldn't seem to stop myself from throwing out ideas. "What about simply calling it The Yard? Kind of a play on Yardley and the fact that it's an outdoor mall? It kind of hints at its past as a brickyard, too."

Mama made a *hmm*-ing noise. "It's not bad," she finally said. "It's just lacking something. But you'll get there. Give it time."

Much to my surprise, Mama had been over the moon with my involvement in the Yardley competition and had gushed on and on about how such an opportunity could bolster my business. If my being in the competition had brought up painful memories, she'd suppressed them in order to support me. Like most mothers, she believed me to be the most talented child in the world and wanted everyone to know it.

But now, as I stared at the eraser shavings scattered on my sketch pad, the lovely feeling her pride had given me slowly evaporated, and in its place a headache bloomed.

Swiveling in my chair, I turned away from my desktop toward the window, though I couldn't swivel too far because my broken foot was resting on the ottoman Emme had pulled over before she left to meet up with Aunt Glory.

I'd actually been a little disappointed to see Emme go this morning. After bringing in my coffee, she'd sat for a few minutes in the overstuffed armchair, chitchatting about the flower bed Glory had set up for her, the bookcase project, and her nerves about the day ahead.

In turn, I'd told her about the Yardley contest, the brick company's history in the community, and Levi's connection to it. I hadn't told her, however, how much my foot hurt.

After last night's one-crutch escapade, I'd awoken to increased swelling. Currently, the chill of an ice pack was doing little to ease the pain, and I swore I could actually feel the pulse in my foot throbbing against my splint. I tossed a look over my shoulder at the clock on my laptop screen. There was still a while to wait before the orthopedic doctor's office opened.

I heard the whistle of Mama's teakettle in the background as she said, "Now tell me, how is it living with Emme? Have you counted your silverware lately?"

I rubbed my temples, though the headache was actually a welcome distraction from my foot pain. "Mama, you have to stop acting like Emme is a criminal. It's not fair of you." Even as I said it, a ribbon of guilt wound around me at how I'd thought the worst of Emme last night. It was a mistake I wasn't going to repeat.

Outside, I heard a loud rumble and the squeal of brakes. I leaned forward for a better look out the window and saw the trash truck next door. I wasn't sure how I hadn't heard it before now, other than my focus had been on telling my mother about the brickyard project.

When my mother said nothing, I added, "Emme is perfectly nice. She's neat and tidy and cleans up around here better than I do. My blinds are dust-free. Do you know how long it's been since my blinds didn't have dust on them? Since I bought them—that's when."

"Of course she's being helpful, Cora Bee. That's the job you hired her for, right?"

The trash truck stopped in front of my house for a moment before rolling on toward Aunt Glory's. "It's more than that, Mama. She's going above and beyond, trying to anticipate my every need."

She *hmm*-ed again. "Aunt Glory mentioned that you weren't able to see Emme's *true* colors, so you don't know what she's like deep down."

I recalled the look in Emme's eyes last night while we stood in the garage. "I know enough to know she's not going to steal my silver."

Mama's voice rose. "You're being narrow-minded."

"Me?" I snapped, suddenly hurting all over. "I think that phrase better suits you right now."

I noticed a black pickup truck roll up in front of my house. The front passenger door flew open and Alice hopped out. She bypassed the full recycling bin, grabbed the handle of my empty trash can, and rolled it up the driveway. She disappeared out of sight for a moment, and I imagined she was placing it in front of the garage door. A moment later, she was running back to the truck, her short hair flying out behind her as if trying to keep up. In a blink, the door closed and the truck drove off, past Glory's house and around the cul-de-sac, heading out to the main road.

Mama exhaled loudly. "All I'm saying, Cora Bee, is that you can't be too careful. I ought to have a background check run on her. Yes. That's exactly what I'll do. It'll set my mind at ease. Somewhat."

"That's going overboard, don't you think?"

"Not at all. But I just realized it's likely Chase has already run a report. I'll check with him first."

I let out an exasperated sigh. "Do what you need to do but leave me out of it." When I heard my father's voice in the background I quickly asked to speak with him since the conversation with my mother felt like it was going nowhere fast.

I spent a good fifteen minutes talking with my daddy, which set my worries about him at ease and lifted my sagging mood.

When my mama came back on the line, her voice was soft and full of heart as she said, "Listen, Cora Bee, I didn't mean to upset you earlier. I'm just trying to look out for our family. I hope you understand that. Glory is too smitten with Emme to see reason, and you're naturally much too trusting."

"We don't need to get into this again."

"I know, I know." There was a beat of silence before she added, "But I simply can't believe you let Emme move in with you. I'd have thought you'd have learned your lesson about trusting the wrong people in your house. As I recall, you thought Heidi was wonderful, too."

Pinpoints of pain and anger exploded behind my eyes. "I do not need to be reminded."

I lived with that knowledge every day. Sometimes every minute of every day.

Mama's voice rose again. "I think you do. Unless you *want* to get hurt again."

"I'm hanging up now," I said.

"Cora Bee, be sensible about this."

"I'm done talking about Emme. Done."

"*Fine*," Mama said, the word hot and fiery.

With that, the line went dead. I stared at my phone, disbelieving that my mother had hung up on me. My mother had *never* hung up on me. We rarely even fought. But if there was ever a time, this was it. How dare she be mad at *me*, when *she* was the one who brought up Heidi.

Heidi Merrill. We'd met at the University of Florida when we'd been assigned as roommates our freshman year, and we soon became best friends. We'd stayed best friends right up until the day three and a half years ago when I found her in bed with my husband.

The laughable part was that Heidi was the one who had initially warned me about dating Lucas when I was a college senior and he'd been a teaching assistant working on his master's degree. She'd heard rumors of his flings, his graveyard of broken hearts, his cheating. I'd listened, I'd looked for clues. I studied the color around him, looking for any hints, but he emanated only confidence since, unfortunately, this all happened before I could fully see secondary emotions.

Finally, I asked him flat-out about his reputation and he hadn't denied it. Instead, he'd told me how he'd changed, because of me.

Because he finally fell in love. True love. Till-death-do-us-part love. I'd fallen for every word. I'd fallen for him. And later, for his one-year-old son, Wiley.

I hadn't thought twice about inviting Heidi to stay with us while she was down on her luck, unable to make ends meet. We'd been like sisters. Her primary color was a beautiful magenta that spoke only of her ambitious nature, so I knew how hard it had been for her to ask for my help in the first place. She was supposed to have stayed with us for only a couple of months, just enough time for her to get back on her feet.

Now she was living my old life.

She was sleeping in my old bed.

She was the one holding Wiley's hand and making him peanut butter and potato chip sandwiches.

Feeling like I wanted to scream, I shoved away from the desk, grabbed my crutches, and stood, cursing my foot, my mother, my ex-husband, and my ex–best friend.

I made my way into the kitchen, fighting waves of pain from my headache, my broken foot, my broken heart. Using my hip, I balanced against the farmhouse sink and reached for the bottle of prescription painkillers on the windowsill.

If I took two, I could sleep away this pain. I could drift off in a haze of nothingness where I didn't hurt. Didn't *feel*. Emme wouldn't be home for hours yet, my work could wait, and didn't I need the sleep? It'd been so long since I slept through the night. Years. The *relief* would be so welcome. So very welcome.

The amber bottle warmed in my hand as I pushed down on the white lid, twisted it, and popped it off. I stared inside, feeling tears welling in my eyes. I shook two small round pills into my palm. Then I added another for good measure. Through my tears, the tablets blurred, a dangerous yet lovely white cloud that would be a soft fall but a hard landing.

Folding my fingers over the pills, I closed my eyes. I'd lost my way on this path before, after my car accident, and it had taken months to find my way back to myself. Or what was left of me. I'd made bad choices, desperate choices. Without Glory's help and my will to heal, to fully heal, I don't know where I'd be right now, what my life would look life.

I'd sworn to myself I'd never lose my way again, yet here I was, staring at relief, blissful relief, in the palm of my hand, questioning why I couldn't handle a couple of pills. Three pills were not going to do anything other than put me out of my current misery. I wasn't going to relapse. I had more self-control than that.

Didn't I?

Was it a risk I was willing to take?

At the squeak of the porch door, my head snapped up. Footsteps followed the noise, then came a knock at the front door. My heart pounded with guilt, with shame, as I quickly dropped the pills back into the bottle, put the lid back on, and placed it on the windowsill.

I wiped the tears from my eyes and crutched into the living room, where I found Jamie's face looking in through the panes of glass on the front door.

He smiled when he saw me, but it faltered when I pulled open the door.

"Hey, are you okay?" In his arms, he held a cardboard box full of tools. "Rough morning? Is it your foot? I saw you using one crutch last night, and I was worried you'd pay for it today."

I breathed in deeply through my nose and tried to muster up a smile. I failed. "It's a little of everything."

He studied me, and it was like those pale eyes of his could see right through me to what I needed most. "I only stopped by to drop off some supplies for Emme"—he lifted the box—"but if you have a little time, how about I take you out for some coffee?"

The offer hung in the air, a silver-tipped arrow on a guidepost that swayed in the wind, swinging between my past and my future. I didn't particularly want to have coffee with him— the two of us at a small table in a coffee shop would feel too personal, too much like friendship, if not something more. But if I stayed, I might make a choice I'd regret forever.

Finally, I said, "Coffee sounds good."

A few minutes later, as I followed Jamie out the door, I glanced back toward the windowsill, to that amber bottle. Even though I knew I'd made the right choice by accepting his offer, I couldn't deny that I still longed for the relief those little pills could bring me.

It wasn't a small table in a crowded coffee shop where we sat, but rather a bench overlooking the bay. A surprisingly cool breeze coasted across the water, ruffling the feathers of a pelican perched on a pylon not too far away.

"It was nice of Alice to bring up my trash can this morning, but she doesn't need to do that." My hands were wrapped around the to-go coffee cup, its heat sinking into my palms. Before I left the house, I'd swallowed two Tylenol to battle my aches and pains—at least the physical ones—and was feeling a little less on edge.

"She likes to help," he said simply. Whorls of beige floated through his iced coffee as he swirled the liquid in his clear plastic cup. "And she likes you."

My broken heart ached just a little bit more. "She's a great kid."

"I've lucked out. I was a hellion. Every time I got into trouble, my mother said that one day she hoped I had a kid just like me."

"A hellion? Really?" I tipped my head. I couldn't see it.

Soft blue light filtered around him. In my world, that meant calm, stoic, salt of the earth. But there were a few wisps of juniper green floating around him, too, the same color I saw drifting around Emme. Jamie was keeping a guilty secret.

But weren't we all? That color probably drifted around me, too, not that I could see it. I couldn't see colors around myself at all.

"I mean, I didn't get arrested or anything like that," he said, "but I liked to try her patience, push my boundaries. When I was young, I wanted nothing more than to be a grown-up, make my own rules, live my own life."

"And now?"

"Now I want to call my mother and apologize, but she passed away twelve years ago."

"I'm so sorry." I ran my finger over the cup sleeve, suddenly swamped with guilt for fighting with my mother this morning. Not so much for the fight that had taken place but more that it had ended so badly. We shouldn't have left things off with so much anger.

"Yeah, me too." He stared into his drink. "But luckily for Alice, she inherited her mother's good nature."

Alice definitely had a good nature about her, but I'd seen some sassiness in her, too, and now I suspected that had come straight from Jamie. "You get along with your ex-wife, then? I mean, if she is an ex-wife?" Could be she had been a girlfriend or a one— "Oh Lord." My cheeks burned. "Sorry; I'm being nosy."

With an understanding smile, he said, "It's fine, really. I don't mind talking about it. Autumn and I had dated for a couple of months and had already broken up by the time we learned about Alice. We knew we weren't right for each other, but we both agreed to be the best co-parents we could be. There've been some challenges, but overall, we've all been happy. Autumn's been married to Phil for a few years now. Nice guy."

Autumn and Alice. The cuteness almost did me in. My emotions were so raw this morning I wasn't sure how I was going to get through the rest of the day. Once upon a time, I'd dreamed of having children of my own, of continuing the tradition that had started with Cain and me to use names that start with C. Carolina, Cody, Charlotte, Christopher. I'd had a whole list on my computer—a list that had since been deleted.

But even though those dreams had been shattered, I could still feel them pulsing with life from deep within me, faint heartbeats destined to fade away.

A flock of birds flew overhead, heading south toward the open waters of the Gulf, and for a moment I watched them, wishing I could fly along with them.

He looked out over the bay, watching those same birds. "Glory mentioned you were divorced."

"Of course she did."

He laughed. "I haven't known her very long, but for some reason she feels like family. A dear old aunt or godmother or something. That probably sounds strange."

"Not at all. Everyone loves Glory the instant they meet her. She's . . ." I swallowed over a sudden lump in my throat. "Utterly loveable. Even when she's oversharing."

Even though Aunt Glory had a tendency to reveal too much, I knew my deepest, darkest secrets were safe with her. "The divorce was . . ." I searched for the right word. Traumatic? Soul crushing? Excruciating? "Messy," I finally said.

"I'm real sorry about that. I can see from the look on your face that it still hurts."

I hated that he could read me so well. "It's been a few years now, and healing has come in dribs and drabs. Certain aspects still hurt."

The betrayal was near the top of that list, but it was Wiley who took the top spot. However, I didn't want to tell Jamie about him, mostly because I literally didn't think I could. Emotion clogged my throat just thinking about the little boy. About how I loved him as if he were my own flesh and blood. How he'd been taken away from me. It was agonizing to mourn someone who was still very much alive. I haven't yet been able to talk about him without sobbing.

"Dribs and drabs is still progress."

I nodded as my phone dinged with a text message.

"Sorry," I said as I pulled it from my purse. "I should check this. My father had surgery last week, and the stuff with Bee, and Glory, and clients . . ."

"It's no problem, Cora Bee."

I shifted, uncomfortable with how my heart warmed when he said my name, like it glowed with pleasure.

The message was from my mother.

I love you, and I'm sorry. I'm right, but I'm still sorry. I shouldn't have gotten so angry.

It was just like her to apologize while still asserting her opinions. Part of me wanted to argue that she hadn't really and truly apologized, but then I thought about Jamie and his mother and simply typed back I love you, too.

My mother was opinionated, and I knew her concerns about Emme came from wanting to protect those she loved. But my goodness, she was stubborn.

I looked at the time before I put my phone away. It was a little past nine. "I ought to be getting back. I need to call the doctor's office, and I should probably get some work done." Then my brow furrowed. "I'm not keeping you from work, am I?"

He stood and lifted my crutches, then held out a hand to me. "I have a little leeway with start times," he said with a smug grin, "since I'm the boss."

Suddenly that smug grin didn't bother me as much as it had when I first met him. I now found it oddly charming.

I slipped my hand in his, felt its warmth, its roughness. "What kind of work do you do?"

"Construction management. I came to town to oversee a new project."

His hands were rough, calloused, so I had the feeling he had also done his fair share of trade labor at some point. Once I was standing, he didn't let go of my hand right away. My heartbeat kicked up a notch and any follow-up questions drifted away as I lost myself in the touch of his skin on mine. The heat. The sudden fluttery feelings I thought had died long ago.

Finally, he let my hand go, and I set the crutches under my arms and tried to tell myself that there hadn't been anything to

what had just happened. That there still wasn't a trace of heat
on my palm.

"As soon as the project is done," he said, his tone turning
somber, "Alice and I will be moving back to Birmingham."

And with that, my hand chilled and my heart froze.

For a moment there, I had thought . . . Well, it didn't matter
what I'd thought.

They'd only been more impossible dreams, their heartbeats
left to fade away.

Chapter
11

February 10, 1964: She's here! Lillian Elizabeth Gipson was born on February 6. She's perfect. Absolutely perfect. I'm ecstatically tired and wishing Levi didn't have to work such long hours so he could be as happy as I am right now. He's been moodier than ever lately. When he's not working late, he's out somewhere socializing up a storm. My bees should be waking from their winter nap soon, and I'm looking forward to seeing them again. Sometimes it feels like they're my only friends.

Emme

It had been a long day. An exhausting day. Not only for me, but it seemed it had been the same for Cora Bee. She'd been quiet for most of the afternoon, offering little in terms of conversation. She'd mentioned her foot hurting and having a headache, but I suspected there was more to the explanation of her mood. But whatever it was, she wasn't saying.

At her first appointment of the afternoon, with a client a few blocks away from Hickory Lane, she'd glanced in the car's sun visor mirror and pasted a big smile on her face. "Fake it till you make it, right? How do I look?"

"That smile's terrifying. Are you trying to lose business?"

At that, she gave me a real smile—a small one, but it still felt like some kind of victory. While she was meeting with her clients, I had stayed in the car with the windows down and tried to lose myself in a book, but my thoughts kept wandering to Glory and what was wrong with her.

Now, Cora Bee and I were currently on our way back to Sweetgrass from her second appointment of the day, which had been in Fairhope, a quick ten-minute drive away. Traffic was relatively light, and the route kept revealing glimpses of the bay, undulating strips of silvery blue that glistened in the afternoon sunlight.

The air conditioner blew coolness throughout the car and rustled the pages on a pad of paper Cora Bee was using to jot notes about her latest consultation. She yawned, covering her mouth with the back of her hand and murmured, "Whoa. Excuse me."

"How could I not when it's my fault you were up half the night?"

"You didn't wake me—I was already up and heard you go out. I don't sleep much. I'm lucky if I get a few hours a night."

"I don't know how you're not a zombie."

"You get used to it."

I was happy she was talking more, coming out of her funk. Her consultations seemed to have drained some of the tension from her shoulders, a sign that she truly loved her job.

"This is such a pretty area," I said, catching sight of the water once again.

Cora Bee's last appointment hadn't been too far from a hardware store, so I'd shopped while she consulted, picking up some of the items I needed to paint the bookcase. By the time I'd collected and paid for my items, I didn't have time for sightseeing, but I hoped to come back one day to window-shop at the boutiques and stroll along the pier.

"It truly is. Even though Sweetgrass is my mama's hometown, I'm fairly new to it. I had a horrible car accident when I lived in Gainesville and moved here not long afterward. I broke vertebrae in my back. Hurt my head. The beauty of this area helped me heal, along with Aunt Glory's nurturing nature, of course."

Immediately, the photo of her in the hospital bed filled my mind, along with Glory's words about how some of the most beautiful flowers bloomed in harsh conditions. The new me, the one trying my hardest to build a friendship, forced myself to say, "How long were you married?"

She took so long to answer that I thought she wasn't going to. But finally she said, "For six years, and I've been divorced for three and a half. I met Lucas when I was a senior in college. We were married only a few months later, right after I graduated."

"Fast," I said.

"Love tricks you into thinking that time doesn't matter. That it feels right, so why wait? Sometimes I wonder, What if I had waited? If I'd dated him longer than a few months, would I have seen the real him and made different choices?" Her voice drifted away into a whisper. "I don't know."

"The what-if game can be dangerous."

"Oh, I know." She leaned back, relaxing her shoulders, letting them rest against the seat. "My parents had a love-at-first-sight story, and I think I convinced myself that I'd been gifted one, too. Have you ever been married?"

"No. I've barely dated."

"Really?"

"When I was younger, I moved around a lot. When I was older, I was still moving around and too busy trying to take care of myself to invite someone else into my life. And I have trust issues, so that doesn't help. Plus, my mother was a serial dater, and I knew that wasn't a life I wanted."

Of course, she dated only to scam those poor, unsuspecting men, but still.

"I guess I'm waiting for my love-at-first-sight story, too. Where did your parents meet?" I asked, not wanting to talk about me anymore. I walked a fine line while sharing bits about my past. One slip and I might reveal too much.

"They met in Destin, Florida, while my mama was on spring break from Auburn and Daddy was on leave from his navy base in Pensacola. They married not long after and have been happily married since, so I know long-lasting, loving relationships can happen. But I've come to believe that they're rare. Like blue moon rare."

"Like white peacock rare."

"Like getting hit by lightning."

I smiled. "That took a dark turn."

She laughed and said, "Well, love feels like that sometimes."

I wouldn't know but trusted her about it. "And your dad is still in the military?"

"He is. His current orders are in San Diego, but I'm not sure where he and Mama will go when he retires. I'd love for them to move here, but . . ."

"But what?"

She gave a slight smile. "Just not into my house."

I was amused by the wry humor in her tone. I wouldn't want my mother living with me, either, but it seemed to me that Cora Bee and I had vastly different motives behind our reasoning.

Looking over at her notepad, I asked, "What does one of your consultations consist of, exactly?"

Shifting in her seat, which had been pushed all the way back to give her more legroom, she adjusted her foot. She had an appointment with the orthopedist scheduled for Wednesday afternoon, and I hoped she got good news from the doctor because it seemed to me that being forced to slow down and depend on others was part of the reason for her bad mood today.

"The first appointment? It was with a couple who want to paint their house but can't decide on a color. So I met with them, snapped some pictures of the exterior, took notice of the landscape and other houses in the neighborhood, checked which direction the front of the house faces, chatted with them about their design styles and the colors they gravitate to. I'll go back home and create three virtual renderings of the house with different color palettes that they can choose from."

"Do you know right off the bat which colors you're leaning toward? Or do you study your color swatches to see what pops out?"

She tapped her pen on the notepad. "You know how you had a feeling the bookcase should be teal? You didn't even really have to think about it. It was a gut instinct and you trusted it."

I glanced her way and nodded. "I have a knack for first impressions. It's mostly with people, but sometimes it pops up in other areas, like with furniture."

Her eyes widened. "Really? I'm the same way but I see impressions solely through colors, and I see those colors on just about anything organic. I'm thinking the house I saw today should be smoky grayish purple with creamy-white trim and a soft butter-yellow door."

In my mind's eye, I could see it. "That sounds *perfect*."

She smiled then, a real smile. It lit her whole face, setting off emerald sparks in her eyes. "I can't make my clients choose it from the three renderings I'll send them, but I'll definitely nudge them in that direction. How'd your day go at the marketplace?"

This was the most in-depth conversation we'd had yet, and I liked it. I liked *her*. She was making *friendly* feel easy. "A little overwhelming. There was a lot to learn."

"It'll get easier," she said. "But I need to know, with your knack for first impressions, what do you think of the courthouse and its clock tower?"

There was a light tone to her voice I'd come to recognize as her playful tone, one she used when cracking jokes or using self-deprecating humor. "Honestly? It looks like a swamp monster rising up to terrorize an unsuspecting small town."

"That's my take on it, too," she said, laughing. Then she tapped a pen on the notebook and added, "I know today was overwhelming for you, but can you see yourself liking the work at the Sweetplace eventually?"

"I actually can. I liked the busyness of it, and everyone seemed nice."

She kept tapping. "Do you think it's something you'd like to do long-term?"

I didn't understand why there seemed to be more to the question than what was on the surface, unless she was trying to gauge how long I planned to stay in Sweetgrass. "I mean, maybe. I'm not sure it's sustainable financially. Part-time work hardly pays the bills. Even though you and Glory have been so generous to me, one day I'd like to have a place of my own."

"What kind of work would you like to do? Would you go back to customer service?"

Sunshine broke through a stand of trees and glinted off the window. I lowered the visor. "I'm not sure. Whatever pays the best, I guess. I was never one of those kids who grew up wanting to be something. A teacher, a doctor, a lawyer. My dream was to have a home. That's it. Just a home to call my own. I'd work just about any job to get one."

"You've never had . . . a home?"

Emotion swelled, pushing and pulling. It was a risk sharing so much of myself. "I've had places to live, but no, never a home. Not one single place filled with love and light and the things that make me happiest." I lifted my chin. "One day, though."

Cora Bee's breath caught and she reached out to offer a comforting touch only to pull her hand back as if reconsidering; then she reached out again and gave my arm a gentle rub. "I can't even imagine the life you've led."

I tried for a smile. "I don't recommend it."

Her return smile faltered. "You're here now, with us. Glory and me. And I know my place isn't quite the home you're wanting, but it's a start."

"It's more than a start," I said. "It's a whole new beginning."

She nodded. "Day by day."

Warmth flooded me, but as we entered the Sweetgrass town limits, I tapped the steering wheel and gathered up my courage. "One strange thing kept happening today. At the marketplace. Nearly every person who talked with Glory asked about her health. I've noticed she's had a few stumbles and sometimes mixes up her words. What's going on with her? I feel like it's something everyone knows but me."

From the corner of my eye, I saw Cora Bee using the pad of her right thumb to rub the pink-painted fingernail of her left thumb. It was the only movement on her side of the car, as she otherwise sat perfectly still, staring straight ahead.

"She didn't want to tell you straight off," Cora Bee finally said, her voice steady but threaded with remorse. "She wanted you to get to know her before you knew about her health situation, so the foundation of your relationship wouldn't be built on pity. I tried to explain that it was hard to hide, but she's a bit stubborn, if you haven't noticed yet."

I'd noticed. "Is it dementia?"

"No. She has," her voice faltered, "brain tumors."

My heart rose into my throat and beat there wildly as Cora Bee explained about Glory's health problems. The doctors, the hospitals, the treatments. "So, she's in remission now?"

Cora Bee looked down at her notebook. "Yep."

I couldn't see her eyes, but I had the feeling she was lying. I swallowed hard. "If she wasn't in remission, how much time would she have left?"

Cora Bee's gaze slowly lifted. Grief pooled in the depths of her eyes, muddying the light brown. "Six months or so."

By that look in her eyes, I knew without a doubt that Glory was dying. My heart broke. "That's not much time."

"No, it's not. But I hope you know how happy you've made her by moving here, by being part of her life. So, so happy. She's been looking for you for a long time."

My breath hitched and I tried to breathe deeply through my nose. There was a lot to sort through from this conversation. So much to think about. But most of all, I hurt for Glory. I hurt for Cora Bee. And everyone, really, who loved Glory Wynn.

⤳⤶

An hour later, we arrived back at Cora Bee's house after making a spur-of-the-moment stop at the library. I'd signed up for a card and we each stocked up on books. My stack included several hardcovers about the language of flowers and flower gardening, a little homework to go along with my garden lessons. We were in the midst of talking about what to eat for supper when I walked into my bedroom to set the books on the nightstand.

Immediately, I knew someone had been in the room, and it took only a moment to realize who it had been.

I walked over to the bed, set the books down, and picked up the purple bunny that had been propped against my pillow. I hugged it to my chest.

Thoughts and emotions swirled in my head, too many to sort out, to untangle. Knowing Glory's diagnosis broke my heart. It also threw my plans, my goals, into the unknown. But if Glory had less than six months to live, I wanted those days to be the happiest they could be.

That meant I knew one thing for certain.

I had to make sure that Glory never, ever found out that I wasn't really her granddaughter.

Chapter 12

Hon, surely you've taken a close look at these glads by now. With their height, their grace, gladiolus—gladioli?—have a way of capturing attention without really trying. That's probably why they symbolize love at first sight. I certainly fell hard when I first saw them. The flowers inspire me with how they start blooming from the bottom of the stem and work their way up to the top, one bud slowly opening after another. Climbing diligently, always reaching for that sunshine. They also represent sincerity and honor, preparedness and generosity, and strength of character. What's that? Oh, yes—I agree wholeheartedly. They remind me of Cora Bee, too.

Cora Bee

It had been nearly two weeks since Emme had moved in with me. It turned out I liked her company more than I ever thought I would. She didn't question my insomnia, or my obsessive need to stay busy, or the fact that I didn't drink wine with supper, because she'd never known me any other way. Beyond that, she was funny, kind, thoughtful, and a great listener.

As a favor to Glory, I'd been extra friendly to Emme, but somewhere along the way, without me quite knowing it was happening, she'd become a friend. I had the sneaky feeling Glory knew this would happen all along.

The two of us, Emme and I, had fallen into a semblance of a routine, of waking early, of eating breakfast together while trying to solve one of the crosswords in her puzzle book. She'd then carry my coffee into my office and sit with me for a few minutes before getting on with her day. That's where we were now.

Emme sat in the wide armchair, sipping from a cup of coffee. Even though I sat a good three feet away, I could see that her coffee was pale in color, deeply infused with cream. It hadn't taken me long to turn her to the light side where coffee was concerned.

I sat at my desk, studying the architectural renderings for the Yardley project on my computer screen. I frowned as I zoomed in and out. I took in the sleek lines, the metal, and the tinted glass as I tried to find inspiration. Tried *desperately.*

"I don't know what I was thinking," I said. "I'm in way over my head. *Name finding?* I don't name find. I color find. What do I know about names? Brands? Concepts? Nothing—that's what."

"You were thinking that it'd be great for your business," she said.

Right, my business. I'd had such hopes for this contest, but maybe the pressure was too much for me to handle, because I saw only computer-generated gray scale when I looked at these graphics. "Even if I win, there's no guarantee they'll use the design. It's in the fine print of the contest."

She balanced her mug on her lap. "Even if they don't, the PR is priceless. Which leads us back to how the contest is great for your business."

I frowned at her.

She smiled at me and kept on sipping.

I gestured at the screen. "I'm just not connecting to the project. Not like I do with my other designs. Something feels off."

It was almost seven in the morning, and she was due to leave for work with Aunt Glory soon. Fridays were busy at the Sweetplace, and Emme looked like she was ready to tackle the day ahead with enthusiasm. It amazed me how quickly she had settled in, found her place. It was like she'd always been here. Always belonged here.

Over the past weeks, I'd seen her taking Aunt Glory's flower lessons to heart and faithfully tending her own small planter box with loving devotion. Aunt Glory had also been giving her baking lessons during stretches of free time, teaching her the recipes she used for the items she sold at the marketplace, and Emme had already started taking over the production of some of the inventory. In that regard, Glory's grand plan was working like a charm.

Neighbors had become smitten, to use my mama's term, with Emme as well. A lot of that was due to Emme herself, who was first to volunteer to help when it was needed. I'd seen her carry in neighbors' groceries, play with the twin hellion toddlers who lived on the other side of the cul-de-sac so their mama could take a nap, and take a shift at May's gift shop when one of her part-timers quit with no notice. Nearly every afternoon, she and Alice talked books like no one else had ever read one.

The most recent project she'd completed was helping Glory replant the rhododendron that had been dug up by the police. They'd also added new black-eyed Susans, daisies, and pine straw mulch to the bed.

The black floaters that usually drifted around Emme had recently faded to a pale gray. Her spirit was healing here on Hickory Lane.

I glanced out the window toward the gazing pool. By the time Emme and Aunt Glory finished cleaning up after the police in the garden, it almost looked like nothing untoward had happened there at all.

Almost.

Despite the TLC, the earth around the gazing pool still bore the scars of the police investigation, an unnecessary reminder of the grieving limbo we were all stuck in. Not one single person in this family—or this neighborhood, for that matter—had forgotten. Bee was never far from my thoughts or my mama's lips when she called. And even though Aunt Glory still refused to discuss the matter, my mama had been in touch with the local funeral home to make plans for when Bee could finally be laid to rest properly.

"Is it something in particular in the Yardley design that's bothering you?" Emme asked.

I looked at the building on the screen. Frowned at its grayness. Its computer-generated grayness. It had become painfully obvious that my ability to see colors around objects and people didn't extend to renderings of buildings that did not yet exist. It was rather disconcerting, if I was being honest.

"I can't pinpoint it. I know the brickyard has been razed, but maybe if I see the land in person, I can get a better feel for the project."

"We can go this afternoon."

I nodded and smiled. "Thanks. It's not far. I know you have plans tonight."

This evening, *finally*, Emme and Chase would start work on the garage apartment, now that everything Glory ordered had arrived.

"I'm sure Chase can get started without me if I'm late. Honestly, I'd rather be doing it myself."

I lifted an eyebrow. "Do you not like him? Or do you like him too much?"

Her cheeks colored. "I don't feel one way or another."

"Mm-hmm. What was your first impression of him?"

She took a sip of coffee. "Inquisitive. It holds true. He's nosy."

I laughed, then realized that with her talent for first impressions, she might be able to help me with the Yardley project. I turned my laptop toward her. "What do these renderings say to you? First instinct?"

Emme leaned in for a closer look, careful to keep her coffee cup level. Her eyebrows shot up and she made a sour face. "Incongruous."

"What do you mean incongruous? How so?"

She shrugged. "It's not Sweetgrass. It doesn't fit in. That building there is like a snooty rich auntie coming to town who starts intimating that everything you know and love isn't good enough."

Dang if she hadn't put to words what I'd been feeling.

"Compare that building to the Sweetplace, for example," she added.

"To be fair, I don't think the new shopping center is looking to attract the same kind of consumer as the Sweetplace."

"Exactly my point," she said, leaning back in the chair. "The Sweetplace is for everyone. It feels down-home, all heart and soul. That place feels big-city, cold, and impersonal. Not many around here will take a liking to it. I haven't even been in Sweetgrass very long and I know that."

I jotted *down-home* on a piece of scrap paper. "I don't necessarily think it's a bad thing for Sweetgrass to offer an upscale place to shop. It can only help the town grow and expand. And not all big cities are cold and impersonal. But this . . ." I shook my head. It was too much.

"Upscale is fine, but not cold and impersonal. That's not going to fly around here."

It wasn't. Even the wealthiest Sweetgrass residents, those who enjoyed all the finer things in life, prided themselves on their Southern charm and hospitality. That, I suddenly realized, was what was missing from the rendering. Charm. "Color will help. A soft blue? A light green?" I ventured, but neither felt quite right.

"Maybe," she said, sounding like color wasn't going to help at all. "Where's the brick? I mean, they don't have to use hideous Yardley brick—I know I wouldn't—but it's a former brickyard. You'd think there'd be a nod to its history somewhere. Did the Yardleys sign off on these design plans? Did they do a business model? Unless they make some big changes, it seems to me like they're destined to fail."

I laughed at how riled up she had become. "I have no idea."

"Soften it up, Cora Bee. Put a little bit of Sweetgrass into it. Put a little bit of *you* into it. It needs your warmth, your connection to nature. It's the only way it's going to succeed in a town like this." After looking at the clock on the computer screen, she stood up. "I need to get going. Do you need anything before I head out?"

I glanced around. "I think I'm good."

She gestured to my foot, housed in a black cast that started at the bottom of my toes and ended a couple of inches below my knee, which was propped on the ottoman. My toes, painted a radiant peony pink, peeped out from the bottom of the cast looking cheerful in the morning light, reminding me of how grateful I was that I hadn't needed surgery. Sure, four to six weeks in a cast wasn't ideal, but at least it didn't require hospitalization.

"Keep that elevated as much as possible," she said.

"Yes, ma'am." Like other mornings, I found myself wishing she didn't have to go. It was a shocking thing to admit, even if only to myself. I had convinced myself that I had enjoyed living alone.

I'd been wrong.

"Call Glory's phone if you need me."

"I will, but once again I'll ask when you plan on getting your own phone?"

"Soon," she said with a smile as she headed out the door.

I didn't quite believe her. I had the feeling she liked being unreachable.

As I turned back to my computer, I heard her moving about her bedroom, the kitchen, and finally the living room. The front door squeaked open and then a second later squeaked closed. Despite my reminders that Emme didn't need to lock the door while I was home, I waited to hear the sound of the dead bolt and finally heard the metal click. Before she'd moved in with me, I rarely locked the dead bolt at all—only the handle—but I had changed my ways since she'd been here, simply for her peace of mind. She took security seriously, and once again it made me question what she'd been through in life.

If I read between the lines of what she'd shared with me, I could picture the places she and her mother had stayed while moving about the country. The motels, the short-term rentals, the seedy rooms for rent. What had life been like for a young girl in that situation? What did she do while her mother, a serial dater according to Emme, went out on the town? I couldn't imagine that Kristalle took her daughter along with her when she met men.

It was no wonder Emme locked the doors.

Out the window, I watched as she walked along the sidewalk, waving to Dorothy, who was in the garden wielding her pink trowel, and to May, who was picking up the newspaper on her front lawn.

Tomorrow would mark two full weeks since Emme had first stepped foot on Hickory Lane. But for some reason it felt like I had known her forever, even though I truly knew very little about her at all.

↘ ↙

Hours later, I yawned and stretched and tried to work a kink out of my neck. My eyes were blurring from looking between paint swatches in my hand to my laptop screen. It was time for a break.

Pushing back from my desk, I grabbed my crutches and set them under my arms. Emme had found armpit pads and hand grips made for crutches at the pharmacy, and they'd made all the difference in terms of comfort. She'd taken the extra step of creating covers for the pads with scraps of fabric Glory had on hand, so they looked cute, too. I'd watched in awe as she had cut a pattern, then hand sewed the covers with neat, even stitches.

"Where'd you learn how to sew?" I'd asked.

"There was a sewing program at a library once. In Omaha?" She'd tipped her head upward as if searching her brain for information. "No, it was Des Moines. I always get those Midwest cities mixed up."

It was another thing I had learned about Emme. She'd spent a lot of time at libraries. Each time we visited the Sweetgrass library, I was amazed at the variety of books she'd select—and how many. It was obvious she was a well-read bookworm.

As I crutched past her bedroom, I glanced inside. The bed was made, and the little lavender bunny sat in front of fluffed pillows. Glory had told me how Emme had taken a liking to the stuffed bunny, and it had filled me with happiness that Glory had bought it for her.

I crutched into her bedroom to steal a peek at the connected bathroom, just to make sure she had enough supplies. Everything was spotless. Even the towels were hung neatly. As I headed for the hallway, out of curiosity—and pure nosiness—I opened one of the dresser drawers near the door.

It was empty. I checked another. It was empty, too. All of them were empty.

I'd suspected that Emme had been living out of her suitcase—which was stowed away in the closet—and wondered why she hadn't unpacked. Not that she had much to unpack, as she had very few items of clothing, but still.

It made me realize that Emme likely viewed my home as just another temporary place to live. Technically, I supposed it was. Emme would eventually move back to the apartment above Glory's garage. For some reason, the thought of her leaving—even if it was only to move next door—made my heart hurt.

Feeling guilty for snooping and suddenly restless in the house, I made my way outside to the porch. The last week of April had brought with it a pattern of abundant sunshine and pleasant weather. It wasn't bound to last, all this good weather. Storms would roll through. Hurricanes would form. There would be nights spent hunkered in the hall closet while tornado sirens blared. But for now, I was going to enjoy the clear skies.

I bypassed the rocking chairs and porch swing and headed for the wooden door. I carefully made my way down the steps and paused to catch my breath as I reached the walkway. Stairs were challenging. Before I'd broken my foot, I'd taken my mobility for granted. I had never really considered the agility required for simply getting up for a glass of water, or rolling over in bed, taking a shower, or driving a car.

Once I'd resigned myself to wearing the cast for the next four to six weeks, I realized that I had to cut back on in-home consultations. It was too exhausting to lug myself around people's homes, in and out, up and down. I'd contacted the clients I already had scheduled, explained the situation, and switched them to virtual consultations. Fortunately, all had been agreeable to the modification.

The sun shone brightly overhead as I crutched across the street, headed for the gazing pool. The natural spring had been a favorite spot of my grandmother's, and it was a favorite of mine as well. As soon as my left foot hit the ground in the island, a gentle buzzing vibrated under my foot. I could even feel it radiating in the handles of the crutches.

I waved to a neighbor who was working on a vegetable bed, leaned my crutches against the stone ledge of the gazing pool, and sat down. My gaze went to the rhododendron that amazingly looked none the worse for wear after its uprooting, but I couldn't bear looking at the roughed-up ground without tearing up until I remembered how much Bee had loved this spot. This garden. This land. She wouldn't want a single bit of it to cause me sorrow. What happened here hadn't been the garden's fault. It was good, also, to remember that we'd be laying Bee to rest near this same spot. With that in mind, I took a look around, focused on the beauty. I saw it in the curve of an oak leaf, the veins on the ferns, the numerous shades of gold on the black-eyed Susans.

Just last week a county engineer had come by to look at the garden. Ultimately, he claimed the sinkholes were a rare aberration. The ones that had opened in the 1960s had developed because of a drought. The newest one had apparently opened because of the excessively rainy early spring we'd had. He deemed the garden safe but warned that caution should be used in the area during extreme weather patterns, especially near the gazing pool.

Aunt Glory hadn't seemed the least bit worried about another sinkhole opening up, which eased the minds of everyone in the neighborhood. Where she led, we followed. I had no idea what any of us were going to do without her.

I gently lifted my casted foot onto the pool's stone ledge, since I'd promised Emme I'd keep it elevated as much as possible, rearranged my skirt for modesty, and took a deep breath. Closing my eyes, I lifted my face toward the sky and let the sun warm my skin.

"Listen," Aunt Glory would always say when we sat here side by side.

I heard the whisper of wind through the live oak tree, the melodic song of a wren, the soothing murmur of the water in the pool, the buzz of a bee. Tension eased from my shoulders. Worries slipped away.

I glanced at the water, wondering if I'd see anything today, glimpses of times past. Images of life lived by others. I didn't always. The gazing pool was selective in its offerings. I'd only seen three images since I moved to this neighborhood, but not for lack of trying. The most recent had appeared six months ago when I'd seen a doctor in a white coat, a stethoscope around his neck, and sorrow in his eyes. Instinctually I knew what he'd been saying and to whom. If the gazing pool hadn't shown me that scene, Glory might never have told me the truth of her so-called remission.

As the tiny wren continued to sing from atop the bee weather vane on the stone shed, the water stopped murmuring, the quiet a sure signal to pay close attention. The ripples on the surface flattened as images slowly came into focus.

The sun warmed my shoulders as I watched the scene play out. It was dark and hard to see the finer details. It was a motel room, the walls bathed in red and blue police lights. There was a formidable officer, holding handcuffs. Blood on my hands. My heart beat crazily, and I was filled with fear.

The officer reached out, and the scene spun around to face a new direction. It now looked out into the night. At an ambulance. A stretcher. Then I was being walked to a police car, placed into the backseat. As one foot went in, then another, pink flip-flops came into view on the floorboard. The tops of the feet were splattered in blood. The second toes on each foot were just a fraction taller than the big toes.

Emme.

Startled by the realization, I must have jumped because I

nearly lost my balance on the wall. I grabbed the stone ledge to balance myself, and when I looked back at the water, it was bubbling peacefully, as if it hadn't just sent a shock wave through my world.

I set my casted foot down on the ground and reached into my skirt pocket for my cell phone. I had only spoken to my mother a few times since our fight, but we'd texted every day. Quick notes, mostly about my father, who was improving steadily, and about the police investigation, though there wasn't anything new to discuss. And, of course, after my vow to stop discussing her, we'd said nothing about Emme.

But now here I was about to break my word, something that filled me with a sense of shame. Yet when I'd told my mother that I was done talking about Emme, I never expected what I'd seen in the gazing pool.

I was afraid my voice would betray me if I called, so I typed out a text as quickly as I could.

Me: Hey, did you ever check with Chase about Emme's background?

Mama: Why? Did she take something priceless and skip town?

Even though the words were typed, I could hear the pain in them. Kristalle had wounded my mother to her core when she took Emme away. Now probably wasn't the time to tell her that letting Emme into her life would likely be the first step in healing that wound. Not when I was asking about her background.

Me: Just curious.

Mama: Seems like more than curiosity.

Me: Are you stalling answering because the report came back clean and you don't want to admit you were wrong?

Suddenly I prayed that the report had been clean. That she *had* been wrong. That the gazing pool wasn't telling me the whole story. There had to be some sort of reasonable explanation for what I'd seen. Not that an arrest and blood were reasonable, but I was grasping at straws.

Mama: You don't get that sass from me.
Me: I know exactly who I get it from.

It was her. It was all her. My sass came straight from my mama.

Mama: You'll be happy to know that Emme's background check was clear. In fact, it was spotless. By all appearances, she didn't exist in the time frame between her birth and when she got a GED.

Spotless. Even as relief pulsed, the scenes from the pool haunted me. She'd been handcuffed, put into the back of a police car. And whose blood had been splattered on her? Had it been her own?

Mama: Isn't that curious? Where was she?
Me: I don't know for sure. All over, it seems.

I needed to end this conversation before she remembered we weren't supposed to be discussing Emme at all.

Luckily for me, a good reason appeared in the form of a chocolate Labradoodle racing toward me, freedom flying through her curly hair. As Mabel barreled forward, tongue lolling, I put my phone in my lap and braced for her enthusiasm even as I said, "Mabel, sit!"

Her steps slowed and faltered as if she hadn't been expecting a command, but she didn't stop completely.

"Sit," I said again, more sternly this time, lowering my palm like Alice had taught me to do during one of her afternoon visits.

Mabel slowed to a hesitant stop, and her backside lowered. It didn't touch the ground but it hovered closely to it. Her tail wagged like mad, brushing the grass, kicking up dust.

"Sit," I said again.

She sat.

"Good girl," I said in a voice I nearly didn't recognize, all high-pitched and oh so proud.

I swept my hand toward my chest and said, "Come."

With an excited jump, she trotted over and stuck her nose in the crook of my neck and licked my chin. I gave her a good back rub. "Hi, Mabel."

When my phone dinged from my lap, I kept one hand on Mabel's collar and with the other opened the text that had come in.

Mama: I think an alias is entirely possible. Probable even.

Me: I have to go, Mama. I have a dog to return to its owner.

Mama: That excuse is getting old, Cora Bee.

I sent an eye-rolling emoji along with a quick snap of Mabel, who appeared to be smiling for the camera.

Glancing down the street, I saw Jamie's truck sitting in his driveway and sent the same pic to him with a text that we were at the gazing pool. Since Alice had been spending so much time at my house, he'd insisted I put his phone number into my phone, which had certainly come in handy right about now.

I slipped my phone back into my pocket and rubbed Mabel's ears. "We have to stop meeting like this."

Her tail wagged.

"I mean, I'm glad no bones were broken this time, but still. It's not safe for you. There are cars. You could get lost. Stolen, even, since you're so cute." She licked my chin again as if thanking me for my assessment, and I laughed.

She sat at my feet but seemed to be trying to glue herself to my body. She pushed her head and neck against my stomach and chest and left them there. And every so often, she snuck in another sloppy kiss.

So help me, I was getting used to them.

I rested my cheek on top of her head, rubbed her belly, and felt the stress of my morning drain away. "Thanks, Mabel."

When her head snapped up, I looked up and saw Jamie jogging toward us. Her tail started wagging again, but she stayed put.

At the sight of him, I felt something deep within me pang with longing to know him better. To know how he took his coffee first thing in the morning, to know his favorite childhood memory, to know how his arms would feel around me. To become his friend. Maybe more.

I looked down so he wouldn't see any of those things, those impossible things, written on my face. It had been so long since I wanted any of that from a man that it felt strange even thinking about them. After our coffee chat, I'd told myself that I'd stay friendly but keep my distance—emotionally and physically. But the father-daughter duo made that nearly impossible. Beyond Alice's afternoon visits, Jamie often walked Mabel by the house when I was sitting on the front porch, and we'd get to talking and sharing sweet tea, allowing those feelings to grow like out-of-control weeds. I hadn't even known the man two full weeks. It was all such a whirlwind, and whirlwinds scared the life out of me.

As he grew closer, he said, "I thought Mabel was with Alice, but Alice is nose-deep in a book in the hammock, oblivious to the world around her. I also thought we'd dog-proofed the backyard, but we must've missed a spot." He took a breath. "Thanks for finding her, Cora Bee."

"Honestly, she found me." I scratched her chin, and her beautiful brown eyes were alight with happiness. "She's good company. Lifted my spirits right up."

He clipped a leash onto her collar, and then took a moment to study my face. "You were feeling down?"

At his inspection, I felt my cheeks warming. "I'm just tired, that's all. A visit from Mabel is like a jolt of espresso."

"She's a jolt of *something*, that's for sure."

"She sat for me when I asked her to," I said like a proud mom.

He smiled, and I watched the way it transformed his whole

face, softening his sharp cheekbones and crinkling the skin around his eyes. "Good girl, Mabel."

At that, Mabel left my side and went to his for more love and affection. She nudged his hand, and he laughed. "I don't have your treats with me. When I get home, okay?"

I loved that he was having a conversation with her as if she could understand. Then something he had said suddenly registered. "Wait—Alice isn't at school? Is she not feeling well?"

He sat next to me on the ledge, and Mabel edged in between us. We each had a hand on her head. He was rubbing her left ear; I was scratching her right. She probably thought she'd died and gone to doggy heaven.

"Earlier, Alice called me from school, asking to come home. Physically, she's fine, but sometimes she struggles with middle school drama. She had a hard time at her last school—it's why she jumped at the chance to move here with me to finish out the school year. And why her mom was okay with it. I hate that she's already struggling here, too. She has trouble making friends."

I glanced toward their house, to where I could practically envision Alice swaying in a hammock, and I wanted to run over there and give her a big bear hug. Which wasn't exactly keeping my distance, but sometimes personal rules were meant to be broken.

"I don't get that," I said. "She's so . . ." I searched for the right word, and so many came to mind. Wonderful. Special. Friendly. My brain whirled with all the glowing adjectives. "She's amazing—that's what she is. Who wouldn't want to be her friend?"

Besides me. But even I was failing in that endeavor because her charm had broken right through my defenses. Frankly, I was starting to think my defenses were weak to begin with, the price I paid for being so softhearted.

There was tenderness in Jamie's eyes when he looked at me. "She's an old soul. A worrier. Lots of times she sees the bigger picture when other kids her age only see what's in front of them. It's hard for her to relate."

I was wondering if she had ever used the *fake it till you make it* method of enduring awkward social situations, but then in my head, I heard Glory's voice saying, *Best to accept her as is instead of trying to change her. You don't want to go breaking her spirit.*

Alice's inner spirit was what made her so beautiful, and the thought of it being broken nearly made me cry.

Jamie said, "It'll be all right. She'll get through it. We call these kinds of days when she's overwhelmed at school and wants to come home 'personal days,' and I'm happy to let her have them. Sometimes I question how much she even needs friends."

I opened my mouth to tell him that *of course* she needed friends, but then I abruptly pressed my lips together, suddenly seeing myself in the young girl. Closing myself off to avoid pain. Avoiding life when it was too hard to face head-on. Trying to avoid relationships in case people didn't understand why I was the way I was.

Jamie went on talking. "She has me, her mom, her stepdad, Mabel. She has you and Emme and Glory and the other neighbors who treat her like family."

At that, my eyes did fill with tears, and I blinked them away just as my fingers absently brushed against Jamie's on top of Mabel's head.

The world around me suddenly went silent, and I could hear only my own heartbeat thudding crazily in my chest as I slowly lifted my gaze to meet his.

What I saw in his eyes, the gentle heat, nearly made me melt.

His fingers didn't pull away from mine, and our index fingers curled around each other's. As his head slowly came toward me and his gaze narrowed on my lips, I braced myself for a different kind of impact. One I wasn't sure I was ready for, but one I found I wanted quite badly.

His lips were almost to mine when Mabel let out a bark and took off. The spell was broken as Mabel ran toward Alice, who had just crossed the street and was headed our way.

Since my face was surely as red as one of Glory's anemones, I reached for my crutches so I would have a moment before having to look anyone in the eyes.

Jamie was on his feet in an instant to help me. He held me steady while I positioned the crutches, and his warm hands sent flashes of heat into my skin.

"Dad! Why didn't you tell me you were taking Mabel for a walk?" Alice called out as she picked up the leash and walked Mabel back to us. "I came inside for a snack and you both were gone."

Alice looked none the worse for her troubling morning at school. She seemed cheerful enough with her chastising tone and smile. Her hair was loose today and framed her narrow face, making her eyes look bigger than usual.

Jamie glanced at me with a secret smile before saying, "You were so into your book you must not have heard me tell you where I was going."

"It *is* a good book," she said with a slight shrug. "Hi, Cora Bee."

"What're you reading?" I asked.

"*Les Misérables*," she said, comically overexaggerating the French pronunciation. "Emme and I were talking about musicals yesterday, and I told her about seeing the Broadway tour of *Les Mis* with my mom when it came to Birmingham a couple of years ago, and Emme told me that I should read the book, too—that she had read it around my age and loved it. I got it at the school library this morning." Her smile faltered when she mentioned school, but then a grin bloomed big and as bright as one of Glory's sunflowers. "The book is good. A little wordy but good."

Wordy was putting it mildly. If I recalled correctly, it had more than a thousand pages. What would other twelve-year-olds think about Alice voluntarily reading a massively thick book like *Les Mis?* I couldn't help wondering if that had been the source of her upset this morning.

"Did you ask her yet, Dad?" Alice looked expectantly between him and me. She bounced on the balls of her feet, and her eyes were wide with excitement.

It was my turn to study Jamie, and I definitely noticed extra pink in his cheeks.

"Alice . . . we talked about this."

"Dad, I told you who I wanted."

They stared at each other for so long that I fully believed they'd forgotten I was standing there. "Um," I said, gesturing with my chin toward my house, "I'm going to head on home. I'll see you later for flower watering, Alice?"

"Dad." Her tone was rigid, unyielding. "You said I could invite anyone I wanted."

Jamie sucked in a deep breath and pivoted toward me. "Alice and I are going to the drive-in tonight to watch *Jaws*, and I told her she could invite any friend she wanted."

"I chose you, Cora Bee," she said, her big smile stretching even wider.

"I told her that wasn't quite what I meant, but she insisted, and I told her to let me ask you so you wouldn't be put on the spot. That plan worked out real well, as you can see."

"Please say you'll come with us, Cora Bee!" Alice said. "I know Emme's going to be working over at the apartment tonight or I'd ask her, too. We can set up in the bed of Dad's truck, so you're comfortable with your cast, and I don't know if you've ever been to Buck's Drive-In, but they have the best nachos I've ever tasted."

No. Just say no, I told myself.

"You can say no," Jamie said. "We know you're busy with working from home these days."

I looked at Alice and pictured her swaying in that hammock, preferring to be alone than be with kids her own age. Then I pictured myself at home on a Saturday night in front of the TV with my crochet.

My heart hurt.

For her and for me.

I glanced between them, then down at Mabel. Agreeing to go

with them was either going to be the best decision I ever made, or one of the worst. Time would tell, but right now it felt . . . right.

I smiled. "What time do we need to leave?"

Chapter
13

May 22, 1964: Had to slow down a bit because I broke my arm. Fell in the garden. Hard to take care of a newborn with one arm but have been getting help from a woman I met at the plant nursery. Dorothy is married to the police chief and has a son just a little older than Lillian. She's smart and wickedly funny. I don't think I've ever laughed harder than with her. She's also helping me take care of the bees. They seem to like her, too. They haven't stung her once, unlike Levi, who seems to get stung every time he steps into the garden.

Emme

"You're a natural, hon," Glory said to me as I scooped chocolate cupcake batter into a muffin pan filled with gold liners. "I couldn't have done it better myself. I'm right proud of you."

A wash of unshed tears stung my eyes. It was my first time making cupcakes from scratch. It was my first time making cupcakes at all, though Glory and I had made plenty of other goodies since I'd been here. I'd weighed flour, leveled sugar, learned when to use measuring cups and when to use a measuring glass. She taught me about baking powder and baking soda and how buttermilk would react to each. If the pride in Glory's voice wasn't enough to make me tear up, the pride in myself was. "You're a good teacher, Glory."

With a warm smile, she reached over and patted my arm from where she sat on a stool pulled up to the island. This baking lesson hadn't been on the schedule for this afternoon. Originally

Cora Bee and I had plans to go see the land where the old Yardley Brick Company had once stood, but Glory had been feeling off most of the day. She'd mixed up at least a half dozen orders at the Sweetplace, had called people by the wrong name, and was unsteady on her feet. When she asked for my help this afternoon to prep some of tomorrow's confections, I couldn't say no.

Cora Bee and I had rescheduled our field trip, and I'd donned an apron and jumped into baking, nervous at first that I was going to ruin the cupcakes. But as I stood in Glory's kitchen, which had quickly become my favorite place in all of Sweetgrass, and listened to her talk about the recipe, how she had adapted it and learned its quirks, I'd lost myself in the sound of her voice, the sweet scent of vanilla and chocolate, and the coziness of the late afternoon light filling the room with warmth that made the bees on the floral wallpaper shimmer.

I was going to miss it terribly when I left Sweetgrass.

Because I had come to realize that I couldn't stay here. Not without Glory. When it was her time to go, it would be mine as well, though I'd simply move on to another town. I'd make yet another new start. But in addition to my battered suitcase and dingy backpack, I'd take with me all I learned from the woman who I wished with all my heart was my grandmother.

I knew I should leave now. Honestly, I should never have come in the first place. But this was likely my only chance to feel what it was like to be part of a loving family, and the thought of leaving hurt so much that I couldn't bear to pack my bags and disappear.

Glory yawned, then said, "Into the oven they go. Set the timer for thirteen minutes and then we'll check to see how they're doing."

It was Glory's unconditional love for me, a perfect stranger, that made me come to this quaint little town in the first place. Her desire to reconnect with her long-lost granddaughter coupled with how badly I'd wanted a family had been an irresistible combination. So I'd agreed, even though I'd known for a long time now that Rowan Wynn wasn't my father.

That knowledge had been a harsh blow, one dealt by my mother after one particularly bad night in Nashville when I had threatened to run away and live with my father.

"Good luck finding him," she'd said with a laugh that had hard edges and no humor. "Even I don't know who he is."

I'd been confused, since my birth certificate had listed his name, plain as could be. When I pulled the paper out of my folder to remind her, she'd ripped it in half and handed it back, then dragged her suitcase out from under the bed.

I knew what that suitcase meant.

"Don't believe everything you read, Emme. You're old enough now to know the truth. Your father can be any number of men. I don't even know all their names." As she hefted the suitcase onto the bed, she'd smiled the coy smile she always thought was cute but just made her look crazy. "Strangers-in-the-night kind of thing."

Gently, I'd held the torn paper in my hands, my heart feeling like it, too, had been ripped in half. "Then why put Rowan Wynn's name on my birth certificate?"

She opened the closet doors and started yanking down clothes from thin wire hangers. "Simple. The hospital asked, and I knew he had money. Lots of money. Now stop pouting and get packing. We're leaving in the morning."

"What're you thinking about, hon?" Glory asked now. "You have the saddest look on your face."

"My mother," I said honestly.

"Bound to happen, being here, and with Mother's Day coming up next weekend."

I nodded, though I hadn't given two thoughts to Mother's Day, which was often a painful day for me, spent wishing for a mother who was everything mine wasn't. I was glad Glory brought up the holiday, though, because I'd like to do something nice for her.

I might not be her granddaughter, but I was damn well going to be the best pretend granddaughter I could be. For her. For me.

If I only had six months here with Glory, then I was going

to make the most of every minute. I was going to soak in every story she told me, every recipe she shared, memorize every flower and its meaning.

I'd lap up her affection, her attention, her love. And I'd return it, tenfold, as I'd come to realize I wanted to give love as much as I wanted to feel it. I'd use these last months with Glory to let all that love fill my heart right to the brim.

And maybe, just maybe, it would be enough to see me through the rest of my shallow, rootless life.

On the counter, the recipe for the cupcakes was written with a sloping hand on a stained four-by-six-inch index card decorated with whisks. There was a part of me that wanted to steal that card, so I'd always have a piece of Glory with me, wherever I ended up. I'd add it to my collection of favorite things in my old backpack, the things that meant the most to me in all the world.

"I wish I'd found you sooner," Glory said. "So much time lost. Rowan looked for you, you know."

The scent of chocolate permeated the kitchen as I said, "He did?"

"He hired a private investigator, but time after time there were only false leads and dead ends. It was like Kristalle vanished into thin air."

That didn't surprise me. She was quite good at disappearing.

"It was his greatest disappointment not being able to find you."

I made myself ask, "What was he like? My mother never spoke of him."

Part of me didn't want to know, simply because I had no right. But another part of me, the one that wanted so badly to be part of this family, couldn't be denied.

A smile ghosted across her face, glowing brightly, then fading quickly. "He was a sweet boy, so loving. He adored animals and the outdoors. I was forever making him come down out of one tree or another to eat supper. Like you, he had a way of reading people, and that steered him through life. Helped him choose friends. Showed him who to avoid. It led him to his career as a professional poker player, where reading people was half the challenge. He had a strong sense of self, of what he wanted in life, and he chased it, never settling. I admired that about him. I was always one to settle for what felt easiest. Especially when it came to marriage."

"You settled?"

"My family didn't have a lot of money when I was growing up. So when my former husband showed up in my world, having a good job, a car, and a little money in the bank, I thought he was offering me everything I'd ever dreamed of."

"Did you love him?"

Sadness shadowed her eyes. "I liked him. I thought it was enough. I was wrong." She let out a sigh. "I know Rowan likely had my marriage in mind when he told Kristalle he wouldn't marry her. He didn't want to make the same mistakes I had. Yet, I also saw how much the decision hurt him, because she took you away. Sometimes life feels like a no-win situation. Hard choices are made. Consequences are suffered. Some are more painful than others."

I suddenly thought of Jamie. Cora Bee had told me of his co-parenting situation. My life could've been so different if my mother hadn't wanted Rowan to suffer from the choice he'd made, the choice to reject her. Yet, if she had stayed and he eventually requested a DNA test as part of a custody agreement, then her game would've been up. At least in leaving, she got to see him suffer.

"Your father was curious, kind, giving, and creative. Just like you. He brought me such joy. And so do you, honey."

I willed myself not to cry.

"I wish you could've known him," she added.

"Me too," I said, nearly choking on emotion as my heart beat wildly in my chest. I wished a lot of things that would never come true. My own set of consequences.

"In the hospital, just before he passed away, I made him the promise that I'd find you one day, bring you home. For a while, I didn't think I'd be able to keep that promise. Year after year, the PI I hired kept hitting those same dead ends. But then you threw us a lifeline. You got your GED, so we knew you were still out there. Then you got a steady job and a driver's license and we were able to find out where you were staying. I'm just so happy you're here now. Home, where you belong. Where you've always belonged."

I couldn't stop the tears this time, and she shimmied off the stool to give me a hug. I let all my inhibitions go and hugged her back tightly, trying to remember the scents that clung to her—the chocolate, the rose, the lingering sunshine—and the feel of her soft, feathery cheek against mine.

When she pulled away, I wiped my eyes and movement outside the window caught my attention. I squinted and said, "Is that Dorothy in the backyard digging up your vegetable garden?"

She followed my gaze. "Land's sake, it sure is."

Glory headed for the side door, and a moment later, she was outside. I had to race to catch up.

"Dorothy, my love," Glory called out as she wobbled her way along a stone pathway to the raised planter bed. "What are you doing?"

Dorothy was on her knees in the vegetable bed. Dirt clung to her pretty blue muumuu, and her white hair and pink scalp glowed like a pearl in the afternoon sunlight. She yanked out a radish by its leaves, tossed it aside, and stuck her small pink shovel in the hole.

She looked up at our approach, and there was a fire in her eyes I'd never seen before. "I'm looking for that no-account, no-good, slimy, *pitiful* rapscallion. He has to be around here somewhere."

Rapscallion? I had a decent vocabulary, thanks to my lifetime love of reading, but I'd never heard the word before. By her thoroughly disgusted tone, I could decipher its meaning just fine, but even still I made a mental note to look it up.

"Oh dear," Glory said as she climbed into the planter box along with her friend. She peered into the hole. "Is he down there? Do you see him?"

I picked up the radishes, brushed the dirt off their muted red skins, and stood idly by, not sure what to do other than follow Glory's lead. I thought about calling Chase, but I didn't have his number, and I really didn't want to leave Glory to handle this alone.

"Not yet," Dorothy said, still digging. "He's a wily one."

"Maybe try over here," Glory said, pointing to a spot in front of her. She yanked out another radish plant and handed it to me.

"He shouldn't be so hard to find," Dorothy said as she thrust the trowel into the dark soil. "The stench of his putrid soul should lead the way."

Glory nodded as if in total agreement. "There was a rotten smell today in Nannette and May's front yard. Perhaps we should go take a closer look over there?"

"I already checked there," Dorothy said, tossing a shovelful of dirt over her shoulder.

Glory glanced at me as if seeking help, but I wasn't sure what to do until she said, "Have you smelled anything unpleasant lately, Emme, hon?"

Before I could answer, Orville raced past me, and with one smooth leap, he landed in front of Dorothy and Glory in the planter bed. He let out two sharp barks, then sat next to Dorothy and wagged his tail.

It suddenly seemed to me that Orville had been trained to find Dorothy. *Good boy*, I thought. *Good boy*. That also told me Dorothy went on these digging expeditions fairly often. Suddenly I wondered about all those holes in Dorothy's front yard. Had it been *she* who'd dug them and not Orville? It was a definite possibility.

I recalled how Glory had said that Dorothy had squirrel issues, and I suddenly wondered if those "issues" had been a side effect of her brain injury. It seemed likely, considering the way

Glory was playing along with her panicked search for the "varmint," and my heart broke for the darling woman.

A second later, Chase came running into the backyard. With one quick glance, he sized up the situation. He stepped up next to me and said, "Dotty, did you find the dirty son of a—" He caught Glory's raised eyebrow and coughed. "Squirrel?"

I took a small step away from him, uncomfortable with his closeness.

His grandmother threw the shovel down in disappointment. "No."

"It's certainly not for lack of trying," Glory said, as she climbed down from the high bed.

I held out my hand to help her keep her balance until she found solid footing. Her hand curved around mine, holding it tightly.

Chase pretty much lifted Dorothy off the planter, and she *tsk*ed at the dirt on her dress. He said, "The search can wait. Let's get you home and cleaned up before your big night out."

She stared at him, a question in her pale eyes.

"Oh, that's right." Glory finally let my hand go so she could dust off the dirt clinging to her palms. "Nannette and May are taking us to a dance class!" She tried to do a cha-cha-cha but only made it through the second *cha* before she lost her balance.

Chase grabbed her arm, steadying her, and she patted his hand. "Thanks, hon."

I tucked the radishes back into their beds and tried my best to fix the damage that had been done. Orville picked up the trowel by its handle and dropped it in front of me. I patted his head. "Thanks, buddy."

"I don't remember agreeing to a dance class," Dorothy said. "What if I break a hip?"

"You've got a *spare*," Glory said with a wide smile.

Dorothy rolled her eyes but her lips twitched with humor.

After the rough health day Glory had, I didn't think it was in her best interests to attend the dance class, but I knew better than to try and talk her out of it, especially since the reason for attending was Dorothy.

She didn't yet know that the dance class was being held at a local assisted-care facility. Glory had shared with me that for months now they'd been taking Dorothy there to try to get her used to the place. The long-term goal was for her to move in by the end of the year, and now I wondered at the timing of it all. Would Dorothy further decline once Glory was gone?

Chase took hold of his grandmother's hand and tucked it into the crook of his arm and headed for the gate, Orville at his heels. "See you later on for our date, Emme," he said with a cheeky smile. "No need to dress up. Wear something casual."

I threw a glance at the apartment above the garage, then leveled him with a hard stare and tried to think of any excuse whatsoever that would get me out of working alongside him tonight.

"I'm not sure I can make it," I said, wrinkling my nose. "I've got a lot of baking to do. Oh my God—the cupcakes!"

I went running for the side door and skidded my way through the kitchen to grab a pot holder from the counter. The bitter scent in the air told me the cupcakes were burned before I even pulled open the oven and saw their crisp tops.

I set the pan on a trivet on the island and looked over to find the three of them staring at me from the doorway. "Ruined," I said. "I'm so sorry, Glory."

She waved a hand as she stepped inside. "Don't worry any. There are two dozen extra cupcakes in the garage freezer. Plenty for tomorrow, which also means you have plenty of time to work on the apartment tonight as planned."

"Fabulous," I said with a tight smile.

Chase's laugh followed him as he led Dorothy away.

When I was sure they were out of earshot, I turned to ask Glory about Dorothy's squirrel issues, but she was gone, already in the bathroom washing up.

I took a deep breath as I looked at the overcooked cupcakes and hoped to the heavens above that Chase wouldn't ask me any hard questions tonight that would put the rest of my time here in Sweetgrass in jeopardy.

I had the uneasy feeling he'd only volunteered his help because he suspected I was a fraud and wanted to interrogate me. Since he wasn't wrong, I didn't know how to answer his questions without digging myself into a deeper hole. One I wouldn't be able to climb out of.

Chapter
14

 Glory's Garden Lesson #7

There truly aren't enough words to describe the exquisiteness of dahlias. They're simply stunning with their grand size—I have dinner plates smaller! And those rich colors—they're absolutely drenched in beauty. It's little wonder that they represent dignity and elegance. You know, hon, Lillian's named for the white lily, a symbol of sweet purity, but I think Bee missed the mark. Lillian should've been named Dahlia. Maybe when she finally visits, we can talk her into changing it.

Emme

"Where do you want to start?" Chase asked.

"I thought I'd start the wall prep while you tackle that beast." I pointed to the box on the small kitchen table that held a new faucet kit. "I can do small plumbing fixes, but that's a little out of my league."

If I was being honest, I could probably figure out the installation, but I liked the thought of him being in the kitchen, far away from me. Well, as far away as we could get in an open-concept apartment. Besides, I didn't do well with small, enclosed spaces. The thought of crawling into the cabinet under the sink made my stomach hurt.

"Where'd you learn plumbing fixes?" he asked as he poked through the tool box sitting on one of the kitchen chairs.

"Nowhere in—"

"Particular," he finished, as if expecting the answer.

Earlier, I'd peeked at the color chosen for the room by prying off the top of the can and finding it filled with creamy white paint with the barest hint of a yellow undertone. It instantly reminded me of Glory's vanilla buttercream frosting. Cora Bee had picked the color, which meant it was the perfect shade. The color would add brightness, coziness, and complement the wooden beams and trim. "Exactly. Where did *you* learn plumbing?"

Chase had arrived at the apartment right on time wearing a red bandana as a head covering, which both looked ridiculous and oddly attractive. He had a small cooler in hand and was dressed in a sleeveless tee, knit shorts, and old tennis shoes by the looks of them. He'd left Orville at home, due to not wanting to get dog hair in the fresh paint.

I'd arrived early to bring up all the supplies from the garage, because the faster we could get this done, the better. I'd set out tape, sandpaper, brushes, rollers, and paint trays, then covered the wood floors and tried to ignore the pit in my stomach.

"My dad. He's an accountant who has a penchant for DIY. Only, his do-it-*yourself* projects always included me."

I tried to imagine doing homey chores with my father, who-ever he was, and it made me ache with an indescribable sadness. "Did you enjoy it? The projects, the time together?"

He opened the box with the faucet kit, removed the pieces from inside. "Mostly. I could've done without the time we painted ourselves into a corner on the porch. I wanted to cut a screen to get out. He decided we could wait two hours until the paint dried enough to walk on. Any patience I have was learned at his knee."

I thought of the kind way he treated Dorothy and concluded his dad was most likely a saint.

He pulled a phone from his pocket, swiped at the screen. "Any father figures in your life?"

"Nope," I said as I pried the top off a small container of Spackle. I'd learned most of my handyman skills by attending the free classes offered at big home improvement stores. Between those and online videos, I held my own in the DIY department.

When you lived in less-than-desirable apartments or rented rooms, it was necessary to know how to stop a sink from leaking or a toilet from overflowing, because it was unlikely the landlord would care enough to send a maintenance person along.

Music billowed into the air from his phone, the notes a throwback to another time. "Do you like oldies? It's what my dad and I always listen to while working around the house. It's kind of tradition. My phone is a poor substitute for my granddaddy's old transistor radio that we usually listen to." He grinned. "That scratchy reception really adds a little something extra to the sound. Anyway"—he set the phone on the table—"let me know if you prefer something else."

The room filled with the sounds of a man singing about a woman asking him to come a little bit closer. The lyrics made me want to scoot another foot away from Chase. "I don't really have a preference. Is your grandfather why you became a police officer?"

I needed to keep him talking so he wouldn't ask about me, but also not be *too* chatty. It was a fine line I needed to walk.

"Yeah. He was a great guy. One of the best. It about crushed me to leave the force."

"Why did you?" I asked, pretending not to know.

"Broke my wrist chasing after a mugger. Had surgery, pins, the whole nine yards. It didn't work the same afterward. And it was my right hand, my shooting hand, so I couldn't do my job anymore. I could've taken a desk job, but I didn't think I could sit around all day watching other people live my dreams. I tried selling insurance for a while. Then worked as a recruiter. Nothing felt . . . right. My head was still in the police world. It was Dotty who steered me toward writing. She loves true-crime shows. Once, when we were watching an episode about an unsolved mystery, I started throwing out theories. She told me I should stop guessing and get off my rear and solve the case. So I did."

"You make it sound easy."

His laughter rose to the rafters. "It wasn't. It took years of investigating, of conversations, of digging in old files. Then, of course, finding a publisher and all that isn't easy, either."

"How *old* are you?"

"You're not supposed to ask people their age."

I smiled as I used my fingertip to push Spackle into a hole in the wall. "I thought that etiquette rule only applied to men asking about women."

"Nope. It's both. But I'm thirty-three. You?"

"Twenty-five." I'd hoped that would be the end of the questions for a while, but he clearly wasn't done.

"Was it always just you and your mom when you were younger?"

Not always, no. Not if one counted all the men she brought into our lives. I didn't count them. In fact, I wished I could forget them completely. "Until I was eighteen, then we went our separate ways."

When he didn't ask another prying question straightaway, I looked over at him. He was studying me with softness in his eyes.

He said, "That's pretty young to be out on your own, with no family support."

"How do you know I didn't have family around?" I *hadn't* had any family around, but I wanted to see if I could ferret out how much he had already learned about me.

"I found out when I visited *nowhere in particular.*"

His wry tone made me smile. "Or did you find out when you did a complete background check on me? I wouldn't be surprised if you'd slipped away to Louisville for a few days to talk to my old housemates."

After a brief hesitation, he said, "I can't leave Dotty that long. I sent an old friend."

He wasn't joking. It was a strange feeling to admire his honesty. He could've lied easily. Of course, I would've known he was lying, but he didn't know that. "And what did they say?"

"Apparently you don't make much noise. Most of the people who lived in that house said they didn't even know you'd left. I hope you're not upset I checked into you. I have a soft spot for Glory."

Grateful he hadn't found out that I'd once been arrested, I said, "I'd question your investigative integrity if you hadn't looked into my past."

He carried the faucet and hand sprayer to the counter. "I could look only so far. Your early years don't have much information. And if you had a juvie record, it's likely sealed."

My heart darted around my chest like it was trying to escape and run far away. "I don't have a juvie record," I said honestly. "And I've never used an alias, though my mother has more times than I can count."

"Noted," he said.

I took advantage of the break in his questioning to say, "How's Dorothy doing? Feeling better?"

Deep lines creased the space between his eyebrows as he studied the instructional booklet. "She's always happy to get dolled up, go out."

"Glory was excited, too." It was the perkiest I'd seen her all day, and I kind of wished I were with them, watching them dance and laugh, instead of being here, dodging questions about my past. I decided to turn the tables.

"How long did it take you to teach Orville to track Dorothy?"

"So you noticed that, did you? I'm surprised it took you so long since *I've* noticed you're quite perceptive."

"It took so long because I'm not psychic. I'd never seen him find her before today."

"Excuses, excuses."

I smiled. "He's a good boy."

"The best. I can't take credit for training him, though. Professionals did that." As I filled another hole with my finger, Chase added, "You know there's a putty knife on the table, right?"

"If you don't mind getting dirty, fingers do a better job. It's easier to feel if the hole is fully filled, and you don't have a ton of waste."

He smiled, showing off his dimple. "Then carry on."

At some point in the past week, Glory had taken down everything that had previously hung on the walls and carried it down to the garage. She'd mentioned something about a garage sale, and I wondered when she'd ever have the time. It seemed she was always working, at the Sweetplace, or cooking the desserts she sold there, or fussing in the garden.

For as much as I wanted to tell her to rest, to take it easy, I wanted her to keep doing what she was doing. Living every minute. Not missing a beat. Soaking it all in.

She'd yet to say a word to me about being ill, and I wondered when she would. What, exactly, was she waiting for? I couldn't even imagine—mostly because I couldn't imagine what life was like for her right now. Knowing there wasn't much time left.

A song about starting over drifted through the room, filling the silence as surely as I filled small holes, dents, scrapes. I kept an eye on Chase as he picked up a wrench and flashlight and angled himself into the cabinet under the kitchen sink. At the sound of a low, sharp curse, I said, "You okay down there?"

He mumbled something in reply.

I moved a little closer. "What was that?"

There was a clatter of a wrench, then he shimmied out of the space and sat up. "I said it's a knuckle buster."

He turned his hands toward me, showed me the raw skin on his knuckles. I winced, set my supplies on the floor, and glanced around. "I'm sure there's a first aid kit around here somewhere."

"I don't need first aid," he said, stopping me in my tracks on the way to the bathroom.

"You're bleeding."

"Barely."

I set my hands on my hips. "Is this a manly man kind of thing?"

He laughed. "Do I seem like a manly man? Did you not see me reading the *instructions*?"

"Good point. Still, you should wash those cuts."

"Just so they'll be nice and clean for when I go back under and bust them up again?"

"Are you always so contrary?"

He tipped his head, considering the question. "I might be."

I could only shake my head at him. "Do you have work gloves?"

"Despite my quest for gentleman status, no. Let me see your hands."

I curled them into fists. "Why?"

"They're small. No knuckle busting. Come on over." He picked up the wrench.

I eyed the small space. "No thanks."

"It'll only take a second; then I can get back in there." He smoothly rose to his feet and held out the wrench. "A few twists with this bad boy, then you'll be done. Don't make me start questioning if your home improvement skills were fabricated."

I tried to tell myself the cabinet wasn't enclosed. Not really. Not with the door wide open. And the flashlight was still in there, chasing out most of the darkness with its focused beam of light.

But I couldn't chase away the images of hiding in similar cabinets, folding my small body into impossible angles, hoping to stay invisible. Fear washed over me, covering me in goose bumps.

"Emme?" Chase said.

I barely heard him, my mind in another place, another time. My fingers went to the scar on my face, and I could feel my hand shaking.

Despite how good some hiding spots were, if a hunter was determined to find his prey, he rarely gave up.

When I felt a hand on my arm, I let out a scream and jumped backward, plastering myself to the wall. My heart raced; my skin crawled.

"Emme! It's me, Chase." He held his hands in the air. "I'm not going to hurt you. I promise."

I blinked, and as the compassion and kindness in his eyes swam in and out of focus, I saw clearly that he somehow knew why I'd reacted the way I had. Maybe not the particulars, but I guessed that, as a former cop, he'd been exposed to my kind of reaction before. I couldn't stop my tears from falling.

"It's all right," he said, his voice low, soothing, as he inched closer. "It's all right."

It wasn't, not really. And I wasn't entirely sure whether I was crying because of my past misery or my current embarrassment. Every day I tried so hard to hide my past, my emotional scars, and all it took was one kitchen cabinet to do me in.

He leaned against the wall next to me, leaving a good foot of space between us. A second later, he handed over his bandana. "It's clean. Well. Let me clarify. It's not necessarily *dirty*. I don't have a handkerchief on me. What kind of gentleman doesn't carry a handkerchief at all times?"

Grateful for something to hide behind, I sniffled and dabbed my eyes with the bandana, which smelled like coconut and mint. I took a few deep breaths trying to ease the pain in my chest. When I felt like I could talk again, I said, "Do you actually own any handkerchiefs?"

He hung his head. "No. I'm a complete failure as a gentleman."

"I wouldn't say that."

"That's because you're nice."

"I wouldn't say that, either."

He laughed. "No denying it, Emme Wynn. I've seen it with my own eyes."

For the briefest moment, I wanted to tell him everything, get all my sins out in the open, get it all off my chest. But more than that, I wanted to stay in Sweetgrass as long as Glory was here. That meant keeping my mouth shut.

We stood there for a minute or so, the swell of a chirpy Beatles song echoing among the ceiling's wooden beams, making the silence hovering between us less obvious, less painful.

"You know, you weren't entirely wrong that day we first met in the garden."

I thought back to the conversation and how I'd run my mouth so he couldn't ask me any questions. "About what?"

"I am working on a book, and Bee's disappearance *is* a factor."

"*Chase*," I said.

"Not the disappointed tone. I can't take it. Not after the tears. I've been working on this book for months. I can't just go and scrap it. I have a contract. A deadline. And like I said, it's not about Bee. Not really."

I had the feeling he was only sharing this information with me because I'd revealed something so personal about myself—even though my disclosure had been entirely unintentional. I'd suspected he had a big heart before, but now I knew it to be absolutely true. "Who's it about, then?"

"Levi."

At this, I turned to face him. I wanted to see his eyes. "What about Levi?"

"I don't know how much you've heard about him . . ."

"I think I've heard it all. Murderer, abuser, embezzler. Is there anything else?"

"There might be. It's what I've been researching. He had a woman on the side."

My eyes widened. "I'm surprised, but I shouldn't be. What makes you think he was cheating?"

"I found my grandfather's notes on the case at Dotty's house. A whole notebook filled with scribbles of information. Some senseless, some clear as day. One of the pages had a note that said only 'Levi's affair?' and it was circled so many times that the pen nearly tore through the paper."

"Have you found any evidence of an affair?"

"Nothing concrete. But then something happened that made me suspect Levi might not have acted alone the night he killed Bee."

From what little I knew of the case, that would be a huge development. "What happened to give you that impression?"

"The gazing pool happened. A few months ago, I saw in the water what I now think is the night Bee disappeared. I was looking through the eyes of someone shoveling dirt near the gazing pool. And the person doing the shoveling was a woman. I saw her hands, her feet. She was wearing a skirt and low blue heels. It was dark but there was enough moonlight to see by."

I watched his eyes closely as he spoke, and everything he said was the complete truth. I had so many questions to ask but the very first had to be about the gazing pool and how he'd seen images in the water—and believed them to be a glimpse of a past event. It seemed unreal, yet I recalled how the images I'd seen of the man knocking over the bee boxes had felt very real. "The gazing pool—"

I was cut off by the ringing of his phone. He strode forward to the table, frowned at what he saw on the screen, and answered.

I listened to his brusque answers, his *yes ma'am*s, *mm-hmm*s, and finally his "I'll be there as soon as possible."

He turned toward me. "Dotty fainted at the dance class. The retirement home insisted she be taken to the hospital, and she's pitchin' a fit and raising hell. We need to go."

"We?" I asked, taken aback.

"I'm not leaving you alone." He glanced at the cabinet under the sink. "Nope. Not happening."

"I'll go back to Cora Bee's . . ."

His eyes narrowed. "Where you'll be alone. Because she's on a date at the drive-in. The whole neighborhood's talking about it."

Cora Bee was going to hate that, especially since she'd spent a half hour before she left insisting the drive-in was *not a date*.

And I wanted to argue that I was fine being alone, that I was used to it, but I couldn't form the words. I didn't want to be alone with my old ghosts. Not tonight. Not ever.

He held out his hand to me, and I saw his earlier words softly glowing in his blue eyes.

I'm not going to hurt you. I promise.

I didn't trust him. There was a big part of me that suspected he was only being nice to get close to me, to figure out my scam, to run me out of town before I did any damage.

I knew this. I felt this.

Yet, I *wanted* to trust him. I wanted it so badly that it hurt.

For a long moment I stared at his hand and those scraped knuckles, before finally stepping forward to take hold of it and steal some of its strength. And Lord help me, I quickly found that I didn't want to let go.

Chapter
15

October 17, 1964: Levi's been talking about us having another baby. He wants a boy so badly. I'm just not sure. Lillian is only eight months old. There are already not enough hours in the day! Besides, he never seems to be home these days. He's still working long hours, and a few times he's come home smelling of perfume. I'm starting to wonder if he's __working__ at all. At home, he's started criticizing everything. The house, my housekeeping, the way I cook, the way I dress. And don't get me started on the bees. You've never seen a man so jealous. He wants me to get rid of the bees, saying I spend too much time with them. We had a big fight when I told him I don't spend near as much time with the bees as he does working overtime. It just doesn't feel right to bring another baby into our lives amid so much uncertainty.

Cora Bee

"Filmmaker Hitchcock? Is this puzzle maker even trying?" I asked, staring down at the crossword puzzle open on the kitchen table.

My pulse beat against my temple in a steady rhythm, silently punctuating my words. I'd awoken with a throbbing headache to go along with my aching foot, which was extra angry that I'd overdone it yesterday, spending too much time out and about and not enough elevating my injury. The headache I blamed on a combination of lack of sleep and the storm front blowing in— sharp changes in the air pressure always brought on a headache.

It was early Saturday morning, just after dawn, and dark clouds had crowded out any sunshine, leaving the sky gray and moody. Light from the gold fixture above the table glowed down on Emme and me, its reflection swimming in the pale coffee in our mugs.

Emme smiled and used a gel pen to write *Alfred* into the appropriate squares. "As much as I like a challenge, some days— like today—I appreciate an easy clue. I feel like my brain is only half working this morning."

It had been a long night for her. For both of us, really, since I hadn't been able to fall asleep until she had come back to the house. She was already sipping from her second cup of coffee when normally she had only one, but she didn't seem to be affected by the extra caffeine at all. Dark smudges of exhaustion sat under her eyes, and she covered a yawn with her hand.

"Do you want another turnover?" I asked as I reached toward the plate in the middle of the table, hoping that eating would help my head pain.

"No thanks," she said as she continued to fill in boxes.

Once Dorothy came home from the hospital, after having cursed out the entire emergency department's staff, Glory had stayed with her while Emme and Chase went back to the apartment to put a few more hours of work into the makeover. She'd come in at a little past one in the morning and had already been awake when I came out of my room at five.

Emme threw a look at the clock on the microwave. "I should probably get moving. Before I head off to the Sweetplace, I want to do a little work on the bookcase. It's so close to being done." But instead of getting up from her seat, she picked up her mug and leaned back against the chair. "How was the movie last night? I've been dying to ask but didn't want to crush you with questions first thing in the morning before you even had your coffee."

I shifted the puzzle book so it sat squarely in front of me and picked up the pen she'd abandoned. I tried to bullet point the night as best I could. "You haven't seen *Jaws* until you've seen it on a giant screen—I might never go swimming in the ocean again. I was thankful I remembered the bug spray or we all would've been eaten alive, as sharks have nothing on Alabama's mosquito population. Buck's in fact does have the best nachos in town, dripping in cheese and jalapeños and spicy chopped tomatoes. Maybe too much cheese. I woke up with a headache."

"Is there such a thing as too much cheese on nachos?"

"You're right. It was probably the tomatoes that gave me the headache. Who puts healthy stuff on nachos?"

She laughed, such a quiet sound that I barely even understood what I was hearing before it was gone. I'd never heard her laugh before. When she kept looking at me, like she was expecting more information about my night, I added, "Mabel was on her best behavior."

The sweet dog had spent most of the time snoozing with her head in my lap. Jamie had decked out the back of his pickup with a cushy blow-up mattress and a ton of pillows. Alice had sat in between us the whole time, gasping and groaning at the screen. Okay, perhaps not the whole time. She'd made several trips to the concession stand and the restroom, each trip growing noticeably longer.

Emme had her mug cupped in her hands, as if she was trying her hardest to absorb its warmth. "You should probably know that the whole neighborhood thinks you were on a date. Everyone's waiting to hear how it went. At the hospital last night, May said she was hoping there'd be a wedding soon."

"Oh my God." I gave up on the crossword clue—a three-letter card game—and pushed the puzzle away, now thinking its creator was just plain mean. Picking up my mug, I said, "You know it wasn't a date."

Humor filled her green eyes. "*Mm-hmm.*"

I sighed. "It *wasn't.* But I do think Alice was trying to play matchmaker. It became obvious after her fourth trip to the concession stand."

Every time she returned, she'd look at Jamie and me expectantly, then sigh dramatically as she plopped down between us once more.

"Were there any matches made?" Emme asked.

"No, of course not."

One of her eyebrows lifted. It was odd, the feeling I had that she knew when I wasn't telling her everything.

"I mean . . ." I shifted on my seat, trying to get comfortable when the cast made comfort nearly impossible. "No. Once Jamie's job here in Sweetgrass is done, he and Alice are moving back to Birmingham. There's no point in getting involved."

I took a deep swallow of coffee, wondering why it hurt to even *talk* about the fact that they'd be leaving soon.

"Okay, so maybe no *wedding* plans, then, but why not have some fun while he's here?"

"There's no maybe about it. I'm never getting married again."

Her eyes darkened with sympathy before she said, "I hate to hear that. I was hoping to be a bridesmaid. May thinks that your bridesmaids should wear pink dresses, to match the roses in the garden, where of course your wedding would be held. I'm not sure I could pull off the color, but I'd be willing to give it a shot."

"You really weren't kidding about her planning my wedding, were you?"

She laughed again, and this time I soaked in the sound. "We were in the waiting room a long time."

I jumped at the change of subject. "Anything show up on all the tests they ran on Dorothy?"

"No, which is a good thing. The doctor said she was dehydrated and that was why she fainted. They treated her with an IV and sent her home. Personally, I think they were happy to get rid of her. An angry Dorothy doesn't make a good patient. I was shocked at the words coming out of her mouth, and I didn't grow up around Goody Two-Shoes."

"I once heard her cuss out a squirrel that was digging up her vegetable bed in the garden, and it was the most colorful vocabulary lesson I'd ever had."

"There's really a squirrel? I thought it might have been imaginary."

"Well, there *was* a squirrel. I'm not sure it's the same one she's still searching for. She only started looking for him after her head injury . . ."

"Poor Dorothy."

It was truly heartbreaking to see her digging holes all over the neighborhood, but I was beyond glad she was still here with us and often fought the urge to help her dig.

We sipped our coffee in silence for a moment before she returned to what we'd been speaking about before veering off track with talk about Dorothy. "Do you like Jamie? Like, really *like* him?"

I wavered on how to answer and finally opted for honesty. "I think I might. But I also think that's why we need to stay friends."

She nodded as if she understood fully, which was a relief. I didn't want to spell out how healing from a broken heart had almost killed me once—I didn't think I could go through it again. And a fling was out of the question. I was an all-in kind of person.

As she slid her bare feet out from underneath the table, I couldn't help noticing the Y-shaped tan line from her flip-flops, which reminded me of what I'd seen in the gazing pool. Although Emme's background check had come back clean, my mother's words about aliases echoed in my head. I couldn't very well ask Emme straight out if she'd ever been arrested. Well, I *could*. But I had the feeling the question would change things between us forever.

She carried her plate and mug to the sink, rinsed them both, and set them into the dishwasher she'd emptied earlier. "Do you have any plans for the day? Other than our trip to the brickyard?"

"Just work," I said, already outlining the projects that needed to get done.

She wiped her hands on a dish towel, then carefully rehung it, making sure its edges draped evenly. "Do you ever take any days off?"

"Rarely. It feels like there's always something to do. Today I'll throw myself into client designs since I have to hit pause on my Yardley proposal until I get more information. But it won't be all work today. I'm sure Alice will be by at some point after her soccer game this morning to water the flowers, even though it looks like it's going to rain." I ran a thumb around the lip of my mug. "We'll probably end up watching a couple of *Gilmore Girls* episodes."

It hadn't taken long before I started looking forward to Alice and Mabel's visits every afternoon. Mabel would stay with me while Alice worked outside, watering flowers and tending to other odds and ends. Afterward, we'd usually have a snack together and watch a TV show.

I said, "I should probably start thinking about what to get my mother for Mother's Day so I can ship it out. Do you need to shop for your mother? We can go together."

Her chin shot up as she folded her arms across her chest, and her hands curled into fists before she tucked them under her elbows. "I don't even know where my mother is. I'd like to look for something for Glory, though."

My head told me to leave it alone, but my heart told me to ask. "How long has it been since you've seen your mother?"

"Since I turned eighteen."

"Any phone calls? Emails?"

She shook her head and her nose wrinkled for a second before she looked away, out the kitchen window into the backyard. Even though her expression was all but hidden, I could see the tension in her neck, in the stiff set of her slim shoulders and sharp jawline. "I have no way to contact her, other than hire someone to track her down, and I'm not sure that would work, either, because she's really good at not being found."

"Is your mom . . ." I couldn't bring myself to finish the question. "Never mind."

"What?" she asked.

I lifted a shoulder. "Is she really . . . that bad?"

Emme kept looking out the window, and I noticed the once-gray floaters that drifted around her were darkening again. "She's worse. Besides, I don't really want to see or talk to her. We don't have the kind of relationship you and your mother have."

I thought that might be the understatement of the year. "I'm sorry."

I wasn't sure my apology was for her having a rotten mother or for bringing up the subject in the first place. Maybe it was a bit of both.

And as I continued to watch those hazy charcoal spots float around her, I wanted to take away all the pain she'd ever endured. My mom and Aunt Glory had always believed Uncle Rowan to be Kristalle's biggest victim, but I suddenly had the feeling that title belonged to Emme.

Emme

Out in Cora Bee's garage, I had the door open, and a sulfur-rich breeze drifted through the space, promising rain. Since rescuing the bookcase, I'd spent a good amount of time out here, usually late at night, sanding, filling dings, dents, cracks, and priming and painting the piece.

Crouching down, I stirred the paint, taking care so that it didn't splash up into the grooves of the can. The teal color was an equal mix of blue and green that reminded me of a peacock. I dipped the tip of the paintbrush into the can and then carried it to the bookcase, careful not to drip on the tarp that covered a section of the garage floor.

I ran the brush along one of the shelves, completely in awe at how the bookcase had been transformed. There was such a sense of satisfaction in turning trash to treasure, and I let myself get lost in that feeling for a moment. The pride. The accomplishment.

I let it drown out the rising tide of guilt threatening to make me do something stupid.

Like confess.

I'd wanted to spill all to Chase last night, and at breakfast with Cora Bee this morning, I'd had the same thoughts. The more I fit in outwardly, the more I hurt inwardly. I wanted them to care for me, the real me. Not the Emme I was pretending to be. The granddaughter. The cousin. The family friend.

But if I told them the truth, that I was no blood relation, then I knew I'd lose them all.

Birds sang morning songs as I took my time to finish the last coat of paint, losing myself in the work instead of my troubling thoughts. Once done, I stepped back to assess the job I'd done and smiled. It was beautiful, the rich color the perfect balance for the hefty wood. I quickly washed my paintbrush in the slop sink, cleaned the sink itself, and put away my supplies. Tonight, after Chase and I finished our work at the apartment, I'd give the bookcase its topcoat, and tomorrow morning, I'd apply the wallpaper to its backing.

And with any luck, there would be another treasure for me to rescue in this week's trash. It was a longshot, I knew, but I couldn't help feeling hopeful.

I closed the garage door on my way out, crossed the driveway, and fought the urge to take a stroll through the garden to check on my flower bed. There wasn't time this morning.

Once inside, I looked around the kitchen for any cleanup to do, then walked down the hallway to Cora Bee's office. Her crutches were leaning on the side of the desk, easily at hand, and her foot was propped on the ottoman. An insulated water bottle sat on the table next to her desk where she could easily reach it, along with a banana, a pack of crackers, and a sleeve of Glory's butter pecan cookies.

She glanced up from her laptop when I tapped lightly on the door, and winced as if the motion hurt. "Heading out?"

I nodded and said, "Anything I can get for you before I go?"

She cracked a smile. "Some motivation to do these design boards would be nice."

"You're not going to get it from me. I think you deserve a day off. Work-life balance is important."

"You're starting to sound like my mother. The nagging genes must've skipped me."

My heart squeezed painfully whenever she compared me to someone else in the family. I wanted so badly to be one of them. "We nag because we care."

Absently, she rubbed her temples. "I promise to watch an extra episode of *Gilmore Girls* with Alice."

"It's a start. Did you take a pain pill with breakfast? Will one of those work on headaches, too?"

"I think they work for everything. I'm good. Really. I'm sure it'll go away soon. It's just the weather."

"And the tomatoes."

"And the tomatoes. I'll never make that mistake again."

I left her with a wave and my regret that I couldn't stay with her all day, to coax her out of the office and into the fresh air.

After gathering what I needed for a day at the marketplace, I headed for the front door. As I passed the kitchen doorway, I hesitated, my gaze slipping to the amber pill bottle on the windowsill.

I glanced down the hallway, then walked quickly to the sink and turned on the faucet to cover any noise. I opened the bottle and spilled the pills into my hand. It took only a moment to do a quick count before putting the pills back into the bottle.

The prescription had been for twenty-eight pills.

There were still twenty-eight pills in the bottle.

I'd suspected she hadn't been taking her medication but couldn't for the life of me figure out why when she was in so much pain.

Chapter
16

Glory's Garden Lesson #8

How much do you love the wildflower field? I adore it myself.
The whimsy, the freedom. The cosmos are a particular favorite
of mine, and I'm happy as all get out to see them blooming
early. That sometimes happens here—flowers blooming out of
season. I'm not sure why, but who am I to question such a gift?
Are the cosmos not the sweetest flowers? And such variety of
colors, too. Pink, purple, orange, yellow, white, magenta. It's all
here. Look at the scalloped edge on the petal and how the yellow pollen florets provide such a nice contrast. Oh, how nature
amazes me! These darlings represent peace and harmony, and
I surely feel it when I'm standing out here among them. Don't
you, hon?

Emme

"You'll be just fine, Emme. Just fine."

I leaned against the island and stared at the wallpaper in Glory's kitchen, which seemed to have lost some of its golden shine.
"I'd rather stay here with you."

"Oh, what a lot of fun that would be," Glory said, "watching
me sleep. Though my snoring might keep you entertained."

I'd walked through Glory's *unlocked* side door this morning to find her still in her housecoat and slippers. She'd been
waiting to tell me she was calling in sick and that I'd be on my
own at the marketplace. Today's goods had been stacked on the
kitchen table and bench, where we had placed them last night

before going our separate ways. Her to the dance class, me to the apartment above the garage. The box on top was filled with colorful flowers arranged in mason jars.

"I don't like leaving you here alone." Not that I wanted to run her booth by myself, either. But leaving her here by herself took the top spot on my do-not-want-to-do list.

"I just need a little rest, Emme, and I'll be good as new. Just the idea of missing two Saturdays in a month's time gives me palpitations. No one wants palpitations, most especially me. My heart and soul are in that marketplace, in Glory and Bee, and to see it suffering would make me suffer *endlessly*," she added with a dramatic sigh.

Even though she was laying it on thick, trying to convince me to go alone, I noticed she was slurring her words a little. Just the slightest bit, like part of her mouth was still asleep. I wished I knew whether she was simply tired, like she said, or if it was more than that. After all, she hadn't been feeling well yesterday, either.

She hobbled over to me, placed her soft palms on my cheeks, and noisily kissed my forehead. "You'll do great. Now, git on with ya. Time's a-tickin'. I trust you, Emme, to take my place, to take good care of my heart's work and my customers. Push the honey lollipops, will ya? They're getting close to their expiration date."

Thirty minutes later, I sat in the parking lot adjacent to the courthouse, staring at the homely clock tower. The lot was slowly filling with the cars of other vendors, and an ice-cream-themed food truck dubbed The Frozen South had pulled right up to the marketplace gates.

I was doing myself no favors sitting here, since there was a lot to get done, but I couldn't seem to make myself get out of the SUV. Being here without Glory just wouldn't be the same. The work was almost fun with her at my side, with her teaching me the ins and outs, showing me how to be personable, teaching me things I'd never be able to learn in a book or classroom. But was I ready to deploy all the lessons I'd learned? To be here on my own? It felt too soon. Much too soon.

I trust you, Emme, Glory had said.

No one had ever said those words to me before. They stung, because I knew I was a big phony, but they also filled me with a swell of love for Glory and how it somehow seemed like she could see the real me. That she somehow *knew* the real me. And knew I'd do everything I possibly could to help her. Because even though she wasn't my real grandmother, I'd already come to love her like she was.

"Helloooooo!" someone shouted, the voice loud enough to carry through the closed window. "Incoming!"

I turned to find a smiling Chase walking my way. He lifted his hand in a quick wave.

Heat rose into my cheeks as I waved back. I shut off the car and pushed open the door. "That's a much better approach than sneaking up behind me," I said. "Thanks."

"I'm a quick learner."

He didn't look any worse for wear after last night's events, and I wasn't sure how, since he couldn't have gotten much more sleep than I had. The bags under my eyes were nearly as large as my battered suitcase. But Chase . . . He looked too handsome for his own good. With his inquisitive eyes and his long hair still damp from a shower and the tawny stubble that covered his chin and cheeks.

"And an early riser, apparently." I closed the door behind me and walked to the back of the SUV to open the hatch. "What're you doing here?"

"Glory sent me. Reinforcements."

I was torn between happiness and anxiety. Chase already knew too much about me as it was. Spending even more time with him was a dangerous game—but it was a game I found I enjoyed a little too much. "What about Dorothy?"

From the back of the SUV, he pulled out the hand truck, set it on the ground. "She's with Glory. They'll keep an eye on each other until we get back."

"I'm not sure that comforts me."

He laughed. "Cora Bee and Nannette are on call for emergencies."

I had the sudden image of Cora Bee corralling the two of them with her crutches and smiled. "Maybe we'll sell out early."

He eyed the twelve boxes stacked in the SUV. "That's an optimistic attitude."

"Just call me Pollyanna." I grabbed a box and set it onto the hand truck.

With a shake of his head, he said, "No way. I prefer Little Miss Sunshine."

"I'm assuming you mean the book version and not the character from the movie."

"You've read those books?" Reaching past me, he picked up two boxes and hadn't even bothered to hide the surprise in his voice.

"Hasn't everyone?"

"No."

I shrugged. "Am I wrong?"

"Not at all. The resemblance is uncanny. The freckles, the braids you wear sometimes, the kind disposition, the radiating warmth."

Warmth rushed through me now, the surge making my hands tremble. "I sense you're purposely avoiding mentioning her spherical figure."

He swept his gaze over me, assessing with a raised eyebrow. That warmth in me turned to straight-up heat. He said, "I don't think she actually has bones, so I felt it improper to make a comparison."

I smiled. "Fair enough."

I appreciated that he didn't comment that I was too skinny, something I already knew. Instead, he only looked like he approved of me exactly the way I was.

It was unbearably unsettling.

We worked quickly to secure several of the boxes to the hand truck, and I carried the box of flowers. As Chase and I walked under the arched marketplace sign, I heard him mutter, "What in the hell is wrong with this thing?"

I glanced back and laughed. Suzanne the hand truck kept tipping sideways. "She likes to be babied."

"She?"

"Just go with it."

"Women," he groaned, then said, "C'mon, darlin'. That's right. Nice and steady."

I wished I'd had a cell phone to record the moment so I could relive it forever and ever. I'd been putting off buying one, oddly enjoying being free of its invisible ties. I'd found I hadn't really needed one, not with always being in the company of either Glory or Cora Bee, but if I was going to be running Glory's booth on my own more often, I definitely needed a phone so I could text her any questions.

I busied myself unpacking while Chase went back for more boxes. I glanced over at the tent next to Glory's booth and was surprised to see May working there, chatting with another vendor who was oohing and aahing over a set of note cards. May looked on like a proud mama as the woman gushed about the watercolor artwork. May must've sensed that she was being watched, because her head turned slightly my way, and she smiled when she saw me. A real smile, no phoniness about it.

Lightness filled my chest, and I gave her a quick wave and went back to carefully stacking cake boxes the way Glory had taught me. A moment later, May wandered over.

She said, "Please tell me you have caramels here somewhere."

"I do. I packed them myself last night. Let me see if I can find them."

"Oh, thank goodness. They're my biggest weakness, and my one weekly indulgence, since Nannette has us on the latest diet trend, which consists of a whole lot of lemon juice and little else."

I dug around in the box of candy. "Sounds horrid."

"I give it a zero-star rating. I also suspect it won't last. I saw the way Nannette eyed the pints of Blue Bell Cookies 'n Cream at Publix last night. Ice cream is *her* biggest weakness."

I found a bag of caramels and handed them over to her. She passed a five-dollar bill to me. I glanced around. "I don't have the cash drawer out yet—can I give you the change in a few minutes?"

She had already pulled the ribbon from the top of the bag. "Keep it. The caramels are worth it. Plus, I'm hoping it'll buy your silence." She held up the bag. "This never happened."

I smiled. "I'll keep your secret for free and make sure Glory gets the extra money." I'd put a note in the cash drawer explaining the overage. "I didn't realize you had a stall here." She hadn't been here last weekend, and during the week, the space had been occupied by others. A woodworker, a blacksmith, and a ceramicist. I didn't think it was a coincidence that the nearest food stall was five booths away, and they sold vegetables.

"I'm only here every other Saturday." She stuck a caramel in her mouth and rolled her eyes in bliss. When she finished chewing, she said, "Some of the other vendors have been talking about how you fit right in and help Glory at every turn. She's lucky to have you."

"I'm lucky to have her."

With a warm smile she said, "We all are."

The morning passed quickly and the threatening rain continued to hold off. Working alongside Chase made the time fly by. He'd made it a personal mission to sell all the honey lollipops, and I watched in awe as he sold one after another.

I tried to be as engaging as humanly possible, using the lessons I'd learned from Glory. People stopped to chat with me simply because they didn't see her at the booth. Almost all of them bought an item or two, a show of support that made me tear up more than once.

It hadn't taken me long at all to start recognizing faces, remembering names. When a woman I didn't know approached, her gaze intent on me, I tried to recall how Glory interacted with tourists, spouting tips on great places to dine and shop.

But as she stepped up to the counter, I swallowed back my sales pitch as I sized her up. *Opportunist.* I might not know who she was or what she was after, but I was wary, especially since Chase had stepped away to get us some drinks. It felt like she had waited for him to leave before she approached.

"Emme?" she asked, a question in her voice.

"Yes, ma'am. Have we met?"

She tucked a strand of bright-red hair behind her ear. "Once, a long time ago. You were just a little thing, all big eyes and big lungs. Cried the whole time I held you."

Even my younger self had good instincts.

"I'm Scarlet. A friend of your mama's. We hung out in the same circles."

I could only imagine what kind of circles those were, all dark and dingy.

"I heard you were in town helping Glory and had to see you for myself. You sure did grow up right pretty," she added. "You were a wrinkly thing last time I saw you, so I wasn't sure you'd get your mama's looks, but you did. Thank goodness. Your daddy wasn't much of a looker, no offense to the dead. He was all ears and so . . . big." She shook her head as though she still pitied the man.

I assumed Scarlet was talking about Rowan, and I thought she might have a screw loose since the pictures I'd seen of him showed a ruggedly attractive man. Big and brawny with a toothy, friendly smile. I hadn't noticed his ears, which told me they hadn't been *that* big.

She adjusted her purse strap. "I never understood what made your mama so gaga over him, chasing after him endlessly. I thought Kristalle would just about lose her mind when he kept rebuffing her."

"Well," I said with a tight smile, "since I'm here, she obviously found a way to win him over."

Scarlet laughed. "Win? No. More like take advantage of after a night of drinking. Good ol' Kristalle. If she sees an opportunity to get what she wants, she takes it, and she wanted your father. Seems to have worked out for her for the most part. She got you, didn't she? And with you turning out so pretty? She must be real proud."

"*Mm*," I said vaguely, wishing she'd just leave.

She picked up one of Cora Bee's delicate crochet dolls, frowned at it, then dropped it back into the basket. "How's your mama been? I haven't talked to her in, oh Lordy, it's been more than a year now. Is she still in Destin?"

I hoped not. Destin was too close for comfort. A mere two-hour drive. "I never quite know where she is," I said, skipping the first question and dancing around the second. "You know how she likes to pack up on a moment's notice."

Scarlet laughed, loud and obnoxious. "Ain't that the truth? It's been ages since I've seen her, but we talk every now and again. Usually when she's on the road between towns."

Between men, Scarlet meant.

My mother has always had two cell phones. Cheapies that could only be used with prepaid cards. One of them she replaced every time she moved somewhere new. New town, new mark, new phone, new trouble. The other one was as old as dirt. I thought she used it only for banking purposes but now I suspected she used it to talk to old friends once in a while, too. Friends like Scarlet, who I'd never even known existed until now. It was like my mother had a whole side of her life that even I didn't know. What else had she kept from me? As soon as the thought came, I shoved it away. I decided I didn't want to know.

Chase returned, stepping into the booth with two drinks and a tight smile on his face as he assessed my uneasy body language. He handed me a cold drink before facing Scarlet. "The Frozen South has the best Cheerwine slushies around. Have you tried one?"

She stood straight, thrusting her chest toward him. "You've got good taste, Chase Kistler. I've been drinking them since I was knee-high."

"Do you know Scarlet?" I asked. "She's an old friend of my mother's."

She scowled at me when I emphasized *old*.

I willed my heart to stop pounding. This woman had spoken to my mother recently. Over a year ago, but still. They kept in touch.

"Never had the pleasure," he said.

She turned her frown upside down and tugged down her tank top to reveal more cleavage, of which there had already been plenty on display. "Everyone around here knows Chase," she said. Her eyes lit. "The town's going to name a street after him."

I smiled. "I heard something about that."

"Scarlet," he said, "if you have a sweet tooth, you're going to love these honey lollipops. Best ones I've ever tasted, so light they practically melt right on your tongue. You want to take some home? We're having a sale. Five for ten dollars. And look at that—there are only five left."

They were actually a dollar apiece, but I didn't correct him. Suckers for the sucker.

"If you love them, I know I will," she said with a titter as she reached into her handbag for her wallet.

Chase set down his cup and bagged the lollipops quickly. When he handed the cash to me, he gave my cheek a peck, right on the spot where my scar was. It nearly knocked me clear off my feet with surprise.

"Those lollipops aren't nearly as sweet as Emme," he said. "But you probably already know that."

Scarlet shoved the lollipops into her handbag and said, "I didn't know you two were dating. That was sure fast." She raised a judgmental eyebrow toward me. "Guess you got more from your mama than just her looks." She then gave Chase a pointed look. "Best you keep a close eye on how much you drink around her."

With a fake smile, she turned and threaded her way back into the crowd.

Chase said, "Sorry to plant that kiss on you, but I thought if I didn't, she might climb over the counter to eat me alive."

I pressed my fingers to my cheek. "No big deal."

He grabbed his chest. "I'm wounded. *No big deal*? I clearly need to work on my technique."

I'd have teased him back, but I couldn't stop staring at Scarlet's retreating form. Her visit had left me shaken, as if something in my world had just tilted the wrong way. My house of cards was threatening to fall.

He picked up his cup, took a long pull through his straw, then said, "Hey, what did she mean that you got more from your mother than her looks? And that stuff about the drinks?"

"I'm not sure," I said, circling wide around the truth.

"Such a mystery," he said around the straw in his mouth.

I set the ten-dollar bill into the cash drawer, tucking it in nice and neat, and added an addendum to my earlier note about the overage. "What is? Scarlet? I think her intentions with you were clear."

"Not her. You. Such a mix of contradictions. You said yourself that you're uneducated, yet you're well-read and smart as a whip. You're friendly yet closed off. You seem fully here but I sense you're hiding, too."

"Me?" I asked, pasting on a fake smile. "I'm hardly mysterious. I'm Little Miss Sunshine, remember?"

I wanted him to remember. I didn't want him to see the tattletale dark cloud that had hovered over me my whole life long. My first crime—as an accomplice—had occurred when I was just days old after my mama lifted a woman's wallet on the way out of the Sweetgrass hospital, tucking the spoils into my baby blanket as she sailed out the door. Until I turned eighteen, it was a story she told every year on my birthday, affectionately brought out and proudly displayed with my cupcake and my unwrapped—likely stolen—present. The stories of how she used me for her misdeeds were my mama's version of a baby book.

And also her subtle way of reminding me that I wasn't as innocent as I looked, and that if need be, she'd throw me under the bus to save herself. It had been a relief, truly, when she cut me loose on my eighteenth birthday, leaving me to my own devices. Until today, I hadn't even known if she was dead or alive. Was ashamed I didn't care either way. Was grateful that I wasn't so dead inside that I could still feel shame.

Yet, I sensed Chase could absolutely see that cloud today, could see every last one of my sins.

He held my gaze, and I saw the million questions he had about me in his eyes. "Who are you, Emme Wynn?"

I couldn't bear him staring into my soul, so I looked away as I said, "I'm no one in particular."

Chapter
17

*January 6, 1965: I was doing my best to properly over-
winter my beehives, but all the bees have died. It feels like
a piece of me died, too. I should've done more to protect them.*

Cora Bee

The police presence lured me away from my desk and out onto the
front porch. A police car, an unmarked sedan, and a search-and-
rescue cargo van had pulled up to the curb, not too far from where
the gazing pool stood. I recognized Bob Graham, the detective in
charge of Bee's case, straight off, and wondered why he had returned when he'd told us the police were done in the garden.

In addition to Bob, three men and a woman conferred at the
curb before pulling a piece of equipment from the back of the
cargo van that looked like a cross between a lawn mower and a
hand truck.

Glory and Dorothy were quick to join them in the garden,
full of energy as they gestured this way and that. When I had
checked in with the pair earlier, after Chase had texted me
about Glory calling in sick to the marketplace, it had seemed
to me that Glory had made a miraculous recovery. She hadn't
appeared the least bit under the weather. Even Dorothy, who'd
been in the hospital the night before, seemed full of life as they
played gin rummy and ate omelets.

I had the suspicion Glory had been planning this day off for a
while as part of her grand plan. She wanted to get a feel for how
Emme could handle the Sweetplace on her own.

The sneaky, sneaky woman.

As I watched the goings-on across the street, I was so intent on rubbernecking that I didn't hear Jamie and Mabel until he tapped on the screen door.

"Come on in," I said, unable to stop the small flutter in my chest at seeing him.

Mabel rushed over to me and I leaned over to give her some love. She licked my face and gave me her paw. I laughed. "Did you learn a new trick this week? Good girl."

Her tail thumped.

"What's going on there?" he asked with a jut of his chin toward the garden as he sat in the rocker next to mine.

"I don't know. They showed up about fifteen minutes ago. I'm sure Aunt Glory will fill us in when she's done talking to them." I glanced over at him, felt that stupid flutter intensify. "Where's Alice?"

"Her mom took her home with her after the soccer game. She'll be there until Monday morning."

The flutters died, drifting slowly into the dark, gaping pit in my stomach. I hadn't realized she wouldn't be here this weekend. "Oh. Well, that's good. I'm sure she's missed her."

"She has," Jamie said. "Living between two houses isn't ever easy, but she shoulders it well enough since it's all she's ever known."

"It probably helps that you and her mom have a good relationship and are willing to do what's best for Alice. Not every kid is so lucky."

I glanced at my hands, remembering how Wiley's small fingers used to curl around mine, and how he'd laugh, open-mouthed, showing off the gaps where his baby teeth had fallen out. When Lucas and I divorced, I'd tried to get visitation rights to see Wiley. They were impossible by law, but Lucas could have allowed it. Instead, he was intent to cut me clean out of his life, as if I'd never existed at all. He'd told me that it would only confuse Wiley if I was still around. There was no changing his mind, no amount of begging, of offering to forfeit my divorce settlement, of throwing myself at his mercy. I'd have done *anything*, because I'd wanted desperately to keep Wiley in my life, wanted it more than life itself.

When I lost him, I'd wanted to die.

I'd *tried* to die on a wet road on a dark day.

But fate and Glory had kept me alive.

I pushed the memories away, irritated at how often they popped up unbidden. Would they ever stop hurting?

"It's not always easy," he said, watching me closely, "but I know it's worth the hard times. Alice is why I'm here, actually. I know I'm a poor substitute, but she made me promise to water the flowers. And I was hoping to take you to lunch."

The flutters rose from the dead.

"If you're not busy," he added when I didn't answer right away. "I know you work on weekends."

I ran my fingers over Mabel's head and through her soft curls. "I do, that's true, but I've wrapped up all the work I had planned for today." Because I thought I'd be spending the afternoon with Alice. "I have a big project I'm working on, a contest, but I'm kind of in limbo with it."

"The brickyard contest? Why the limbo?"

I turned slightly to face him head-on. "How do you know about the contest? Did you read about it somewhere?" I know I hadn't told him. I'd barely told anyone. Just Emme, my mother, and Aunt Glory. *Glory.* The oversharer. "Did Glory say something?"

Confusion swept over his face, darkening his pale eyes, drawing his eyebrows down low. "No. She hasn't said a word about it. I know because the shopping center is my project." He tipped his head, as if truly puzzled.

I opened my mouth, closed it again. "You're managing the Yardley job?"

How had I not known his temporary work in town was connected to the Yardley brickyard? It seemed a major detail to

miss, though I *had* tuned out his particulars when he first arrived
in town, once I learned he was a single dad. Could be the whole
neighborhood had been talking about it, but I'd tuned it all out.

He half smiled, yet there was still a puzzled air about him.
"You don't know, do you?"

"Know what?" I said more sharply than I intended. Or
maybe I intended it. I wasn't sure. I was annoyed, feeling like I
was missing something obvious.

"I'm Jamie *Yardley*. It's my land that's being built on, Cora
Bee. I inherited it from my father when he passed away a few
years ago. I know about the contest, because I'm the one who
came up with the idea. I'm lousy with concepts. Truly terrible.
I'm more of a spreadsheet kind of guy."

No.

It was the only word that went through my head. It circled,
growing bigger, louder.

No, no, no.

"You really didn't know?" he asked. "It's not a secret."

"No," I said, voicing my thoughts aloud. Mabel licked my
hand. "I didn't know. This is . . . terrible."

He laughed, then sobered as he realized I wasn't kidding.
"Why?"

"It's just that I can't be in the contest if we . . . you and me,
I mean . . ." My cheeks felt blazing hot, and I couldn't bring
myself to say anything more for fear that I'd self-combust from
pure embarrassment.

"The contest committee knows we're acquainted, Cora Bee,
that we're neighbors, friends. I've been assured it's not a problem. I'm not a judge, so there's no conflict of interest. It's a small
town. People know each other. I also know the other two designers. Worked with them a couple of times on difference jobs.
The judges are from out of state and completely impartial. If
you drop out now, the only one you'll be hurting is yourself.
You're talented. Let that talent speak for itself."

Bits of juniper green continued to float around him indi-
cating there was still something he wasn't telling me, a secret

he was keeping to himself. I didn't know whether it revolved around something to do with his private life or his work life, but whereas it hadn't bothered me too much before, it did now.

"I don't know," I said. "It's not sitting right. This whole contest has never sat quite right. I thought maybe that was why I was struggling, but now, knowing who you are . . ."

He held up a hand. "Let's put me aside for a moment."

"As if that's possible."

He cracked a smile. "Let's *try* to put me aside for a moment. Why are you struggling?"

I debated how to explain it before saying, "I'm more comfortable with color consulting. And though that's an aspect of the contest, it's not everything. And with my color work, I've only designed for structures that already exist. I can't get a good feel for the Yardley complex's personality from a mock-up. I know that probably doesn't make sense to you, but it does in my head. I'm hoping that seeing the land will help. If it doesn't, maybe the historical society has photos of what was there before it was razed, and I can find inspiration there."

"I have pictures," he said. "Plenty of them."

Before I could beg to see them, I noticed Glory and Dorothy heading up the walkway. Mabel was on her feet, her tail wagging as they climbed the steps.

Jamie leaped up to open the door.

As they came onto the porch, Dorothy kept looking over her shoulder at the police and bright color sat high on Glory's cheeks.

As they sat down on the porch swing, I said, "What's Jamie's last name, Aunt Glory?"

She tipped her head and gave me a strange look, as though wondering if I'd lost my mind. "Is this one of those mental acuity tests? Because I can pass this one, easy as can be, hon. He's a Yardley."

Why hadn't she said anything about him when I brought up working on the Yardley contest? It seemed an odd thing not to mention. *Unless.* I narrowed my gaze at her.

She looked me dead in the eye and grinned. "A dang hand-some one, too, don't you think?"

Apparently, Alice wasn't the only one around here hoping to be a matchmaker.

Before I could say anything, Dorothy bounced in her seat and said, "Can I play, too? My brain isn't as sharp as it used to be, so it can use all the testing it can get."

Dorothy liked a good competition.

"Sure can," Glory said. "What's Jamie's granddaddy's name? The one that Levi stole from?"

"Joseph," Dorothy said, beaming. "His wife, that's who Levi was cattin' around with, was named Margot, with a fancy *t* at the end. Jamie here has his granddaddy's smile. Cut from a fine cloth, he was. A fine, fine cloth."

"Well done," Glory said, putting her arm around her. "Your brain seems to be working just fine to me."

I stared wide-eyed at Dorothy, who was puffed up with pride. Because of Bee's diary, I'd known she suspected Levi had been cheating, but I hadn't known it had been with *Mrs. Yardley.* If I was this shocked by the news, I could only imagine how Bee had felt at the time.

"I told you my name wasn't a secret," Jamie said softly to me.

He was a *Yardley.* I couldn't wrap my head fully around it.

At the sound of voices, Glory looked across the street. "I don't know if I can abide watching the police tromping through the garden all day. I might lose my head. They were supposed to be done."

Jamie said, "Cora Bee and I were thinking about going out for lunch. Why don't you and Dorothy come with us? We can take our time, and hopefully the police will be done before we get back."

I opened my mouth to argue but then snapped it closed again. If getting out of the neighborhood would help Aunt Glory in any way, I was all for it.

"Happy to!" Dorothy said. "I worked up a powerful appetite whupping Glory at cards this morning."

With a roll of her eyes, Glory wiggled off the swing. "Her memory might be just fine but her arithmetic skills are questionable. Lunch is a good idea. Give us a minute to get freshened up; then we'll be ready to go."

"Why're the police even here?" I asked; otherwise, my curiosity might just kill me.

Glory huffed, then shook her head. "I'll fill you in in the car."

🌿

We were an unlikely foursome. *Fivesome*, really, if one counted Mabel, and she wasn't the type to be overlooked.

"He's being tight-lipped," Glory said from the backseat of Jamie's truck.

He being Bob the detective.

Jamie's truck was surprisingly spacious and fit us all—and my crutches—with room to spare. Mabel sat in between Dorothy and Glory, her nose sticking out of the small sliding rear window, her tail slashing against the console. It was the same spot she'd taken last night, when we'd gone to the drive-in. It was like the space had been designed just for her.

"Tight-lipped and squirrelly," Dorothy added, sounding like she was wanting to cuss him out the same way she'd done with the squirrel who'd dug in her vegetable garden.

"He wouldn't tell us much." Glory rubbed Mabel's neck, then let out a laugh when Mabel licked her chin. "But he was using some sort of fancy radar or sonar or something. Ground penetrating, he told me. So he's obviously looking for something underground."

The radar must've been the lawn mower–looking machine I'd seen. "What else is there to find?"

"More bones is my guess," Dorothy said over a yawn.

I winced at the words. It was an upsetting, unsettling thought.

As I thought of Bee my eyes filled with tears, and I looked out the window. I had believed this investigation was all but over. Now this. When would it end?

Glory said, "Bob said he'd let us know more when he could."

"Squirrelly," Dorothy repeated.

I wiped the tears from my eyes and noticed the landscape. How unfamiliar it was. Clearly, I hadn't been paying attention to where we were going. "Where are we?"

"I'm taking the scenic route to lunch," Jamie said. "There's something I want to show you."

"I haven't been out this way in forever," Glory whispered. "Feels like a different world, even though it's only five minutes from home."

Dorothy, I noticed, had nodded off. Her head was tilted back, her face suddenly looking peaceful instead of troubled.

Glory caught me watching. "Had herself quite the night."

"Is she feeling better?"

"She was never feeling badly." Glory's hair blew across her face, and she tucked what she could behind her ears. "She faked fainting. An actress she isn't. But she sure made her bed, because the staff insisted she go to the hospital."

"She faked it? Why?"

"She figured out why we were there and couldn't think of a faster way to get home. She confessed the whole thing this morning. Chase is going to have his hands full with her."

Glory tried to cover the wistfulness in her voice with humor, but I caught it anyway. She knew her days of helping to manage Dorothy's care were coming to an end.

We drove along a two-lane country road lined by the Sweet-grass River on one side and woods on the other. Soon enough, Jamie put his blinker on and turned into a gravel lot marked up with survey sticks.

Glory said, "Sure has changed since the last time I saw it. Didn't realize *all* the buildings were gone. Those kilns were something else."

"Sure were," Jamie said as he put the truck in park.

"Is this where the old brick company used to be?" I asked, staring out at the flat, naked expanse. The lot must've been graded quite recently, because there wasn't so much as a weed growing on the property as far as my eye could see.

Glory chuckled. "I don't suppose you're willin' to scrap your fancy retail plans and sell this land to me on the cheap? It'd be perfect for the marketplace. That river view is something I'd never tire of."

He smiled at her. "My investors might have a collective stroke."

She winked and said, "It was worth a shot."

Jamie looked at me. "Do you want to get out?"

I sat up straighter in my seat. "Just for a minute. Dorothy worked up an appetite, remember?"

He left the truck running with the air on while he helped me with my crutches. He stood at my elbow as I carefully crutched forward on shifting gravel.

I took a deep breath and tried to imagine the glass-and-steel shopping center here. I could see it. Barely. But it was like Emme had said the other day—the building was too cold for this land. It needed warmth. It needed *nature*. "Are you married to your building plan? The architecture? The glass? The steel?"

"I wouldn't say married. Maybe engaged. A breakup would be ugly. And costly. Why?"

I shook my head, not wanting to get into it with him. I probably shouldn't be talking to him about it at all. It wasn't fair to the other designers.

"You're not still thinking about dropping out of the competition, are you?" he asked. "Sleep on it, at least."

It was hard to argue when he was so insistent. A little time couldn't hurt any. "Since it seems so important to you, I'll sleep on it." I eyed him. "But why do you care so much if I drop out or not?"

He stuck his hands in his pockets. "I just think you deserve the chance to showcase your talents."

I watched him closely, wanting to believe him, but I couldn't. Because as he stood there, talking about my talents, the juniper green that floated around him intensified in color.

Whatever guilty secret he was keeping apparently involved me.

Chapter
18

 *Glory's Garden Lesson #9*

Coneflowers are always a crowd-pleaser at the Sweetplace. And no wonder, with their happy demeanor and their purple petals that look almost pink in certain light. The coneflower's proper name is *Echinacea*, and extracts of it are used in cold medicines, which is probably why it symbolizes strength and healing. Oh, get this. Because of the prickly nature of the flower's stem, the plant was named after hedgehogs. That's right, hon. *Echinacea* derives from the Greek word for hedgehogs! Oh, I sure do wish we had hedgehogs running about the garden to go along with all the healing that's going on around here. Wouldn't that be something to see?

Emme

The rain had rushed through the night before, leaving Hickory Lane glistening on Sunday morning as sunlight bounced off shallow puddles.

I stood in Cora Bee's garage, ready to make a grand reveal and a sales pitch to Jamie. He'd been heading up the front walkway with a manila envelope in hand when I'd called out to him.

"You claimed first dibs, so . . ." I pulled the sheet off the bookcase. "Otherwise, it's going to the marketplace with me tomorrow." I had decided to sell the bookcase since I needed the cash. I didn't know how much time I had left in Sweetgrass, so the bigger nest egg I could gather, the better.

Jamie's jaw dropped. "My God, Emme. It's amazing. You're serious about selling? You don't want to keep it?"

I wanted to keep it. I truly did. But hauling a bookcase around would *not* be considered traveling light. "I'm serious."

"I need to get Alice on the line, make sure she likes it." He held up a finger, tucked his manila envelope under his arm, and ran his fingers over his cell phone screen. He then held the phone up to eye level, and I saw that we were both pictured on his screen while the phone made a strange ringing noise that indicated a video call.

A moment later, Alice's face filled the screen instead. She smiled when she saw me. "Hey, Emme!"

"I'm chopped liver since she became friends with you and Cora Bee," Jamie said to me.

"Hi, Dad," she said loudly with a hint of exasperation.

"Al, Emme finished the bookcase she's been working on," he said, flipping the screen to show the bookcase. "Do you want it for your bedroom?"

"Is that the same wallpaper that Glory has in her kitchen?" Alice asked, her voice lifting with excitement. "I love that wallpaper."

"It is. She had an extra roll that she graciously gave to me." I'd made sure to get as many shimmery bees onto the backing of the bookcase as I possibly could.

"I definitely want it," Alice said. "I can't wait to fill it up with all my books. I'm halfway done with *Les Mis*, Emme. Soooooo good. I need to get a copy of my own, one that's not all beat-up like this one. It's *dog-eared*," she said, her voice full of disgust. "Who does that to a library book?"

"Barbarians." We'd been brought up in two different worlds, but there was something about Alice that reminded me of myself. The good parts of me.

"Ignoramuses," she said.

"Monsters!"

Jamie flipped the screen back. "All right, you two, don't be so hard on the poor dog-earers."

I looked at him in horror. "Don't tell me . . ."

He hung his head. "I promise to stop."

"He's been saying that for years, Emme. *Years*."

"Okay, time to say goodbye," Jamie said with a light laugh. We said our goodbyes to Alice and he crossed his arms over his chest. "Looks like we have a deal for the bookcase, Emme. How much are you asking for it?"

I took a step back, sized up the bookcase. I hadn't thought this far ahead. I mentally calculated the cost of supplies; plus, there was my time to consider . . . But the number I came up with seemed much too high—I certainly wouldn't pay that much—so now I was mentally subtracting.

"Don't undervalue it," he said as if reading my mind. "No friends-and-family discount. I'm happy to pay full price. It's worth it."

"You're a lousy negotiator. How do you own a company?" I'd been stunned when Cora Bee had told me Jamie was a Yardley. She wasn't the only one who hadn't a clue.

He laughed. "The old-fashioned way. I inherited it."

"Now who's undervaluing?"

Over pints of ice cream last night, Cora Bee and I had fired up her laptop and searched online for everything we could find about James Yardley. It was true he'd inherited what was left of the Yardley Brick Company, but a few years out of college (Clemson), he had started and grown The Yardley Group, a multifaceted industrial, commercial, and residential development and construction company.

"All right, you want tough?" He put his hands on his hips, narrowed his eyes. "I refuse to pay more than three hundred dollars. Take it or leave it."

I about fell over. Three hundred? "That's too much, Jamie. You're just being nice."

He held up a finger again as he pulled out his phone. I thought he was going to get Alice back on the screen, but after a moment, he held the phone out to me. "My niceness only goes so far. Know your market, Emme."

I studied the screen, which was full of listings for hand-painted bookcases. Most weren't nearly as nice as mine and were priced between four and five hundred dollars.

He said, "I wasn't lying when I told you I'd been looking for unique pieces for Alice's room. There's a big ol' market out there for what you do."

What you do.

As the words sank in, sank in *deep*, a sense of purpose came over me.

Could I make a living doing this? Others did, if this website was any indication. Why couldn't I? Okay, so maybe not straightaway. But I could work toward it. After all, look where Glory had started with the marketplace.

With a burst of resolve, I thrust out my hand, and said, "Three-fifty and we have a deal."

"My God, you're a fast learner." His big hand enfolded mine in a firm handshake. "I'm guessing you only take cash or check?"

"Cash is preferable."

"I'll get it to you by the end of the day."

Smiling, I nodded. "That's just fine, but you can take the bookcase now, if you want."

My sadness at parting with the bookcase had ebbed with knowing it was going to a good home. The best home.

"I'll do that." He held out the manila envelope. "Could you give this to Cora Bee for me?"

"She's inside—you don't want to give it to her yourself?"

He glanced toward the house, looking like he very much wanted to see her. "I don't want to seem like I'm pressuring her. They're the photos of the old brickyard."

I took the envelope. "I'll see that she gets them."

Last I'd heard, she still hadn't decided whether to continue on with the contest. She'd asked my advice, but I hadn't much to give. This kind of thing was out of my league. I'd simply told her to trust her instincts. Mine had rarely led me astray.

"Thanks, Emme." He hefted the bookcase, the same way he

had the night it had been rescued from the curb. With his long strides, he was down the driveway and halfway home before I knew it, but I swore I could still see those bees twinkling in his wake, as if proud of me for seeing beauty where others couldn't.

I started grinning and didn't stop for a good, long while.

↘↙

By midafternoon, I'd cleaned Cora Bee's house, read a few chapters of a book, took a walk around the neighborhood to examine the trash at the curb ahead of tomorrow's pickup but didn't find any furniture in the mix, and checked on my flower bed, smiling at the growth in so little time. I sat by the gazing pool for a while, where I'd seen nothing in the water but bubbles. I'd been putting off asking Glory and Cora Bee about the gazing pool for one reason or another, but I was determined to bring it up today when we were all together, prepping Sunday supper. But as soon as I walked into Glory's kitchen, she had put me straight to work.

Now I stood at the island, my hands slick with butter. "This seems inappropriate."

Glory laughed. "Don't be shy. Get on in there; shove it on in. You got enough butter?"

I glanced at Cora Bee for help, but she was smiling ear to ear as she watched, too entertained to intervene. "Maybe too much," I said.

Glory shook her head. "No such thing, hon. We want lots of it, so it'll slowly melt into the meat as it cooks. *Mm*. So good."

As if removing the giblets hadn't been bad enough, now my hands were in between the skin of a raw roasting chicken and its breasts. I tried to flick butter off my fingertips the best I could, the way Glory had showed me. "I might have to become a vegetarian."

"Not today you don't," Glory said. "Not after all this work. Once you're done with that, wash your hands up good and we'll add the seasonings." She crossed to the pantry and pulled open the door. "A little salt and pepper, some fresh rosemary and thyme."

Cora Bee, who was sitting in front of the sink with a basket of potatoes, turned the water on for me when I walked over, and then squirted some soap into my hands.

"How do I get potato duty?" I asked.

She smiled sweetly. "You'll have to fight me for it."

I wrinkled my nose and washed up. I could take Cora Bee in a fight pretty easily, but I couldn't imagine scrapping with her. Fighting her would be like fighting a puppy. "I think I'm more of a baker than a cook. Maybe I can take over dessert from now on."

Glory laughed. "The baking is yours for the taking, Emme, honey. I bake so much during the week I wouldn't mind passing the torch. I wouldn't mind it at all."

Now she told me. After I'd already abused the poor chicken.

Glory looked around the kitchen. "Where on earth did I put the salt and pepper?"

I glanced at the knife block. The pair of ceramic chickens were sitting in front of it as usual. "I found them," I said as I dried my hands. I picked them up and handed them over to Glory. I was growing used to overlooking her slipups, acting as though they never happened.

"I swear they move around on their own." She set them on the island and started pulling leaves off a sprig of rosemary.

I shared a meaningful look with Cora Bee before returning to Glory's side.

As the rhythmic clicks of the potato peeler filled the air, I thought about how to broach the subject of the gazing pool. Straight out with it was probably best, but I didn't quite know how to form the words. So we went on with our roast chicken lesson, and not long after, the chicken was in the oven, which I'd made sure was preheated.

Opportunity to talk about the gazing pool finally came when Glory pulled dirty carrots from her harvest basket.

"Puny little things, but they'll do just fine for supper." She faced me, which I noticed she did whenever she really wanted me to pay attention to what she was saying. "Carrots aren't one of my finer crops, but they're one of my favorite vegetables, so they're worth the effort. We're going to glaze these babies with some butter and honey, and whew—just wait till you try them. Go on and grab the honey from the pantry while I wash these up and have Cora Bee peel 'em for us."

I opened the pantry door, found the honey, which I noticed had come from a local farm that had a booth at the market-place. Glory left the carrots with Cora Bee and filled a large pot with water and put it on the stove top. It took two tries for her to turn on the correct burner. Then she headed to the fridge.

I still held the honey as I said as casually as possible, "This honey is beautiful. Did Bee ever keep bees?"

The peeler stilled. Glory's hand froze on the refrigerator handle as she turned to face me. "Why do you ask?"

I almost chickened out and made a quip about how it seemed like something someone named Bee would do, but I took a shallow breath and said, "I saw something in the gazing pool that made me think that maybe she did."

Glory threw her hands in the air with excitement. "You saw something in the gazing pool? Did you hear that, Cora Bee?"

Cora Bee smiled. "I sure did."

Glory wobbled over to me and gave me a big hug, squishing me and the honey against her chest. "The gazing pool doesn't show the past to just anyone. It has to be someone special. Someone worthy."

It doesn't show the past to just anyone.

Glory pulled away but gave my forehead a noisy kiss. "Bee did keep bees, according to her journal, which was saved only because it had been in her purse in the car when the farmhouse burned down."

"She also wrote that the bees didn't survive," Cora Bee added as she passed a plate of peeled carrots to Glory. "Something about overwintering."

Overwintering? Hardly. The weather had nothing to do with the bees' fate. I could clearly see the man push the boxes to the ground, the man I assumed was Levi.

"What did you see in the gazing pool?" Glory asked, her eyes full of curiosity.

"I saw two bee boxes not too far from the gazing pool. The land looked a lot different then." I wouldn't tell her how the bees had been killed. It would serve no purpose. "How does the gazing pool . . ."

Glory held up a hand. "We stopped asking why and how a long time ago. The first time I saw something, I took myself off to the doctor, afraid I was having hallucinations. Everyone knows the South is full of magic, so why shouldn't we have a little of it in our lives?"

"I will say," Cora Bee piped in, "that it seems like it doesn't show you something unless it thinks you need to see it for whatever reason."

"True, true," Glory said.

I couldn't imagine why I'd needed to see Levi being a terrible person. His reputation had been well-known by the time I arrived in Sweetgrass.

Unless it hadn't been Levi?

I asked, "Do you have any old pictures of Bee? Or Levi?"

"Oh, hon, I have plenty of Lillian and Rowan growing up, but none of Bee's photos survived the fire, and I lost the only album I had in the move from Georgia. It's possible Dorothy might have a couple from parties around town and whatnot."

Cora Bee perked up. "Really? I'd love to see if she has one of Bee. I can get it framed for Mama for Mother's Day."

"What a sweet idea, hon. I'll ask Dorothy." Glory handed me a knife. "Okay, Emme, honey, we're going to slice up these carrots and steam them till they're soft. Then we'll—Oh! Someone's come early."

Her attention had been drawn away by footsteps on the porch, and before Glory could even wipe her hands on a dishcloth, the door swung open.

"Surprise!" a woman shouted as she rushed inside, arms open wide. "Who's missed me?"

Glory squealed with happiness as Cora Bee reached for her crutches and exclaimed, "Mama!"

While they hugged, I was busy hoping no one had noticed the way I'd held the knife when the door had been flung open, ready to protect myself and those I'd come to love.

Some old habits were hard to break.

Chapter 19

February 19, 1965: I've been planning my spring garden, gathering seeds and corms and bulbs. I have to admit my heart isn't quite up to the task. I've decided not to replace my bee boxes since I can't guarantee they'll be safe under my care. Life feels a bit unsettled at the moment and I'm considering visiting my mama for a long spell. She recently moved to be closer to the ocean, and I'd like to see her new place and make sure she's settling in okay. It's been much too long since I've seen her, and sometimes you just need to surround yourself with your mama's love to remember to believe in tomorrows.

Cora Bee

"It was like she was a cast member of *West Side Story*, ready to rumble," Mama said later that evening while mimicking jabbing someone with a switchblade. She held a glass of wine in her other hand and managed not to spill a single drop during the demonstration.

Mama was talking about Emme, of course.

A bee drifted around the clematis as Mama and I sat on my front porch in the rocking chairs, watching the sky turn pink then orange as the sun sank on the western horizon.

Mama had done plenty of theater productions in her time, so she had a flair for the dramatic and didn't mind attention in the least. She was used to it, I supposed. Her outer beauty, with her deep-auburn hair, fair skin, and brown eyes, hadn't seemed to wane with age. But I'd always believed it was her inner beauty, a light so bright that it drew everyone closer, one created by her big heart, her giving nature, her quick smile and attentive ear, that made her utterly lovely.

I glanced at her now, sad to see that inner light doused by her unsympathetic feelings for Emme. I'd been so thrilled to see Mama when she popped through Glory's kitchen door earlier, a rush of pure sweet happiness, but now . . . Now I was glad she was only staying a week. Her plan was to stay through Mother's Day, then she'd be on a flight back home the following Monday afternoon.

"You did take us by surprise, bursting through the kitchen door," I said. "You scared her, that's all."

I couldn't say that Emme's had been a normal reaction, but she hadn't exactly had a normal life. Her fears colored her every waking moment. From locking doors and windows to being afraid of the dark and strangers.

Thank the good Lord above, Mama been on her best behavior all through dinner. It had helped to have a full house to distract her. Nannette, May, Chase, and Dorothy had been there as well. Jamie had been invited but declined, already having other plans with a business colleague. I tried telling myself I wasn't the least bit disappointed that he hadn't been there but couldn't quite pull it off.

Glory had the wisdom to buffer Emme by having her sit at her side, with Chase on the other side and May across. Mama had been seated the farthest away, next to Nannette and Dorothy. And though most of the dinner conversation revolved around my parents' travels, I noticed the way Mama's gaze kept slipping back to Emme. Taking in every detail, every word said, every small movement.

Seeing it had brought out my protective instincts, like I was a mama bear protecting a cub, and my hackles were still raised. I loved my mother more than life itself, but she was being plain ol' pigheaded.

"It would hardly have been a surprise if I'd *knocked*. This is

Sweetgrass, for land's sake. Where exactly did Emme grow up to have learned such things?"

Nowhere in particular. I could practically hear Emme saying the words in my ear. "A little bit of everywhere. She's mentioned Omaha and Des Moines. She was in Louisville for a while. She moved around a lot. Her mother didn't like to stay in one place very long."

"No surprise there. Kristalle would probably be in jail right now otherwise." Mama picked up the wine bottle sitting on the low table between us. "Are you sure you don't want any?"

"I can't," I said. "My medication, remember?"

The overhead fan stirred the loose auburn hairs that framed her face as she topped off her wineglass. "Is the pain so bad? Your daddy's doctor already has him weaned off the strong stuff."

Glory's advice about telling my mother the truth floated through my head, and I let it keep going. I couldn't. I wouldn't. I was too ashamed. "It's getting better."

And it was. My foot was feeling better with each passing day. And my emotional pain, the pain that had come from my divorce, from losing Wiley, from losing myself, hadn't been nearly as sharp this past week. It was more a dull ache, pulsing with each breath I took.

I noticed movement in the garden across the street and saw Emme walking around, yanking weeds from unsuspecting beds. As soon as my mother had shown up here, Emme had excused herself, saying she had some gardening to do. Afterward, she had plans to meet Chase at the apartment, which was still undergoing its makeover. I had the feeling she was going to make sure my mother was gone before she came back here tonight.

Mama noticed her, too. "Emme is here now, so why hasn't she cleaned herself up? She has to see the way you dress and carry yourself, Cora Bee. Glory too. Why doesn't she get a nice haircut and some new clothes?"

In the garden, Emme was walking toward the gazing pool

but then suddenly turned her head and smiled as Chase and
Orville approached her.

The smile lit the darkening night, a bright spot in my current
gloom.

At some point, I'd come to realize that Emme looked the way
she did on purpose. She was hiding behind her street urchin
look. For some reason, she didn't want people to see beyond her
rough exterior, to see her value.

"I think she doesn't want to be seen, be noticed. Most likely
it's another remnant of her horrible past. But once you get to
know her, to really *see* her, there's no hiding her loveliness."

Mama stopped rocking as she looked over to the gardens, at
Emme.

I said, "I'm pretty sure it was you who taught me that in order
to see someone's true beauty, you need to look beyond what's on
the surface. Could you please try to get to know Emme while
you're here? Really get to know her, without all your judgments
and criticism? Without thinking she's just like Kristalle? I know
Kristalle hurt you terribly, hurt this *family*, but Emme is not her
mother."

Mama tore her gaze away from Emme and searched my face.
The look in her eyes softened, and I saw that inner light within her
spark to life as she said, "All right. For you, Cora Bee, I will try."

"Thank you."

"But," she said as her eyes sparkled with mischief, "in return,
you have to do something for *me*."

With the way she was looking at me, I couldn't imagine what
she wanted. "What's that?"

"A little birdie told me that you're dating someone. Tell me
about this Jamie of yours."

Since May had apparently been planning my nonexistent
wedding, I could only deduce that she was the birdie in question. "Jamie and I are not dating."

"The drive-in? Lunching together? I heard tell he's been seen
over here a lot."

"We're friends. *New* friends. I've only known him a couple of weeks. He has a daughter. Alice. She's twelve. And he's a *Yardley*. Did May tell you that?"

The sparkles in her eyes sputtered but didn't go out. "I can see why some of that might scare you, but does he make you happy? In the reports I'm hearing, you positively glow when you're around him."

I was going to strangle May the next time I saw her. I barely knew Jamie. Yet, nearly every time I saw him, my first reaction was a smile. "We're friends," I repeated.

Mama reached over and took hold of my hand, squeezing it tight. "With the possibility of more?"

I shrugged. "I just don't know . . . It's complicated."

"Love often is. But, my darling girl, with the right person, it's worth the complications. Love hurt you, yes, but it can also heal you. It's worth a second chance."

"I'm not so sure."

"All I ask is that you don't slam the door on the possibility of happiness only to hide alone in your office with your work and yarn."

I lifted an eyebrow. "That was rather specific."

She smiled. "I call it like I see it."

A plane droned overhead as a dog barked. I smiled when I saw Mabel towing Jamie down the sidewalk until I realized they were headed here.

"The smile on your face suggests this would be your Jamie now," Mama said.

"He's not mine," I whispered as Mabel veered up the walkway like she owned the place, and Jamie dutifully followed.

Mama laughed. "Like I said, I call it like I see it."

Mabel barked when she heard a new voice and broke into a run, nearly making Jamie trip in order to keep up with her.

"She's getting obedience lessons," I said quickly, so Mama wouldn't judge her, too.

Mama stood up and opened the door for the pair, and Mabel stretched her leash to its limits to rush right past her to get to me. She licked my face.

My mama kept on grinning. "*She* might be yours, too."

"*Shh*," I said as my cheeks flared red-hot.

She paid me no mind as she welcomed Jamie inside. "Beautiful night, isn't it? Come on in. I'm Lillian, Cora Bee's mother. I've heard so much about you that it's nice to finally meet you."

"Ma'am," he said with a shake of her hand. "It's nice to meet you, too."

"She heard all about you from May," I added quickly, hoping he didn't think I'd been the one gushing. As if this moment couldn't get more embarrassing.

He laughed. "Did May invite you to my and Cora Bee's wedding? I heard it's being held in the garden at the end of summer." He then looked my way with humor in his eyes. "The whole neighborhood is talking about it."

My mama laughed. "No formal invite yet. Just a verbal save-the-date."

I groaned.

He glanced between us. "I didn't mean to interrupt—I didn't realize you had company. I can come back later to water the flowers."

"Don't leave on my account," Mama said. "I was just going myself. It's been a long travel day, and I still need to unpack." She walked over to me, leaned down, and kissed my cheek. Into my ear, she whispered, "*All* yours."

Then with a lick from Mabel, she was gone, down the sidewalk to Glory's, where she'd be staying for the week, since the apartment wasn't yet done.

"I didn't realize your mom was coming to town. Come here, Mabel." He unclipped the leash from her collar.

"None of us knew. It was a surprise." I stood—I was getting good at standing on one foot—and reached for my crutches. "I don't think the flowers need water since it rained last night."

"Oh. Okay."

He looked so disappointed that I couldn't help smiling. "Do you like cake? Glory sent me home with plenty."

His gaze held mine for a long second. "Love cake."

Love.

Give it a chance, Mama had said.

I motioned to the doorway with my chin. "Let's eat it inside, okay? I feel like the whole neighborhood is watching us."

He stood firm. "Me coming inside is only going to fuel the fire."

I laughed. "I don't see why, seeing as how we're getting married soon."

"True, true." He followed me in, taking the wine and Mama's glass with him.

He set them on the kitchen counter, and I said, "Would you like a glass?"

"Nah. I gave up drinking a long time ago when I realized I was thinking about my next drink before I finished the one in my hand. It had started taking over my life, and I hadn't even noticed."

My heart thudded. I lifted my chin. "Me too." I swallowed hard and added, "I don't take prescription pain medicine, either. Just over-the-counter stuff."

It was the first time I'd talked about it with anyone other than Glory, and I found it wasn't as hard or painful as I'd feared. Maybe because he'd shown me how easy it could be. Just say it. Own it.

His gaze skipped to the amber bottle on the windowsill, a question in his eyes.

"It's full," I said.

"Why keep it?"

It was a question I'd asked myself a dozen times. "I'm not sure. A reminder, maybe, of a place I don't want to go back to? I shouldn't have gotten it filled, but I'd been too embarrassed to say anything in front of you."

His eyes softened. "You don't ever have to be afraid to be embarrassed around me, Cora Bee. I think you're pretty perfect the way you are, warts and all."

"Warts?" I said, laughing. "When did I get those?"

"You never know when one's going to pop up," he said with a playful shrug.

Mabel had followed us into the kitchen, where she now sniffed every available surface.

His gaze fell to the kitchen table, where the leftover cake sat as well as the manila envelope Emme had brought inside earlier. "Have you had a chance to look at the pictures?"

"Not yet, but now seems a good time. With an expert in the house and all."

I crutched over to the cabinet next to the stove top and took down two dessert plates. Jamie took them from me and set them on the table, along with the napkins, forks, and knife I gathered.

Mabel sniffed the area rug that lay in front of the sink and apparently decided it was a good place to nap. She plopped herself down, let out a tired sigh.

I felt that sigh in my soul.

I leaned my crutches against the table and sat down, and Jamie pulled his chair closer to me. I cut cake slices, set them on the dessert plates. Then I opened the envelope, slid the eight-by-ten photos onto the table.

The picture on top of the stack was an aerial view of the brickyard, and I picked up the photo for a closer look. There were numerous outbuildings, wooden and brick, but there were several round, domed buildings at the edge of the photo that caught my attention. "What are these?"

He leaned in so close I could smell the chocolate on his lips. "I thought those might interest you. They're the beehive kilns, where the bricks were fired. The area where the kilns were located was called the bee yard. Those kilns were your grandmother's idea—she'd seen them in a magazine after the term *bee yard* caught her eye in a caption. She chatted about them with my grandfather at a company function. He did some research on his own, met a guy in Montgomery who had a similar setup, and made it happen. Seemed like it was meant to be, doesn't it? Bee's bee yard?"

The bee yard. Chills swept down my arms, raising goose bumps. Instantly, I knew I'd found my inspiration. The BeeYard sounded like the perfect name for the shopping center, and I knew just how I'd design it. "All right, you've convinced me. I think I'll stay in the competition."

He was still leaning in, his face so close to mine I could practically feel the stubble on his cheeks. "You haven't even looked at all the pictures."

I turned to face him. We were practically nose to nose. "I don't need to see them. I've seen all I need."

"The kilns?"

As I put the photos back into the envelope, I smiled. "You're just going to have to wait and see. Thank you for loaning these to me."

"My pleasure, Cora Bee."

Oh my heart. The way he said my name filled me with pure, sweet bliss.

He leaned in just a little bit more, bumping the table, and I felt my pulse pounding in my ears as his lips brushed against mine.

Absently, I heard metal sliding against the table but didn't realize what was happening until the crutches hit the floor with a bang. Jamie and I jumped apart at the sound, laughing at the absurdity.

Mabel leaped up from the rug and rushed over to us, taking turns slurping our chins.

"All right, we're okay; it was just the crutches. Down, Mabel," Jamie said, his voice round with exasperation, sounding just like Alice had the first time I'd met her. "It's *my* turn."

Then he reached out, gently cupped my face with his rough hands, and kissed me.

And as my hopes and dreams picked themselves off the floor, dusted themselves off, I thought maybe giving love a second chance wasn't such a bad idea after all.

Emme

While Cora Bee was with her mama on the porch, I stayed out in the garden. I'd pulled all the weeds in sight, not only those from my planter bed but also those around the grounds as well.

I'd quickly run out of tasks to do, so I wandered about, touching and sniffing and trying to remember all the names of the flowers Glory had taught me and their meanings. Chase was supposed to meet me at the apartment soon, and while I could go over early, I was enjoying the garden. It was calm and peaceful out here, a judgement-free zone, something I needed right now more than ever.

I stopped at Dorothy's vegetable bed, admired the orange marigolds sprinkled among the vegetables, the scent of the flower popular to keep rabbits and hornworms away, and thought about what I'd read in my library book about them. About how marigolds represented sorrow and despair, and that was why they were popular flowers for funerals and cemeteries. But I also read that marigolds offered comfort to the heart, and I liked that symbolism very much.

I worked my way out of the vegetable garden and was walking toward the gazing pool when I heard dog tags jingling and looked up to see Chase and Orville headed my way. I smiled, unable to help myself, when Orville dashed toward me with that ratty green tennis ball in his mouth.

"Hey, buddy," I said, wrestling the ball from him and tossing it as far as I could. He took off.

"I'm starting to think he likes you more than he likes me."

"Dogs like me," I said simply. "Cats too."

"Not surprising. Animals are usually a good judge of character."

I wiped my hands on my shorts. "Or they just recognize someone willing to play with them."

He glanced over at Cora Bee's house as Lillian opened the porch door for Jamie and Mabel, who were headed up the walkway.

"Hey, did you know Jamie was a Yardley?" I asked.

"Yeah. I've talked to him about my book. Why? You didn't know?"

I shook my head. "Not until yesterday. And neither did Cora Bee."

"I can excuse Cora Bee, but *Miss Perceptive* didn't know? I'm shocked."

I rolled my eyes and tried not to notice how charming I found his nicknames.

"You wouldn't happen to be hiding out here, would you?" he asked with a knowing smile.

"Of course I am. Lillian hates me."

"*Hate* is a strong word."

Orville returned with an exuberant gallop, his tail wagging. I patted his head and threw the ball for him again. "Do you have a better word?"

He thought for a moment before saying, "*Distrust*. She distrusts you. You held your own at supper. I was impressed."

It hadn't felt like I'd held my own. It felt like I had shrunk into myself. All my work of trying to be present, be visible, be friendly had gone straight out the window under her intense scrutiny.

Formidable was the first impression I'd had of Lillian, and I could only imagine what hers had been of me. But *formidable* didn't quite do her personality justice. Cora Bee had once described her mother as take-charge, and I could see that, too. Lillian looked like she could take over running the world if someone would simply give her the go-ahead.

And Glory had been right, as well. Lillian was elegance personified. All through dinner, she'd sat perfectly straight, shoulders back, chin high. Her clothes, a rich blue tailored skirt suit and white pleated blouse, hadn't dared wrinkle on her long journey from California. A colorful, chunky triple-strand beaded necklace hinted at a creative, artistic side. The necklace had thrown me off a bit, a touch of wildness in an otherwise tamed landscape. It told me that there was more to her than met the eye.

But still, her personality wasn't a landscape I cared to explore. I'd keep to myself as much as possible while she was here. That was why I had escaped to the garden when she'd shown up at Cora Bee's with a bottle of wine, looking to stay awhile.

When Orville returned once more, I noticed that Lillian was headed back to Glory's, and I let out a sigh of relief that she wouldn't be at Cora Bee's when I returned. Cora Bee's house had become a comfort zone, a safe place. It made me feel secure for once in my life. But if Lillian stuck around, her negative energy was bound to ruin something I'd come to cherish.

Because she had good reason to be distrustful.

To hate me, even.

"You ready to get to work?" Chase asked with a nod toward the garage apartment.

We should've been done by now, but Glory kept adding little projects. New knobs for the kitchen cabinets and drawers. Shelves in the closet. Wainscoting in the bathroom. Liners added to drawers. The front door painted. New curtains. Every day it seemed like a big truck rolled up and dropped off another delivery. A couch. A coffee table. Even two armchairs. And all that didn't even include the time she'd handed over her credit card and sent Chase and me off to "find knickknacks to pretty up the place." I had been thinking about staging an intervention for her online shopping when she'd announced that there was nothing else on order.

I nodded, and as we started walking toward the apartment, I saw Nannette come out of her house, carrying some sort of wooden shelf. She set it on the curb next to the trash can that had been put out earlier, gave us a stiff nod, then went back inside.

In my mind, I could already see what I'd do to transform the piece, bring out its beauty.

From the corner of my eye, I noticed another neighbor walking down their driveway with a nightstand. I looked down the street and saw that many of the houses suddenly had furniture at the curb. A dresser, a bookcase, a side table. In front of Dorothy's house sat a console table.

With a start, I realized that this wasn't coincidental. This had been organized. This was . . . acceptance.

My gaze swung back to the piece Nannette had set at the

curb and my chest squeezed tightly. Maybe she was a wild card after all, because I never thought she'd see me as anything other than an outsider.

I blinked back tears as I looked at Chase. "Did you do this? Set this up?"

He reached his hand up, like he was going to tuck my hair behind my ears, but then dropped it again. There was softness in his eyes as he said, "No, Emme. Don't you see? This was all you."

Chapter
20

Glory's Garden Lesson #10

Peonies are a gift from the heavens above. I mean, just look at this flower, so big and round. The ruffled petals that look like they belong on a ball gown? Absolute perfection. That scent? It always reminds me of rose and jasmine. I sell these stems at the Sweetplace, but there's no better place for them than in a wedding bouquet, since peonies represent a happy marriage and a happy life. Mix them with some stock in a bouquet, and well, you're kicking married life off right. From what I hear around the neighborhood, there might just be a wedding around here sooner than we think. Though I'm not sure pink is the best color for the bridal party.

Emme

By the following Thursday, I'd become quite adept at dodging Lillian. It helped that she seemed to be avoiding me, too. I felt her, though. When I was helping Glory bake, I could sense Lillian nearby, watching. I'd also sensed that she'd been in my bedroom at Cora Bee's. Yesterday, after returning from the marketplace, I'd caught a faint whiff of her perfume in the air when I'd gone into my room. Nothing was out of place; nothing had been taken. Yet, I knew without a doubt she'd been in there.

It had made me want to pack everything and run. Run far.

Away from Sweetgrass. Away from my guilt.

I was grateful she wasn't here now and wasn't expected back for a while. And this evening should be peaceful as well, since

Lillian had volunteered to take Glory to see several parcels of land for sale, and then out to dinner.

"This is all very exciting," Glory said as we crossed her driveway.

She was smiling ear to ear, reminding me why I stayed here with my growing guilt.

"Will Chase be joining us?" she asked.

"I asked him to, but he said he'd leave the grand reveal to us girls."

She gave me a sideways glance. "He's a good boy."

"Who? Orville? I adore him."

Glory laughed. "Don't sass. I knew Cora Bee was going to be a bad influence on you."

I stepped over a dandelion growing up from the driveway bricks. "Chase is a nice guy," I agreed. And also extremely inquisitive, which meant he was dangerous. Dangerous mostly to my heart at this point, since I found his endless curiosity with just about everything attractive. I looked forward to seeing him just a little too much.

As Glory and I climbed the metal staircase alongside the garage, she glanced back at me, a knowing glint in her eye, and I could feel my cheeks heating. I said, "You're as bad as Alice."

She gripped the hand rail, hauled herself up another step with a loud exhale. "Who do you think she learned it from? I have to confess, however, that she just may be better at it than I am."

I took each step slowly so as not to rush her. "Or perhaps Cora Bee and Jamie are better suited?"

Watching them together this week had been amusing. Cora Bee was still trying to hold back a little, but Jamie was all-in. Seeing them dance around each other and their attraction had caused endless entertainment for Alice and me.

Alice was convinced there was a happily ever after in their future.

I wasn't so sure. Not yet.

Cora Bee was terrified to love again, and Jamie . . . Well, I couldn't shake the sense that Jamie was hiding something from her.

I wondered if Cora Bee sensed it, too, because something was certainly bothering her these days. If not Jamie, then perhaps it was her mother's return or the brickyard contest that was making her anxious. She'd barely slept at all this week. The sound of her crutches on the hardwood floor had awoken me many times in the last few days, all during the wee hours. Inevitably when I checked on her, I found her at her desk or on the sofa with a ball of yarn or a book in her lap, an apology on her lips, bags under her eyes.

"Or sometimes," Glory said, "we're too blind to see what's right in front of us."

I didn't argue, though I wanted to. Even if I saw it, it wasn't mine for the taking.

At the top of the steps, Glory started coughing. Tight barks that robbed her of her breath. I reached out, rubbed her back. I didn't think it helped, other than it made me feel better to offer what little comfort I could.

"I'm all right, hon," she said once she caught her breath.

"Mm." I slipped a key into the new door handle, heard the satisfying click of the tumbler turning over.

"Did I order that?" she asked, staring at the new lock.

"No, I picked it up." The door had needed a good dead bolt, and I was happy to use a portion of my first paycheck from Cora Bee to pay for it.

"Thought I'd lost my mind for a second there. It's a lovely finish."

Turning the knob, I pushed the door open. "It matches the new faucet you bought for the kitchen."

"You've got a keen eye for details, Emme."

If Chase had been here, he'd have called me Miss Perception again, and I smiled as his voice echoed through my head.

"And an unhealthy sense of fear," she added, patting my cheek before she stepped inside. "Oh, Lordy be. Look at this place!"

I stepped in behind her, closed the door. A surge of pride washed over me at the look on her face. "It's amazing what a little paint can do."

"Oh, Emme. This is more than paint. I can practically see your heart beating in here."

What she was seeing was my love for her.

It was in the cut flowers on the kitchen table. The dried flowers I'd put into shadow boxes. It was in the burnished gold and purple accents. The vases, the frames, the trays.

She walked deep into the living room and looked at the canvases hanging on the wall. I'd taken pictures of flowers in the garden and had a local shop put those photos onto canvases. There were two hanging above the couch.

One of gladiolus shining in the morning light.

And one of a sunflower, the sun behind it making it glow.

She wiped the corner of her eye with her thumb, and I felt tears welling in my eyes.

Trying to keep my composure, I said, "I've been studying my language of flowers book. Did you know that sunflowers actually turn toward the sun? I suppose that's why they represent warmth and devotion and loyalty. Of all the flowers, they're considered the happiest. My favorite sunflower, however, seems to radiate light instead of turning toward it. I swear sometimes you downright glow, Glory."

"Oh my goodness. Emme, honey, I have no words." She put her arm around my shoulders, pulling me in tightly next to her. "I don't know if I've mentioned it yet, but you're a very good student. The *best* student. So observant. So astute. So sensitive. And it just goes to show that educations come in all different shapes and sizes."

We stood side by side for a few moments, simply studying the pictures, and I didn't mind it a bit. Not with her arm around me. Not with the way she made me feel like I was a part of her.

"You do know it's missing one, though?"

"I put the dahlia in the kitchen by the fridge."

She smiled. "I'm surprised you included it at all."

"Family," I said with a shrug.

"You have a big heart, Emme. But I wasn't talking about Lillian." She waved a finger at the canvases above the couch. "I was talking about you, my little dandelion."

I faked shock. "A dandelion? Are you comparing me to a *weed*?"

"Ah-ah," she chastised. "Don't you know the saying about how some see a weed, while others see a wildflower? Dandelions are wildflowers, and they're the picture of survival, resilience, determination. Just like my Emme."

My tears overflowed, spilling down my face.

She slowly faced me. "I hope that you'll be happy here. Even after I'm gone."

"You're not going anywhere." My voice was a mere whisper, choked with emotion. "Not for a long time."

"I know you know that's not the truth, Emme honey. It was written plain as day on your face the day you found out. You can hide from some but not from me."

I pressed my lips together to keep them from quivering, but my chin trembled.

"I know it's not fair," she said, "me leaving so soon after we found each other. But life's rarely fair. No one knows that better than you do. But we have right now."

More tears leaked down my face, leaving scorching hot trails of grief and regret.

Taking my hands in hers, she squeezed tightly. "Listen here now. I want you to always live for the moment, Emme. *In* the moment. Don't look back. Don't look too far ahead. Don't let fear stop you. Don't let safety be the only thing that drives you. Forgive yourself for the things you've done that have hurt others. Let go of the things that hurt you."

It was all I could do not to dissolve into a full river of tears. "I don't know how to do any of that."

"That's why I'm here. To help you."

I flung myself at her, hugging her tightly, holding on for all I was worth.

"There, there," she consoled. "It'll be all right."

Right here, living in this moment, I allowed myself to believe her.

"Now," she said after the long hug, "what else does this place need? I've got a credit card and I'm not afraid to use it."

"It doesn't need anything else."

"Do *you* need anything? I'm happy to take you on a shopping spree, plump up that wardrobe of yours. I owe you decades of birthday and Christmas presents."

I wiped my eyes and sniffled. "You don't owe me anything. All I've ever wanted was a loving family, and you've already given me that."

"A gift that keeps on giving," she said with a smile. "Even after I'm gone, you'll have Cora Bee. And Lillian, who *will* come around—I assure you."

I only nodded, because I knew that as soon as she was gone, I was going to leave the only place that had ever felt like home and the only people who had ever felt like family.

Cora Bee

I was working on the brickyard project on Thursday afternoon when Alice and Mabel let themselves in with a cheery, "Cora Bee! We're here."

I glanced at the clock, surprised by how fast the time had flown by while I worked. My design was coming along, but I wasn't ready for anyone else to see it yet, so I minimized the screen.

Mabel raced into my office, her whole body seeming to wiggle with happiness at seeing me. She didn't jump on me but instead zoomed around my chair, letting out little yips of joy as I gave her love and attention.

Alice appeared in the doorway seconds later. Her short hair was pulled back in a stubby ponytail that reminded me of the first time I'd met her. "She loves you."

"I've grown mighty fond of her, too. Yes, I have," I said to Mabel in a high-pitched voice.

She licked my hand, and as she settled down, she started sniffing around the room, beginning with my foot that was propped on the ottoman. When she started to lick the cast, Alice snapped her fingers. "No, Mabel," she said, and the dog moved on to smell the chair Emme usually sat in, the chair where Mabel preferred to nap in the afternoons. As usual, she jumped up and lay down.

"Are you still not sleeping well?" Alice asked as she moseyed into the room, one arm behind her back.

"Does it show that much?" I asked as I picked up the glass of iced coffee Emme had made for me before she left to see Glory.

Alice lifted one shoulder and winced as she said, "A little."

She was honest—I'd give her that. "It'll get better soon, I'm sure." I wasn't sure at all, but I didn't want Alice to worry about me. "What have you got there?"

I'd noticed she still had one hand behind her back and there was an impish light in her eyes.

With a big smile, she swung her hand toward me, and on it sat a wrapped gift. The paper, I noticed, had "happy birthday" written on it.

I took the gift. "You know it's not my birthday . . ." We'd talked about birthdays last week. Mine was in August; hers was in November.

"Oh!" She rolled her eyes. "That's the only gift wrap Dad had in the house. Ignore that. Open it!"

I carefully removed the paper and smiled at what was slowly revealed. It was a ceramic bee, its rotund body painted black and gold, its wings white. It still smelled like clay. "Did you make this?"

She nodded. "In art class."

She'd made a gift just for me. Tears gathered in my eyes. "It's beautiful. Thank you, Alice. I love it. Absolutely love it."

Alice came over to me and before I knew it, she was giving me a hug. "I'm sorry Mabel knocked you down, but I'm glad she did. Well, you know what I mean."

I hugged her back. "I do know what you mean."

A minute later, she was outside, and I heard the squeak of the spigot.

As I set the bee on my desk, I stared long and hard at it, thinking that there might just be enough room inside my heart for a few more people . . . and one happy dog.

Chapter 21

June 1, 1965: Strangest dang thing is happening near the gazing pool. A perfectly round sinkhole has opened up, about the width of a manhole cover, unsure how deep. A neighbor said it's because of the drought. Have a call in to the county engineer to see what to do about it, and I'll be sure to keep Lillian away from it since she's walking all over the place now. Another strange thing . . . since that sinkhole has opened, I've started seeing the glowing bees near the gazing pool again. Every day, I sit out there with them for a long while, listening to their soft buzzing. It feels a bit like visiting with old friends.

Cora Bee

Friday had dawned with a full-on hissy fit. Thunder had shaken the house and rattled glassware in the cabinet while rain pounded the roof. The forecast had called for intermittent storms throughout the day, and so far, the prediction hadn't been wrong. The temperature had steadily risen throughout the day, too, which most likely meant the storms would become more severe as the day went on. Tornado watches were already in effect.

At least the bad weather had kept me alert through the morning. I was feeling the effects of my insomnia, yawning all the time, dealing with sluggishness, and I was plagued with a constant low-level headache. I had tried just about everything to sleep and stay asleep, except for a bath before bedtime because even though my cast was made of waterproof material, I didn't want to deal with it in the tub. Tonight I was going to try diffusing lavender oil, which Emme had brought home from the Sweetplace for me to try. At this point, it couldn't hurt.

Now that it was midafternoon, the skies were still angry but at least it had stopped raining for the time being. I was trying my best to keep my eyes off the sky and on my computer screen. I consoled myself with the fact that tornadoes weren't common here—there hadn't been one that touched ground in more than twenty years. Still, years of living in the South had taught me that weather was the most unpredictable enemy.

I felt for Emme and Aunt Glory, who'd been at the Sweetplace all day and had come back looking like they'd gone for a swim in the bay. Sales had been lousy but both seemed in good enough spirits, though they often were when they were together.

Emme was currently across the street in the garden, tending to her beloved flowers, and then she had plans to work in the garage on some of her new upcycling projects. Aunt Glory, Dorothy, and my mama were taking a quick trip for a second look at a plot of land not too far from the old brickyard. Aunt Glory thought the proximity would prove beneficial for the Sweetplace, as drivers would have to pass the Sweetplace before getting to the new shopping center. Afterward, they were planning to stop at a local retirement home under the guise of Glory looking at it for a possible place to move should she become too weak to live on her own. Dorothy, I was quite sure, would see right through that plan. I smiled as I wondered if there was going to be a fainting spell in her near future.

My gaze fell on my desk calendar, and I realized I still didn't have a gift for my mama for Mother's Day this Sunday. Dorothy had promised to check for photos of Bee, but so far she hadn't found any. I couldn't wait much longer.

I glanced out the window again, then forced my gaze back onto the rendering on my computer screen. At what I saw, I felt a sense of pride, even though I had gone off the rails in terms of what had been asked of me by Turner & Gebbes.

With my design plan for the BeeYard, I'd altered the original renderings the firm had sent me, adding brick columns, rich wooden accents, subtle honeycomb patterns, lush landscaping, and touches of gold everywhere. The branding would include bees, and I had made a note to have hundreds of the bricks stamped with a small bee design, so that visitors would catch a glimpse of one every here and there as they shopped. Overall, the design exuded elegant warmth, hinted at the past, and above all, it felt *right*.

Which had made my decision to drop out of the contest that much harder.

Still, it had to be done.

My professional integrity was on the line, and I refused to compromise it. If I wanted Jamie in my life, my heart, then there was no other option. And I wanted Jamie in my heart. With him, there were glimpses of hope. Hope and promise for a future I'd never dreamed possible.

Feeling like I was absolutely making the right choice, I picked up my phone and called my contact at T&G, letting them know of my decision.

What I heard in reply had me storming out the front door before I could think twice. I made sure Jamie's truck was in his driveway before I crutched my way up the sidewalk and turned up his walkway. I was glad Alice wasn't home from school yet, so I didn't have to fake a happy face for her. Mabel heard me before I knocked, her cheerful barks doing little to diffuse my anger.

The front door swung open, and Jamie's welcoming smile dissolved when he saw the look on my face.

"What's wrong?" he asked, closing the door behind me as I crutched past him into his entryway.

Mabel danced around my legs, and I petted her because I couldn't help myself, though I really just wanted Jamie to explain himself.

"Come, Mabel," he said, leading her outside, as if he knew no one but us should hear this conversation. Not even the dog.

When he came back, I looked straight in his eyes. "I called

Turner and Gebbes to pull out of the contest due to my relationship with you."

"But Cora Bee," he started.

I held up a hand, stopping him. "They were real kind about it
but perplexed, since they were aware of our relationship."

"I told you," he began.

I held up my hand again. "They told me they'd keep me in
mind for other projects, that they'd been impressed with my
portfolio, that they might have overlooked me had you not
insisted I be issued an invitation to the competition. Why, Jamie? Why? Why did you insist I be invited to the competition? I
hadn't even met you at that point."

He dragged a hand down his face. "I can explain."

"I'm waiting."

"Let's sit down."

"I'm fine standing."

He sighed. "You're right—I'd never met you. But I knew of
you. Knew exactly who you were. A Gipson. Specifically, Levi
Gipson's granddaughter."

"What does this have to do with him? Is this because of what
he did at the brick company? Some kind of revenge?" Oh God,
how that thought hurt. Had he been using me all this time as
some sort of plan to seek justice for his family? As if Levi hadn't
already hurt my family enough?

"Of course not. No. It's because of what Levi *didn't* do at the
brick company."

Now I kind of wished I'd sat down, but I stood steady, gripping my crutch handles. "I don't understand."

"Levi didn't steal anything from the brickyard. He was set
up. Framed. The money was never missing, just moved around
to make it look like it was."

The words swirled in my head, and I tried to make sense of
them but couldn't. "What? By whom?"

"My grandfather. For revenge. Because Levi *did* steal my
grandmother's heart."

The affair. I'd almost forgotten.

"It's a long story," Jamie said, "and I only found out because when my grandfather was dying, he lost his head a bit and started talking about all kinds of things he probably otherwise would've taken to the grave. When he admitted he framed your grandfather, it got me to thinking. Were the embezzlement accusations the thing that pushed Levi over the edge, made him snap? After all, he was facing a decade in jail and no one believed he was innocent. Or—and I hate to even think this—what if my grandmother was the reason Levi did what he did to Bee? Did Bee know about his affair? Had she confronted him? Was the affair the reason for the fight they had the night she disappeared? Or what if Levi just wanted Bee out of the way so he and my grandmother could be together?"

My head started to spin, and I felt dizzy. "Did the police ever question your grandmother?"

"Not that I know of. She left town shortly after Bee disappeared, moving to Tuscaloosa to live with family up there. My grandfather stayed behind in Sweetgrass for a while but ultimately closed the brickyard and opened a new one up along the Black Warrior River. He and my grandmother stayed together—but had separate bedrooms—until her death six years later."

"So we'll likely never know what really happened."

"Probably not, but the shame of my family's possible, *probable*, involvement in Bee's death weighed on me. When I came to Sweetgrass to start the brickyard project, I found out Levi still had family in the area and that you were a designer. I thought, I don't know, that if I could give your career a boost, it would somehow make some of the shame go away."

As he spoke, the bits of juniper green around him paled. *This* had been the big secret he'd been keeping. "So you were going to rig a contest for me to win?"

"No." He shook his head. "I'd never do that."

Suddenly he was awash in a plum color—remorse. At seeing it, my anger lessened but didn't fade away completely.

"All I did was get you invited," he said. "You would've been judged fairly, just like the other designers. I never expected to meet you in person. I didn't know you lived on Hickory Lane when I came up with the idea for the contest. I didn't know Mabel would knock you down. I was just trying, in my own small way, to help you out, to make some sort of amends."

Now that my adrenaline was wearing off, I was beginning to shake. "I don't need your help. I was doing fine before you came along trying to make yourself feel better."

He winced. "This is a shock, I know. And I'm sorry. I've been thinking long and hard about Sweetgrass this week. And the brickyard. Being here . . . being with you, has been the best thing to happen to me in a long time. I decided I want to sell the brickyard land to Glory for the Sweetplace. It feels like the right thing to do."

My head hurt, my heart hurt, and I was so damn tired. This was all old news to him, yet it had only just been sprung on me. "You can't be serious. Years of work has already gone into the brickyard project. All that time, all that effort, all that money . . . You're just trying to appease me. You don't need to do that."

"I don't make decisions lightly. I want to stay here in Sweetgrass. I want to be with you. I want *us*." His sorrowful eyes pleaded with me. "What do you want, Cora Bee?"

My heart thudded against my ribs. I couldn't listen to any more of this. And Alice would be home soon, and I didn't want her to see me upset.

I turned toward the door, pulled it open. It had started to rain again. "I don't know what I want other than I don't want to be here right now."

With that, I crutched outside and let the rain wash the tears from my face as I made my way home.

ﹰﹰ

An hour later, the skies had gone black as night. As soon as I'd gotten home from Jamie's, I'd taken four ibuprofen and shut off my computer for the day. I would've crawled into bed, but one of the tips for insomnia was to stay out of bed until bedtime, and right now my longing for sleep outweighed my desire to hide under my covers.

To occupy my brain, I'd taken my latest crochet project to the couch, where I'd spent more time pulling out stitches than completing them because my concentration kept wandering.

To Jamie. To Alice. To Bee.

Would she still be here?

All my anger drained away as I replayed over and over again what Jamie had said, but it always kept straying back to one aspect in particular.

I want us.

Did I want us, too?

It should've been a simple question, yet it wasn't.

I heard footsteps on the porch stairs and hoped it wasn't Alice. It shouldn't be. Beyond the fact that she didn't need to water because of the rain, she should be on her way to her mom's house—she was spending Mother's Day weekend up there.

When Emme came rushing into the house, her hair plastered to her head, my shoulders loosened with relief.

Laughing, she said, "I've never seen it rain so hard." She then took one look at me, held up a finger. "I'm going to put some dry clothes on, and then you're going to tell me what's wrong. I'll be right back."

Five minutes later, I said, "I had a fight with Jamie."

At the compassionate look in her eyes, I let it all spill out.

She said, "The first time I saw Jamie, I pegged him as honorable, and my first impressions are rarely wrong. I truly think he meant to help, not harm. He was trying to make things right between the two families in his own way."

The wind picked up and thunder rocked the house. "He still lied."

"Yeah, he did. But on the lie-o-meter, it's a one or two at most. A small white lie."

I arched an eyebrow. "The lie-o-meter?"

She smiled. "I just made that up."

"It's just that after my divorce, I decided not to let anyone else into my life. I'd decided that love wasn't worth the inevitable pain. But these last couple of weeks, I haven't been so vigilant. I've gotten attached to Alice, to Jamie, even to Mabel. I'm afraid something is going to happen and I'm going to lose them. Whether it's a fight with Jamie or they move away or *anything*. I'm scared." So very scared.

A bolt of lightning hit somewhere close and the hair on my arms stood up and the power cut out.

Emme let out a yip and jumped up to look out the window. "I don't see any flames, but that was way too close for comfort."

I used my cell phone data to look at the local radar. An angry red line was inching across the bay toward us. Suddenly, my cell phone let out a warning alarm, which I shut off only to hear the county sirens blaring.

"Tornado sirens," I said, grabbing my crutches to stand up.

Emme didn't back away from the window. "Glory's out there somewhere."

My mama and Dorothy, too. And Jamie and Alice, on their way to Birmingham. How far were they ahead of this storm? I swallowed hard. "We need to take cover. But first I need to grab my laptop."

She finally turned away from the window. "I'll get it."

"And the ceramic bee on my desk?"

The wind howled, nearly drowning out the sound of the tornado siren, as she nodded and darted down the hallway.

I crutched quickly into the kitchen, opened a cabinet, and grabbed a flashlight. I flipped it on, only to find it was dead. I looked for spare batteries but didn't have the right size. In my head, I could hear my daddy's lecture about always being prepared and pushed it out of my thoughts.

Emme came rushing into the kitchen with my things, plus her backpack and the crochet bunny. "Do you have a storm cellar?"

"No, unfortunately." Wobbling on my crutches, I moved into the hallway, pulled open the closet door. I yanked out the sweeper and rolled it aside. "This closet is our safest spot. Inner room, no windows. It'll be tight, but we'll both fit easily." I saw the rising panic in her eyes as she stared into the dark space. "It'll be okay, Emme."

She started to tremble. "It's so dark."

I slipped my phone from my pocket, used its flashlight feature. "Let there be light. Now, come on." I crutched into the closet, then waved her inside.

With a deep breath, she stepped into the closet beside me, set down our prized possessions, and stowed my crutches next to my winter coat. She helped me down to the floor, then sat opposite me. Her back was on one side wall, mine on the other. I thanked the stars above that the closet was wide enough for me to stretch out my legs. Emme had her knees pulled up to her chin, and we were so close I could feel her shaking through my cast.

The cell phone light was surprisingly bright, but I was already worried about how long it would last. My phone had only 60 percent battery life left, but that charge would drain quickly with the light on.

I quickly typed out a note to Glory, and relief flowed when I saw response bubbles. I read the message to Emme as soon as it came in. "Glory says she, Dorothy, and my mama took shelter at the courthouse. She says she loves us and to be safe." I typed back that we were safe in the hall closet and that we loved them, too.

My heart was in my throat as I texted Alice next. Are you on the road yet? Bad storm here.

As I waited for a response, I reached over and picked up the ceramic bee, ran my finger over its delicate wings, and tried not to worry as time stretched on. I told myself that Alice and Jamie were fine. That they had found cover on the road like Glory had. That the cell phone coverage was spotty because of the storm.

I didn't even care anymore what Jamie had done. I just wanted to make sure he was okay. That Alice was okay. *Please, please let them be safe.*

Emme was still shaking, and I knew it had nothing to do with what was going on outside.

I started talking to keep her mind away from her fears. "You know, when I pictured my innermost circle, the one around my heart, it held only the people I loved and trusted most. Glory, my parents, my brother. But now I'm starting to think that maybe *I* was the only one in that circle this whole time. And that everyone else stood just beyond. I hid myself away in there, afraid to open myself up again. Afraid for people to see the real me. The person I became after my divorce. I didn't really like that person, so I was hiding her so no one would know."

Emme's voice was weak as she said, "Why didn't you like her?"

It was an easy question so I wasn't quite sure why it was so difficult to answer. "I felt weak. Unable to handle the betrayal, the pain, the heartbreak of my divorce and its aftermath, I fell apart. I didn't want to live."

"The car crash?" she asked softly.

"Yeah. Then, after the crash, I smothered my pain with pills and alcohol. It took a long time to get better. But I was still ashamed of myself, my behavior. So I kept on hiding it. Only Glory knew what happened. I cut myself off from people. I didn't deem myself loveable."

"Not loveable? Impossible."

"Well, I didn't love myself anymore. And if you don't love yourself, healthy relationships *are* impossible. But now, looking back, I think maybe I wasn't as weak as I thought. I was trying to cope the best way I could. Lousy ways, mind you. But now I see that I'm stronger than I thought."

Love is worth a second chance.

I owed it to myself to love *me* again.

"And you, Emme Wynn, are stronger than you think."

"I'm not so sure about that," she said. "Can't you feel me shaking?"

I was hoping she'd open up a little, so I asked, "Were you always afraid of the dark?"

After a long moment, she shook her head. "No. When I was younger, I actually spent a lot of time in closets and cabinets."

"Really?"

"Closets, because I was endlessly hopeful my Narnia was out

there somewhere, waiting for me to find it. Cabinets, because I was small and it was usually the best place to hide."

"Hide from what?" I asked, somehow already afraid of the answer.

"When my mother would bring men home, I'd need to be invisible. Sometimes the men knew about me and came looking when they knew my mother wasn't around. Those dark spaces that used to be safe became filled with fear."

My heart fell.

"A couple of the men found me." She touched the scar on her cheek, then dropped her hand. "This scar came from a man that realized my mother was playing him for a fool. He took his anger out on me until my mother came home and bashed him on the head with a cast iron pan."

"Did you call the police?" I asked, thinking of the scene in the gazing pool.

"No. We were off to the next town before the guy hit the floor. My mother made up some story to tell the hospital staff that patched me up; then we were off again."

"Oh, Emme."

"After that I started carrying a switchblade I'd found at a pawnshop. And, well, the next time a man came after me, I fought back. A neighbor called the cops when they heard the fight. When the cops arrived, and the man was writhing on the floor covered in blood, I was arrested. My bruises, my torn shirt didn't mean anything to them. Only that guy's word, because he was some bigwig somewhere—by the way, he ended up needing stitches but was fine otherwise."

She didn't sound pleased by that outcome, and I couldn't blame her.

"Luckily for me," she went on, "the detective on the case saw through what had happened. Saw through a lot, actually."

"Where was your mother during all this?"

"This happened days before my eighteenth birthday, and she hovered in the periphery until that day. Then she showed up and gave me a cupcake and a fifty-dollar bill as a gift and said she had taught me all I needed to know and that I was old enough to take care of myself. She left, and I haven't seen her since."

I had no words. Not a single one. But I realized I was crying. Tears flowed down my face.

"Not sure what to do, I contacted the detective who'd helped me initially, and he put me in touch with some charitable nonprofit groups around Louisville. Eventually, the charges against me were dropped. I stayed in shelters for a while, took on odd jobs that paid under the table. I was finally able to save enough to live on my own, even if they weren't the safest places, and to hire a lawyer to make sure my arrest was expunged from my record since I hadn't been formally charged. I got my GED. I found a decent job. Then I lost that job when my boss wanted more from me than the hard work I'd put in for my promotion. Then I came here."

It was no wonder she didn't like darkness, and why she was surrounded by it.

"You're the strongest, bravest person I've ever met," I said.

"Stop. I'm not. Look at how far you've come. I've seen that full bottle of pills on the windowsill."

I wasn't surprised—it seemed like she noticed everything.

My phone dinged and joy shot through me. "It's Alice. She's had bad reception. They're okay—driving ahead of the storm."

Thank goodness. I wanted to weep with relief. And to talk to Jamie, to make things right between us.

Another text came in.

Alice: Dad's staying at his place in Birmingham this weekend so don't worry about him driving back either.

My shoulders slumped with disappointment. I told myself that he was simply giving me space, but I wasn't sure I believed it.

Emme tipped her head, listening. "I think the storm has moved on." She cracked open the door, peeked outside. "The sky has lightened up, and it's not raining anymore."

So caught up in Emme's past, I hadn't even noticed the lack of thunder, of wind.

As soon as we were out of the closet, she looked back at the dark space. "That wasn't *too* terrible."

"Day by day you'll find your way, Emme," I said, then reached out to hug her tightly, one of my crutches falling in the process. "You know, I've become attached to you, too, and am so glad you're here to stay, because I can't imagine my life without you in it."

Chapter

22

 Glory's Garden Lesson #11

Come with me over to the pergola. See the border plants here? They don't have flowers yet, only that gorgeous lobed foliage, but in a few months, these plants will be bright with autumn colors. You'd recognize them straight off if they had their flowers, since you've probably seen them hundreds of times around Halloween, sittin' in front of grocery stores, in big pots with their orange and yellow flowers. Mums symbolize loyalty, friendship, happiness, and devotion. Generally speaking, mums—chrysanthemums—shouldn't do well in this area. It's too hot. They like cooler weather. They're a tad bit finicky. But here on Hickory Lane, all cuddled up close together, they're flourishing despite the odds, which just goes to show that sometimes you just need to be planted in the perfect spot to be able to thrive. Don't you agree?

Emme

Early the next morning, I spent a little time in the garden to check on the flowers after all that rain before loading up Glory's SUV for our day at the Sweetplace. I was halfway across the street when I saw Dorothy storming through the garden with the pink shovel in her hand.

I quickly detoured toward her. "Good morning, Dorothy!"

Determination was stamped on her face, in the drawn brows, the purse of her lips. She wore a purple muumuu but didn't have on any shoes. Her hair was flat, smushed against her delicate scalp.

"The ground's nice and soft after all that rain," she said by way of a hello. "It's a good day for diggin'!"

I had the uneasy feeling she wasn't talking about working in her vegetable bed. As I studied her face and noted the distant look in her eyes, I wasn't sure if she recognized me or not, but that didn't matter at the moment. "Sure is. Don't you think the day after a storm is one of the most beautiful? Just take a look around. The way the sun glistens on wet leaves and grass makes it seem like the whole garden is sparkling."

She lifted an eyebrow. "You talk a lot."

I laughed. "I think it's the first time I've ever been accused of that."

"Humph."

"Are you hungry? I'm sure Glory's got some breakfast cooking and some coffee on. Do you like French toast?" I walked as I talked, hoping she'd follow me. She did.

"Only if it's fixed proper."

"I know you're not questioning Glory's cooking skills."

She cracked a smile. Finally. "Her French toast isn't as good as mine since she doesn't use thick cuts of bread, but she does turn out a mean omelet."

"I could go for an omelet right about now with some peppers and onions."

"Don't forget the ham."

"Never. What kind of cheese?"

Grass stuck to her feet as she walked. "Good ol' American. Don't need none of that fancy stuff."

We'd reached the curb, where she stopped dead in her tracks and looked back at the damp gardens. "Breakfast can wait. I've got to get digging."

Glory's house was just across the street, and I looked at it longingly. "Don't you think a hearty breakfast will give you more energy?"

She stared at the shovel in her hand. "But he's out there. I've got to find his sorry self, make sure he's really gone."

That squirrel must have really ticked her off for her to hold a grudge this long, even if it was her head injury that kept her looking for him years later.

I heard a bark and knew without turning around that Orville was on his way. Which meant that Chase would be here soon as well.

Lillian stepped out onto Glory's front porch and yelled, "Everything okay over there?"

I took hold of Dorothy's free hand and started walking across the street. "Yes, ma'am. Dorothy's worked up an appetite this morning. I'm going to fix her an omelet."

"I thought we were having French toast?" Dorothy said, stopping in her tracks at the edge of Glory's lawn.

She tried to free her hand, but I kept holding it. I would've kept walking, marching her straight inside, except Orville raced up, barked twice, and sat, his tail sweeping the ground. He'd done his job well. "Good boy, Orville."

His tail swept faster. I glanced over my shoulder and sure enough, Chase was jogging toward us.

Glory stepped out onto the porch next to Lillian. "What's going on?"

Lillian said, "It looks like Emme's trying to kidnap Dorothy."

My head snapped up at the hint of humor in her voice. For the first time since she'd arrived, she smiled at me. A smile was the last thing I'd expected. Especially since I figured she knew I'd been arrested once. Last night, after having shared my past with Cora Bee, I thought it best to tell Glory, too, so Cora Bee didn't have to carry the weight of my secrets. Glory had tut-tutted throughout the retelling, her heart in her eyes. I'd told her it was okay to tell Lillian as well. By this time tomorrow, I suspected the whole neighborhood would know.

Which was fine by me. I was grateful to finally be rid of the secret.

This morning, I'd fully expected Lillian to be filled with I-told-you-sos. Yet, she was smiling. It brought unexpected tears to my eyes. I quickly blinked them away and said, "Dorothy's wanting to take advantage of the soft ground to do a little digging, but I think she'll have more energy if she gets some food in her belly first."

Glory's gaze dropped to the shovel in Dorothy's hand, and in the most cheerful voice I'd ever heard, she said, "Come on up here, Dorothy! I can whip up some pancakes in no time flat. Stuff you nice and full."

Dorothy said, "I thought I was getting an omelet? What in tarnation is going on around here?"

Chase was breathing hard by the time he reached my side. His hair was damp and curling around his ears.

Dorothy looked him over, then said, "And my doctor questions *my* health. You don't see me breathing like that. Maybe he should be the one looking at *convalescent* homes."

Chase rolled his eyes. "How about we go home and get some breakfast, Dotty?"

She looked between us. "Why is everyone trying to feed me? I've got diggin' to do!"

As a car rolled up the street and slowed to a stop in front of Glory's, we all fell silent, except for Dorothy.

"What's Bob doing here?" she asked. "Did you invite him for breakfast, too?"

I patted her hand. "I don't know."

Glory came down the porch steps and waited for him to get out of the car.

Bob dipped his chin in an all-around hello and said, "Glory, I was hoping to catch you before you went to the Sweetplace. Can I have a moment of your and Lillian's time?"

"Sure thing," she said. "Care to come inside for some coffee?"

"No, no. This won't take but a minute."

Lillian hurried down the stairs. "Is this about my mama?"

"In a way," Bob said. "I finally got the go-ahead to let you know that there's been a positive identification on the body."

Lillian latched on to Glory's arm.

Bob said solemnly, "It wasn't Bee we found in the garden. It was Levi."

Dorothy gasped, then muttered, "Levi? That no-account, no-good, slimy, *pitiful* rapscallion."

The words, I noticed, were the same ones she'd used when looking for the squirrel in Glory's vegetable bed.

Before I could give that too much thought, she whispered, "I *knew* he was around here somewhere. He couldn't hide forever, the varmint."

Chase and I both stared at her, then my gaze dropped to her shovel. After her accident, when she'd started digging holes, had others simply jumped to that conclusion that she was looking for the squirrel that had once dared forage in her vegetable bed? It made sense, I supposed, since she often used the term varmint when on her digging expeditions.

But what if she hadn't been looking for a squirrel this whole time? With her head injury, it was hard to be sure, but I couldn't shake the feeling that it was really *Levi* who she'd been searching for.

Grateful that we stood far enough away from the others for them to have overheard, I snatched the shovel from Dorothy's hand, pushed it into Chase's chest.

As our gazes met, I somehow knew he was thinking along the same lines as I was where Levi was concerned. I whispered, "You should take Dorothy home, don't you think?"

"We're going to head home," Chase said loudly, "and give y'all some privacy."

"But—" Dorothy sputtered.

"Now, now, Dotty," he said sternly. "This isn't our business. Come on."

He put his arm around her, whistled for Orville, and led his grandmother away as fast as her little legs would carry her.

As soon as they left, I didn't quite know what to do with myself until Glory held out her hand for me. I stepped up and put my hand in hers, felt her strength even though her hand trembled.

"Are you sure, Bob?" she asked him, her voice shaking, too.

"We're sure. We had his dental records on file from when it was believed he might've died in the house fire."

"How?" Lillian asked. "Is there a cause of death?"

"The body was found in a vertical position, feet first, which isn't very common for graves. Did some research, and 'round about the time this all happened, sinkholes were opening up all over Sweetgrass, most of the openings no bigger around than a person. Just like the one that opened up here a few weeks ago."

Glory nodded. "Bee's diary mentioned there was one in the backyard."

Lillian frowned deeply. "He fell in a sinkhole?"

"Yes, ma'am. Looks that way. There were no signs of trauma. Due to the narrowness of the sinkhole, the county coroner says it's likely he suffocated right quick."

I tried to imagine what it had been like to fall into a sinkhole, to be stuck in the darkness, and I almost started hyperventilating.

"But what about my mama?" Lillian asked, grief etched in her brown eyes.

Bob looked over toward the garden. "We brought out sonar equipment to see if we could find any evidence that she might've fallen in a sinkhole, too, but didn't have any success. We'll be back next week to keep on looking. Since this land was all wild back then, we'll expand the search to cover the paved street. We need permission from homeowners to check yards, so I'll be knocking on doors later on."

"I can make some calls," Glory said, her voice still strained. "So people know to expect you."

"I appreciate it," he said. "As long as Bee's still missing, we'll keep looking. As for Levi, his death has been ruled an accidental asphyxiation."

He talked a bit more about contacting the local funeral home and then murmured his condolences. As he walked back to his car, we all watched him slide behind the wheel, but my gaze soon wandered over to Dorothy's picture-perfect house.

Glory's gaze followed my own, and I held her hand a little

more tightly as her trembling intensified. I couldn't help thinking that she was wondering the same thing I was.

If Levi's death was accidental, how had Dorothy known he was buried in the garden?

It had been a day. A long, drawn-out day.

First there had been the news about Levi, which had sent shock waves through the neighborhood. Then, since Glory hadn't been of a mind to work, I'd volunteered to run the stall at the Sweetplace by myself.

I wasn't sure how she'd done it on her own all these years, because I'd been busy from the moment I set up until the moment I broke it all back down. Happily, I'd sold both the furniture flips I'd brought with me—the spice rack Nannette had put in the trash earlier this week and the console table from Chase and Dorothy—along with most of Glory's inventory.

The quick sale of my pieces boosted my hopes that I could refinish furniture as a career. And although I'd planned to launch that career in another town, ever since my time in the closet with Cora Bee yesterday, I found myself questioning whether I should really leave Sweetgrass.

For the first time ever, I felt like I belonged somewhere. The neighbors had accepted me, the Sweetplace regulars always called out a hello, and then there was the garden, where I had fallen in love with nature.

Then there was Cora Bee.

How could I leave her knowing that she was losing Glory, too?

Currently it was a little past ten at night, and we were sitting together on the couch watching *Mamma Mia!*, which we'd both seen a dozen times, while she tried to teach me how to crochet.

She had been as stunned as I was that it had been Levi in the garden, but she hadn't said much about it. I had the feeling she was still processing the matter, trying to decide whether she was sad about his death or not.

Because no matter how he'd died, he'd been a truly terrible man.

"Then you pull the yarn through, like this," she said.

I glanced at her. "What?"

Dropping her hands, she laughed. "I don't know if you're not paying attention or if I'm not making sense because I'm too tired. You know what? It's late and it's been a long day. Let's save the lesson for another time."

I was more than happy for a reprieve. My thoughts were too scattered for a tutorial. "You should go to bed," I said, studying the darkness that rimmed her eyes and the droop in her shoulders from exhaustion.

"So I can lie there with my eyes open? No thanks."

Her insomnia was worrying. I hesitated to suggest a doctor, but she couldn't go on like this much longer. Nothing seemed to be helping, and she had seemingly tried all the tricks and tips. "Well, if we're staying up, how about I make some popcorn?"

"Sounds good."

"Need anything else while I'm up?"

She yawned widely, then said, "Not unless you can magically produce a picture of Bee that I was hoping to give my mother for Mother's Day."

"Sorry," I said. I thought about my gift for Glory, a framed photo of the two of us. I'd hand painted the frame with sunflowers and dandelions that turned out better than I'd ever dreamed possible. In my excitement to give her a gift, I'd already presented her the wrapped package thinking she'd open it straight off, but she'd surprised me by insisting on not opening it until Mother's Day.

"I have a blanket I made her for Christmas. I'll give it to her early."

I placed the popcorn bag in the microwave, set the timer. "You already finished her Christmas present?"

"Don't you remember that before you moved in, I didn't have a social life? I already have a dozen other Christmas presents done, too. Though, I need to make something for Alice. A pillow maybe?"

I leaned against the archway that separated the kitchen from the living room. "She'll love anything you make her. And what about Jamie? What're you thinking for him?"

"I don't know," she said softly.

"Have you forgiven him yet?"

She nodded. "I didn't realize exactly how much I cared about him until I was scared to death yesterday when he was on the road. Since I'm already attached, I might as well see where it takes me, right?"

I smiled. "For what it's worth, I think it's going to take you to good places."

"Well, no one can say I didn't know the risks going in."

"Have you talked to him yet?"

"Not yet. He's staying in Birmingham this weekend, and I'd rather not talk about this over text message."

The microwave dinged, and as I poured the popcorn into a big bowl, a loud blast from outside had me ducking for cover, then running into the living room to look out the front windows.

"Was that a shotgun?" Cora Bee asked, reaching for her crutches. "It was close."

Too close. I hadn't heard gunshots since leaving Louisville.

A second later, her cell phone dinged, then dinged again.

"Oh my God," she said. "Mama texted that Glory's caught herself a burglar. The police are on the way. She says to get over there ASAP."

I knew it was just a matter of time before someone broke in. "Caught a burglar or *shot* a burglar?"

"It says 'caught.'" She crutched to the front door, flung it open.

I followed, my heart racing as the concrete bit into my bare feet. Neighbors were already gathering outside their houses and sirens wailed in the distance.

Cora Bee had gotten so fast on her crutches that it was hard to keep up. As we hurried along Glory's driveway, toward Lillian, who stood on the porch, I noticed someone had stepped on one of the dandelions. It lay limp, its normally bright, cheerful color dull and lifeless.

"What happened?" Cora Bee asked.

Lillian's voice was hard, cold. "Maybe you should ask that question of Emme."

I tore my gaze away from the flower. "Me? Why?"

She gestured farther down the porch, toward the backyard. "Take a look."

I walked to the edge of the porch. Just around the corner, Glory held a shotgun like she handled it every day. It was aimed at a person sitting on one of Glory's rockers, acting as if nothing out of the ordinary was happening.

"There's my girl," my mother said.

My jaw dropped.

Glory, for all her wobbliness, kept the shotgun nice and steady. "Caught her trying to break into Lillian's room."

"I keep telling you, old woman, that I wasn't trying to break in. I thought it was Emme's room. I was simply trying to see my girl on Mother's Day weekend."

It had been seven years since I'd last seen her, but little had changed. She had one of those faces that aged at a snail's pace. A baby face. She'd used that to her advantage, too. There was very little about her to hint that she was a seasoned con woman. Not with the way she dressed—in white jeans, a modest yet feminine green blouse, and wedge sandals. Not in her cloud of curly blond air, big green eyes, and petite frame. She barely wore any makeup. Just a lot of mascara and lip gloss. She knew the stereotypes women like her possessed—the hoochie mama type—and had strived for the complete opposite, appearance-wise. Men tripped over themselves when she asked for help or a ride or a few dollars to buy some groceries.

Her gaze swung to me. "Don't you have some sugar for your mama, you sweet thing?"

I shook my head. I was standing too close as it was with a good three feet between us.

"Have you ever heard of knocking, Kristalle?" Glory asked. "There's a perfectly good front door around the other side of the house."

Glory's delicate floral earrings were glinting in the light, and I saw my mother eyeing them. She'd steal them in a heartbeat if given half a chance.

"It was late. I didn't want to disturb the rest of the house." My mother smiled the smile she always thought was cute. "My bad."

A siren grew louder, then silenced as a police car rolled into the driveway, its lights flashing. I glanced over my shoulder and saw that a crowd had gathered on the sidewalk.

"What are you doing here?" I said, my voice low, harsh.

"What a lovely way to greet your mother. Less than a month in this town and you've already lost your manners."

She made to stand up and Glory said, "Nuh-uh. Stay right there." Glory glanced at me. "She already tried to run off once. Had to give her a warning shot to make her understand I was serious."

"She shouldn't be holding that thing in her old age," my mother said. "I heard she has some health issues. *Bless her heart.*"

"You shouldn't have come here," I said. "No one wants you here."

Her brows snapped downward and her eyes went cold. But before she could say anything, a police officer stepped onto the porch.

"Miss Glory," he said, "I got this now. You can put that gun on down and tell me what happened. Do you know this woman?"

Glory lowered the gun. "I surely do, Dave."

Of course Glory knew the officer. Glory seemed to know everyone.

"Ain't this rich," my mother said. "You callin' the police on *me*. I'm not the one here with a criminal record."

Ah, so she was already firing her own shots.

"I don't have a record," I said. "But Glory already knows about the time one of your boyfriends tried to assault me and I defended myself."

There was a flash of surprise in my mother's eyes before they hardened. She hadn't expected I'd tell the truth about my past and had been hoping to use it against me.

Why was she here? What did she want? Because I knew she wanted something. She always wanted something.

Another police car rolled into the driveway as Dave pulled out a notebook and wrote quickly as Glory explained how Lillian had been asleep when she heard someone trying to open her window. She slipped out of the room, found Glory in the kitchen baking, and called the police. Glory grabbed her shotgun and went outside to investigate, only to find my mother still trying to get the window open.

She was used to being invited into the homes she robbed, rather than breaking in. Apparently her skills were rusty.

The officer put the notebook away. "We can cite her with criminal trespass or take her in for attempted breaking and entering, or we can give her a warning and send her on her way."

My mother always wiggled out of trouble, one way or another. She looked harmless to most, those who couldn't see through her act, her lies. When would she ever be held accountable? I wanted her taken in, charged, locked up, but it wasn't my decision. I couldn't believe she'd come here. Again, I wondered why. I didn't have anything she wanted. No money, no nothing.

Glory stood next to me. "Give her the warning, Dave. Next time, I won't be so generous."

My mother stood up. "Fine. I'll go. And I won't even come back . . . on one condition. I get a minute alone with Emme."

"You don't have to, Emme," Glory said. "If she comes back, she'll be charged."

Charges meant nothing to my mother, and I knew that once she had her sights on something, she rarely veered from her course of action. Currently, her sights were set on me. If I didn't talk to her now, she'd simply find me at the Sweetplace come

Monday or pop up at the grocery store or library when I least expected it. It was best to find out what she wanted now so she could move on.

"*One* minute," I said.

"Ever so gracious." She motioned me into Glory's backyard, to the edge of the patio near an arbor covered in roses. We kept our backs to the porch, but I felt the eyes on me. Once we were clear of eavesdroppers, she whispered, "I see the game you're playing, Emme. Smart. I should've thought of this years ago."

"I'm not playing a game. I'm living my life. And you're not welcome in it."

She laughed. "Too bad I'm already here. I didn't really take them for fools, but since you're still here, they must not have asked you to take a DNA test. And I'm guessing you haven't voluntarily told them you're not Rowan's pride and joy?" She glanced over her shoulder, at the porch where everyone stood watching us. "I wonder what they'd say if they knew the truth? What would they think of you worming your way into their lives? Their *hearts*. Oh dear, I can only imagine. It'd be a shame if they found out. A damn shame."

My stomach rolled. "What do you want?"

"What I always want," she said easily. "Money."

"I don't have any." My piddling savings wasn't the kind of money she was looking for.

"Rowan was rich, Emme. Where'd that money go? Shouldn't it go to his only child?" She squeezed my cheek hard. "I want a cut. I *was* the one who put his name on your birth certificate. I deserve that money."

I slapped her hand away. "Impossible."

"You have one week to make it happen, Emme, or I start talkin'." She smiled that sickly sweet smile again. "I'll be in touch."

She walked off, waving to Glory as she passed by the porch. At the curb, a car pulled up, and I saw a flash of red hair in the light from the streetlamp. Scarlet. My mother pulled open the passenger door, slipped inside, and a moment later the car drove off. She hadn't looked back.

"Emme?" Glory asked.

I made my way back to the porch. Glory, Lillian, and Cora Bee were all waiting on me. Dave the police officer was already walking back to his car. The neighbors were inching inward, waiting for the go-ahead from Glory to swarm her with questions.

Glory said, "What'd she want, hon?"

"Money," I said honestly. "She thought I was living the high life, living here, working a steady job. I set her straight. I don't think she'll be sticking around long."

"Are we supposed to believe you didn't call her?" Lillian asked. "That she miraculously knew where to find you after all these years?"

"Lillian," Glory said sternly. "Enough."

"It's a little too convenient if you ask me," she shot back, holding her ground. "Just when I was starting to think that you might be the real deal, Emme, I'm reminded that you can't be trusted. We don't know who you are at all."

"Enough," Glory said with such anger in her voice that Lillian pressed her lips together.

It was on the tip of my tongue to explain about Scarlet, but ultimately I decided it wouldn't matter. Lillian had already made up her mind.

Trying not to fidget, I waited for Cora Bee to stick up for me, but she kept quiet at her mother's side, studying me as if searching for the truth. Doubt floated in her pretty brown eyes.

I suddenly realized that nothing was ever going to change. Not really. No one was ever going to trust me fully—and they shouldn't.

Because I wasn't being fully honest.

Before I burst into tears, I simply walked away. Once past the open stares of the neighbors, I practically ran all the way back to Cora Bee's house, wishing the whole way there that I'd never stepped foot onto Hickory Lane.

Chapter
23

June 27, 1965: The county engineer came by to examine the sinkhole. He said since it's shallow, only ten feet deep, to fill it with dirt. Will wait to do that until I start work on my big grading and irrigation project later this summer when there will be a tractor here, borrowed from a neighbor. My flower garden is stunning this year. It's small now but I have big plans. One day I hope to sell bouquets at a roadside stand. It'll be nice to have a little money to set aside, too. Money of my own. Levi is still working long hours, and I've all but accepted that there's another woman. There's been talk floating through town about some missing money at the brickyard and how Levi might be involved. I'm not sure what to think other than more often than not these days, I'm happiest when he's not home.

Cora Bee

Emme was avoiding me.

I'd woken up to find the dishwasher emptied, the coffee prepped, and the crossword puzzle book open on the kitchen table next to a note that said she was out in the garage. Her bed had been made, the corners tucked in neatly, but the purple bunny no longer sat in a place of honor in front of the pillows. I didn't see it at all, and my heart broke thinking about her tucking it out of sight.

I didn't blame her for avoiding me. I shouldn't have kept quiet last night when my mother tore her to pieces, and I wished I could go back in time, stand at her side, say *something*, defend her. If there had ever been a time to be strong, to voice my opinion, it was last night. And in all the fuss and confusion, I'd blown the chance.

By now I knew Emme well enough to know when she was barely holding it together, and when she'd seen her mother sitting on Glory's back porch last night, I thought for sure she was going to break clean in half. And even if I didn't know her well, I'd seen her colors shift, the gray turning back to black, and there'd been a burst of indigo blue around her when her mother came into view. *Surprise*, and not the nice variety.

I leaned back in my office chair and rubbed my temples, trying to ease a nasty headache. I hadn't slept a wink last night, and I was running solely on caffeine and determination. For a few blissful hours last night, as I sat with Emme on the couch, my headache had vanished, and I had hoped that maybe I would finally get a good night's sleep.

Then the shotgun blast had brought back the pain full force.

My cell phone rang and I glanced at the readout. My mama was calling. Again.

I dismissed the call without a shred of guilt, even though it was Mother's Day.

Emme was avoiding me, and I was avoiding everyone else.

I'd already texted my mama and Glory earlier today to tell them I wanted some time alone and would see them this afternoon to help prep dinner.

Glory had simply texted back that everything would be okay.

My mama had started calling. Thankfully, she hadn't come over here yet, and I suspected that it was Glory keeping her where she was, telling her to give me time.

Heat flooded my cheeks at the memory of the way my mother had talked to Emme last night. And at how Emme had shouldered it all so gracefully.

Although she had said she'd be in the garage, when I went out there to apologize, the space had been empty. Her supplies were still out, so I knew she hadn't gone far, but the longer I waited around, the more I felt like she was staying away until I left again.

Finally, I'd come back inside to practice my apology a little bit more. I hoped that I wouldn't sob my way through making it and that she'd forgive me.

Last night, my mother had said that we really didn't know Emme at all. Those words had echoed through my head all night, haunting me. Because my mama was wrong. I knew exactly who Emme was. I'd seen who she really was these last few weeks. I'd seen her love for Glory, her care for Dorothy, her work ethic, her thoughtfulness. I'd seen her fear, her bare soul, and I saw the way she had cautiously opened up, like a flower unfolding its petals for the first time.

I let my head fall back, my eyes close. If only I could sleep for a while. Then maybe I could convince my mother to look at Emme the way I did. To see her and not Kristalle. She'd been trying—I had seen her efforts. But then last night had ruined everything.

Eventually, as I sat there with my eyes closed, my thoughts drifted to Jamie. He hadn't yet returned from Birmingham, and I missed him. I missed his smile. His beautiful milky-blue eyes. The way he always seemed to support me physically, with his steady hand, and emotionally, in the way he believed in my design talent.

I wished he were here to talk about the news that it had been my grandfather in the garden, and about what had happened with Kristalle. I wished he were here to hug me. I simply wished he were here.

What do you want, Cora Bee?

Why did the answer to that suddenly seem so clear?

Lifting my head, I rubbed my eyes and glanced at my computer screen.

The only silver lining to my sleepless nights lately was that it allowed my mind to run free with design ideas. It was almost as if I was simply too tired to edit myself, to rein in my crazier concepts. And for some reason, my brain wouldn't stop thinking about the BeeYard. So much so that I'd gotten up in the middle of the night to tweak my design. I'd added an L-shaped open-air extension to the current project that had a domed roof and a series of brick domed structures at the back—open-air stalls that resembled the beehive kilns that had once stood there. I'd labeled this extension "The BeeYard's Sweetplace." Combining the retail area with the Sweetplace was a compromise that benefitted everyone.

Even while I worked on the project, I recognized it was a pointless endeavor, since I was no longer in the design competition. Still, I couldn't have stopped myself if I'd tried. I'd needed to get the design out of my system, see it come to life in the renderings.

Picking up my coffee mug, I found it empty. I didn't even remember drinking it. Deciding that more caffeine was the only way to make it through the rest of this day, I reached for my crutches. I stood, wobbled, and nearly fell over. My arms and legs felt leaden. My eyes drooped. I skipped the coffee pot and went straight to the couch and propped myself up for a nap. Just ten minutes would do me wonders. Ten sweet minutes. I closed my eyes, waited for sleep to take over.

But my mind whirred with thoughts.

About my grandfather and his fate. Had he been chasing Bee when he fell into the sinkhole? Why hadn't anyone found him in the sinkhole when they searched the property? Where was Bee? What was the secret behind the juniper green floaters that lingered around Emme? They hadn't dissipated after she shared her assault with me. Why was my mama so stubborn? I missed Mabel. I should bake peanut butter cookies. Emme's favorite. A peace offering. How had Kristalle known where to find Emme? Would Dorothy ever agree to a retirement home? Would she ever find the picture she had of Bee? Would I ever get a good night's sleep again? Where was Bee? Would we ever find her?

I started counting sheep, then reciting song lyrics in my head, then counting sheep backward. When I couldn't stand lying there anymore, I sat up. My leg under my cast itched, so I used a crochet hook to scratch it and swore under my breath in utter frustration. *I'm so tired.*

I should just get up and make those peanut butter cookies for Emme. Wiley used to love peanut butter cookies, too. Peanut butter anything, really. Especially peanut butter and potato chip sandwiches.

A fuzzy image of Wiley formed in my mind, as if I was starting to forget what he looked like. Tears gathered instantly as I desperately tried to force the picture into focus. To fill in the gaps of the life I was missing out on.

I felt tears rolling down my face. It was clear to me that the pain of losing him would likely never go away. It might fade, like the image of him in my head, but it was now a part of me, same as the scars on my scalp and back. But where there had never been comfort in knowing I wasn't part of his life anymore, today, for some reason, I found some consolation with the knowledge that I'd had seven wonderful years with him. That I'd been a good mom to him. No, a *great* mom to him. Maybe someday, if the stars aligned just right, our paths would cross again. And he'd see in my eyes that I never stopped loving him. And I'd see in his that he'd never forgotten me.

Wiping my eyes, I sat up, took a deep breath, and felt a sense of peace wash over me, one that had been missing from my life for a long time now.

Slowly, I stood and crutched into the kitchen, still a little wobbly and woozy. As I ran water to refill the coffee maker, my gaze fell on the amber bottle on the windowsill. Jamie had asked why I had kept it around if I had no intention of taking the pills. I'd said something about using it as a reminder, but I hadn't been telling the whole truth.

I shut off the water. Picked up the bottle.

I'd kept it because I recognized the relief it held, the power.

I'd kept it because while I wasn't the same woman I was three years ago, the one who had wanted nothing more in the world at that moment than to die, parts of her still existed.

But the thing was, I wasn't even the same woman I was when

this prescription had been filled. I'd made mistakes in my life-time, yes, but now I recognized that my whole life shouldn't be defined by them. My questionable choices didn't make me a bad person.

The amazing thing about life was the ability to constantly re-invent yourself. To change. To evolve. To learn. To heal. To make new friends. To fall in love. To *grow*.

I'd seen it firsthand with Emme. Now I could see it in myself.

After opening the bottle, I stared at the little pills and then tipped the container upside down into the sink. I turned the wa-ter on, then the garbage disposal, and let my past go.

Emme

I was hiding. Again.

Old habits died hard. Real hard.

I'd worked on my furniture flips most of the morning in Cora Bee's garage with the door closed, shutting myself off from the rest of the world. When I couldn't take the paint fumes any longer, I had taken a break and walked the woods behind Cora Bee's house. I lost myself in the scent of the earth, the rustle of the leaves.

It was almost two in the afternoon now, and I was expected at Glory's soon for supper. Honestly, I should be there now, helping with the preparation of the meal. Fixin' dessert. We'd talked about me making a cobbler this week, but I couldn't stand to be in that kitchen with the way I was feeling right now, beneath the knowing watch of those shimmery bees and Lil-lian's discerning gaze.

My emotions were scraped raw. I was barely holding myself together. Guilt was eating me from the inside out. I couldn't keep lying to Glory, to Cora Bee. But if I told them the truth, I'd have to leave Sweetgrass immediately, walk away in shame.

All I'd ever wanted was a loving family. For a blissful while, I'd gotten one. Leaving them was going to be the hardest thing I'd ever done in my life.

Knowing I couldn't put off the inevitable indefinitely, I'd finally gone back into the house to clean up for dinner, grateful to find that Cora Bee wasn't there. She'd left a note on the kitchen table that she'd gone over to Glory's house, as if I didn't know where to find her. The note had been sitting on top of a plate of peanut butter cookies and was signed *Love, Cora Bee.* There was a PS that said the cookies were a peace offering and that she was sorry, so very sorry.

Another piece of my heart broke off.

After washing up, I took a second to look at myself in the mirror. I'd come to Sweetgrass wanting to become a better person. A bigger person. The version of me I'd always wanted to be, had I ever been given half a chance. Now I knew that the only way to do that was to say goodbye to the people I'd come to love.

In doing so, I also took the power away from my mother to do any more harm around here. We'd both move on, hopefully far, far away from each other.

Tonight, I'd talk to Glory and Cora Bee, tell them everything, and then head to the bus station. I'd already packed my suitcase, listening to it telling me "I told you so" over and over again the whole time.

I ought to march myself over to Glory's and confess right now, but sharing one last meal with them, one last supper, was too much of a gift for me to pass up.

Once I stepped outside, however, I gave in to the strong desire to wander into the garden for a few minutes. I picked suckers off Dorothy's tomato plants, said hello to my budding flowers, telling them I'd be leaving soon and that Glory would take over caring for them. Lastly, I sat on the ledge of the gazing pool, feeling the fern fronds brush against my calves. I closed my eyes. An airplane flew high overhead, a lawn mower droned on from down the street, a dog barked.

What am I listening to?

Life, Emme. Life.

I opened my eyes and gazed down at the water in time to see a bee skim its surface. A cloud drifted in front of the sun, changing the light, and the burbling quieted. A milky image appeared in the water, and at first I had no idea what I was seeing. Gradually the image became sharper, clearer.

It was a living room. Two sofas sat in an L-shape, and next to a low wooden coffee table, a baby, a year old or so, sat on the floor. She was crying. A man was yelling, his face florid as he gestured wildly. In one hand he held a lit cigarette, in the other a short glass of amber liquid. It was the same man who'd knocked over the bee boxes, dressed the same way as well. Dark trousers and a white T-shirt. Levi, I assumed, and I immediately knew I was watching this scene from Bee's eyes. She was sitting on the couch, a hand held to her face, and when she pulled it away, blood covered her fingers.

Levi kept yelling, motioning toward the screaming baby, his anger making him look like a monster. He threw his glass against the fireplace, where it shattered, making the baby cry even louder. Then he tossed his cigarette at Bee, who ducked out of its way. He surged toward the baby, his hands fisted. Bee leaped up and grabbed the little girl, cradling her protectively, and Levi came after them both. She dodged his punch, and when he lost his balance after throwing it, she shoved him. He toppled back over the coffee table. Fury lit his features, making them glow red as he tried to scramble to his feet.

Bee ran. She ran toward the front door, stopping only for a brief second in the hallway to grab her handbag, which sat on a console table in the entryway. In the mirror above the table, I saw her face for the briefest moment, and I nearly cried at the sight of the blood, the swelling, the panic in her eyes.

She dashed into the night, practically throwing the baby through an open window of a car parked in a circular driveway, then tossing her handbag in next. But before she could get inside, lock the doors, Levi came flying out of the house. She fled on foot, around the house, into the moonlit night, toward the garden. Just beyond the gazing pool, she stopped to hide behind the live oak tree in order to catch her breath. Her chest heaved.

Using the cover of the tree, she looked behind her, and I wanted to scream to never look back.

In the murkiness of the night, a dark silhouette moved steadily across the backyard toward her, illuminated by the golden glow of the lights from inside the house and the brightness of a full moon. It was as if he knew exactly where she was hidden.

Bee looked down at her feet. They were bare, cut, and I wondered if she'd twisted an ankle. When she looked back at Levi, he was glancing over his shoulder, toward the house. When he faced front again, there was panic in his eyes and fear etched into his face. He started to run faster but kept looking over his shoulder.

I squinted, trying to see what he was seeing, but I realized the scene was fading away. The clouds shifted once again, and the water offered up its sympathies with soft burbles.

My heart thumped wildly. As I waited for my pulse to calm, I could hear Glory telling me that the gazing pool didn't show the past to just anyone. It had to be someone special. Someone worthy.

I had no idea why it had shown me what happened the night Bee had disappeared.

I wasn't worthy. I wasn't special.

I was just Emme, and I didn't really know who I was anymore.

Chapter
24

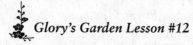 *Glory's Garden Lesson #12*

Oh! Look at your bed, hon. It's coming right along, isn't it? Your anemones are trying to outshine all the others, aren't they? Usually they're so meek, but these are cheeky little darlings. If you can't tell by those delicate rosette faces, they're related to ranunculus. So you know charm is in their genetic makeup. But did you know they represent anticipation? And it's also said that anemones are protection plants that ward off evil and ill will. *Huh*. Maybe with your mother in town, we should plant a few more? Certainly can't hurt, and this kind of protection is a sight easier on the ears than a shotgun blast. I'll get the shovel.

Emme

Sunday supper had been oddly lively, full of false cheer. It was as if everyone, except me, was going out of their way not to talk about the night before, not to talk about me. No doubt Glory was behind this merry show, her way of trying to protect me. But behind the forced laughs, the exaggerated stories, I felt the sideways looks. The curiosity. I hadn't been able to eat a single bite. I'd simply pushed my food around my plate and kept my mouth shut, even though May and Cora Bee had tried hard to draw me into conversation. When I saw the frame I'd gifted Glory sitting proudly on the mantel with the other family photos it had taken everything in me not to start sobbing.

When the time came for clearing the table, I jumped up to

volunteer, ready to be away from the rest of them, to settle my stomach, to not feel so *naked*. To hide. Yet again.

Chase volunteered to help as well. After following me into the kitchen, he set down the stack of plates he'd carried in and quietly said, "No one but Lillian thinks you knew."

I almost smiled at him jumping straight to the point without any sugarcoating, but I couldn't quite. "It doesn't matter."

"I think it does."

Tears stung my eyes and I blinked them away. "It really doesn't."

I was leaving. This would all be behind me soon. Painful memories. Important lessons.

He leaned a hip against the counter as I rinsed dishes and then set them into the dishwasher. "I wanted to thank you."

"For?"

"For protecting Dotty yesterday when Bob showed up."

Chase hadn't sugarcoated with me, so I didn't with him. "Did she say anything about knowing Levi was buried out there?"

"No. Once I got her home, she napped for a bit and then woke up not even remembering being out in the garden that morning. I took her to see my parents over in Dothan, spend the day with them. I don't know how hard to push."

I glanced at him, saw the fear in his eyes.

He crossed his arms. "My job is to uncover the truth, but now I'm not so certain I want to know what happened."

If he didn't know the details, he wouldn't have to report it if Dorothy had done something criminal. "How will all this fit into your book?"

"I'm not sure yet. All I know is that it's hitting a little too close to home for my comfort."

I rinsed another plate and wondered why no one had ventured into the kitchen to check on us. It was probably another one of Glory's edicts at work. I could almost hear her telling everyone to leave us be. I was going to miss her something fierce.

He bumped my arm with his elbow. "I'm worried about you."

I forced a smile. "Me? Why?"

He narrowed his eyes, those lovely eyes of his. "You're not fooling me."

"I've never been able to, have I?"

"You didn't stand a chance, not with Orville around. He's the ultimate judge of character. He can sniff out a good soul a mile off."

I looked at him, his face blurry from my tears. I was about to tell him the truth, but Glory swept into the kitchen, and I looked away, toward the wallpaper with the shimmery bees.

"I think it's time to break out the dessert," she said in a chirpy tone. "Chase, hon, can you slice up this Italian cream cake for me?"

"Sure can," he said, picking up a big knife, but his gaze never wavered from me.

I set the last plate into the dishwasher and dried my hands on a kitchen towel printed with chickens. "Glory, I think I'll skip dessert. I'm not feeling very well. I'm going to go lie down for a while, but I'll be back later on. I have something I want to talk to you about."

She stepped up to me, cupped my face. "Could you stay a little while longer? I have an announcement to make, and I'd like you to be here for it."

I glanced at the door, at freedom.

"Please?" Glory added.

I never could say no to her. "All right."

For Glory, I would do just about anything. Which was why I picked up two dessert plates to take into the dining room, set them in front of Dorothy, who'd patted my hand, and Nannette, who gave me a wan smile, and then sat down, feeling like the biggest phony that had ever lived.

Cora Bee

I watched Emme walk back to the table, her head held high, her eyes glittery with unshed tears. When I first saw her today, when she finally showed up for supper, I'd noticed the black floaters had faded once again to a light gray now that her mother wasn't in the vicinity. She'd healed so much in the time she'd been in Sweetgrass. However, her juniper green floaters were pulsing with anxious energy, and there was now periwinkle blue in the mix as well, which represented sadness or grief.

I wanted to wrap her in a big hug and tell her I was sorry until she heard me. Really heard me.

As soon as Glory returned to the table and proclaimed she had an announcement to make, my mama reached for the wine bottle in the middle of the table and said, "I have the feeling I'm going to need more wine to hear this. Cora Bee?" she asked, holding up the bottle. "I noticed you had Coke with dinner. Are you ready to switch to something a little more comforting?"

"No, thanks," I said.

"Still taking that medication?" Mama asked, worry creasing the fine lines in her forehead.

I gripped the napkin in my lap tightly, looked her straight in the eye, and tried to keep my composure. "No, Mama. Actually, I've never taken any of the pain meds that had been prescribed for me for my broken foot. Only over-the-counter ibuprofen. And I don't drink alcohol anymore."

Mama's eyebrows shot upward and bursts of indigo popped around her. "I don't understand. Since when?"

I glanced around, found all eyes on me. I could do this. Jamie had shown me how easy it was. "Since after my car accident when I turned to alcohol and pain pills to help me feel nothing at all. It took a long time for me to realize that I couldn't heal *without* feeling the pain, so I stopped. And that's when I truly started healing."

Mama blinked.

Under the table, I felt a hand squeeze mine. Emme. I squeezed back and didn't let her hand go, so grateful that she'd reached out to me, that she hadn't judged me for my confession.

"I . . . I," my mama stammered, tears in her eyes. "I didn't know."

"I didn't tell you, and I'm sorry about that. I am. But I was scared. You're a mite bit judgmental, if you haven't noticed."

"I noticed," Dorothy said from her end of the table.

Nannette hushed her, then sighed.

Dorothy *tsk*ed.

I pushed on. "And if I'd told you, you would've swooped in and tried to fix it all, when the only person who could do that was me. Plus—"

"There's *more*?" Mama interrupted, eyes wide with dismay.

"*Plus*," I went on, "you tend to see only what you want to see, so it was easy to hide. But now, I'm tired of hiding the person I've become. I am who I am. So no, I wouldn't like any wine."

I glanced at Aunt Glory, who was smiling at me. She said, "We all have our secrets. There's not a one of us at this table who doesn't have something they'd rather keep to themselves. Maybe one day those secrets will be shared; maybe they won't. And if they're not, I don't see any harm in that if those secrets aren't hurting anyone."

I hadn't realized it, but my secrets *had* been hurting me, and I was finally glad to be free of them. Most of them, anyway. I wasn't sure I'd ever be able to share with my mama about the car accident. Maybe one day. Maybe.

"Was that your big announcement, Glory?" Dorothy asked with an aggrieved sniff. "If so, the buildup was better than the reveal. I was on the edge of my seat, expectin' something juicy. I'm disappointed. Real disappointed. No kidding we all have secrets." She blew a raspberry.

I glanced at Chase, but he was staring at his cake as though he were seeking guidance from the frosting.

"No," Aunt Glory said, drawing the word out. "That wasn't my announcement, but I thought it fit to be said. Now. I consider you all family, and this is a family matter."

Next to me, I felt Emme stiffen.

Across the table, I saw my mama reach for her wineglass, then put it back down on the table. Her gaze shifted to me, her eyes twin pools of remorse.

Aunt Glory said, "I wanted you all to know I've made a change to my will to include Emme. She'll inherit all I inherited from Rowan's considerable estate, since it was rightly hers in the first place. And I'm leaving her my stake in the Sweetplace. The rest of my estate will be divided between Lillian, Cora Bee, and Cain."

This announcement came as no surprise to my mother and me, since we'd known from the beginning that Aunt Glory's big plan included Emme taking over the Sweetplace eventually. But everyone else at the table had wide eyes and dropped jaws.

Emme was shaking, and she pulled her hand from mine. "No," she said, her voice weak.

"Please don't put up a fuss, Emme. It's already done."

Emme stood, held on to the table as if questioning the strength of her legs. "Can you undo it?"

"It's rightfully yours, hon. Rowan would've willed his estate to you if he knew where to find you. I promised him I'd find you, make it right. And I've seen you come alive at the Sweetplace. Aren't you happy there?"

"I can't . . ." she began, then stopped.

The green floaters around her grew and grew, nearly obliterating all the other colors.

"I came here," she said, looking solely at Aunt Glory, "because I wanted to start a new life. I wanted roots. I wanted a family to love, and to be loved by a family. But the truth of the matter is that you weren't mine to love. I was fourteen years old when my mother told me that Rowan wasn't my real father. I don't know who is. I don't know who I am. But I do know you're not my family, and I can't take your money, and I can't stay in Sweetgrass. I'm leaving tonight. I've already packed."

Silence fell across the room. It seemed even the outdoor noises had gone quiet as if the birds and bugs had been taken by surprise, too.

"Now *that's* an announcement," Dorothy said, slapping her hand on the table.

"*Dotty*," Chase warned.

I glanced at my mother, who was still watching me with deep sadness in her eyes. I was waiting for her to say she'd been right all along, and I was stunned when she kept silent.

"I'm sorry," Emme said as tears rolled down her cheeks, dripped off her chin.

Glory drew herself up and said loudly, "*Hogwash.*"

Emme wiped her cheeks. "I really am sorry. I love you and Cora Bee and I never meant to hurt you, not ever, but you need to know the truth . . ."

"No, no," Aunt Glory said with a flurry of hand gestures, "it's hogwash that you're not Rowan's child."

"But—"

"Who are you going to believe, Emme Wynn? Your mama or me? Because I don't have a single doubt you're my granddaughter. Not one single one. Never have. It's true that except for your freckles you don't resemble him much, but I see him in you clear as day. I see it in the way you love animals; I see it in the way you don't mind getting your hands dirty. I see it in the way you love peanut butter. I see it in a hundred little ways. You're ours, plain and simple."

"I think so too," I said, jumping in. "I've thought so from the first day I met you, when you touched the wallpaper in the kitchen. You're connected to this land same as me, as Mama, as Aunt Glory. There's a thread between us."

"I think you're Rowan's, too," Nannette said, and May beamed at her. "Oh, I know I had my doubts at first, but I soon saw the truth of it. Rowan had such an artistic eye. Remember how he used to rip apart old toasters and things to make steampunk art? Emme's got that talent in her. An ability to see something beautiful in what someone else would throw away."

"My mother had no reason to lie," Emme said faintly.

"Seems to me lying is like breathing to her. The shocking thing would be if she told you the *truth,*" Aunt Glory said.

My mama coughed and said, "I might be able to shed a little light on this situation."

All eyes turned to her.

She looked at Emme. "I owe you an apology, first and foremost. Cora Bee is perfectly right when she said I like to see only what I want to see. In you, I only wanted to see your mother. I couldn't get past the misery she put this family through when she took off with you, or the pain she caused me by pretending to be my friend. I was wrong to judge you, and I'm sorry. But while I was desperate to prove you were just like your mother, I did something for which I'm not real proud."

"Mama, oh no. What did you do?" I asked her.

Mama pulled her shoulders back. "I stole Emme's DNA."

Dorothy slapped the table again, and Chase quickly covered her hand with his own and didn't let it go.

"You did *what*?" Aunt Glory asked.

"And I stole yours, too," Mama said evenly.

Oh Lord.

"I took dental floss from Emme's bathroom trash can, and I took hair from your brush, Aunt Glory, since a DNA link would be strongest between the two of you. You see, I want the truth as much as anyone. Last Wednesday, I sent the samples to a lab that does DNA tests. It takes a little longer for the test because it's not the usual mouth swab, so I haven't gotten the results yet. They're due to arrive tomorrow morning by nine. We'll know then whether Emme is related to us."

To *us*.

I met her gaze and could easily read the apology in her eyes.

I hoped that when she looked at me, she saw my heart and all the love it held for her.

"Like I said, I have no doubts," Aunt Glory said, standing firm in her opinion. "I already know. But since I can see Emme is still worried, perhaps the test will lay all questions to rest. So you can't leave tonight, Emme. Not until you know the truth. Promise me you won't leave until you see the results."

Emme's watery gaze didn't waver from Aunt Glory's face, but I could practically see the battle she was waging internally.

Finally, she said, "I promise."

Aunt Glory beamed. "That's a good girl. Now good gracious, can we eat some cake?"

Emme dropped back down into her seat, and this time I reached over and took her hand in mine. She didn't look my way. Only kept staring at her plate.

By tomorrow morning, we'd know the truth.

Which gave me less than a day to convince her to stay here in Sweetgrass, even if the result of the DNA test proved that her mother had been telling the truth for once in her life.

Chapter
25

August 24, 1965: When I got home from the market earlier, I noticed that Lillian had a new bruise on her arm. Levi says she fell. Maybe she had, but he'd started drinking after I left, even after promising he wouldn't, and when he's drinking he's . . . not himself. These days, he's been drinking a lot. There's been some trouble at the brickyard, big trouble, regarding that missing money. The police are involved now. Levi's suddenly talking about moving away, and I know I have some big decisions to make. I can't stop crying. My heart is broken. I thought when we married and moved here to Sweetgrass that I was living my dreams, but now it feels like my life has become a nightmare.

Emme

Monday morning came wrapped in a dreamlike mist. It hovered lazily over Hickory Lane, over me, and glowed goldenly as the sun tried its best to break through the haze.

It seemed fitting, this mist. It matched the fogginess in my head, the confusion, the hope, the fear.

Trying to pretend like everything was normal, perfectly normal, I'd sat with Cora Bee at breakfast. But I hadn't been able to eat, my stomach too anxious for what lay ahead today. My suitcase remained packed, and I had the phone number of a taxi company in my pocket.

I'd lain awake most of the night thinking I should leave in the

cover of darkness, sneak away. It would be so much easier on
everyone if we didn't have to say goodbye.

That, however, was something the old me would do. Not the
new. I'd stay. I'd see this through. I'd promised.

I tried to sleep, but I'd been restless. For some reason I kept
seeing the image of Bee running out of the house the night she
disappeared. It flashed again and again in my head until I simply
couldn't bear looking at it anymore. Why had the gazing pool
revealed it to me? What was I supposed to see? Learn?

At some point during the dark hours, while my night-light
glowed, I'd allowed myself to imagine for the briefest moment
that I really was Glory's granddaughter. Last night, she and
Cora Bee and Nannette had half convinced me it was truly possible. Probable, even. So I let myself feel that happiness, that
euphoria. But only for a moment.

It was best if I prepared for the worst, so I wouldn't fall to
pieces in front of everyone if I wasn't a Wynn after all. I'd give
hugs and kisses and move on, going wherever the wind blew
me. I was a dandelion, after all. The very picture of survival,
resilience, and determination.

"You'll stay no matter what, right?" Cora Bee had said as we
bent our heads over the crossword puzzle at the breakfast table.
"You have to stay, Emme."

"I couldn't."

"Why not?"

"It's not right."

"Who says?" she'd challenged, a fierce look in her clear eyes.
She'd finally slept well last night. Confession had been good
for her soul.

"Family doesn't have to be blood," she said. "Families are
stitched together with love. And we love you, Emme, and you
love us. It's that simple. You're my best friend, even if you might
not be my cousin. Don't you see? You *have* planted roots here,
and you're blooming, so why *not* stay?"

Why not stay?

I hadn't had a good answer for her, especially now that all my secrets had been laid bare. The question had stuck with me all morning, and I carried it along with a rustically wrapped package as I walked the sidewalk, feeling like I was tripping over my heart with each step.

Since Glory had canceled our workday at the Sweetplace, I had time on my hands this morning, and I had a delivery to make. I supposed I could've mailed the package, but I wanted to deliver it in person, just in case today was the day I had to say goodbye.

The light mist drifted around me, brushing my skin with pearly sparkles as I turned onto a brick walkway that led to the steps of a wraparound porch of a large cottage, painted pale gray green with creamy trim. The holes in the lawn had been filled in, and new grass had sprouted. It, too, glistened in the mist.

Before I could even knock, the door swung open, and a man dressed in jeans and a white T-shirt leaned against the doorjamb and didn't even try to hide the pleasure in his eyes at seeing me.

We'd come a long way, Chase and me, since the first time we'd laid eyes on each other.

Just seeing him lifted my mood, lightened it as if he were suddenly carrying some of the weight for me. Orville came racing onto the porch with a stuffed frog in his mouth, his tail wagging, his brown eyes as welcoming as they'd ever been. He'd been my first friend on Hickory Lane.

"What have you there?" I asked him, playfully tugging on the stuffed frog.

Orville bit the toy and it squeaked, which made me laugh as I gave his head a good petting.

"What have *you* got there?" Chase asked me, nodding to my hand.

I held up the bandanna-wrapped gift. It had taken everything within me to return his bandanna—I'd wanted so badly to keep it. "It's for you."

He took it from me, closing his fingers around the package protectively. "Do you have some time for a cup of coffee? I just made a fresh pot."

"I don't want to bother you and Dorothy. I just wanted to drop that off before . . ."

I didn't know how to finish the sentence.

"You're never a bother, Emme. Come on in."

He closed the door behind me as I stepped past him. Somewhere in the house a TV blared loudly with the chatter of a morning talk show.

Chase put his hand on the small of my back, and I was beyond proud that I hadn't flinched at the touch. In fact, I liked it. A little too much, perhaps. He steered me to the left, through a set of double doors that led into a dark-paneled office filled with shelves stuffed with books and knickknacks. A massive wooden desk sat facing the front windows, and a computer monitor glowed with a screen saver picture of Orville as a puppy. My heart melted.

"Dotty fell asleep watching her morning shows, though how she can sleep with the volume that high is a mystery I've yet to solve. Especially since she has better hearing than any of us." He set the gift on a low table in front of a loveseat. "How do you like your coffee?"

"With a little cream or milk," I said, thinking of how Cora Bee would grin if she'd heard me say so. She'd ruined black coffee for me forever.

"Have a seat. I'll be right back." Orville followed him out of the room, his nails clacking on the wood floors.

I sat on the loveseat beneath wide double windows, careful not to knock over any of the books or papers balanced on its arms. My gaze swept the room, trying to take in every detail. Finally, it landed on a side table where a thick Merriam-Webster dictionary sat. It sparked a memory, and I picked up the large book. The book's binding was loose, a sign that it was well used, and as I flipped through the pages, I heard Dorothy's voice in my head muttering about a no-account, no-good rapscallion. I let the musty scent of the old book fill my senses as I thumbed through the pages, and once I hit the *ra*'s, I dragged my finger down the lines.

A rapscallion was apparently a person who causes trouble, a ne'er-do-well.

From what I knew of Levi, the term fit, though I could think of a few other words that would suit him better. Miscreant. Degenerate. Reprobate. Monster.

Again, in my mind's eye, I saw Bee running out of the house. Saw her panic in the mirror. *Felt* it. Why was it haunting me? As far as I was concerned, Levi had found himself a big pit of earthy karma when he stepped into that hole.

Because I didn't want to dwell on him at the moment, I gave my head a good shake and flipped through the dictionary to another word that had been on my mind lately.

Pluck.

The dictionary's definition read, "The strength of mind that enables a person to endure pain or hardship."

"You think I have pluck?" I'd once asked Glory.

Her eyes had sparkled. "You're here, aren't you?"

Why not stay?

With emotion swelling in my throat, I closed the dictionary and set it on the table in front of me just as Chase and Orville came back into the room. As Chase handed a mug to me and set his on the table, Orville jumped up next to me, turned once, and sat down. He still had the frog in his mouth.

"I don't think so, buddy." Chase snapped his fingers and pointed to the floor.

Orville looked at me with his soulful eyes, and I laughed. "I'm going to stay out of this one."

"Down, Orville," Chase said, his voice laced with humor. "You have a perfectly nice bed over there."

My gaze went to the dog bed by the side of the desk, which was chock-full of toys. Reluctantly, Orville stepped down and plopped onto his bed, letting out a huff of air as he did so. He let go of the frog, laid his head on it, and stared at us as if we'd completely and utterly betrayed him.

"I almost want to give him my seat now."

"Don't be fooled by those eyes of his." Chase grabbed a dog

biscuit from a container on the desk and gave it to Orville, who started thumping his tail against the floor. "That c-o-o-k-i-e was what he was really after."

I smiled as he spelled the word. "Smart, smart dog." I sipped the coffee. "Thanks for this. It's good."

"I live on coffee, so I try to buy the best."

The soft cushion dipped as he sat next to me, and I suddenly listed toward him, trying not to spill my coffee as I nearly fell into his lap. "Whoa!"

His strong hands were there, catching me, as if he knew all along I was going to topple.

He laughed. "I really want to make a joke about you throwing yourself at me, but I have the feeling you wouldn't appreciate it."

A blush warmed my cheeks as our thighs pressed against each other. I could feel his body heat on my bare leg as it blazed through the fabric of his jeans. "I might."

Yes, we'd come a long way.

I set the mug on the table, tugged down the hem of my shorts. "You'd be horrified to know how much instant coffee I've drunk in my lifetime."

"I've had my fair share, trust me." He picked up his mug and nodded toward the dictionary. "Were you doing a little light reading?"

"One can never know too many words, am I right?"

"Agreed. Yet somehow when I'm writing, I tend to use the same ones over and over again."

I glanced around, trying to take in every detail. "Is this room where you do all your writing?"

"Since I've been living here, yes. It was my grandfather's study. Dotty loves that it's being used again."

I wanted to keep asking him questions, about his life, his writing, his family, but I recognized this wasn't the best time or place. Maybe later if . . .

I picked up my mug again, took a sip, and ignored the heat I still felt on my leg.

"Before I forget," he said, "Dotty finally found a couple of pictures of Bee. Better late than never, right? Remind me to give them to you before you leave."

"Can I see them now?"

I was so curious to see what Bee looked like without being battered and bruised.

He hesitated only a moment before leaning forward to pick up a small envelope from the corner of his desk. With a look in his eyes I couldn't quite decipher, he handed it over.

I put my mug down and peeked into the envelope. There were two small photos inside, both faded in color and trimmed with scalloped edges. The first one was of Bee standing in front of a grandstand, holding up a blue ribbon. I flipped the photo over. *Bee Gipson, 1st place peach cobbler. Baldwin County Fair. 1964.*

I turned the photo around again and studied the face of Cora Bee's grandmother. She didn't look much like the woman I'd seen in the waters of the gazing pool. Her slender face was unmarred, her blue eyes open and bright. Her light hair was pulled back in a ponytail. She smiled broadly, revealing a chipped tooth, and I wondered if Levi had broken that, too. She was utterly lovely, and it was easy to see that Cora Bee had her nose, that darling little button nose.

The next photo was of four people, two men and two women. The men had their arms around the women, anchoring them to their sides. Only, the man who held Bee seemed to be holding extra tightly, and it was easy to see the pain in her eyes. The man was the same one I'd seen in the gazing pool, and I was surprised his eyes weren't glowing red in the photo as well, him being the monster that he was.

The photo seemed to have been taken at some sort of social event. They were dressed nicely, and in the background were tables topped with fancy place settings and big flower arrangements. I flipped the picture over. It read, *Dorothy and Gil, Levi and Bee.*

Turning it around, this time I studied Dorothy and Gil. Chase resembled his grandfather in coloring—that sandy light-brown hair and tanned skin. They shared similar eyes, filled with shiny curiosity.

Dorothy's smile lit the room, and you could tell solely from the picture that she had a big personality. The style of her fluffy hair was the same as it was now, except for the color. Back then she'd been a brunette. She wore a shiny shirtwaist dress, cinched in tight at her tiny waist, and blue heels.

In my head, I heard Chase's voice clear as day.

The person doing the shoveling was a woman. I saw her hands, her feet. She was wearing a skirt and low blue heels.

I wanted to believe the heels were a coincidence, but I didn't.

As I tucked the photos back into the envelope, I said, "I'll make sure Cora Bee gets these. Thank you."

I turned to see that he'd been watching my face the whole time, and I had little doubt he'd seen me realize that in all likelihood Dorothy had been shoveling dirt on Levi after he fell in the sinkhole. I didn't know how she knew he was there or why she was covering him up, and I didn't need to.

I gave him a faint smile, unsure what to say. Finally, I said, "We all have our secrets. Now, open your present. I've got to be gettin' back soon."

Gratitude flared in his eyes as he set down his mug and picked up the gift. He held it between both hands, letting it rest there as if he was measuring the weight of its meaning. "Why does this feel like a goodbye present, Emme?"

Because I desperately needed something to hold so I wouldn't reach out and touch his face and tell him what his friendship had meant to me, I picked up my mug and held it tightly. "It's more a thank-you gift. For the loan of your bandanna."

"I'm glad to hear that. I didn't want it to mean goodbye."

Why not stay?

Slowly, his fingers untied the loose knot I'd fashioned and the fabric fell open to reveal four folded cotton handkerchiefs tied together with a thin piece of twine.

"For the best gentleman I've ever known," I said, my voice breaking on the last word.

He ran the pad of his thumb over the soft cloths, then set the bundle on the table and took the mug from my hands and put it down, too.

Before I knew it, his arms were wrapped around me in a tight hug, his cheek resting gently on the top of my head. My cheek was pressed to his chest, where it was easy to hear the rapid beat of his heart.

"Please don't go, Emme. No matter what happens, don't go."

It was hard to talk over the lump in my throat. "I don't know if I can stay if I don't know who I am."

"A last name doesn't define you. Your heart does, your actions do."

"I lied to everyone . . ."

"You don't know that yet. Could be you were telling the truth."

"I'm embarrassed."

"Embarrassment fades. Anyone who's taken the time to get to know you knows exactly who you are. They love you for who you are."

Pulling back, he looked into my eyes and wiped the tears that had fallen onto my cheeks. I saw his heart in his eyes, his hopes, and I knew he was seeing the same in mine.

He leaned in a little, then paused, and I could see the question there, too. *Can I kiss you?*

I gave a slight nod and leaned in to meet his lips halfway.

There was a noise in the hallway, and I surely wouldn't have heard it if Orville hadn't lifted his head and rattled his dog tags.

Chase and I both turned our heads in time to see Dorothy shuffle into the room. Orville wagged his tail at the sight of her.

"What's all this?" she asked, swirling her hands at us. "I doze off for two seconds and you two get all lovey-dovey?"

"I'm just trying to convince Emme to stay in Sweetgrass," Chase said.

His cheeks had reddened, which I suddenly found adorable.

"Well, of course she's staying," Dorothy said. "Don't be a

twit. But carry on convincing her. It's been a long time since there was a little lovey-dovey in this house. A long damn time."

She pivoted and shuffled off.

He dropped his head and let out a half laugh, half sigh.

I reached for his chin, lifted it, and leaned in. "Didn't you hear the woman? Carry on."

Chapter
26

 *Glory's Garden Lesson #13*

Cornflowers shouldn't be confused with coneflowers, though sometimes my tongue gets tangled up in the names these days. The charming blue cornflowers represent young men in love, which is why they're also called bachelor buttons. The legend is that bachelors would wear cornflowers as boutonnieres when courting, and if the flower wilted, it was a sign that his love wasn't returned. *Hmm*. Seems to me there are a couple of bachelors here on Hickory Lane who'd be wearing the perkiest cornflower boutonnieres you ever did see. Don't roll your eyes at me. The sass! You know I'm not wrong.

Cora Bee

On the front porch, I balanced on my crutches and watched Emme walk down the sidewalk carrying that sweet gift she'd picked up for Chase, wondering if he'd have better luck convincing her to stay than I'd had.

Over the last few weeks, I'd seen the way he looked at her. Heard the way she talked about him. There was something between them. A seed that only needed a little time and care in order to sprout into something strong and beautiful.

I was about to sit down to do a little rocking in the cool morning mist, when I heard a bark and saw Mabel racing down the sidewalk. Jamie jogged after her. He wasn't calling her name, because it was clear he knew where she was going.

My heart leaped around my chest as I crutched to the porch

door and pulled it open just in time for Mabel to race up the steps. She threw her front paws on my stomach, and I wobbled but held steady.

"Did you miss me?" I asked her, trying to give her as many pets and rubs as I could without falling over. She licked my arm and jumped to lick my chin. "I'll take that as a yes."

"Mabel, *down*," Jamie said on a heavy sigh, sounding just like Alice again.

I loved how alike they sounded when exasperated.

I loved them.

It scared me, because it was all too fast, too soon. But then I thought about my parents' relationship and realized that maybe I'd gotten my love at first sight after all—that jolt when I first met him. The one that had made me string caution tape around my heart. I'd just been too blind to recognize it for what it was at the time.

He stood at the foot of the stairs, and as Mabel ran between the two of us, I simply had no idea how she had so much energy. I said, "I didn't realize you were home. I didn't see your truck or I would've been knocking on your door."

He glanced over his shoulder, toward his house. "Got in an hour ago. I guess I pulled up a little farther than usual. The house is blocking my truck. How long were you looking?"

I held his gaze, shrugged, and gave him a what-are-you-waiting-for smile. "Every couple of hours for two and a half days."

He took the steps two at a time, and as he pulled me into his arms, I let go of the door and it slammed shut on our argument.

"Mabel's not the only one who missed you," he said.

"She's certainly better at showing it."

He rested his forehead against mine, and his voice was low as he said, "I thought I blew it with you. I'm so sorry."

"You asked me what I wanted the other day," I said.

"Cora Bee, you don't have to say anything. I was being pushy, rushing you. I'm just happy knowing you've forgiven me. Everything else can wait. We've got time."

I let him finish then said, "Ask me again."

One of his eyebrows lifted as he pulled back and studied my face, and I wasn't quite sure what it was that he'd seen to make his voice go hoarse with emotion as he asked, "What do you want, Cora Bee?"

"I want *us*. Today, tomorrow, always."

⤹ ⤸

"So, is he *your Jamie* now?" my mama asked not long after Jamie had left for an emergency meeting with his investors.

I'd taken a chance and shown him my design for the BeeYard, and he'd smiled ear to ear the whole time I'd explained the inspiration behind my work. He'd taken my renderings with him to the meeting, and it remained to be seen whether they would be embraced as wholeheartedly by his investors. As for the competition, Jamie decided not to cancel it outright. The bit I'd seen in the contest's legal fine print, about there being no guarantee the winning design would be implemented, would come into play if the investors approved the plans for the BeeYard, and if they didn't, then there would still be a need for a concept.

Mama and I sat on my front porch, and it felt a bit like déjà vu. There wasn't a wine bottle between us, however, but a pitcher of lemonade instead.

"He is all mine," I said to her with a shy smile.

She nodded as if she'd known it all along, and perhaps she had. "It's good to see you happy, Cora Bee. I didn't realize how sad you've been until the happiness came back."

"It feels good to be happy again."

She held out her hand, palm up, and I reached my hand over and placed it in hers. Our fingers curled to hold our hands in place, and suddenly I was a young girl again, holding on to her for dear life.

"I'm real sorry, Cora Bee. I'm going to work on not being so hardheaded and oblivious."

It was such a strange notion to see a beloved parent as human. One who's flawed and can make mistakes. But that didn't mean I loved her any less. In fact, I loved her more for recognizing that she'd been wrong.

"Are we good?" she asked, worry shimmering in her dark eyes.

"We've always been good, but now we're even better."

She squeezed my hand tighter, and I glanced up the street to see Emme on her way back. For the first time, I saw a pink glow breaking though the gray wisps that surrounded her, revealing the color of her true personality. Blush pink. I smiled. I should've known. I *had* known. Emme was nothing but kind-hearted at her core.

Behind her, a delivery truck had just turned onto the lane.

I stood up, and my mama grabbed my crutches and handed them to me. She then held open the screen door, and I hopped down the steps as the truck passed Emme and rolled to a stop in front of Aunt Glory's house.

I met Emme at the end of the walkway, and we watched as Aunt Glory came out of her house to meet the driver halfway, taking a harmless-looking envelope from his outstretched hand. I heard her thank him and tell him to say hi to his mama for her, and then she waved as he drove off.

My mama gave Emme a nod and a hopeful smile. "I'll meet you girls over there."

I took hold of Emme's hand. In the short time she had been here, she had shown me that I didn't want to be alone. I wanted to be more like she was—willing and open to making friends. I wanted to help neighbors. And get involved in the community. I wanted relationships. I wanted all the dreams I'd given up on so long ago.

She had helped me see who I truly wanted to be. And I was grateful I'd been strong enough to become that person. I had finally healed. Heart and soul.

Tears glistened in her green eyes as she faced me. "I've been thinking, Cora Bee."

"About?" I asked.

She smiled wide. "Why *not* stay?"

Chapter
27

*September 7, 1965: I spent most of the day in the gar-
den, reflecting on life as I sat by the gazing pool with
my shimmering bees. I've decided I can't stay married to Levi
anymore. It's too painful, physically and emotionally, and I
need to do what's best for Lillian. To protect her before it's too
late—a lesson I learned from the bees. Dorothy has offered her
support and made me promise I wouldn't talk to Levi about
a divorce or moving out of this house without her and Gil
present. We all fear Levi won't leave without a fight. I'm not
sure what the future holds for Lillian and me, but no matter
where we end up, a big piece of my heart will always be here
on Hickory Lane.*

Emme

It had been a little more than a week since I had decided I'd stay
here in Sweetgrass. As I often did since I first arrived, I found
myself in the garden. My flower bed was flourishing, and I was
already thinking ahead to what I'd add to the bed next year.

My gaze wandered to where the police were working today,
scanning a neighbor's yard for any sign of Bee.

Like her, my visits to the garden usually ended up at the gazing pool as well, reflecting on life. I sat there now, and the water
burbled behind me as I ran my hand over the fern fronds and
across the soft moss. Mothers *should* be a soft place to fall, but
not all were. Mine wasn't. But if I ever had kids of my own one
day, I was going to make sure her painful life lessons ended with

me. I'd create new lessons, drawn from the women around me
who inspired me. Glory, Cora Bee, Dorothy, Nannette, May,
and even Lillian. My *real* family.

As promised, my mother had turned up last Friday, greeting
me at the Sweetplace with that sickly sweet smile of hers. Glory
had stood by my side as I shared with my mother that I'd told
everyone the truth about me and Rowan, and that everyone had
accepted me for who I am. That it didn't matter who my father
was. I added, too, that I still didn't have any money and doubted
I would anytime soon.

That fake smile had stayed locked on her face, but it was
clear she'd been shocked silent by my confession. Then she'd
simply turned on her heel and walked away, disappearing into
the crowd and from my life. I couldn't imagine I'd ever see her
again, unless she somehow heard that I was going to inherit a
good chunk of Glory's estate.

Because it had once belonged to my father, and he had wanted
me to have it.

The DNA test had revealed I was, in fact, Rowan's daughter.

Glory had held my hand the whole time I'd talked to my
mother, keeping me from shouting my fool head off. Why had
she lied to me?

"Trust no one, Emme," she'd always said to me while I was
growing up. "Everyone lies. *Everyone.*"

I should've known not to trust *her*, either. Lying was her love
language.

"Mind if I sit a spell?"

My head snapped up at the sound of Glory's voice. She approached slowly, her wobbly gait more pronounced than ever.
A harvest basket hung empty on her arm as she sat down next
to me.

"You all right, hon?" she asked. "You look a touch pale."

I let out a breath. "Just thinking about my mother and her
lies. She had more to gain by my relation to Rowan than to lose.
So why did she lie to me? If she stayed, she could've gotten child
support at least."

"I've thought about that a fair amount," Glory said. "And the more I thought about it, the more I began to see a little of myself in her."

"No." I shook my head. "You're *nothing* like her."

"Honey, don't go getting all riled up. All I'm trying to say is that I think she wanted to settle. After her hard upbringing, a traditional family in a stable home with good money coming in would likely have made her feel like she had the whole world at her fingertips. It might be the romantic in me, but I think she did love Rowan, as much as she could love anyone. When Rowan shattered her dream, she wanted to hurt him the same way he'd hurt her. By taking away what had become *his* world: you."

I felt flutters of truth in what Glory had said, and for a second, I felt a twinge of sympathy for my mother. "I don't think I'll ever understand what drives her to do the things she does."

On the top of the stone shed, a small wren began to sing as Glory said, "Some things in life aren't meant to be known, only learned from."

I certainly had learned a lot in my short lifetime. Unfortunately, most of those were lessons I could've done without.

"I've seen myself in you and Cora Bee, too," she said. "In how you've learned to forgive yourselves for the mistakes you've made."

Her words wrapped around me like a hug, and I wanted to ask about what mistakes she'd made, but I suspected I already knew—she'd told them to me once, plain as day.

When a car door slammed, we both looked over to see the police packing up for the day. "Have you decided on your tropical getaway yet?" I asked.

An island vacation was on her bucket list, and Dorothy, Nannette, and May planned to go with her as well. I would take over running Glory & Bee while she was away and live vicariously through text messages and video chats now that I finally had a phone of my own.

She nodded. "I'm leaning toward the Bahamas. White sand beaches, turquoise water."

I slipped my foot from my flip-flop, set my toe against the cool, soft moss, and gathered up my courage. "Do you think Dorothy will bring her shovel?"

She set her basket on the ground near her feet and tipped her head, studying me, *reading* me.

I let her, not hiding my thoughts.

I glanced over to the flower bed closest to us, to the large shrub that had once been dug up by the police, and said, "Some say rhododendrons represent caution and danger. Plus, they're poisonous, deadly even, so they seem a fitting grave marker. Has Dorothy always known where Levi was buried?"

We sat with the weight of the sentence heavy on our shoulders until she finally said, "It was she, not Bee, who planted the rhododendrons originally. Mulched them with pine straw, too, so searchers wouldn't realize what the bushes were hiding. Since there had been a lot of work going on in the garden that summer, nothing seemed out of place."

Beneath the rhododendrons, the daisies and black-eyed Susans we had planted were thriving, their contrasting flowers blooming so closely together that it almost seemed like they were one plant, a strange hybrid. "Some say black-eyed Susans symbolize justice and daisies represent new beginnings. Have those varieties always been part of that bed?"

"For almost as long as the rhododendrons."

The bird continued to sing as I asked, "Who planted them originally?"

"Somehow I think you already know I did." She lifted her chin, turned her head imperceptibly toward the sun, just like the true sunflower she was. "I planted them not long after Lillian, Rowan, and I moved here from Georgia."

I reached out, took hold of her hand, clasped it between both of mine. "I'm surprised there aren't any lotus flowers in the gazing pool, seeing that they mean rebirth. After all, this is essentially where Bee Gipson died and Glory Wynn was born, isn't it?"

She looked downward and she smiled when she saw my toes

in the moss. "If anyone was going to figure out the truth, it was always going to be you. You see life in ways no one else can."

I swallowed hard. "The first time I saw you, my first impression was of love. That has never wavered. I doubt it ever will."

She turned her head toward the rhododendrons. "How did you know? How long have you known?"

"Not long. It was mostly the flowers that told the story. Once I knew what the flowers meant, it became clear. Did you want it to be known? Is that why you've been giving me garden lessons?"

"It was never my intention, no." She looked at me with a sad smile. "I've been wondering if the sinkhole opening on the same day you arrived was a coincidence. Now I'm sure it wasn't. I think it was this land's way of letting me know that I'm more than what happened to me, and that it was time for the truth to come out. You were meant to be the one to discover that truth."

"Me? Why?"

"So you could see that you're more than what's happened to you, too. To prove that everyone has secrets. And to show that it's not so much about what you've done in your past that matters as it is what you do in the future. Lessons, Emme. The garden always offers lessons to be learned, and I know that with your inherent curiosity, you will always pay attention."

I thought about what she said, and I realized that since I had been here, I had learned to let my past go, to not dwell, to move on. I wasn't defined by who I'd been but by who I was right now.

Nodding, I blinked away tears and she leaned against me.

As the water behind us burbled peacefully, I said, "The gazing pool also helped me figure out the truth. It showed me a vision of the night Bee disappeared. I saw her grab Lillian and run out the door. There was the briefest glance in the mirror in the hallway."

Her eyes watered. "We'd had a terrible fight. I'd found out he'd been cheating on me with Margot Yardley, and he didn't appreciate the fact that I knew. He tried to blame the affair on me. Tried to blame all his problems on me, and I before I could stop myself and wait for Dorothy and Gil to be there, I told him I wanted him to move out, and all hell broke loose."

Hell. It was a good description of what I'd seen.

I cleared my throat. "The reflection in the mirror had been haunting me, keeping me up at night. I couldn't figure out why I'd been shown the scene at all, or why I was being tormented by it, until I stopped looking at the injuries. I'd been so focused on the horror that I didn't notice the earrings. They're the same ones you're wearing now. The ones you wear every single day. Since they're likely antique and one of a kind, I doubt you both had the same pair."

Her fingers went to her ears and lovingly caressed the gold discs. "I probably should've stopped wearing them, but they were my mother's. She sent them to me for my birthday a few days before . . . well, before my life was changed forever. Besides Dorothy, no one in Sweetgrass had seen them, so I figured it was safe enough to keep them. How much more did the gazing pool show you?"

"I saw you hide behind the live oak tree, then look back. An enraged Levi was heading straight toward you. Then you looked down and he started looking fearful. That's it."

She nodded. "I looked down because I felt the strangest vibration under my feet. A rumbling."

"The natural spring?"

She shook her head. "Bees. They came out of the sinkhole in a glowing swarm and went after Levi. It felt . . . like they were *protecting* me, even though I hadn't been able to protect them. Oh, how I loved my bees."

The pain in her voice tore at my heartstrings.

She went on, saying, "He started cursing and yelling, and I knew I should run, but I was shaking so badly that I could hardly stand. Finally, I crouched down and wrapped my arms around my knees. I closed my eyes and started praying, using the words to block out his anger, his hatred. I don't know how long I stayed there like that. A couple of minutes? Ten? When I opened my eyes again, I realized how quiet it was. Eerily quiet. Every muscle in my body ached as I stood up and peeked around the tree. I didn't see Levi—only the bees flying in circles around the sink-hole. As I limped toward them, they faded away, one by one. I started shaking again because somehow I *knew* Levi was in that hole." She cleared her throat and wiped a tear from the corner of her eye. "When I looked in, I could only see his hands over his head. I tried to pull him out, but he didn't budge. He wasn't moving at all. His hands felt"—her voice cracked—"lifeless."

That her first instinct had been to help him spoke volumes about her character. How easy it would've been for her to walk away. I'd like to say I'd have made the same decision she had—to try to save him—but I wasn't so sure.

"I started digging with my hands and quickly realized I'd never be able to get him out on my own. I ran to the tractor, fired it up, thinking I could somehow scoop him out of the dirt. But it seemed the more I tried, the worse I made the situation. Before I knew it, the sinkhole collapsed, covering him up completely. I was still trying to free him when Dorothy showed up, Lillian in her arms. At the sight of them, I shut down the tractor, suddenly acutely aware that there was nothing anyone could do to save Levi at that point. In hindsight, I realized he'd likely been gone before I'd stepped onto the tractor."

Her hand trembled in mine as she relived that night, and I wanted to take her in my arms, hold her, and tell her how sorry I was, but for now I kept quiet because I knew there was more to the story.

"Dorothy took one look at my battered face and started bawl-ing, which made Lillian cry, which made me cry. And I couldn't stop, Emme. I simply couldn't stop. Dorothy held me for the lon-gest time, and in between sobs, I told her everything that had happened. Only then did she confess that for a moment, when she'd first seen me on the tractor moving dirt around, she'd har-bored the notion that I might have buried Levi deliberately. As soon as the words were out of her mouth, we both realized how bad the scene looked for me. I'd known Levi was cheating. I had sought counsel from others about divorcing him. I wanted him to move out of the house and knew he wouldn't go without a fight. Everyone knew how much I loved this land and didn't want to sell it or move. From a legal standpoint, I had plenty of motives for wanting him dead. It was highly doubtful a jury of my peers would believe that I'd *accidentally* buried Levi while trying to save him."

"Laid out that way," I said, "it does sound particularly damning."

She nodded. "It was suddenly a real possibility that I'd be arrested, tried, convicted. That Lillian would be left parentless. I was at a loss for what to do. As Dorothy and I sat side by side on that moonlit night, eventually it became clear that there was only one way out of the mess I'd made: Bee had to die, too."

Tears gathered in her eyes, and I could only imagine the emotions she'd experienced that night so long ago. As much as I'd hoped a jury would've seen that she'd never deliberately hurt someone, I couldn't fault her for the choices she'd made.

"I left Lillian with Dorothy," she said in a shaky voice, "and took off on foot through the woods to her house, where I hid in her garden shed. Dorothy stayed behind, used the tractor to grade the area, and some of the garden just beyond, making it appear as though it had been done earlier in the day as part of the irrigation work. Then on top of the sinkhole she planted the rhododendrons that I had set aside for fall planting—I'd told her which ones to use, because as you mentioned, they seemed appropriate."

I realized suddenly that was the image Chase had likely seen. Dorothy planting the rhododendrons, not shoveling dirt into the sinkhole.

"After that," Glory said, "Dorothy picked up Lillian and headed back to the house to call Gil, to tell him there'd been trouble and that I was missing. Except by that time the house was on fire. I don't know if Levi set it before he took off after me . . ."

"It was probably his cigarette. He flicked it at you, and you ducked. It probably landed in the couch cushion."

She let out a breath. "I'd forgotten that part. It's probably for the best that it went up in flames. It was easier for me that way, to think that it had never existed at all."

"Did Dorothy hide you at her house for long?" I was wondering what to tell Chase, *how* to tell him. He had to know. It wouldn't be fair of me to let him think his grandmother had killed a man.

"The day . . . after, when Dorothy volunteered to drive Lillian to my mama's house in Georgia, I was hiding in the backseat. Dorothy started the rumor about her husband letting Levi go, though after that, she never spoke his name aloud again. It was always *he* or *him* or *the devil himself*. After her head injury, it was *varmint* she favored most and started talking openly about finding him. It was Nannette who first assumed Dorothy was referring to a squirrel and the rest of us just went along with it, even Dorothy, though I'm not sure she fully understood. While she's in her digging mindset, she's not really thinking straight."

Poor sweet Dorothy. "Did she tell her husband what had truly happened to Levi?"

"Oh, no. She knew Gil wouldn't have stood for our plan, since he was all law and order and justice. Though she did feel badly about throwing him under the proverbial bus, she knew he could withstand the gossip. That it would pass. And it did."

"Do you think a guilty conscience was why Dorothy started her digging expeditions after her accident? She lost the filter to keep the guilt at bay?"

Glory let out a soft laugh. "I thought so at first, but she set me straight at one point. Turned out she wanted to make sure he was well and truly dead. And if he wasn't, I think she had a mind to finish the job."

My gaze wandered to the sunny side of the stone shed and the bed of parrot lilies—Dorothy's garden. I smiled as I recalled Glory's lesson on the flower and how it represented friendships that had deep roots. Strong relationships full of support and devotion. I wished everyone could have a friend as good as Dorothy.

"When I got to Georgia," Glory said, "my mama took over my care and promised to take my secret to her grave, which she

did. She also took me to a doctor, and surprised me by intro-
ducing me as her daughter, *Glory* Wynn. Up until that point, I
hadn't given a thought to a new name. The doctor did what he
could for my broken nose and fractured cheekbone. He was also
the one who discovered I was three months pregnant. I stayed in
Georgia for nearly a year and put on a good amount of weight.
My broken nose and cheek had already changed the shape of
my face and the added weight only made me that much more
unrecognizable. Still, I dyed my blond hair a deep, chocolate
brown and got my teeth fixed. It was alarmingly easy back then
to become a whole new person. I had no trouble at all getting
a new birth certificate and driver's license." There was a brief
flash of humor in her eyes as she added, "And I figured that
since I was starting over, I decided I would be Bee's *younger*
sister and knocked a few years off my true age."

I smiled at that while at the same time thinking that she
looked amazing for her age, whatever it might actually be.

"During my life here in Sweetgrass with Levi," she said, "I'd
been a fairly private person. Dorothy had been my only true
friend. So after I came back here, no one questioned why they
hadn't ever heard Bee mention a sister before. And if anyone
saw similarities between me and Bee, they were easily explained
as family resemblance."

I'd always thought she was strong, but I hadn't realized just
how strong. "Why'd your mother choose the name Glory? Is
there meaning behind it?"

"I thought she had chosen it because morning glories represent mortal life, but Mama told me it was because there had been
a golden light around me when I came back to Georgia. Said it
looked like a full-body halo. Till the day she died, she said that
light was because when Bee had gone to glory, glory had come
to me."

It was impossible not to remember that the first time I saw
Glory, I'd thought she glowed with light as well, as if her innate
goodness shined for all to see.

"But I don't think it's some kind of halo at all," she said, "even though such a big piece of me died that night in this garden."

"What do you think it is?"

She glanced at a bee skimming the water of the gazing pool. "It's always reminded me of honey. Especially since I feel like the bees are looking out for me. I've felt their buzzing underfoot since that horrible night. It never went away. I like to think that the glow—and the buzzing—are their reminders that I'm safe now."

My eyes widened. "So the vibration isn't the natural spring at all?"

She shook her head. "It's the bees. You'll never be able to tell me otherwise."

We sat together listening to the water, the wind, the sweet song of the wren, the gentle buzz of the bees around us.

Breaking the silence between us, she said, "Can I ask you to wait to tell the others until after I'm gone? The news that her mama has been at her side all along will likely break Lillian's heart, and I can't bear to see it. I don't know if she'd understand why I did what I did—and never told her the truth."

I thought she was underestimating Lillian's love for her. As I laid my head on her shoulder, I tried really hard not to think about when she would no longer be here. "Someone I love dearly once told me that we all have secrets. Maybe one day they'll be shared; maybe they won't. And that's all right if they aren't hurting anyone. Right now, as far as I'm concerned, Bee died on a moonlit September night a long time ago. But I have to ask, why did you even want to come back here? Doesn't seeing those rhododendrons all the time bring back bad memories? Doesn't this land feel tainted?"

She faced me and cupped my cheek. "Ah, my sweet Emme. This place is special. It could never be tainted. Sure enough this garden has a dark past, but look how far it's come. Look at the joy it brings. Look at how much it still has to give to others." With tears in her eyes, she looked about, a sense of wonder pulsing around her. "I'm truly grateful to this garden—it gave me a new life. One where I didn't have to live in constant fear. It may seem ghoulish to some, but knowing where Levi was and that he couldn't hurt me or Lillian anymore allowed me to be able to fully live. It helped me believe in tomorrows again. Those rhododendrons don't represent bad memories, hon. They represent hope for the future."

"Sanctuary," I whispered.

"Sanctuary," she repeated.

As we sat side by side, golden bees flew around us, and I realized there truly was a little of everything, including a touch of magic, here in the middle of Hickory Lane.

Epilogue

🌿 *Glory's Final Garden Lesson*

As you can probably tell, another of my favorite flowers is Queen Anne's lace. It's all over this garden! Doesn't the flower look like snowy white lace? Tatted in a starburst pattern? Just gorgeous. And it's not a favorite just because it's also known as wild carrot—you know how much I like carrots, hon. That's just a bonus. This flower is considered a weed, or a wildflower, depending. Remember the saying? I always see wildflowers. Always. Queen Anne's lace isn't colorful and doesn't have any scent, but bees and butterflies are drawn to it. I think it's because they know the flower represents a safe haven, a sanctuary, security. I wonder sometimes if that's why everyone who lives on Hickory Lane was drawn here. We all needed a safe place to land.

Emme

In the middle of Hickory Lane grew a neighborhood garden, a circular patch of vibrant land that fit snugly into the footprint of the wide dead-end street, a cul-de-sac. The landscaped island rose up from the surrounding asphalt road, lush and verdant, beckoning for a closer look, a long stay. It was impossible for me not to notice, however, that among its gravel pathways, trees, shrubs, planter beds, trellises, and flower meadow stood a preacher, a bride and groom, and twenty or so guests.

The peonies for Cora Bee's wedding bouquet had been ordered from Norway of all places, where peonies still bloomed in August. It had been worth the cost to overnight the flowers, simply for the smile on her face when she opened the long box.

Fortunately for the wedding budget, stock was still blooming in the cutting garden, somehow surviving the soaring summer temperatures, as if it knew something important was in store if it just held on a little longer.

I once thought peonies were the most beautiful thing I'd ever laid eyes on, but that was before I saw Cora Bee in her lace wedding gown, standing with Jamie in front of a preacher under an arbor covered in white roses.

May had been right all along, about a summer wedding in the garden. But she was being humble about it now, only smiling knowingly whenever someone brought it up.

I stood next to Alice on Cora Bee's left side as she and Jamie recited vows, and to his right stood Cora Bee's brother, Cain, and Chase. Lying on the ground just behind them was Mabel, a white bow in her hair and two golden bands tied to her collar.

Only twenty lawn chairs had been set up for the intimate wedding, and in the front row sat Simon and Lillian, their eyes shining with pride as they watched their daughter radiate joy.

Next to them, Glory and Dorothy sat side by side, both of them dabbing their eyes with lace-edged handkerchiefs. I was keeping their secret safe as could be. I was waiting to tell Chase what had happened that long ago night until after Glory was gone, like she'd asked. I hadn't decided if I'd tell anyone else. Perhaps some secrets were meant to stay that way forever.

So much had changed these last few months. The Sweet-place had moved to Buck's Drive-In until the work at the much-anticipated BeeYard was completed sometime next year. I'd fully taken over running Glory & Bee and also started The Little Dandelion Company, which specialized in furniture flips.

In June, I'd ordered a new, pristine birth certificate and had a decent haircut for the first time ever. I also hid a stone hedgehog in the cutting garden where it still sat waiting for Glory to find it.

In July, I turned twenty-six. There was a lovely party, but my favorite gift was a first-edition copy of *The Lion, the Witch and the Wardrobe*. It had been given to me by Lillian, which spoke loads about how far we'd come in our relationship. During that same month, I bought two bee boxes to start my own small apiary near my flower bed in the cutting garden and had started a journal to keep track of all Glory's garden lessons that I'd learned so far. I dearly hoped there would be many more entries to come.

I'd also watched every single episode of *Designing Women* with Glory. Unfortunately, Suzanne the hand truck hadn't changed a single bit in all this time, but I couldn't bring myself to part ways with her. And last week, I'd finally moved out of Cora Bee's house and into the garage apartment. My suitcase hadn't said a single word the whole way there, still pouting that it had been wrong.

Cora Bee had gotten her cast off and started sleeping well again. Her business was booming, and she'd begun offering crochet lessons at the library. Last month, she'd started a petition to limewash the courthouse, and surprisingly, she had collected more than enough signatures to get the measure put on the next ballot.

Glory and Dorothy had taken their vacation to the Bahamas with Nannette and May, and Glory had been stopped by authorities at the airport for trying to bring native plants back to the States.

Alice had made several friends over the summer while hanging out at the library during Cora Bee's programs. She was actually looking forward to school starting. And to having a stepmom she loved with all her heart.

Chase scrapped his book on Levi and had started writing a PI novel. When he wasn't writing, we spent a lot of time together. He walked with me almost every night to help me overcome my fear of darkness. And while I was no longer absolutely terrified of being outside at night, I still slept with a night-light on. Old habits were hard to break.

And now, August had brought a wedding.

As the preacher pronounced Jamie and Cora Bee husband

and wife, they kissed, and a loud cheer erupted. Flower petals flew as people rushed forward to greet the newlyweds.

I held back, just watching, taking in every detail, and I thought my heart might just burst from pure happiness. There was a time I believed I'd never fit in here on Hickory Lane, and now I couldn't imagine myself fitting in anywhere else.

Chase cleared his throat as he approached and smiled when he saw the sappy look on my face. He stepped in close, pressed a kiss to my temple, and said, "Has anyone ever told you how pretty you look in pink?"

ACKNOWLEDGMENTS

While there's a little bit of me in every book I write, there are also pieces of many others. For this book in particular, Hickory Lane wouldn't have been nearly as charming and special without the insights of my incredibly talented editor, Kristin Sevick. In fact, at one point I emailed Kristin to tell her that when she's right, she's right. And she was. Thank you for your special kind of magic, Kristin.

To everyone at Forge Books and Macmillan Audio who had a hand in making *In the Middle of Hickory Lane,* thank you so very much. A special thank-you, also, to my copy editor, formatters, proofreader, and cover designers. I appreciate all of you more than I can ever express.

A big thank-you to Jessica Faust and the BookEnds team for all you do.

To all the readers who believe in the magic of books, thank you for choosing my stories to read.

And to my family, my heart. Much love as always.

Turn the page for a sneak peek at
Heather Webber's next novel

AT THE COFFEE SHOP
OF CURIOSITIES

Available Summer 2023

Maggie

"He's losing his dang mind. Maybe even lost it already. Wandered straight off along with the stuff that's missing from his house."

"Desmond's mind is fine, Maggie," Carmella Brasil said, looking up at me as I balanced on a step stool in front of a floor-to-ceiling blackboard inset into a narrow slatted wooden wall at the back of the coffee shop. "Eccentric, perhaps, but fine. The items in his house had simply been misplaced—didn't he tell you he'd found them?"

He had, but I thought the admission proved, rather than discredited, my point about my father's wayward mind. He would be seventy soon. Wasn't that too young for memory issues? For dementia? Alzheimer's? It felt too young, but that might be because he rarely acted his age.

You're only as old as you think, my little magpie, he'd once told me. *And I like to think I'm in my forties. No, thirties. No, twenties. Hoo, boy. My twenties were something, let me tell you.*

He'd been in his late twenties when he first met my mother, Tuppence, at a Mardi Gras parade over in Mobile. After spotting her standing along the route, he'd jumped off the float he'd been riding to give her a MoonPie and his heart. She'd accepted both enthusiastically. She did *everything* enthusiastically. After that they'd been inseparable. Well, until . . .

Nope. I gave myself a good mental shake.

I couldn't go *there* right now.

Truly, I never wanted to go there, but when I was stressed that particular grief wiggled through the cracks in my heart, reminding me of all I had lost.

Of all I still had to lose.

My heart rate picked up, and I forced myself to focus on the task in front of me. Monday mornings meant posting a new recipe on the back wall. After uncapping a white chalk marker, I used my best hand lettering to write *Mrs. Pollard's Mini Vanilla Scones* at the top of the blackboard.

Magpie's had been part of Driftwood for thirty-five years now—my mother had opened it when I was just three years old—and oftentimes mornings here felt more like a neighborly get-together, a time when even the snowbirds and tourists felt a bit like family.

The coffee shop was quiet at the moment with only a handful of customers, the proverbial calm before the storm since I knew the Mermaids would be along soon enough. They arrived every morning around nine after having walked the beach with their buckets and bins, and I knew their usual numbers would be doubled today—maybe tripled—because of last night's bad weather.

I took a moment away from the scone recipe to scan the dining room, knowing that with only eight tables—four two-tops and four four-tops—there was no way to fit all the Mermaids inside, but they'd come anyway, spilling out onto the sidewalk and into the park across the street after ordering. I felt a surge of love for my small Southern town and how supportive they were of the coffeehouse—and all the businesses here in the square.

I couldn't ever imagine moving away, and especially not moving north like Effie Reyes, who quit on me last week to follow her boyfriend to a horse ranch in Wyoming. But then again, I wasn't so goo-goo-eyed over a boy that I'd blindly follow him anywhere. Well, I hadn't been for a long time now at least—and where he'd gone I'd decided not to follow. I *couldn't* follow.

Not because I'd been prohibited in any way, but because I was tied here to this town, to the water. Its magic pulsed in me as sure and strong as my heartbeat. When I was away from the beach for long, the magic disappeared, which felt a lot like I was losing myself.

My gaze swept briefly over the Curiosity Corner, across all

the bits and bobs I'd collected that were awaiting their fated companions, before landing for a brief moment on Estrelle Cormier, who sat at a two-top by the window. She was dressed in black as usual, today's outfit adorned with sequins. She was staring at me through her veil's netting, the look so piercing it felt as though she could see right into my heart, to the part where my deepest darkest fears lived, and was taking notes.

I shivered and looked away, toward Rosemary Clark Hale, a divorced mom of two grown kids, who was also the best employee known to mankind. Rose was humming under her breath as she wiped down empty tables. Since I hadn't yet hired anyone to fill Effie's spot, it would just be Rose and me handling the Mermaid rush, and I had no doubt she was well prepared for the madness about to descend on us—and could likely handle it on her own if need be. She had worked here longer than I had, and I thanked my lucky stars that she wasn't the one who ran off to follow the rodeo circuit.

"Though I admit, *eccentric* may be putting it mildly," Carmella conceded with a smile, pulling me back into our conversation as she rested a slim, deep-brown shoulder against the wall. In her sixties, she'd aged spectacularly well, for which she gave credit to working hard, eating right, her Latina heritage, and the exceptional talents of a local cosmetic dermatologist. "Dez has always marched to the beat of his own drummer."

In my opinion, my father, Desmond "Dez" Brightwood, acted mostly like a teenager, and more often than not, I parented him, rather than the other way around. It hadn't helped that he and my son, Noah, had been best buddies, two peas in a pod, partners in all sorts of mischief until Noah had flown the coop for college, which had been an exciting time for him and a hellish one for me.

I had been so hyper-focused on raising Noah up right and good and *fulfilled* that it felt an awful lot like grief when he went away. It had taken a good while for me to find my footing again once he left, though I had to admit it still wasn't solid ground I stood on but shifting sand. I had assumed since I raised

Noah on my own, he'd be just like me—wanting to stay here in Driftwood always and forever—but instead he was a lot like my mama had been, full of adventure. He wanted to see everything and go everywhere and nothing was going to stand in his way. One of the hardest things I'd ever done was let him go to live his own life, his own way.

These days, Noah was a sophomore at Vanderbilt and didn't come home often enough to suit my needs, especially since he'd stayed in Tennessee the *entire* summer for an internship. He'd promised to visit soon, and while I waited patiently for that day, I filled my time with the coffee shop and stepped up my activity in various clubs and organizations around town, never turning down an opportunity to support my neighbors or this community. Doing so helped fill the ever-present emptiness within me—a chasm that had developed not long after my mama disappeared.

I had to admit, however, that these days my schedule might be too full—something my doctor had pointed out to me after I'd seen her about the headaches I'd been having. She'd noted my sky-high blood pressure; put me on medication, a low-sodium diet, and an exercise plan; and warned me about the dangers of spreading myself too thin. But try as I might, I couldn't see where I could cut back, not without it affecting someone else.

I wrote *2 c flour* on the board, the letters shaky. I erased them and tried again. Working had always helped when it came to calming my inner turmoil. Here at Magpie's, I was in complete control and had been for nearly ten years, which was how long ago my father had handed me the reins of the business, deciding he was ready to switch careers at fifty-eight years old. He'd become a real estate investor, flipping houses in the area, turning them into short- and long-term rentals—all except for the home he'd sold to me on the cheap. The super cheap. Then, last year, he'd decided to get his real estate license and had sweet-talked Carmella, owner of Driftwood Realty, into hiring him on.

When I questioned why he didn't just retire like other, *normal* people of his age, he'd said boisterously, "Waves of change should be welcomed, Maggie. They can uncover beauty and treasures untold."

I hadn't earned the nickname Magpie for nothing—I loved discovering treasures as much as the next person—maybe more—but I also knew how waves of change could be destructive. As evidenced by the innocent-looking folder in Carmella's hand that had seemed to expand since she'd walked in ten minutes ago, doubling in size.

A dull headache was growing, creeping across my forehead, so I kept my voice low as I said to Carmella, "Don't you think Daddy's been behaving oddly lately? Odder than usual, that is?"

Humor flashed in her eyes. "He's always been an unusual man, Maggie Mae."

"He's given up Purty's pulled pork, his absolute favorite food on earth, and has been talking about becoming a vegetarian. This from a man who I've never once seen eat a green vegetable."

"Veggies are good things, remember?"

I frowned at her levelheadedness. "I spotted him jogging on the beach the other day, too. *Jogging.* You know how he feels about regimented exercise."

Her eyebrows rose. "Jogging? Really?"

I nodded. "Plus, when have you ever known him to host a yard sale? I can't tell you how many times he's said he'd rather cut off a limb than get rid of any of his treasures, yet not only is he planning a sale but has made it a whole community event."

I'd garnered the nickname Magpie early on. As soon as I learned how to walk, I was off, picking up anything shiny or unusual. It wasn't until I was a few years older that the focus of my collecting narrowed to very specific objects. My father, however, had always collected anything that struck his fancy. There was no rhyme or reason other than he liked it. Those items filled two storage units and were stuffed into every nook and cranny in his house. He couldn't bear to part with anything. Until now, apparently.

"Are treasures truly treasures if they remain boxed up or covered with dust?"

That wasn't the point. Not at all. But Carmella seemed intent on being reasonable. Didn't she understand that this was not the time for something as practical as common sense? *Land's sakes alive.* "And the coffee shop? How do you explain that?"

The burgeoning folder in her hand held the preliminary paperwork for the sale of Magpie's. My father was selling the coffee shop.

My mother's coffee shop.

I could barely breathe just thinking about it. The pressure in my head increased, and I tried to remember if I took my medication this morning. I had. I was sure of it.

Carmella tucked a long, black curl behind her ear, and her eyes were full of sympathy as she carried out my father's dirty work. As a real estate agent himself, he could've handled this on his own, but he was using her as a buffer to protect himself from my disapproval.

Of which there was quite a lot.

She said softly, "I know it's been a shock."

My father had broken the news of the sale to me over the weekend, and I was still processing it. When I tearfully pushed for a reason why, he only said, "It's time for me to let go."

I didn't understand why. Why let the shop go now? The business was making money. Not a fortune by any means but enough to pay the overhead and expenses plus some. Magpie's was a fixture in this town. It was the *heart* of this town. Closing it would be devastating—not only to me, but to everyone who lived here.

"I'm worried."

"You're always worried," she stated because she knew me well. "This is nothing new."

Carmella had been in my life . . . forever. She'd been my mother's best friend, and from the time I was four years old she had tried to help fill the gaps in my life left behind by my mother's absence. It was an impossible task, but I loved her dearly for trying.

"Be that as it may, he's acting strange. You can't convince me he isn't."

Compassion thickened her voice as she said, "To me, Dez is

acting only like a man who's ready for a change. And change isn't always a bad thing, Maggie. You're letting your heart rule your head."

I didn't like change, not one single bit. It brought chaos and disorder and confusion and emptiness, but what she said struck a chord of truth, especially since Daddy always liked mixing things up. But this time it felt different.

It felt like I was losing him.

"Do you think he's sick? Like, really sick?" My voice wavered as I spoke my fears aloud, and I felt ill. I could absolutely see him wanting to hide troubling health news from me, to keep me from worrying. If that were the case, his plan had backfired in a big way. "It seems like he's pulling out all the stops to get healthy . . . while preparing for the worst."

She shook her head. "Absolutely not. He's the picture of vim and vigor."

I wanted to believe it, but I knew him too well. There was definitely something going on. The changes had begun a few months ago, when he started talking about a ghost haunting his house. Showing up in the middle of the night, making noise, making a mess of his house. He hadn't seemed bothered—in fact, he seemed amused more than anything. He'd always loved a good ghost story.

I'd tried to brush it off as him just having a bit of fun, but one afternoon after I'd let myself into his house to drop off a plate of his favorite cookies, I found his house in complete disarray. Dishes had been piled up in the sink, dirty laundry overflowed, dust covered nearly every surface. His boxes of his treasures had multiplied, clogging hallways, blocking doors. Many of them had been emptied, spilling onto tables, the sofa, chairs.

Dad wasn't persnickety with his cleanliness, but he wasn't a total slob either, so the quick deterioration of his home was completely out of character. When I called him, he'd simply blamed it all on the ghost.

It was unsettling to say the least.

Then, not long after that day, he'd been involved in a sleepwalking incident that could have been disastrous if a neighbor hadn't seen him wandering about in the dark of night wearing only a pair of boxer shorts.

That event had opened a Pandora's box of *what-if*s and *could-have*s. Once the dust had settled on his nighttime adventure, I'd broached the idea of me moving back in with him. It wasn't that I *wanted* to move in with him—I rather liked my house and having my own space—but it seemed the best option for my peace of mind.

He'd turned me down flat, though. Wouldn't even discuss the matter.

I'd tried to let it all go, to believe that whatever was going on wasn't serious. But then, about a month after the sleepwalking episode, I dropped by unannounced and found that his house was still a disaster area. Worse than that, though, was his neglect of Molly. His cantankerous cat's food and water dishes had been empty, which told me more about Dad's mental state than anything else could have.

I'd waited for him to get home and confronted him, floating the idea of hiring an in-home caretaker. I'd even offered to pay for the help. He'd shut down that conversation with a hearty laugh that went on and on until he gently steered me toward the door. "My ghost is messy, Magpie, and I have better things to do than clean. Molly's dishes were full this morning, I assure you. She's fine. All is well here, my little Magpie. Stop worrying. Go home."

Frustrated after that visit, I had marched myself straight home and wrote up the worst possible job description I could think of for an in-home care provider. Even though what I'd written was based in truth, I might have overexaggerated slightly, purely as a source of therapy. Then I saved the document and pretty much forgot about it until *he* forgot my birthday.

He'd tried to play off his absentmindedness when I brought it up, and the conversation quickly devolved into an argument when I once again suggested hiring someone to keep an eye on him, his house. His usually jovial face had clouded over with anger, something so rare it had stunned me silent.

"Enough, Magdalene," he had snapped. "Enough. It would take a divine act for me to even consider it. Let it go. *Let it be.*"

Then his face softened, the anger vanishing as quickly as it had come as he grabbed a garishly painted, porcelain monkey candlestick off the counter and used it as a faux microphone to wail about Mother Mary speaking words of wisdom—he was never one to pass up a chance to sing the Beatles, especially when the lyrics were used to lighten a heavy situation.

I couldn't let it be, though. I *wouldn't*. I was too afraid of losing him.

I was just at a crossroads with what to do about it.

My headache now felt like it was giving my skull a tight, painful hug as I added *1/3 c sugar* to the board, my penmanship barely legible. With a damp rag, I erased what I had written, capped the marker, and climbed down off the step stool. I'd finish the recipe later, when my emotions weren't running so high and the headache waned.

Carmella touched my arm gently. "When was the last time you had a vacation, Maggie? You might be worried about your dad, but I'm worried about you. You look ready to snap in half. You're always working or on the go, doing for others—never taking time for yourself to just be."

Honestly, I hated traveling. I didn't like to be away from home. The most I could tolerate was a day or two away before I started feeling homesick and lost. The last time I'd left home for more than a day's time was shortly after Noah graduated high school. We'd gone to Mississippi to a fossil park for a few days—my paleontology-loving son's idea of a good time.

Tucking the marker into the front pocket of my Magpie's apron, I gave Carmella a faint smile. She was practically family, and I knew she cared deeply, so I rearranged my mental calendar to appease her worries. "I could probably schedule a short *staycation*."

A day or two. It *would* be nice to tackle the home repairs I'd been putting off, and perhaps organize my craft room. Heaven knew it needed it.

"A staycation is a good start, but is it really a vacation if you're doing home projects?"

I shoved a wayward spiral curl back into the claw clip that held my hair off my face and narrowed my eyes at her, suddenly hating that she knew me so well. "Well, that would feel like a vacation to me."

"We clearly need to work on your relaxation techniques."

I crossed my arms. "I'd be able to relax if I knew my father was okay."

She smiled brightly, blinding me with the full wattage of her innate charm. "I was thinking more along the lines of a massage. Or perhaps a mani-pedi? Or even a short road trip to your favorite thrift shops. I know how you love thrifting."

The bell on the door clanked as Sam Kindell pulled it open. Rose welcomed him with a hearty, "Good morning, Sam!" before hurrying behind the counter to await his order, which would likely be his usual iced hazelnut latte and a whippy cup to go.

I kept my attention on Carmella. It didn't escape my notice that she had tried to steer the subject away from my father, and I suddenly had the unsettling feeling she knew more about what was going on with him than she was letting on. I narrowed my eyes at her. "Carmella, do you know what's going on with my father?"

She shifted her weight on her high-heeled sandals and wouldn't meet my eye. "What? No."

I laughed, but it sounded more like a cry to my ears. She might be the number one real estate agent in these parts, but she was a lousy liar.

"Carmella," I said, her name a plea.

As she lifted her head, I saw resolve gleaming in her deep, dark eyes, and I held my breath, waiting, hoping that I'd finally know the source of my father's odd behavior, once and for all.

"You should really hear this—"

"Magdalene Mae Brightwood, a word?" Estrelle stomped toward me, the sequins on her gown glinting like moonlight on water.

"Can it wait a second?" I asked her.

"No, it most certainly cannot."

Relief washed over Carmella's features at the reprieve she'd been given. "I should be going, anyway. I have a showing at nine thirty," she hastily added, knowing I wouldn't likely push for her to stay if she had an appointment scheduled. She shoved the ginormous folder into my hands, gave me a kiss on my cheek, and practically ran to the door, shoving it open.

The folder felt like it weighed a hundred pounds.

Sam followed her out the door, his order in hand, and I winced at how the usually dulcet sound of the bells now rattled my nerves and stoked my headache.

Trying my best to ignore my troubles and my throbbing head, I forced my focus away from Carmella's hasty retreat and onto the woman standing in front of me. "Is something wrong, Estrelle?"

Estrelle owned the fabric and notions shop next door, Stitchery, and also offered tailoring services and custom work. She had to be eighty if a day but bristled with life, showing no signs of slowing down, despite her age. Her thin, pale skin was practically translucent, a maze of blue veins easily visible. Her fingers were gnarled, her manicured nails painted hot pink. Her crystal clear, silvery stare was unwavering behind the black netting of her veil. Her back was hunched, which pitched her head slightly forward, as if she was always leaning in to hear better, not that she seemed to have hearing issues. In fact, all her senses seemed as sharp as ever.

Outside, the church bells began tolling the nine o'clock hour, one resonant peal for each hour.

Estrelle's gravelly voice held no quaver as she spoke. "You *will* hire her."

ABOUT THE AUTHOR

VTJ Photos

HEATHER WEBBER is the *USA Today* bestselling author of more than thirty novels and has been twice nominated for an Agatha Award. She loves to spend time with her family, read, drink too much coffee and tea, bird-watch, crochet, watch cooking competition and home improvement shows, and bake. Webber lives in southwestern Ohio and is hard at work on her next book.

heatherwebber.com
Facebook.com/HeatherWebberBooks
Instagram: @booksbyheather
Twitter: @BooksbyHeather